"A third body was lying on the floor of the car a dozen feet away, the nylon pistol-grip butt of a Siles nickel-barreled police shotgun a few inches from its outstretched hand. Unlike the two uniformed corpses, the third man was dressed from head to toe in black—combat boots, paratrooper pants, and a black shirt-and-combat vest combination...."

"We've got to get out," he repeated, panic rising in his gut and squeezing his throat. He backed up a pace, eyes still glued on the corpses. "I just wanted to rob the train," he whispered. "This is...this is..."

"Murder."

MAXWELL'S TRAIN

MAXWELL'S TRAIN

Christopher Hyde

A TOTEM BOOK
TORONTO

Author's Note

The information regarding the North American rail system, international terrorist organizations, and U.S. Treasury currency shipments is accurate. However, in the interests of public safety some specific technical information has been slightly altered, so anyone who wishes to travel in Harry Maxwell's footsteps will have to do his own research.

Christopher Hyde

This one is for my parents, Laurence and Bettye Hyde, who set the example and nurtured my love of books, even though they always wanted me to have a steady job.

First published 1984
by Collins Publishers
100 Lesmill Road, Don Mills, Ontario

This edition published 1985 by TOTEM BOOKS
a division of Collins Publishers

© Christopher Hyde 1984

Canadian Cataloguing in Publication Data

Hyde, Christopher, 1949–
   Maxwell's train

ISBN 0-00-222859-9

I. Title.

PS8565.Y34M39 1985   C813'.54   C85-099197-8
PR9199.3.H97M39 1985

Printed and bound in Canada.

Prologue

Special Air Services
Intelligence Division
Whitehall, London

The nine SAS group leaders, none of them in uniform, sat in the darkened projection room and listened to the senior intelligence officer give his commentary on the slides that flashed onto the screen in front of them.

"These pictures were taken last week in Algiers. The café is on the Rue Didouche Mourad, and is a well-known safe house for terrorists. In an apartment across the street from the café we operate a joint surveillance team with our French counterparts, the Gigene. Next." The wide shot of the sidewalk café changed to a closeup of a narrow-faced young man with wispy blond hair. "Dieter Haas. Dutch, twenty-eight years old. Suspected of being involved in more than seven kidnappings, and one of the planners of the Iranian Embassy takeover in May 1980. Next." The slide showed a scowling, long-haired Oriental woman. "Sheila Teng. Member of the Japanese Red Army. Identified at Lod, identified again at a bank robbery in Milan. Known to have been with Fusako Shigenobu, the woman the Arabs call Samira. Thirty-two years old. Next." A lean Semitic face, deeply colored, with heavy five-o'clock shadow. "Mohamet Kawi, twenty-nine years old. Libyan. Identified by Italy's Squad R in connection with the Dozier kidnapping. An instructor at the Ras Hilal training camp, the old German U-boat installation. A demolitions specialist. Next." A couple, linked arm in arm. The woman with short, dark brown hair, the man broadshouldered and slightly overweight. "Lisa Ruffio and Raoul Attendera. These two are always seen together, lovers clearly. Ruffio comes out of the Italian Red Brigade and was identified by Squad R in connection with the Moro kidnapping. Attendera is a long-time Sandinista. Both of them have been in Jordan for the past three years, in-

1

active. He is thirty-one, she's thirty. Next." A short, hawk-nosed man with deep set eyes, a cigarette dangling from an almost feminine mouth. "Amal Akbar. Often associated with Mohamet Kawi. They are close friends and possibly there is a sexual connection as well. Libyan, of course, trained at the main camp at Torca in Libya, took the three-month explosives course at Camp Mantanzas, near Havana, as well as the urban-warfare course at Guanabo. He's thirty. The profiles we have on him indicate that he is very unstable mentally. Probably a sadist. Nasty. Next." The slide showed a stunningly beautiful woman with shoulder-length black hair, a high-cheek-boned face, and the body of a fashion model. The skirt-and-top ensemble she was wearing looked American and expensive. "The best for last. This is Annalise Shenker. German. Thirty-four years old and virtually the last surviving member of the Baader-Meinhof group. Ulrike Meinhof's protégé, so to speak. Involved in no less than four kidnappings and three hijackings, she is thought to be the organizer of the OPEC headquarters attack in Vienna in 1975, and was identified at the terrorist summit at Benghazi in 1979. She has been linked romantically with Carlos the Jackal on a number of occasions, but there is no concrete evidence of this. She has been working as an instructor at the Karlovy Vary training camp, outside of Prague, for the past year or so. Of all the people identified coming into the café last week, she is undoubtedly the most important and the most dangerous. Lights, please."

The lights in the room flickered on and the beautiful face on the screen faded and disappeared. The intelligence officer stepped in front of the screen and looked out at the nine men seated before him.

"From what we can gather, it would appear that these eight are involved in the planning of a major operation. As of this moment there is no evidence to show that such a project has the United Kingdom as its target, but we thought the group leaders should be advised in any case. Questions?"

A tall man with a grizzled shock of salt-and-pepper hair and a weather-seamed face stood up in the back row of the projection room.

"Major Simpson?" said the intelligence officer.

2

"Yes. You say there is no evidence that the group is considering the U.K. as a target. Can we assume then that you have some idea of what the target country is?"

"We believe it will be the United States," said the intelligence officer. "We have discovered that with the exception of Ms. Shenker, the group is traveling by various means to New York over the next month or so. Ms. Shenker, it seems, is heading for Montreal."

"That's a bloody awful bunch to have coming your way," commented one of the other group leaders.

"The Intelligence Division agrees with your assessment, Captain Laird. As a matter of courtesy we have sent copies of these photographs to both the Royal Canadian Mounted Police Security and Surveillance Division and the United States' Delta Group. We've also sent copies of our files on each of these individuals, as well as our comments stressing the potential danger these people represent."

"Better them than us," said Laird.

The intelligence officer smiled thinly. "Quite," he said. "And now, gentlemen, if you please, tea is being served in the other room."

Part One

PREPARATIONS FOR DEPARTURE

*I never wanted to be a folk hero;
I just wanted to be stinking rich.*

Harry Maxwell,
the Playboy Interview

Chapter 1

When Harry Maxwell was eighteen and in the midst of obtaining a second-rate degree in an obscure discipline, he, like everyone else he knew, often indulged in the game of "where will I be ten years from now?" Sometimes he saw himself as a working anthropologist on some South Seas island, following in the footsteps of Margaret Mead, or working as a marine biologist with Jacques Cousteau. But his best fantasy was projecting himself onto the campus of a small New England university, bearded, graying with dignity at the temples, a pipe in his mouth, the idol, both intellectual and erotic, of enough leggy, small-breasted coed freshmen to keep himself from going stale.

At twenty-eight—his dreams, ideals, and degree long since lost in the anticlimax of life-after-Woodstock—Harry was making his living as a courier, working the sweaty-palm routes from Morocco to New York and from Bogotá to Miami, as afraid of the people he worked for as he was of the police. He no longer thought in terms of ten years ahead, and rarely even five. When he thought of the future at all, he saw it as a shadowland of half-hidden images where the best he could hope for was a full night's sleep unbroken by the paranoid nightmares of his profession.

But no idle fantasy or considered prediction had ever come close to imagining the reality of his thirty-fifth year. Harry Maxwell—son of a Seattle corporation lawyer, IQ 145, the soft good looks of his adolescence darkened into a leaner, harder image through time and events—was now a full-fledged employee of the Washington Terminal Company, working in the D.C. Coach Yard with a vacuum blower strapped to his back, flushing sandwich wrappers and cigarette butts out of the Amtrak cars used on the Northeast Corridor. Taking home $176.50 a week, he was on a thousand-runged ladder of promotion that might see him getting half that much as a pension after twenty years, if he managed to stick it out that long. He'd been on the job for just over a year now, and his only advance had been the honor of getting transferred to the eight-to-four shift from the midnight-to-eight. But as Mosley, his supervisor, was so fond of telling his "boys": "Be glad you got a job at all, shithead."

"True enough," said Harry to himself. "True enough." In fact, after seven years running coke, he was glad enough just to be alive. His final run a year and a half before had ended beside a Miami drainage canal with a sawed-off shotgun under his nose while two other guys carrying Dirty Harrys made sure that his partner, Daniel Pendergast, handed over every last ounce of the hard-won powder. The ripoff had broken Harry's nerve as well as his wallet. His friend Daniel had gone back to being an artist, and Harry had eventually taken the job with the railroad until something better came along. Nothing had.

He swung the wide-mouthed nozzle of the blower back and forth as he walked along the aisle of his fourteenth car that morning, bending and tucking to get at the spaces under the seats and occasionally lifting the corrugated plastic pipe to take a swipe at the overhead luggage racks in case somebody had dumped a load up there out of sight. The worst were the people who filled up a litter bag with junk and then crammed it down between the seat and the wall panel, and that happened at least twice for each car he cleaned. He'd have to turn off the blower, pull out the bag, and then resume his normal sweep. There was no way to ignore the "jammers," either, because Mosley checked every single car before it went out to the classification tracks for assembly into consists. Every consist—the railway term for an assemblage of various cars making up a scheduled train—had to be spit-and-polish clean, as far as Mosley was concerned. The barrel-chested man had been putting trains together in the Washington yards for thirty-five years, and he took a great deal of pride in running a clean shop. One jammer was enough to get you put back on the graveyard shift; two would get you the honey-wagon job—cleaning out the toilet holding tanks; and three, in addition to getting you fired, would also win you Mosley's curse of eternal damnation.

By the time Harry reached the far end of the car, there was a pile of garbage almost a foot high surging in front of him, piling up in a sloping wall against the back of the vestibule between the cars.

Even after a year it never ceased to amaze Harry that eighty people in an Amtrak coach—and even fewer in a sleeping car—could dump that much garbage in such a short time. The cars coming off the longer runs were the worst, especially the Montrealer, the joint VIA Rail Canada–Amtrak consist that came in daily. The seven-hundred-mile run produced enough garbage to fill two or three trucks every time. The 702 was almost as bad. The Capitol did the Chicago-Washington run on a daily basis, and that was a 775-mile route—plenty of time to lay down a monstrous barrage of litter for Harry and the other cleaners to wade through. Fortunately, the Capitol didn't get into Washington until midafternoon, and by the time it had been cut and the cars humped into the maintenance yard, the train was work for the night shift and not his problem to deal with anymore—at least so long as he didn't miss a jammer.

For all the dirt, grime, and litter, the job did have a few points of interest. On any given day, Harry would work his way through approximately forty to fifty cars that had found their way into the D.C. Coach Yard from every point of the compass. By picking and choosing, Harry could find newspapers and magazines from Detroit, Chicago, Boston, New York, Philadelphia, New Orleans, Tampa, Jacksonville, and Miami. As well as periodicals, there were also occasional love letters, small jewelry, money, books, and sometimes even luggage left on the overhead racks or under the seats and overlooked by the porters in the station. Anything of value was supposed to be turned in to the terminal's lost-and-found, but even Mosley and the other supervisors turned a blind eye to most of the pilfering. Reports of goods left in the cars just meant more paperwork and lost time for everybody concerned. The lost-and-found didn't do much business anyway. The color television set in the maintenance lounge had been there for two years and no one had even inquired about it, let alone put in a claim.

When all the garbage from the car was gathered in the vestibule, Harry unstrapped the blower, pulled one of the outsized garbage bags out of the pouch on his belt, and began to fill it. As he filled each bag, he pitched it out through the open doorway leading to the platform, aiming for the dumper on the back of his electric maintenance cart.

It wasn't until he was twisting the tie onto the last bag that he noticed the doorway leading to the next car. The other coaches in the cut he'd been working his way through had all been Pullman Standards from the fifties and sixties, equipped with regular pull-handle doors fitted with a large window that let you see into the next car. The door facing him had no window at all and was sealed off from the rest of the cut by three chains looped through heavy eyebolts set into the frame. Where the pull-handle should have been, there was a rectangular metal plate welded into place. In the center of the plate was a round heavy-duty Chubb lockset.

Mildly curious at the heavy security, Harry Maxwell flipped the last bag into the dumper, then dropped down the three steps to the sun-brightened platform. He reached into the breast pocket of his coveralls, took out a mutilated pack of Lucky Strikes, and lit one, using a kitchen match from the supply he kept snugged in between the package and its cellophane wrapper. Squinting in the bright sunshine that beat down on the coach yard, he looked up at the coach with the strange entranceway.

At first he thought it was a baggage car like others that occasionally found their way into the coach yard, but he dismissed that thought almost immediately. No baggage car he'd ever seen had a row of windows, and instead of a single or double pair of wide doors, this car had three small doors—one at each end and one in the center.

Harry took a quick look up and down the platform. Except for the banked rows of empty coaches stretching into the distance, the coach yard looked deserted. There was no sign of Mosley and the lime-green golf cart he made his rounds in. Harry took a drag on his cigarette and flipped the butt away. Hooking his foot into the bottom rung of the three-step metal ladder welded to the frame of the car body below the nearest door, he swung himself up and clutched the protruding U-handle. He dragged back on the handle, and the sliding door rolled into its slot. Using the small grab-irons on either side of the dark opening, Harry hauled himself up into the car.

The interior was a gloomy vault, lit only by the steeply

10

angled shafts of sunlight coming through the windows on either side, illuminating the slow-motion dance of thousands of tiny golden motes of dust. Harry grinned. As a child he'd been terrified of sunbeams like that, and upon encountering them he'd walked around them the way other people avoided ladders, assuming that the dust was somehow magnetically attracted by the light. It had come as a terrible shock to him at the age of five when he discovered that the dust motes were *everywhere*.

The strange car was divided into three obvious sections. Most of the forward third was literally fenced off from the rest of the vehicle by a cage of heavy chainlink fencing that went from floor to ceiling and half the width of the car. The central portion was fitted out with a couple of overstuffed chairs, a small coffee table, and a bar fridge with a single-burner hotplate on top of it. On the wall beside the fridge was a painted metal contraption of hooks, pegs, and padlocks that Harry recognized instantly: a gun rack four tiers high, empty of weapons. From the size of the supports, it looked as though it might be used for automatic weapons or shotguns.

The rear section, closest to the door he'd first noticed in the vestibule, was some kind of communications center. There was a wooden office-type swivel chair in front of a plain metal table that held a complex array of radio equipment. Harry crossed the car to the radio table for a closer look, his footsteps echoing dully. He'd spent almost two years as a backup driver for a large Oregon trucking company, and he knew he was looking at a CB'er's version of heaven on earth. There was an all-channel scanner, a single sideband rig, a large General Motors base-unit transmitter, and a pair of very professional-looking handheld units as well.

Harry leaned over the chair and flipped the power toggle on the base unit. Instantly the LED panel lit up: 164.25. The unit was locked onto a VHF channel well up in the A-license range. The frequency was as professional as the equipment. Harry spotted a thin cable snaking out of the rear of the transmitter, and he followed it with his eyes. It led up the rear bulkhead and across the roof of the car to a small circular vent grille. The aerial.

"Maxwell!" The single word rang out like a pistol shot.

It was Mosley, the five-foot-tall man with the ten-foot-tall voice.

"Shit," whispered Harry, grimacing. Quickly he turned off the radio and headed for the open door of the car, crossing the floor in three long strides.

Mosley was waiting on the platform, perched on the seat of his golf cart, a bright orange hardhat pulled down low on the top of his perfectly round head. To Harry, there was no person alive who looked more like Elmer Fudd than Bertram Orville Mosley.

"Goddammit, Harry! What the hell are you doing in there?"

"Just looking around," answered Harry. "I thought maybe I was supposed to blow this car as well as the others."

"Horseshit," said Mosley, scowling up at him. "You were sticking your goddamn intellectual nose in where it doesn't belong." Harry was the only man in any of Mosley's crews who had a university degree, and calling Harry an intellectual was the supervisor's favorite way of needling him.

Harry turned and climbed down the short ladder, pulling the door shut with one hand. He dropped down onto the platform and turned to face his boss again. Beads of sweat were glistening all over the pudgy little man's features, and the skintight, zippered coveralls he wore made him look like some kind of animated sausage. Harry could barely keep himself from laughing. He also knew it was worth his job if he so much as cracked a smile, so he bit his lip and kept a straight face.

"I should burn your ass for being in there, Maxwell. You realize you could get thrown in jail for what you did?"

"For taking a peek into an old baggage car?" said Harry. He knew perfectly well it was more than a baggage car, but playing dummy to Mosley's expertise had got him out of trouble a couple of times before.

"Christ!" muttered the supervisor. "Shows how much you little shits these days know about the railroad." He took a deep breath and let it out in tandem with a melodramatic headshake. "That's no baggage car. You see any Amtrak stripes on that car? Or markings from any other company?"

Harry knew what was expected of him. He looked over his shoulder at the car, then turned back to Mosley. "Nope," he said.

"That's because she doesn't belong to Amtrak. Or the Pennsy or the B&O or the goddamn Rock Island Line. That's an RPO, sonny boy, a bona fide Railway Post Office made by the Budd people back in the early fifties. A classic. You were trespassing on federal government property, Maxwell."

"I thought they stopped carrying mail on trains years ago," said Harry.

"They did," answered Mosley. "Went out of service in '62. The post office doesn't use this car. She's run by Treasury. She goes out head-end every Sunday on the Night Owl, the same consist that all those diplomats use to get back to the United Nations first thing Monday morning. From the time we start making up that train in the afternoon, this place is crawling with Treasury cops and Secret Service agents. If they knew you'd been fooling around in that car, they'd have your nuts, sonny boy."

Harry frowned. "I understand the Secret Service protecting U.N. people, but what does the Treasury have to do with it?"

Mosley drew himself up on his seat importantly and puffed out his chest against the already overtaxed fabric of his coveralls.

"Money, Maxwell," he said. "All the goddamn money in the world. Once a week they send out a shipment of new currency from the Bureau of Printing and Engraving for the Federal Reserve banks in New York and Boston. It's the most important train on my schedule, Maxwell. But you wouldn't understand that kind of responsibility."

"No, I guess not," said Harry.

"Just keep your ass where it belongs from now on," said Mosley. He turned on the little humming engine of the golf cart, grasping the steering bar with both fat hands. "You so much as put a finger on that car again, and it won't just be Bert Mosley you'll be answering to, it'll be the goddamn FBI. You got that, Maxwell?"

"Yes sir," said Harry. He raised his hand in a gesture that he knew Mosley would interpret as a salute. The rotund supervisor nodded curtly and put his cart into gear. He frowned at Harry for effect, then jerked the golf

13

cart around and headed back down the platform. He swung left at the first crossover and disappeared from view. Harry waited until he was gone before turning to stare at the RPO thoughtfully for a long moment. Standing there, Harry had what he later said was the closest he'd ever come to a religious experience. Two words began to form in his mind in full-blown 1960s-psychedelic Peter Max color, complete with squiggly, mind-altered lettering like a Fillmore poster.

Why Not?

Old FBI agents don't die, and they don't fade away; they wind up on park benches, peeling oranges and wondering what happened to their lost youth. Walter Linberg knew that to be a fact, since it was precisely what he was doing. When he had finished peeling the orange, he broke it into single sections and methodically began to eat them, one by one, squinting in the sunlight, staring at the fortress-like architecture of the J. Edgar Hoover Building. Idly he wondered if perhaps he had a streak of masochism somewhere within him; he could have chosen a bench on the Mall, on the other side of the Museum of Natural History, or one looking up the Mall to the Washington Monument, but each day in the spring and summer he took his brown-bag lunch to the same bench strategically located under a shady maple in the little park between Seventh and Ninth Streets, along Pennsylvania Avenue. The bench gave him a perfect three-quarters view of the new FBI Building, and staring at it each day never failed to bring back all the old memories.

At fifty, Walter Linberg, had spent exactly half his life working for the Bureau, and the deeply etched lines on a face that some people said looked like James Coburn's said a lot more about his experiences than the gold-key service pins on the lapel of his off-the-rack J. C. Penney three-piece.

Walter Linberg's history with the Bureau was classic. His father had joined the Bureau when it was known as the General Intelligence Division of the Justice Department, and had stayed there until his death, soon after World War II. Walter had idolized his father, and although he'd graduated from the Georgetown University

School of Law, he'd never wanted to be anything but an FBI agent. The Bureau, riding high on the fifties wave of McCarthyism, had snapped him up. After graduating from the Quantico Training Academy, Walter had begun a zigzagging course through the FBI's bureaucratic jungle, working in more than twenty field offices around the country, from the renowned bank-robbery squad in Los Angeles to the jewel-theft squad in Miami. After the flurry of hijackings in the late sixties, several of which cases Walter was involved in, he became a specialist and came back to Washington to work as special agent in charge of an anti-hijacking squad within the Internal Security Branch of the Bureau. During the seventies he was regularly offered assistant directorships, but the last thing he wanted was to come in from the field.

Then, in 1982, a regular physical showed that he was suffering from high blood pressure, and his days in the field were over. There was an austerity program under way at the time, and there were no positions available for him. He was offered a choice: early retirement on a reduced pension, or a research officer's job at the newly formed United States Institute for Studies in Terrorism. He'd never married during his career with the Bureau, so the pension would have supported him well enough, but the thought of being without work terrified him. He took the USIST job.

And now he was regretting it. Once past the impressive name, you were left with a rundown office on Fourth Street, across from the Juvenile Court which was staffed by a crew of aging law enforcement and intelligence types like himself who'd been put out to pasture. For all intents and purposes, USIST was nothing more than another acronym on the General Interest Memo mailing list.

USIST had supposedly been organized to do continuing research into international terrorism, specifically with regard to terrorist activities directed against the United States or its citizens in foreign countries. In fact, it did almost nothing, and the only thing Walter Linberg had learned since taking his job was that no one in government was even slightly interested in the possibility of terrorist activity in the United States. Georgetown University's Center for Strategic and International Studies put out a lot of reports, and the Cabinet Committee to

15

Combat Terrorism still met from time to time, but there was no official group within the United States capable of neutralizing a terrorist threat. Both the Black Berets at Fort Lewis in Washington and the ultra-elite Delta Group were supposedly commissioned to deal with terrorism, but neither group had very much in the way of experience. The only time the Delta Group had seen action was the attempt to rescue the Iranian hostages, and that had ended in utter and embarrassing disaster.

For some reason the government of the United States refused to believe that any terrorist would dare violate the nation's sovereign boundaries. Walter called it the Stop Sign Syndrome. In the same way that city hall refused to put up a stop sign at a dangerous intersection until someone had been killed trying to cross the street, the federal government wasn't going to invest millions of dollars to fight terrorism until terrorists actually struck. In Walter Linberg's book, that kind of tunnel-vision was both stupid and dangerous—especially in light of the circulating file he'd read that morning.

The file, which had originated weeks before in the United Kingdom, discreetly suggested that a particularly vile selection of internationally known terrorists were en route to the United States. The file had blossomed as it made the rounds of the law enforcement and intelligence organizations it had skipped through, each office adding its own words of wisdom just to show that it was on the ball. Immigration and Naturalization, for instance, stated without equivocation that no one on the list had entered the United States, while at the same time the INS field office in San Francisco said that photographs of a recent bank robbery in Oakland bore a remarkable resemblance to two of the terrorists thought to be en route to the States. The CIA people shrugged the whole thing off, saying that the Brits obviously had terrorists on the brain, and the file was absurd, since, according to their records, Annalise Shenker had been killed during a CIA covert operation in Berlin two years before.

In other words, thought Walter, as he finished the last section of orange, no one had the slightest idea what was going on. He spit out a pair of seeds into his palm and stood up. He scooped the peel into his brown bag, added the pits, and headed back toward his office. He knew it

16

was probably a waste of time, but he intended to follow up on the information in the file. A quarter of a century at the Bureau had given him high blood pressure, but it had also given him a nose for trouble, and this stank to high heaven.

Harry Maxwell sat sprawled in an overstuffed chair, a beer in one hand and a cigarette in the other, waiting for his friend Daniel Pendergast to digest the proposal he'd just made. Pendergast, wearing nothing but a pair of sagging blue boxer shorts, stood in front of the immense canvas he was working on, delicately brushing in the details of a single pink nipple on the giant nude study.

The chair Harry sat in was close to the front of the large cigar factory loft that Daniel used as a studio and living quarters, and Harry could look down onto the slightly dingy E Street façade of the Bellevue Hotel, across the way. At this time of night, downtown Washington was dead, and except for an occasional taxi and the odd person coming into or leaving the Bellevue's bar, the street was deserted.

It was almost midnight, but the air outside was still hot and muggy. The open clerestory sections of the floor-to-ceiling windows at the front of the loft did almost nothing to move the air around, and even in shorts and a T-shirt, Harry was sweating.

"If you got famous all of a sudden, you could afford air conditioning for this place," commented Harry, speaking to Pendergast's back, thirty feet away across the tobacco-stained floorboards of the loft.

"If I got famous all of a sudden, I wouldn't need to be here at all," answered Pendergast without turning. He wiped paint off his brush with a rag, then dipped the bristles into a fresh daub of pink on the taboret palette beside him.

"Right," Harry said, grinning. He took a swig from the now lukewarm bottle of beer. "Exactly my point. You could be in a nice Georgetown Federal townhouse right now, with some honey from the Hirshhorn Museum nibbling at your ear."

"The Hirshhorn has no honeys," muttered Pendergast hollowly. "They have men in gray suits who won't even

17

look at you until you're eighty-five and so arthritic you can't lift a brush."

"You could give up driving a cab," offered Harry. "You could afford B&B instead of Budweiser."

"I *like* Budweiser," said Pendergast. "And anyway, they don't serve beer *or* scotch in prison."

"You wouldn't go to prison," said Harry. "You'd probably get probation. And even if we did get sent up, it would be a short sentence, and I can guarantee you we'd get a book out of it. Probably movie rights, too. Win or lose, we can't fail."

Daniel Pendergast swung around and stared at Harry, the brush poised in his hand. The stark glare from the ceiling lights high overhead threw the lower part of his narrow face into shadow, and together with his long nose and deep set gray eyes, the effect was to make the slim-hipped, slightly-shorter-than-average artist look like some kind of benign, two-legged rodent in a blue loincloth. "You're really serious about this, aren't you?" he said, frowning at his friend.

"Absolutely," answered Harry. He took a last drag on his cigarette and slipped it down the neck of the beer bottle.

Daniel winced. "I wish you wouldn't do that. It's really a filthy habit, you know."

"So spring for an ashtray," said Harry.

The artist went to the old-fashioned refrigerator that stood against the wall to the right of the canvas, found a can of Pepsi, and popped the top. He crossed the room to the window and dropped down onto a ratty-looking camel-saddle stool that was just about the only piece of furniture in the loft, except for Harry's chair and a slab of ticking-covered foam that passed for a bed, lost somewhere in the gloomy shadows at the rear of the loft.

"It's comic-book stuff," said Daniel, sipping his Pepsi. "Nobody robs trains anymore."

"Not true," said Harry, shaking his head. "Ronnie Biggs and his pals did it in 1963."

"That was England," said Daniel. "And they all got caught."

"Because they were stupid," said Harry. "We're not."

"You're an idiot to even contemplate something like that."

"Any more of an idiot than I am for working at that job for very much longer? Or any more of an idiot than you are for pounding your head against the brick wall of the cultural establishment, as you're so fond of calling it? Face it, Daniel, old pal—we're already idiots. This is a chance to get smart, for once in our lives."

"I don't understand you," said Daniel. "You sound like an old Edward G. Robinson movie, for Christ's sake. You got some problem you're not telling me about?"

"Just the one you've got, Daniel. We're getting old. Pretty soon we're going to be forty, you realize that? Forty! Jesus! You and I went through high school together, and it seems like yesterday. We used to wander around Rock Creek Park looking for action at night, remember?"

"Sure," said Daniel, smiling. "And we never found any."

"We used to talk about what we'd do when we got out of school. You were going to be the next Picasso and I was going to be a combination of Jean-Paul Sartre and Jack Kerouac. We were hot back then, Daniel. We had a lot of fun. We laid the same women, sometimes together, we did tons of dope, drank ourselves into oblivion, raised hell on three continents, for Christ's sake, and what did it all come to?"

"We've lived a pretty good life. I don't regret anything," said Daniel, shrugging his shoulders.

"*Je ne regrette rien*," grunted Harry. "You sound like a Charles Aznavour song, for God's sake."

"So what's wrong with Charles Aznavour?" said Daniel.

"He's a symptom of the disease we've got. Mellowness. We've accepted defeat. Remember after I married Carol? I got a job in a bookstore and started smoking a pipe. You barely spoke to me for the year and a half we were married. You told me I'd gotten mellow then. You were right."

"You think robbing a train is going to give you back your lost youth?" said Daniel, laughing.

"Not my lost youth, my lost balls. I've written some good stuff in my time. You've painted some good paintings, but it doesn't matter a crap, Daniel. We don't have the right connections. We never did, and we're going to be just like this twenty years from now. You're going to be an old man driving a Yellow Cab, and I'm going to be a janitor somewhere. The only way you and I are going to make it before we're old and flaccid is with money, instant fame, or both."

"It's crazy," said Daniel.

"No, it's not. There's lots of precedent. Look at Clifford Irving. He'd been writing half-assed books for years, but no one paid any attention to him until he pulled off the Howard Hughes hoax. Christ, he blew that one totally and he still wound up filthy rich."

"And John Hinckley wound up in a mental hospital."

"We're not going to shoot the President," said Harry. "That's the whole point. When Ronnie Biggs robbed the Glasgow Mail he had the whole country on his side. The same thing happened when that D. B. Cooper guy ripped off the airline and parachuted into the Oregon woods. He was a folk hero. The same thing applies to my idea. Who's going to be unsympathetic to somebody scoring off the Federal Reserve? It's a victimless crime."

"I wonder how much the train carries," murmured Daniel.

"About thirty-five million dollars," said Harry quickly. He'd been Daniel Pendergast's best friend for more than twenty years, and he could almost see the wheels turning inside his head.

"How did you find that out?"

"I asked," said Harry simply. "I took the tour at the Bureau of Printing and Engraving. I asked how much new currency New York and Boston go through each week."

"And they told you?"

"Sure," said Harry. "Why not? It's a standard question, apparently."

"Thirty-five million dollars?"

"That's a three, a five, and six zeros," said Harry.

"Son of a bitch," said Daniel softly, taking a thoughtful hit of Pepsi.

"My sentiments exactly." Harry grinned. "And with less personal risk than when we were bringing in coke from Bogotá."

"I wonder," said Daniel.

"Look," said Harry intently, leaning forward in his chair, "let's do it this way. We plan it out. We figure all the

20

angles and then get it together step by step. If it looks too risky anywhere along the line, we forget about it."

"No violence," said Daniel.

Harry nodded. "Absolutely not. We have to keep things mom-and-apple pie. After I took the tour yesterday, I went down to the Library of Congress and did a bit of reading. This doesn't even qualify as bank robbery. From what I can tell, the crime is described as theft from an interstate shipment. The maximum sentence is five years."

"You're very thorough," said Daniel, grimacing.

"I try my best."

"I think I'm going to regret this," Daniel sighed.

Chapter 2

Walter Linberg's superiors at USIST were surprised at his interest in the British terrorist file, but as a gesture of bureaucratic benevolence coupled with a chronic need to spend surplus budget dollars rather than have their funds cut back, they let him have his head, assigning him a secretary, unlimited use of the Xerox machine, WATS telephone privileges, and even a modest travel budget. On paper, the project was referred to as a "pilot investigative program," and Walter's job was supposedly to come up with a research paper outlining the systems that investigators from various law enforcement agencies might need in case of a serious terrorist threat. In reality, Walter could do exactly what he liked as long as he spent his money, kept receipts, and didn't make any waves.

Walter Linberg had a nose for people, and after a quarter-century of conjuring faces and personalities out of files, rap sheets, and mug books, that nose had become something close to precognitive. His superiors had often grumbled that his "acting on hunches" was nonprofessional, but his batting average was so high that they usually kept their muttering to themselves.

When he read over the file from the U.K., Linberg's nose had taken on Karl Malden–like proportions, and when he utilized the USIST files to fill in the blanks, the first faint whiffs had become full-blown and foul.

Of the six terrorists, two were clearly second-string. Attendera, the ex-Sandinista, was a dilettante, drifting through the dark shadows of international terrorism for kicks more than anything else. The very fact that he had formed a long-term romantic relationship with Ruffio, the Italian woman, showed an inherent weakness. Terrorism was combat, and in a combat zone there was no place for love or romance. Ruffio was probably not much more than a hanger-on, the terrorist equivalent of a groupie.

The other four, however, were obviously made of much tougher stuff. According to her record, Sheila Teng was a 1980s incarnation of a Kamikaze warrior. At her university she had written a term paper extolling the virtues of a publication from the Second World War entitled *Sen-Jin-Kun* or "Battle Ethics." One of its quotes—"fear not to die in the cause of everlasting justice"—was her avowed motto. She had taken part in at least a score of terrorist operations, had executed nine "enemies of the people," and was responsible for the mutilations of two members of her group discovered in a homosexual relationship. She was a Bushido warrior to the core. If she'd ever had a heart or a soul, it had long ago been forged into gleaming steel. Teng was no leader, though; she was a weapon to be used.

The two Libyans, Mohamet Kawi and Amal Akbar, were neither leaders nor weapons. If his dossier was anything to go by, Akbar was one step up from a mad dog. Steeped in a bizarre and utterly illogical combination of Marxism and the Koran, the man was capable of anything. Psychotic, sadistic, and sexually twisted, Akbar's first radical act had been the disemboweling of the man who was fornicating with his sister, which he had followed by insisting that his sister succumb to the ancient clitoridectomy ritual required in such cases. The local mullahs in his village had agreed, and Akbar had performed the hideous surgery himself, cauterizing his sister's genitalia with a white-hot iron used for branding sheep. Akbar had been fourteen at the time. His later history among Qaddafi's minions had done nothing whatsoever to change him.

Kawi, the older of the two, was slightly more sophisticated, but his early years in a PLO camp had shaped him easily to the terrorist mold, and by his late twenties he had taken part in a dozen operations that would have made Adolf Eichmann wince. A hard-core terrorist, a professional without any visible vulnerabilities or obvious neuroses to interfere with his work, Kawi was without doubt an extremely dangerous item.

And then there was Annalise Shenker, the most dangerous of them all, not because she had been party to acts any more outrageous than the others, but dangerous because of her intelligence and her apparent "normalcy." Five feet four inches tall, black-haired and black-eyed, she had a face like an avenging angel, a body made for Calvin Kleins, and a steel-trap military mind that Erwin Rommel would have appreciated. Out of sixty major terrorist operations mounted in Europe between 1975 and 1983, Shenker had played a part in forty, usually as a planner and strategist, but often enough as a front-line soldier to show that she was perfectly capable of carrying out anything she'd ever ordered anyone else to do. A psychiatrist would probably be able to come up with some reason why she was the way she was, but cause was irrelevant; Annalise Shenker was effect and nothing else. Whatever fiends dogged her heels, they had created a woman capable of any murderous act without need of dogma, politics, or any other justification. Putting down her file, Walter Linberg shivered slightly. She was death personified, a disease looking for a host to infect. If the host was anywhere in America, then America was in trouble.

Linberg's first concern after reviewing the files again was to establish whether or not the terrorist group really had chosen the United States as its target, and that meant finding out if any or all of them had come into the country. Using the information in the Special Air Services file, he began to trace their movements from the time they had left Algeria. He pinned up a large chart on his office wall and began filling in the blanks.

Using a variety of domestic airlines, the group had begun to hopscotch over Europe, watched at a distance by surveillance teams from the SAS, Gigene, Germany's Gruppe 9, and the Special Assistance Unit of the Dutch Marines.

The terrorists studiously avoided landing in countries where they were wanted by the local police. Dieter Haas, the Dutchman, went to Marseille and from there to Lyon, where he rented a car under the name Marbeau, which he drove to Paris. Mohamet Kawi and Amal Akbar, the two Libyans, flew to Cairo and then to Athens, backtracked to Rome, and then went on to Frankfurt. Lisa Ruffio and Raoul Attendera, also traveling together, went to Amsterdam. Annalise Shenker, after a brief stop in Paris, traveled by train to Geneva, Switzerland. By the end of the month they all seemed settled, and surveillance was reduced. Then, in the first week of May, all six members of the group dropped out of sight. Bulletins were immediately issued to customs and immigration authorities, complete with photographs and the names on the passports the terrorists had been using up to that time, but it was soon clear that the group had made their getaway undetected. The only lead available was from a Swiss police informer who said that a woman answering Annalise Shenker's description had been in the market for a number of passports. The informer gave the police the name of the document forger she had gone to, and the authorities picked him up for questioning. After twenty-four hours of rather aggressive interrogation, the forger admitted that Shenker had purchased six passports—five of them American and one Canadian. Shenker had provided photographs, and the forger had made them up to order, filling in all the blanks except for the names. The passport with Shenker's photograph in it had been the Canadian one. Shenker had picked up the finished documents on Tuesday; by Friday, all six terrorists had disappeared. At that point the trail went cold, and no further attempts were made to track down the group's whereabouts.

At first glance, it seemed as though Walter Linberg was faced with an impossible task, but working methodically the ex-FBI man slowly began to whittle his way down to the essentials.

It stood to reason that the sudden disappearance of six terrorists meant they'd left their respective countries by air. The fact that the four cities involved were major travel and communications centers bore that out. Assuming that Shenker had mailed out five of the passports to her colleagues the day she got them, they would have been received two days later—Thursday. Given that the documents had a limited life span before they were discovered as false, it followed that the terrorists would have used them as quickly as possible to avoid detection. Which meant that the five U.S. passports had probably been used on Friday, while Shenker had used her Canadian passport on Tuesday or Wednesday. It also meant that all six had probably booked themselves on direct flights rather than take the chance of being picked up on a layover. Assuming that the terrorists' ultimate destination was North America, Shenker had probably gone to Montreal or Toronto, while the others had almost certainly flown to New York.

After that, it was simply a matter of legwork. Walter borrowed an airline schedule directory from a travel agent and began listing all direct flights from Paris, Amsterdam, and Frankfurt to New York, and all the direct flights from Geneva to Montreal and Toronto. Within a couple of hours he had a list of more than twenty flights on seven different airlines, all of them 747s, except for a DC-8 Stretch out of Amsterdam. At a rough guess, that meant a total of around eight thousand passengers.

Undaunted, Walter kept slogging away. After a fair amount of bureaucratic wrangling he managed to pry the passenger lists loose for the various flights, and began crossing out all those not traveling on U.S. or Canadian passports. After three days he'd culled a list of just over four thousand names. Using that list of possibles, he used the old-boys' network at the Bureau to get the names run through the Immigration and Naturalization computers for the Americans, while the RCMP did the same thing at External Affairs in Canada. Any names not matching bona fide passport applications would stand out like a crop of sore thumbs.

Ten days after beginning his investigation, Walter Linberg had what he wanted: a list of six names used on forged passports traveling to New York and Montreal. He had verified the original assumption made in the SAS file.

The first to arrive had been Mohamet Kawi and Amal Akbar, traveling as Lebanese-Americans under the names John and George Haddad, coming into JFK on a Lufthansa DC-10 at twelve-thirty in the afternoon. Two hours later, Ruffio and Attendera, traveling as Mr. and Mrs. Vittorio Romano, came in on a Trans-American flight from Amsterdam, and ten minutes later, at ten to three, Dieter Haas alias Peter Paul Maartens, came in on Pan American 115. Just as Walter had thought, Shenker had left Geneva three days earlier and had arrived at Mirabel Airport, outside of Montreal, using the name Jeanette Lanctot and giving an address in suburban Laval.

All of which left Walter Linberg with a problem. By utilizing nothing more than basic investigative techniques, a little common sense, and a bit of imagination, he'd proved that six of the world's top terrorists were now in North America. The obvious thing to do would be to send out a memorandum to that effect. The obvious thing, however, was not necessarily the *smart* thing. Any formal notification would be embarrassing to the Bureau, the Central Intelligence Agency, and the immigration authorities, all of whom had seen the original file and ignored it. If he was going to go public with his information and expect it to do any good, he'd need much harder evidence.

It was his search for harder evidence that brought him to St. Augustine, Florida, exactly three weeks after he'd first seen the file and eight days after Harry Maxwell's conversation with his friend Daniel Pendergast.

For someone who had been referred to consistently as an academic underachiever, Harry Maxwell threw himself into the task of researching their project with remarkable vigor. Even before broaching the idea to Daniel, he had begun to read everything about trains that he could find, from O. S. Nock's *World Atlas of Railways* to *The Train Robbers* by Piers Paul Read. With Daniel enlisted, Harry took a week's sick leave that was due him, and the two got down to work in earnest.

Within a couple of days the E Street loft had become their headquarters, littered with charts of the Night Owl's schedules, topographic maps of places where the train could possibly be stopped, and large, neatly drawn diagrams of the various cars in the train, including the RPO, the plans having been culled from a book entitled *An Illustrated Treasury of Budd Railway Passenger Cars*, which Harry had purchased at a hobby shop. By Friday evening, over air-conditioned burgers and fries at a Hot Shoppe, the two would-be criminals had reached an inescapable conclusion.

"It's not going to work," said Daniel, cautiously inspecting the interior of his hamburger before biting into it. "There's just too many problems."

"There has to be some way," said Harry, spiking a french fry with his fork.

"Why?" asked Daniel. "Don't you think the Federal Reserve, the FBI, and the Amtrak security police thought there might be an attempt made on that kind of shipment someday? They've covered all the angles."

"Maybe we've overlooked something."

"We went over everything this afternoon," said Daniel, shaking his head. "The line between D.C. and Philadel-

27

phia is too built up. According to the schedule, the train makes five stops in the first hundred and twenty miles. There just isn't enough time. If we screw around with the signals like they did during the Royal Mail job, the next station down the line is going to know something's wrong in ten or fifteen minutes. Not to mention the radio you saw in the mail car. The guards would have an SOS out within thirty seconds. Even if we did get away with the robbery, they'd catch us before we had a chance to get five miles. Suicide."

"What about farther up the line? We figured somewhere between Trenton and New Brunswick would be good, remember?"

"Sure," Daniel said. "Twenty-six miles of fairly barren ground, and Highway One no more than a mile or so from the tracks. But we've still got the time factor. Those guys aren't going to just open up and hand us the money, and you said you saw a gun rack in the mail car. That probably means riot guns. Face it, Harry, the logistics just don't come together. According to that Train Order manual you swiped from work, the people at the Trenton Tower are going to know the instant the train stops, whatever the reason. Even if we figured out some way to stop the guards in the RPO from radioing for help, the clock is ticking from the second the train stops. The Royal Mail robbery took eighteen minutes from the time the train stopped until they drove off, and that was with half a dozen guys working flat out. Say, by some miracle, we do it in the same amount of time." He held up one hand and began counting off with it. "Minute one: Trenton Tower knows the train has stopped. Minute two: they notify Central Traffic Control in New York, and at the same time they try and raise the train themselves. Minute three: after several attempts they can't get the train, and CTC New York can't get the guards in the RPO on the radio. Or if they can, the guards report that the train is being hit. Minute four: every cop from New York City to Philadelphia is alerted, and since it's a federal crime, the FBI gets called as well. By minute five they'd be organizing roadblocks and putting helicopters in the air. Everybody and his brother would know what we were doing and we'd still be picking the lock on the mail car door. It's hopeless."

"You don't have to be such a pessimist," said Harry, grimacing.

"I'm being a realist, Harry. Face it, m'boy, we just ain't cut out for this kind of thing. We're amateurs."

"Amateurs make the best criminals," Harry responded. "Deviant Psych, second semester. Statistically, the amateur criminal is more intelligent and is less likely to repeat his crime."

"The benefits of a university education. Thank Christ I went to art school instead."

Harry pushed his plate away and lit a cigarette. There were only two or three people left in the Hot Shoppe, all of them looking about as dejected as he felt. "So," he said at last, exhaling, "you figure we should throw in the towel. The crime of the century goes bust in a fast-food greasy spoon at ten o'clock at night."

"I think so." Daniel shrugged. "It's the time element."

Harry leaned back against the plastic padding of the booth and closed his eyes, a trail of smoke wafting slowly up to the fluorescent fixture directly above his head. He stayed like that for a minute and then let his head drop forward again. He opened his eyes and stared across the Formica tabletop at his friend.

"No," he said.

"What's that supposed to mean?"

"It means no," answered Harry. "I refuse to believe that it's impossible. We're just not going at it the right way. We've been following the classic stick'em-up-and-hand-over-the-strongbox scenario. Added to that, we've got a nice liberal codicil as well—no violence. You can hardly make the stick'em-up routine work without a threat."

"So what are you getting at?" asked Daniel.

"We've got to do some original thinking," Harry said slowly. "We've got to figure it out logically."

"You're making it sound like one of those philosophy exercises you used to show me years ago. If John smokes Luckies, Edith smokes Kent, and Bob smokes Marlboros, what does Dick smoke?"

"Something like that," said Harry.

"No amount of intellectual game-playing is going to give you the method for lifting thirty-five million bucks off a moving train," said Daniel.

"Bingo. You've come up with a basic element. The train is moving. To rob the train, you have to stop it. Stopping the train invites disaster."

"Marvelous. Now what does that prove?"

"Nothing, except that we can't rob the train while it's stopped. Ergo, we have to rob the train while it's still moving."

"You're nuts, Harry."

"No, listen. It solves a lot of problems. Time, for instance. If we stop the train, our time frame is the length of time it takes the cops to get to us, against the length of time it takes us to get the money, right?"

"Right."

"But if the train is still moving, the time frame becomes the period between the time the train leaves D.C. and the time it arrives in New York. We go from five minutes to almost four hours."

"I still don't get it," muttered Daniel.

Harry was beaming now. "We've changed the whole structure of the event," he said, his words falling over each other. "Instead of trying to do the impossible in five minutes, we now have four hours."

"Three hours and forty-eight minutes, if you want to be accurate. I still don't see how that changes anything. It's still a lot of intellectual bullshit to me."

"Screw you, Pendergast," said Harry, still smiling. "Listen up. What we have to do is come up with a way of robbing the train while it's still on its run between D.C. and New York. If the train is still on its scheduled run, no one's going to get wise. Correct?"

"Fine," said Daniel, "except for the radio you saw."

"Okay, that's the second phase. We have to figure out a way of making sure the guards don't use the radio."

"And what about getting away with it?" said Daniel. "What use is it to rob a train that you're still traveling on?"

"That's the third phase. We've got to get off the train before it gets to New York, and we have to get off with the money."

"I still say you're out of your mind."

"No, I'm not. Instead of one insoluble problem, we now have three problems that may well have solutions."

"Christ!" groaned Daniel. "Okay," he sighed. "What's the next step, then?"

"We have to take the Night Owl to New York this Sunday. A dry run."

The city of St. Augustine lies roughly midway between Jacksonville and Daytona Beach. The oldest city in the United States had been little more than a coastal backwater until the mid-sixties when, eyeing the tourist successes of Daytona and getting a jump on Walt Disney's plans for Orlando, less than a hundred miles away, the city began to capitalize on its only asset—its age. The old section of town, from Avenida Menendez, overlooking Matanzas Bay, to Cordova Street, up until then little more than a slum, was elevated to the lofty status of a historic site, cleaned up, renovated, and stuffed with restaurants, T-shirt emporia, and mini-museums. Pulitzer Prize-winning playwright Paul Green was even commissioned to write a pageant covering the town's history. Once known as a shrimp-fishing center and still the world's largest producer of commercial shrimp trawlers, St. Augustine successfully transformed itself into a tourist center catering to an annual average of 672,000 visitors.

Even though it was still early in the season, Walter Linberg would have had trouble getting accommodations in the town if it hadn't been for the clout of the resident agent in Jacksonville. Swanson, the RA, an old friend of Linberg's from his Miami days, had called Linberg in response to the ex-agent's quietly circulated memo asking for any information on recent major weapons thefts. From personal experience and from the extensive reading he'd done at USIST, Linberg knew that the subject of weaponry was the key to terrorist psychology, and had been since Chevalier had designed the first time bomb in an attempt to kill Napoleon. Without weapons, a terrorist could not instill the fear he required in his victims.

Shenker's group had come into the States clean, Linberg was sure of that. Customs and security procedures at airports left a lot to be desired, but it was unlikely that they would have risked bringing arms into the United States or Canada. That in turn meant the group's first priority would be weapons acquisition, and the arms they wanted wouldn't be the kind you could buy over the counter at the local sporting goods store. Florida, with its almost nonexistent gun laws, was at the top of Linberg's "hot list" of likely places for the Algiers group to hit, and when Swanson called from Jacksonville, his investigative antennae began to twitch. From the way Swanson had described things, Linberg was almost positive that the terrorists had been in St. Augustine.

Swanson—driving one of the ubiquitous green Chevrolet four-doors common to every FBI regional office in the States—picked Linberg up at the Spanish Quarter Inn just after breakfast and headed up Avenue San Marco toward the scene of the crime. They passed the massive bulk of the Castillo de San Marco and jogged to the right onto the Avenida Menendez. Looking to his left, Linberg could see the bright blue water of Matanzas Bay and the darker blue expanse of the Atlantic, beyond the protective arms of Vilano Beach and Anastasia Island.

"Pretty," commented Linberg.

"It's okay if you like living in a history textbook," replied Swanson. The two men were close to the same age, but Swanson wasn't wearing it as well as Linberg. His paunch had grown while his hair receded, and there were little raspberry explosions around his eyes and on his cheeks. Booze tracks, thought Linberg to himself.

"More than that, if what they say about this guy Ungar is true," said the ex-agent.

Swanson made a snorting sound. They went around the intersection at the Bridge of Lions and continued south. "It pisses me, you know," grumbled the resident agent. "The slimy little son of a bitch has been right under our noses for years. We've just started going through his records, but from the looks of things he'd been in the business since the fifties. It looks like he was supplying everybody from Castro to Che Guevara out of here."

"Was he a registered dealer?" asked Linberg. Out of the corner of his eye he noticed they were passing something called Potter's Wax Museum.

Swanson shook his head. "No. He had himself listed as a gunsmith. We asked around and it looked like he was in business doing custom work for the Historical Society and getting his bread and butter from the State

Arsenal—repair work, that kind of thing. His place was only a few blocks away."

"So where did he get his arms from?" asked Linberg.

"Everywhere," grunted Swason. "We've found inventory that goes from A&E submachine guns made in Argentina to Cao Dai .45 automatics from Vietnam."

"How was he getting them in?" asked Linberg.

"His ex-brother-in-law has a string of shrimp trawlers. From what we can tell, he was offloading from boats beyond the limit and smuggling them into St. Augustine in false-bottom holds. Ungar's in the morgue, but at least we've got the brother-in-law."

"You said you found prints?" asked Linberg.

"Sure, lots of them. We ran them all through NCIC and came up with zip. Whoever knocked over Ungar never so much as had a parking ticket."

Linberg nodded. The National Crime Information Computer had criminal files on half a million offenders, and the Ident Section in Washington had a hundred and sixty-five million-odd fingerprint cards.

"You think you can ident the prints?" asked Swanson, pressing for information.

Linberg shrugged noncommittally. "Maybe," he said. In fact, he'd taken the precaution of having Mylars made up from the SAS file, and had a full set back in his hotel room. "Don't worry, Bill, if I can give you a hand on this, I will," he soothed.

"You think it might be some terrorist group?" asked Swanson. "I mean, that's what you're doing these days, isn't it?"

"Yeah, that's what I'm doing, Bill. Like I said, if I come up with something, you'll get the information first."

"I could use an 'attaboy' on my file right now," said Swanson, turing the car onto a narrow, tree-lined street. "I've been RA in Jacksonville for five years now. If I'm going to get an AD, it's going to have to be soon."

Linberg glanced across the seat at Swanson. The chances of the man getting an assistant director's post were slim, in his condition. A transfer to Knoxville or Oklahoma City was more likely.

Swanson parked the car and both men got out. Across the street was a three-story brick building that had seen better days. From what Linberg could see, they were in a light industrial neighborhood of some kind.

"That it?" asked Linberg, nodding toward the building across from them.

"That's it," said Swanson. "And a very neat piece of work, too. You'd never figure it out unless you were wise."

"What? That it's an arms warehouse?"

"Better than that," said Swanson, grinning. "Take a close look at the building."

Linberg did so. Three stories, brick, with a double-door entrance at the front and a wide graveled lane leading to the rear. The windows on the front of the building were filthy with half a century's worth of grime. A sign painted on the side of the building above the third-floor windows said FLORIDA STEEL AND WIRE PRODUCTS CO. in white letters on a green background. It looked like a perfectly ordinary building of its type.

"You don't see it?" asked Swanson.

"I see a building," answered Linberg, his irritation rising slowly. He wasn't interested in Swanson's histrionics.

"Come on, then," said the resident agent.

They crossed the street, and using a key he took out of his pants pocket, Swanson opened the front doors of the building. Linberg found himself in a dusty reception area, complete with abandoned office furniture and the shriveled remains of a potted plant on one windowsill. A steep flight of stairs rising along the rear wall led up to the second floor.

"Ungar had his workshop in the back," said Swanson, indicating the partition wall halfway down the floor. "He never used the front entrance, normally. Follow me."

Swanson headed up the stairs to the second floor, with Linberg close behind. The second floor was open from front to back, lit dully by long rows of windows almost opaque with dirt. The center of the long room was filled with an assortment of machinery, and there were several bales of rusting wire piled in one corner.

"Figure it out yet?" asked Swanson, breathing hard from his brief climb up the stairs.

Linberg scanned the room more carefully. Except that the ceiling over his head seemed lower than the one on the main floor, he couldn't see anything out of the ordinary. "No," he said. "Let's get to the point, Bill. I'm really not in the mood for hide-and-seek."

"Sure," said Swanson. He turned and headed for the stairs again.

Linberg wasn't sure whether it was encroaching old age or his imagination, but the climb up to the third floor seemed longer. Like the second floor, the third was filled with machinery, reels of wire still threaded through various cogs and spindles. Once again the ex-agent noticed that the ceiling here seemed lower than that of the main floor.

Without speaking, Swanson led Linberg across the room. He stopped beside some kind of drill press device, flipped a light switch on the wall, and leaned down. Barely noticeable on the floor, there was a small ring-pull set into the boards, large enough for a single finger. Swanson lifted, and a square trapdoor two feet on a side opened up. A ladder led downward. Supporting himself on the sides of the trapdoor, Swanson eased down the ladder and Linberg followed.

"Good Lord!" Linberg whispered. "Unbelievable."

Stretching into the distance, lit by a string of low-wattage bulbs, were rows and rows of weapons, all carefully racked. Linberg could see everything from mortars to fifty-caliber machine guns. The room also contained stacks of ammunition boxes and piles of what looked like body armor.

"We probably never would have found the place, except that Ungar's body was hanging half in and half out of the trapdoor," commented Swanson. "Somebody phoned in a gunshot call and the local police found him. Incredible, isn't it?"

"Amazing," said Linberg, peering down the long rows of ordnance.

"It's an old Chinese trick, actually," explained Swanson. "I heard about it a long time ago, when Laura and I went on a trip to San Francisco. Business taxes were figured on the basis of square footage in the old days, so the Chinese sweatshop owners made these buildings with whole floors that you couldn't see from the street. The Chinaman would get taxed for three floors instead of four, and meanwhile his secret room would be packed with little old ladies and kids doing piecework."

"Shrewd," said Linberg. "Do you have any idea what's missing from this stockpile?"

"Pretty fair guess," said Swanson. "Apparently, Ungar kept good records. So far we figure about ten or fifteen nine-millimeter automatics of assorted make, at least one Kalashnikov PK .50-caliber machine gun, two crates of MDF polyvalent hand grenades, a box of Israeli number-twelve anti-personnel mines, and six Ingram MAC-11 submachine guns. Ammunition for it all, as well. There was also some plastique in the back that looked like someone had gone through it, but there's no way of telling how much was taken."

"That's enough to start a war," said Linberg. "They would have needed a truck to haul it all away."

"They *had* a truck. Dark blue Dodge van with three people in it. Two men and a woman. The van had New York plates. Long gone by now. Probably stolen."

"Okay," said Linberg, taking a last look around. "Get me the prints, a list of what was taken, and anything you've got from witnesses."

"You really think you might have a lead, Walt?"

"Maybe," said Linberg.

"Christ! It sure would be a feather in my cap if I could lock this one up," said the RA.

"Don't worry," Linberg lied, "you'll be the first to know if I come up with anything. I promise you."

"So what's the next step?"

"The next step, unless I miss my guess, is all hell breaking loose."

Chapter 3

Seen from the outside, Washington, D.C.'s Union Station is the epitome of a classic railroad terminal, complete with huge granite columns, sweeping stairways, and massive entrance doors. Looming to the north of the Capitol Building is a turn-of-the-century architect's grandiose vision of Imperial Rome brought to life.

Unfortunately, by the late sixties a quarter of a century of declining rail traffic had taken its toll, and the station had become a refuge for derelicts, home turf to the kind of people who lurk in public toilets and make their livings by checking the coin-return slots of pay phones. With the establishment of the National Rail Passenger Corporation—Amtrak—in 1971, and a need for a National Visitors' Center, the entire station was completely refurbished and overhauled. However, the Visitors' Center, a major Washington Bicentennial project, received most of the attention and money, and the passenger terminal itself was literally given a back seat, relegated to a few thousand square feet at the rear of the immense building and fitted out with vending machines and rows of plastic waiting-room seats. In the final analysis, the massive infusion of funds to the old station didn't really change much at all; by ten o'clock in the evening, the fluorescent-lit, low-ceilinged anteroom that served as a rail terminal was still populated mainly by winos and pay-phone vagabonds.

"We're probably going to get mugged before we have a chance to board the train," muttered Daniel Pendergast, keeping the heavy suitcase firmly clamped between his knees.

"Relax," said Harry. "There's only another five minutes."

"My palms are sweating, for Christ's sake."

"Why? We haven't done anything yet. Calm down. You're starting to *look* like a criminal."

"It's my Methodist heritage. Somewhere God is looking

37

down on us and saying to himself, 'Those little peckers are in deep, deep trouble now.'"

"I don't think you're taking this seriously enough," said Harry. "I'm not screwing around with this; I want it to work."

"I can't take it seriously," said Daniel. "Anybody who examined what we were doing objectively would have us committed or arrested for conspiracy. If this is the crime of the century, Harry, then understand you've got a chickenshit for a partner. I'm so nervous right now I'm almost wetting my pants."

"I don't want to hear about it," Harry said tersely. There was an almost incomprehensible crackling voice coming over the public-address system. The only words Harry could make out were "New York" and "Boston."

"That's it," he said. He stood, picking up his own bag, and headed for the narrow tunnel entrance that led onto the platform. Daniel followed, the suitcase dragging his right arm down.

They reached the platform and followed a trainman's directions to the right. The Night Owl was ready and waiting, a gleaming silver behemoth snugged up against the concrete walkway, light from the scattered overhead bulbs reflecting off the polished aluminum of the blunt-nosed F-40 diesel-electric engine. With the exception of the Montrealer, the Night Owl was the only Amtrak train on the Washington-Boston run that wasn't all electric. Both trains still utilized the older Budd and Pullman Standard sleepers, which were equipped with steam braking systems, making use of the eleven-thousand-volt overhead catenary system impossible.

As he went past the locomotive, Harry paused and half turned, as though waiting for Daniel to catch up; in fact, he was taking in as much detail as he could about the activity around the RPO coupled directly behind the F-40.

The Railway Post Office was shut up tight, the glass in the doors and all the windows covered by roller blinds. There were four men standing beside the car, watching as the thin stream of passsengers wended its way down the platform. The men made no attempt to disguise their purpose; two were in Treasury Police uniforms and carried pistol-grip-equipped, nickel-barreled TP-8 police shotguns. The other two, both tall and wearing suits, carried attaché cases. Harry, who'd seen the attempted assassination of Ronald Reagan on television ad nauseam, had no doubt that the innocent-looking cases held Uzi machine guns or something just as lethal.

Daniel caught up with Harry, who fell into step beside him. Together they continued down the platform past the RPO and the baggage car behind it.

"You son of a bitch!" whispered Daniel, once they were out of earshot. "What have you gotten me into, man? Did you *see* those guys?"

"Shut up and keep walking," gritted Harry. "If you throw a tantrum out here, you'll get us arrested before we even do anything, goddammit,"

They continued on in silence, Harry mentally checking off the cars in the consist. The baggage car was followed by a pair of tubular Amfleet coaches, an Amdinette, and their car, a stainless steel Budd sleeper. The last car in the train was a Budd sleeper/observation car. The Pennsylvania Railroad nameboards above the windows on both cars had been painted out, and both of the outdated cars now bore the same red, white, and blue "pointless arrow" striping of the other cars. A tired-looking black porter stood at the bottom of the steps leading up into the sleeper.

"Where to?" he asked, eyeing Daniel's large suitcase.

"New York. Bedroom D," said Harry.

"Fine," said the man. He looked at the suitcase again. "You want me to carry that?"

"No thanks," said Harry. "We can manage."

They followed the porter up into the vestibule and down the narrow corridor of the sleeping car. He led them to their room and opened the door. The bunk beds had already been let down, and the canvas webbing on the upper was strung to clips on the ceiling. The window blind was up, giving them a view of the deserted platform outside, while beneath the thinly carpeted floor, machinery clicked and steam conduits hissed softly.

"See your tickets?" said the porter dully.

Harry, standing in the doorway, reached into the inside pocket of his sport jacket and took out the folder of tickets, while behind him in the bedroom, Daniel dropped the suitcase with a sigh of relief.

The porter flipped open the folder, checked the tickets

briefly, and then looked up at Harry, his expression sour. "What's this?" asked the black man.

Harry swallowed, feeling his heart rise up into his throat. For a horrible second he wondered if he'd given the porter the wrong set of tickets. The other set, made out for their return, were for the corresponding train that was now preparing to leave Boston, en route to Washington. The train they were on now was due to arrive at Penn Station in New York at 2:18 in the morning, and their return tickets were for the 3:33 train to the capital. The last thing they needed was to have a porter telling stories to his friends about the two guys who rode up to New York on one train and came back on another one an hour later.

"What's what?" asked Harry, as calmly as he could.

"Says here 'Smith, Mr. and Mrs.' You don't look like mister and missus to me, Smith or otherwise."

Harry squeezed his eyes shut for an instant, and tried not to let his relief be too obvious. He'd tried for the cheapest rate he could, which had been husband and wife. It had never occurred to him that the man taking their tickets would actually read them.

"You have some objection?" asked Harry, trying to sound severe. The porter lifted one eyebrow and curled his lip simultaneously. He snapped his copy off the carbon set and handed the folder back to Harry.

"I'd rather not say," he grunted. "We get into New York at a quarter after two or so," he said. "Should I wake you up?"

"That won't be necessary," said Harry.

The porter gave him one last look. "No, I bet it won't," he said. He turned away, shaking his head, and Harry closed the door. He slumped down onto the lower bunk and dug into his jacket for his cigarettes. Daniel sat down beside him and stared blankly out the window.

"First you get me involved in a train robbery, and now the porter thinks we're a pair of faggots. Jesus!"

"Quit crapping around and get out the stuff," said Harry. "I don't want to miss any of it."

Daniel nodded and lugged the big suitcase up onto the lower bunk. Harry edged around his friend in the tiny room and climbed the short ladder to the upper bunk. Taking a screwdriver out of his jacket pocket, he leaned

40

out and began working on the small half-moon-shaped ventilation grill in the ceiling.

Below him, Daniel pulled down the window blind and snapped open the catches on the suitcase. Inside, nestled in a cut-out block of foam, was a Radio Shack Pro 2002 fifty-channel programmable scanner, a twelve-volt snow-mobile battery, a battered Sony cassette player, fifty feet of coiled shortwave radio antenna wire, patch cords, battery cables with an adapter jack, and an assortment of tools. Daniel lifted out the scanner and the tape recorder, placing them carefully on the hinged cover over the recessed sink in the wall of the compartment. He got to work quickly, connecting the battery leads and linking the scanner to the cassette recorder. He twisted the exposed copper ends of the antenna coil to a universal jack, plugged it into the back of the scanner, and handed up the coil to Harry.

Taking a roll of masking tape and a tape measure out of his jacket pocket, Harry measured off a six-foot section at the other end of the coil, marked it with a strip of tape, and began feeding the wire up into the exposed ventilator duct. According to the sleeper car plans, six feet of wire would bring him to the outer grating in the roof of the train, with a foot or so of wire to spare. Just as he hit the taped mark on the wire, there was a small jerk and a hard metallic rattling from the bogies beneath the car as they got under way. Using another piece of tape, Harry fixed the wire to the ceiling and skidded down the ladder.

"Turn it on, quick."

Daniel turned on the power, set the LED clock at 00:00:00, and hit the program button on the keyboard. He tapped in the 162.25 frequency, entered it, and switched on the tape recorder. An ear-splitting crackle filled the compartment, and Daniel lunged for the volume knob. He turned it low and adjusted the squelch.

"If that porter comes back now, we're dead meat," he whispered hoarsely.

"He won't," said Harry. "Turn it up a bit so we can hear." Harry opened his own, much smaller suitcase, took out a steno pad, a felt pen, and sat down on the bunk. He leaned forward, his face tense as he tried to listen to the scanner over the creaking rattle of the gently lurching train.

For a minute there was nothing but empty air. "You sure it's working?" asked Harry nervously.

"It's working," said Daniel. Suddenly there was another voice.

"*Federal Mobile One, this is Night Owl, how do you copy?*"

There was brief pause and then a reply, slightly weaker. "*Night Owl, this is Federal Mobile One. We read you loud and clear.*"

"*Thank you, FM One. Code Able King Able. We're just out of the station.*"

"*Thank you, Night Owl. We'll relay to Baltimore. FM One out.*"

The airwaves were silent again.

"What the hell was all that?" asked Daniel.

"I think it means they've got some kind of mobile unit riding shotgun on the train," said Harry. He tapped the felt pen against his teeth thoughtfully. "It makes sense. Route One runs within a mile or so of the tracks all the way to Baltimore, and they could use Ninety-five and One again into New York."

"They've probably got a truck with a SWAT team in it or something," said Daniel.

"Whatever," said Harry. "They're riding pretty close herd anyway. I was right, we wouldn't stand a chance if we managed to stop the train."

"What about the other stuff?" asked Daniel. "The 'code Able King Able'?"

"Some kind of ID, I think. Lets the mobile know the calls are bona fide."

"A bit paranoid, don't you think?"

Harry grinned. "They must have seen us coming."

At 10:51 the radio came to life again. "*FM One, this is Night Owl. How do you copy?*"

"*Night Owl, this is FM One. We copy loud and clear.*"

"*Thank you, FM One. Code Able King Able. We're twenty out of Baltimore.*"

"*Okay, Night Owl. Security is confirmed on the mark. Your next transmission will be to Baltimore Base. Out.*"

"What do they mean by 'security is on the mark'?" asked Daniel.

Harry looked up from his notebook. "I'm pretty sure it means the mark the engineers use when they come into a station. The platform is marked off so the driver can tell when to brake. They've probably got security people waiting where the RPO is going to end up, like they had in Washington."

"Uzis and shotguns," muttered Daniel.

Harry ignored the comment. "I'm going up to the head end," he said, standing up. "Maybe I'll be able to see something out the window. I want to check a couple of other things out, too. You keep on the radio. And watch that the tape doesn't run out."

Harry opened the door fractionally, peeked out, and then stepped into the corridor, closing the door behind him. He waited until he heard the click of Daniel throwing the lock, then headed forward, feeling slightly awkward as the erratic pitch and sway of the train tried to catch him off balance. He reached the end of the car, hauled open the heavy door, and moved out into the vestibule. He stepped sideways into the shadows and waited for a moment. If anyone in the cafeteria car up ahead had noticed anything, no one was coming to investigate. He lit a cigarette and stood silently, swaying with the train and examining the flexible diaphragm that connected the sleeper to the Amdinette.

Ever since his discussion with Daniel in the Hot Shoppe a few days before, an idea had been forming. If anything, it was even more bizarre than the initial plan to rob the train, so he hadn't said anything to Daniel. Harry knew his friend well enough to understand that Daniel was just as frustrated as he himself was with the way his life had gone in the past few years, but he'd never been quite the risk-taker that Harry was. He needed to be coaxed along until it was too late to turn back, but once he'd reached that point, you couldn't ask for a better comrade-in-arms.

Harry inevitably found the coaxing process an irritation, but it had its good points. For one thing, it forced Harry to stop and think things out instead of just barging ahead, and if there were any flaws in his thinking, Daniel's cold and fishy eye would find them. It had been Harry's idea, for instance, to get into the cocaine-smuggling business, but it had been Daniel who'd come up with the idea of faking a car accident in Bogotá and having himself brought back into the States in a body cast made of the drug, aided by a Pan Am stewardess to push

43

his wheelchair through customs, and an ambulance-driver accomplice to take him to a "convalescent hospital."

But that was a long time ago; both men were a lot older, and as Harry knew full well, age was a great destroyer of more than the rock-hard teenage erections you once counted on. Age killed imagination, innovation, and initiative. Whether Daniel knew it or not, taking the Night Owl currency shipment was their last chance at anything really great. It was their last chance for glory, and perhaps for a little more than Andy Warhol's fifteen minutes of fame.

Harry dropped his cigarette butt onto the floor of the vestibule and ground it out, annoyed with himself for wasting time thinking. He reached into the pocket of his jacket and took out a small shoemaker's awl and a jeweler's hacksaw.

The diaphragm that connects two railway passenger cars is actually composed of two parts, one of which is connected to each car. The two open ends of the diaphragm couple together to form a flexible seal that allows the train to negotiate curves while providing passengers with a safe passage between cars. The diaphragm itself is a bellowslike arrangement of fiber-reinforced rubber stretched over a skeleton of metal ribs and tie-rods that keep it from sagging. Eyeing the diaphragm, Harry grimaced. If the train came to a sudden stop when he was partially through the gap he was about to create, the steel ribs embedded in the rubber would collapse together, slicing him in half like a pair of scissors. He was suddenly very glad that this was only a dry run.

He dropped down to his knees and rammed the awl into the rubberized fabric of the diaphragm, puncturing it neatly. He worked the awl back and forth until he had a good-sized hole, then inserted the squared end of the little saw. Using a rapid back-and-forth action, he began to rip upwards, keeping the growing tear close to the jutting shape of the reinforcing rod in the bellows. It took him less than thirty seconds to create an opening a foot and a half long. It was all he needed. When the time came to do it for real, the possibility of being interrupted wouldn't be a factor, and he'd have lots of time.

He dropped down onto his stomach and, using both hands, pulled the opening wider. He looked out into the darkness, squinting as the blast of rushing outside air tore through the hole.

After a few seconds he stood up, grinning happily to himself. He brushed the dirt off his shirt and jacket and lit another cigarette. It was going to work. Still smiling, he stepped back and looked down at the tear in the diaphragm. It was barely noticeable from a standing position, and if anyone did notice it, the rent would look like natural wear. He moved out of the shadows and slid open the door into the Amdinette.

There were only three people in the rear section of the car: a late-middle-aged couple silently consuming microwaved slices of pizza with plastic forks while they looked out at the lights of suburban Westport on the outskirts of Baltimore, and a tired-looking businessman nursing a can of Schlitz. The steward behind the U-shaped counter in the middle of the car was reading a newspaper, occasionally sipping from a styrofoam cup of coffee.

Harry moved through the car, nodding to the steward as he passed. The front half of the car was completely empty. Reaching the forward exit, Harry pressed the "open" panel and the automatic door swished back into its slot. He stepped across the vestibule into the first coach.

The lights had already been dimmed and the car was dark except for a few scattered beams from overhead reading lamps. Harry moved through the car slowly, balancing himself by holding on to the backs of seats and taking a rough head count as he went along. By his estimation the coach, capable of seating eighty, was less than half full. Most of the people looked like the guy with his can of beer—businessmen on their way back to New York or Boston.

There were even fewer people in the next coach, and only one reading light was on. Everyone else appeared to be asleep. Keeping things casual, Harry continued forward, stopping in front of the closed door of the washroom. He paused for a split second, then touched the "open" panel on the door. It slipped back and he stepped out into the vestibule.

Moving sideways into the protective shadows, Harry waited again, letting a full minute pass. No one seemed to be paying any attention to him. Another tick on the

45

checklist in his head. He lifted his wrist and glanced at the glowing dial of his watch: 11:08. Two, maybe three minutes before they pulled into Baltimore's Penn Station. He touched the door plate again and stepped back into the darkened coach. No one even looked up. It would be more obvious, bringing two people out into the car, but the diversion he had in mind would take care of that. Satisfied, Harry slipped into the vacant double seat to his left and lit a cigarette. He dropped his chin onto his palm and his elbow onto the window ledge, trying to look like any other bored passenger. Ninety seconds later the Night Owl pulled smoothly in under the arches of Baltimore Station.

The train paused for less than five minutes, but it was enough time for Harry to confirm his suspicions about the security present for the RPO. Four men in suits stood on the platform, each of them with an attaché case and each looking in a different direction. They were so obviously plainclothes cops that they might as well have been wearing signs. All four stood far enough back from the train itself so that Harry could see them without craning his neck. He hoped that meant there was no visual check with the occupants of the RPO. If there was a physical check of the RPO guards, Harry's plan would be down the toilet. He watched as one of the men took a walkie-talkie out of his jacket and spoke briefly. A radio check. No meeting. Ten seconds later the train began to move again. Relieved, Harry stood up and made his way back to the sleeper.

He knocked softly at the door of Bedroom D and waited.

"Who is it?"

"The Queen of Sheba. Open up."

The lock clicked and Harry opened the door. He slipped into the bedroom quickly, shutting and locking the door behind him. Daniel was sitting on the edge of the lower bunk, listening to the radio, the steno notebook on his lap.

"Find out anything interesting?" he asked.

"Just as I thought. They had security types on the platform."

Daniel nodded. "I know. I heard them talking. They're Federal Mobile Two, in case you're interested."

"Any special codes?"

"Nope," said Daniel, shaking his head. "Just the Able King Able."

"Good," said Harry, smiling happily. He kicked off his shoes and flopped down on the lower bunk, thrusting his legs out behind Daniel.

"It's all coming together rather nicely."

"What's coming together?" asked Daniel.

"Ze plan, my friend, ze plan."

"I didn't know we had one," said Daniel suspiciously.

"We don't . . . not entirely," admitted Harry. "But it's brewing."

"Don't be shy," said Daniel sourly. "Lay it on me."

"Not yet," said Harry. "You'd shoot it full of holes and ruin my concentration. I'll tell you one thing, though, we're going to need at least two more people. Remember Benovoy?"

"The geek who drove the ambulance for the Great Snow Job? Sure, I remember him. Why?"

"We're going to need him and his ambulance again. And one other person. You know anybody who's smart, poverty-stricken, and desperate enough to get involved in this scam?"

"Adrian Tucker," said Daniel, without even stopping to think.

"Who's Adrian Tucker?"

"An actor. He's got no talent at all, but he keeps on going out for auditions all the time. He's been a waiter at Sardi's for years now. He insists it gets him closer to the stars."

"You sure he can handle the pressure? He sounds like a wimp."

"Relax," Daniel said. "He'll be okay. Anything else?"

"Yeah," said Harry, cupping his hands behind his head and yawning again. "We're going to need a coffin."

"I beg your pardon?"

"A coffin," Harry repeated.

"Oh God!" moaned Daniel, quietly.

Walter Linberg and his old friend and one-time partner, Inspector George Reikoff, knelt in the dirt in front of the fourth-floor window of the warehouse and watched the freight-loading doors at the rear of the low, windowless building on the other side of the alley. Reikoff, a thin, beak-nosed man in his late forties, took the binoculars from his eyes and pinched the bridge of his nose. The two men had been watching out the window since dawn, almost three hours before. The warehouse and the buildings around it were located in an old commercial area off Water Street in Washington, D.C., just east of the Navy Yard. From what Linberg had been able to tell in the predawn hours, at least half of the buildings in the area were abandoned.

"I hope to hell they're in there," said Reikoff. "For both our sakes."

"What's this 'both' business?" answered Linberg, looking away from the building for a moment. "You're the one who ordered in a full SWAT unit, not me."

"Acting on your information, Walt."

"Just a concerned citizen," said Linberg, smiling. He took a sip from a long-cold thermos cup of coffee, and winced.

"Horseshit," muttered Reikoff, putting the glasses to his eyes again. "You're ex-Bureau. If this turns out to be a pig in a poke, then you're in as much crap as I am."

"Don't worry about it," said Linberg, "You're just doing your job. It's National Firearms Act stuff. Those people ripped off enough small arms and explosives to take out a good-sized city."

"So you say."

Linberg shrugged, but made no reply. He knew he was already walking a thin line, and if things went wrong he was going to need all the friends he could get. He took another sip from the plastic cup and tried to ignore the foul taste of the bitter black liquid.

So far, he'd had incredibly good luck. The prints Swanson had picked up from the St. Augustine weapons dump had matched the ones he had from the U.K. file. It was definite that, at the very least, Haas, Sheila Teng, and Mohamet Kawi had been involved in the robbery and murder of Malcolm Ungar. That in itself was enough to prove that the terrorists had come to the United States, and Linberg was sorely tempted to take the information to his superiors at that point. But he hadn't. The smell of the chase was in his nostrils, and knowing that he was

48

a fool for doing so, he'd decided to carry on his investigation a little longer.

He had some reasonably good contacts at FBI headquarters, but instead of using them and perhaps making his investigation too public too soon, he'd gone to George Reikoff, Special Agent in Charge of the Washington, D.C., Field Office. All Linberg had wanted to do was to use Reikoff as a pipeline into the NCIC computer, and he was stunned when, less than a week after the St. Augustine affair, the SAC called him with the information that the van with the New York plates had turned up as a positive on the D.C. police wanted list. The van had been found abandoned and stripped on a service road beside the Conrail tracks under the John Philip Sousa Bridge. Linberg had called in every marker he had with Reikoff, and finally persuaded the FBI inspector to do a block-by-block sweep of the area, questioning potential witnesses and using photographs of the six terrorists. The effort had resulted in two people picking out Dieter Haas as having been seen in the area, once buying groceries at a corner store close to the Chamberlain Vocational High School, and once entering the building they now had under surveillance. Since Linberg and Reikoff had taken their positions three hours before, there had been no sign of Haas or any of the other terrorists.

Reikoff had managed to find out who the owner of the building was, and from him the FBI man had been able to get a reasonably good idea of what the interior was like. According to the owner, the building had originally been an automotive body shop specializing in painting large trucks. The body shop had vacated the premises two years before, and since then it had been empty, except for an occasional short-term warehousing contract. He'd rented the building three weeks ago to a man who had said he wanted to warehouse some liquidation stock until he moved into his new store. The man, who spoke with a slight accent that the owner thought might have been German, had paid one month's rent in cash, plus a damage deposit. The owner identified a photograph of Dieter Haas as that of the man who had rented the building.

The building had no windows and only three doors—the double doors facing the alley and two fire doors, one on either side of the building. There were three rooftop ventilation ducts. Reikoff had men at the side doors, a truck and half a dozen men ready to go in through the front, and two men on the roof with tear-gas canisters. The D.C. police were providing backup with a SWAT team of their own, and had cordoned off an area bounded by M Street, Water Street, Virginia Avenue, and the Anacostia Bridge approaches. A total of almost fifty people were involved in the stakeout.

"How much longer do we wait?" asked Linberg.

Reikoff put down his binoculars again and checked his watch. Linberg did the same. It was 8:30 A.M. "We don't wait," said Reikoff.

He picked his walkie-talkie off the floor. "Inspector to all units. Go." His expression unchanged, Reikoff carefully placed the walkie-talkie back on the floor and picked up the binoculars again. Linberg followed suit.

Everything went with machinelike efficiency. On Reikoff's command, the two men on the roof pulled the pins on the dark green cylinders of the tear-gas canisters, popped the release levers, and dropped them down the air vents. Their main job done, the two men raced across the rooftop to the rappelling lines at the back of the building. At the same time, a high-bodied vehicle that had begun its life as a UPS delivery van—and was now used by the D.C. field office SWAT team—came roaring up the alley, veering sharply as it reached the wooden double doors leading into the building. Unfortunately, no one had checked to make sure that there was enough clearance for the truck to get in under the top of the door, and instead of bursting into the interior, the truck rammed into the doors with a splintering crash and then stopped dead, eight feet of its roof peeled back like a tin of sardines. From his observation point, Linberg could see wisps of tear gas begin to curl out of the newly created opening.

"Oh shit," said Reikoff, staring down at the ruined truck.

Undaunted, the six SWAT officers poured out of the rear of the vehicle, gas masks obscuring their faces and their bulky body armor making them look like awkward green insects. The first four men to enter the building carried pistol-grip shotguns, while the last two were armed with standard-issue 5mm Colt Commando assault rifles equipped with special long-box sixty-round magazines.

Reikoff's strategy was simple. The two fire doors were located on opposite walls to the left and right of the main entrance. The three SWAT men to the left would direct their fire into the upper right quadrant of the building. The men at the right would fire into the upper left, and the men at the main entrance would fire toward the rear, both left and right. In that way the men wouldn't be firing at each other, and theoretically anything in the building that wasn't hanging from the ceiling would be turned into hamburger.

As the SWAT team raced into the building, the air was filled with a crackling, thundering roar as the men opened up with their weapons. Then there was silence. From beginning to end, the entire operation had taken less than sixty seconds.

"I guess we'd better go and see what the score was," said Reikoff. His features were still expressionless, but Linberg knew that the older man was pleased with the way things had gone, despite the embarrassing damage to the truck.

As the two men reached the main floor of their building and stepped outside into the cool early-morning air, the driver of the SWAT truck began backing the vehicle out of the hole it had created, the curled metal of the demolished roof making a grating screech as it pulled away from the concrete door frame. Reikoff and Linberg stepped aside to let him maneuver, and then crossed the alley to the gaping hole in the side of the building. The darkened interior was filled with a haze of dust and tear gas, making any observation impossible. A SWAT officer appeared, a gas mask dangling from his neck. He was wearing a baseball cap with an FBI crest.

"You looked good going in, Norton," said Reikoff.

The SWAT man shrugged and began peeling off his body armor. "By the book," he replied.

"Anyone hurt?"

"None of ours," said Norton. "We'll have to wait until the smoke clears to see what we did to the other guys. It was pretty dark in there. Couldn't see much at all."

Norton picked up his armor, gave Reikoff a nod, and walked down the alley to where the SWAT truck was parked. Reikoff and Linberg waited for another minute, peering into the building. When the clouds of tear gas had dissipated, they entered, their feet crunching on the rubble created by the truck's violent entrance.

"Shit," said Reikoff for the second time, as he surveyed the scene. In just under thirty seconds the SWAT team had loosed 640 rounds of 5mm expanding bullets and thirty-two rounds of 12-gauge number-one buck pellets into the building. The general effect was catastrophic. The walls, relatively smooth only a few minutes before, were now pitted, torn, and gouged, and thousands of chips of concrete littered the floor. A small partitioned office space of glass and plywood in the rear of the warehouse had been turned to glistening fragments and matchstick splinters blown out over a third of the floor area. A compressor, two fifty-gallon drums, and several hand trucks had also been demolished. Except for several SWAT team members picking through the litter, however, the building was empty. Not only was there no sign of the terrorists' bodies, there was no evidence that they'd ever been there at all.

"Shit," said Reikoff for a third time.

Chapter 4

▐▐

The four members of what Daniel Pendergast had taken to calling the Night Owl Gang met together for the first time on Thursday, June twenty-third, only three days before the projected heist from Amtrak train number 66. During the eleven days since the trial run on the Night Owl, Harry and Daniel had enlisted Martin Benovoy, the pudgy, whey-faced, free-lance ambulance driver, and Adrian Tucker, Daniel's actor acquaintance from Sardi's. Benovoy was immediately enthusiastic, since for a quarter share amounting to around seven million dollars, all he had to do was provide some equipment and do a little driving. Privately, Benovoy thought the whole idea was crazy, but after seven years of pirating ambulance calls and low-level drug dealing, he was willing to give anything a shot, and his previous experience with Maxwell and Pendergast had been successful enough for him to justify what he'd calculated was a minimal risk.

Tucker, on the other hand, had been wary, at least at first. He was considerably more intelligent than Benovoy, and his imagination was good enough for him to visualize all sorts of horrors if something went wrong with the plan. Like Harry and Daniel, though, he had reached a point in his life where he realized that fame and fortune had passed him by. His mustache, muscle, and Marlboro Man good looks were beginning to fade, and his "temporary" work as a waiter was starting to look more and more like a lifetime profession. His confidence in the future had been further eroded by a recent split with a boyfriend he'd been living with for almost five years. After he'd thought about it for a while, the potentially suicidal nature of the project began to appeal to him. It was also the best part he'd had in years.

Harry and Daniel had interviewed the two men separately for security reasons, then assigned them their various tasks. By Thursday everything necessary had been accomplished, and the meeting was called at Daniel's loft for a final run-through.

Over the weeks since Harry had originally broached the plan to Daniel, the loft had lost any visible association with contemporary art. The earlier litter of plans and schedules had given way to a hodgepodge of arcane equipment that ranged from several large compressed-air tanks to a strange rod-and-tripod contraption that looked like a badly made pair of sloping parallel bars. The centerpiece of it all was an immense gray fiberglass casket that sat in the middle of the room, enshrouded by a painter's plastic drop sheet. Benovoy was proud of his acquisition, having purchased it at a fire-sale price from a funeral home that had used it as a showroom model and was now dropping that particular line. Harry and Daniel were pleased with the discount purchase, since the costs of setting up their escapade had been a lot higher than they'd originally thought, and their small savings were running dangerously low.

The four men sat around the work table that Daniel used for stretching his canvases, sipping at bottles of beer and enjoying the coolness of the shadowed room. The last of the day's sun was slanting in through the tall front windows of the loft, covering everything in shades of muted gold.

"Well, we certainly don't look much like the Dirty Dozen," said Tucker, looking around the table with a smile.

"More like the Futile Four," said Daniel. "Every time I stop and really think about what we're doing, I wonder if I shouldn't be committed. It really is crazy."

"Of course it's crazy," said Harry, at the head of the table. "All the great events of history have been based on craziness."

"Let's not have a lecture about it," said Benovoy curtly from the other end of the table. The short, pear-shaped man squirmed uneasily on the hard seat of the straight chair. "We should get down to business, don't you think?"

"Okay," said Harry. "One more time: the Plan."

"For the fiftieth time," muttered Daniel, one finger rubbing the long, curving line of his nose.

Harry ignored his friend and continued. "I've gone over everything, and as far as I can tell we're ready." He glanced down at the typewritten sheet in front of him. "I'd like to go over the schedule, each of us describing what he's supposed to do, just to make sure we've got it right. Martin, you start it off."

Benovoy took a short swig of beer and began, his reedy voice echoing slightly in the big room. "At nine P.M. I pick up the ambulance from the garage on I Street. I checked this afternoon, by the way, and the paint's just about dry. When I spray on the sign, it'll look just like a mortician's meat wagon. Okay. I make sure I've got the other sign under the seat, and then I head over here. I figure it should take about fifteen minutes on Sunday evening, so that puts it at nine-fifteen, right?"

"We've got some flexibility there, but that sounds okay. Go on," said Harry.

"Right. I pull into the back here and then I come up and help load Harry into the coffin. We check to see that the spring release is working on the end panel we put in, and then we hand Harry the rails and the tripods."

"I'll already have the tanks and the masks on me when I get in," interrupted Harry.

"Right," said Benovoy. "Anyway, after we get Harry and the stuff loaded, Daniel, Adrian, and I take the coffin down to the hearse. According to the test times we've done, it should take about twelve minutes to get the box into the freight elevator and down to the car. That makes it, uh, nine-twenty-seven, give or take a couple of minutes. From here I drive to the station and go in the H Street freight entrance at the back. I hand the coffin over to the freight handlers there at around nine-forty-five."

"You've got all the paperwork figured out?" asked Daniel.

"No sweat," said Benovoy. "Picked them up this morning, and it went just like Harry said. They asked me to bring in the stiff as late as possible so they can make sure it gets put close to the doors. They only do the Princeton Junction stop on specials like this, so they have to get it off the train as fast as they can. I think the Amtrak guy said the stop was only three minutes."

Harry nodded. The coffin was the key part of the plan. Other than at major scheduled stops, the only way to offload baggage from any of the Amtrak Northeast Corridor trains was by special dispensation, and those were most commonly given for cadavers.

"So," Benovoy went on, "as soon as I hand over the box, I split out of town for Princeton Junction. When I figure I'm in the clear, I pull over and paste on the new signs. I go from being Arlington Memorial Gardens to the Woodglen Funeral Parlor."

Harry nodded again. Both were the names of real companies, and after the robbery that fact would help to further cloud their escape. He figured on at least a couple of hours being wasted while the authorities ran down the two morticians and discovered that neither one had transshipped a body to or from Princeton Junction.

Benovoy went on, "I should get to Princeton Junction about one o'clock in the morning, which gives me about twenty minutes. Even if I'm a bit late, it won't matter, because they'll just keep the coffin on the platform until I pick it up."

"Don't be late," said Daniel.

"All right," Harry said. "That takes care of you. Daniel?"

"I board the train just after Adrian does. I'll be there early to make sure that I'm pretty close to being first on. I get a seat as close to the exit door as I can, in the coach nearest the baggage car.

"At ten-thirty the Night Owl leaves Union Station. I sit there twiddling my thumbs until twelve-forty-five or fifteen minutes after the train leaves Philadelphia, in case it's late. At twelve-forty-five I get up, go to the washroom, and come out about a minute later. When I'm sure that no one is paying any attention, I go out into the vestibule. If everything has gone according to plan, Harry should have opened up the baggage car door from the inside by then. I help Harry get into the sling that holds the gas bottle on his back, and then he goes out into the vestibule between the baggage car and the RPO. While he's cutting through the diaphragm with the bolt cutters, I'll be setting up the conveyor. Harry and I tested it today, and it works perfectly."

Wearing a pair of Harry's Amtrak coveralls and carrying a toolbox, Daniel Pendergast had bluffed his way onto the Night Owl platform just before the currency shipment was loaded the Sunday before. Watching out of the corner of his eye from a hundred feet away, he'd seen the uniformed Treasury guards transferring the money onto the RPO. From what he could see, the money was contained in plastic or fiber boxes about a foot square and six inches deep. He could only keep a rough count, but he thought there were about a hundred of the boxes loaded onto the train.

On the basis of that information, Harry had devised a system of rapidly moving the money from the RPO into the baggage car, and from there into the casket. Using full five-hundred-sheet boxes of typewriter paper as dummy money parcels, they constructed a simple conveyor system. Using stainless steel tubing lengths of diminishing circumference, they built two rails that were twelve feet long when fully extended. Daniel then sewed a long sleeve of lightweight nylon sailcloth that could be slipped over the rails. When metal braces were added at the ends of the rails, the nylon sling became a taut, almost frictionless trough slightly less than an inch deep. The two end braces were then screwed on to aluminum photographer's tripods, one with its telescoping legs set two feet higher than the other. By placing a box of the typing paper at the high end and giving it a quick push, it was possble to move the box down to the low end without any trouble. Harry and Daniel had practiced for most of the afternoon, timing their performance with a stopwatch. After four hours of cold-start assemblies, Daniel could put the whole thing together in two minutes and tear it down in ninety seconds. The two men figured that, working at top speed, they could load the coffin to its maximum capacity of ninety-six boxes in approximately fifteen minutes. The boxes of typing paper weighed just over four pounds, so if the money weighed roughly the same, the coffin would be loaded with 392 pounds, which was only ten pounds more than Harry and the equipment he was taking with him.

Daniel continued to outline his schedule. "By the time the conveyor is set up, it'll be twelve-fifty. By twelve-fifty-five Harry will have finished gassing the RPO, and I'll punch out the lock. We should be able to start loading a couple of minutes after that, as long as the gas masks Martin got us don't leak."

"They won't," put in the ambulance driver. "The gas is pretty heavy anyway, and it dissipates fast. Just make sure you put vaseline around the seals before you put them on, and you'll be okay."

"I hope so," said Daniel. "Anyway, as soon as we finish transferring the money, we break down the conveyor, collect all our tools, and put them into the coffin. Then we close it up and wait. At one-twenty-three, or four minutes outside Trenton, we go back into the coach under cover of Adrian's diversion. The train will stop at Princeton Junction at one-twenty-six but we stay on until Metro Park at one-forty-eight. That gives us roughly half an hour before the shit hits the fan in New York, which should be plenty of time." Daniel turned to his old friend and smiled. "Your turn, Harry."

"Okay. I climb out of the coffin at twelve-forty with the gas and the tools and the subassemblies for the conveyor. The first thing I do is turn the latch on the baggage car door to let Daniel in. Then I strap on the tank and go to the vestibule with the bolt cutters. I cut through the bellows frame on the diaphragm and climb out onto the coupler. There are lots of grab-irons on the end of the RPO, so I don't think I'll have any trouble getting onto the roof. Once I'm up on the roof, I cut their antenna with the wire cutters and then I push the outlet nozzle into the nearest of the two rear vent chimneys and crack the valve. According to Martin, it will take less than a minute for the stuff to empty, and another couple of minutes after that for it to take effect."

"That's the part that worries me," said Adrian Tucker, frowning. "This whole thing depends on the gas working. If the two guards aren't completely out of it, you're likely to get killed when you come in through the door."

"Ask Martin," Harry said with a shrug. "He's the one with the medical background."

Benovoy, whose "medical background" consisted of his ambulance driving and three years as a paramedic at a NATO base in Germany, gave a brief nod. "It should work," he said. "Nitrous oxide isn't the best anesthetic in the world, but it's a debilitant as well. That tank has eighty cubic feet at three hundred PSI. That'll saturate the inside of the car pretty thoroughly, more than the blowers can handle, and by the time the two guys pick up on the smell, they'll be too stoned to move. There's nothing else you could use safely. Anyway, it was the only thing I could get in any kind of quantity. The nitrous and the Noctec will put out their lights for a good four to six hours."

"Satisfied?" asked Harry.

"I guess so," answered Tucker, his expression still worried.

"All right, where was I? Twelve-fifty-two. I climb down from the RPO, dump the tank, and come back through the diaphragm. By then, Daniel has the conveyor set up. We put on the masks and then Daniel punches out the lock with the sledge and the cold chisel. I take the Noctec syringes from Daniel and inject the two guards while Daniel uses the bolt cutters to cut into the mesh around the money boxes. I go back to the baggage car and Daniel starts sending out the boxes. After that, it's just like he said. Back into the coach at one-twenty-three, off the train at Metro Park in New Jersey at one-forty-eight." Harry sat back and lit a cigarette, looking toward Adrian Tucker, the man he figured as the weakest link in the chain.

"My basic job is to monitor the radio," began the actor. "I get on the train at ten-fifteen and go to Bedroom C. I set up both the scanner and our own transmitter, running the antenna wire up through the ventilator like Harry showed me. I monitor the transmissions from the RPO at Baltimore, Aberdeen, Wilmington, and Philadelphia, making sure that I have that night's code group. I also make sure that the transmissions are still coming through at their regular intervals. At one o'clock exactly I make my first transmission, covering for Harry and Daniel. I make my next transmission at one-twenty, right on schedule, informing the mobile unit that my next transmission will be from the stop at Princeton Junction. As soon as I finish, I leave the bedroom and go forward to the first coach. Halfway up the coach I pretend to slip and make a big production of falling down. While I'm doing that, Harry and Daniel slip into the coach and sit down. I limp back to the bedroom and make my one-twenty-six transmission from Princeton Junction. I keep on making regular transmissions all the way into New York. When the train pulls in, I get off immediately, leaving everything behind. I grab the first cab I see and get the hell away from the station as fast as I can. How's that?"

"Fine," said Harry cautiously. "Are you sure you can handle it?"

"I think so," the actor said, frowning thoughtfully. "But I have a question, if you don't mind," he added.

"Shoot," said Harry.

"Well, I don't mean to be negative, but it occurred to me that you're really the biggest problem we've got."

"How's that?" asked Harry coldly.

"You work for Amtrak. That's going to be the first place the police check. They'll be looking for anyone who might have had access to that mail car. If you stay at your job, you're going to be questioned, and if you suddenly quit, that will draw attention to you. It might take them a while, but eventually they'll figure it out, and that means we're all in trouble."

Harry nodded. "You're right, but I've taken care of the problem. I'm going to have the perfect alibi, you might say."

"How?" asked the actor. "Alibi or not, they're going to question you."

"They can't question me if I'm dead," said Harry.

"Excuse me?"

"The coffin gave me the idea. When you think about it, my dying is the only way, really. I'll be ruled out automatically as a suspect. Mr. Benovoy there, at the end of the table, has taken care of everything. According to the files at D.C. General Hospital, I will be admitted to their emergency room in the early hours of tomorrow morning as a DOA drug overdose. Smack. My boss, Mosley, will believe that without thinking twice about it. The file will have a fully completed death certificate filled in and signed by a bona fide doctor in the ER who does so much speed, according to Martin, that he wouldn't remember one patient from another twenty minutes after working on him. The file will also show that I was carrying a cadaver-donor card stating that I sold my body two years ago to Georgetown University Hospital. Martin even came up with a transfer slip showing that I was shipped off to Georgetown U. Even if the FBI was as suspicious as hell, it would take them weeks to go through all the bureaucratic bullshit."

"Wear a paramedic's whites with a few old bloodstains on it, and you fade right into the background," said Benovoy. "You can go anywhere in a hospital and no one pays the slightest bit of attention to you."

"Marvelous!" breathed Tucker. "You really have thought of everything."

"I sure as hell hope so," said Daniel.

Harry lifted his shoulders in a shrug. "I think it's a pretty good setup," he said. "We're amateurs, and this is a one-shot proposition, so I think we stand a decent chance of getting away with it cleanly." He paused and looked around the table. "On the other hand, I'm not giving any guarantees. Even a single wrong move could screw things up, like Ronnie Biggs's fingerprints at that farmhouse after they'd robbed the Scottish Mail. This whole thing is a risk. A big one."

"Come on, Harry," chided Benovoy. "What could go wrong?"

"Who knows?" said Harry. "Maybe nothing, and then again, maybe everything."

By Monday afternoon, the FBI forensic team had completed their work at the supposed terrorist hideout in the Water Street area. By Wednesday, George Reikoff had managed to sneak a copy of their findings to Walter Linberg, along with a terse note informing the ex–FBI agent that as far as Reikoff was concerned, Linberg was persona non grata at the Washington field office from now on. Late Friday morning, Linberg received a copy of a memo that had been sent from the FBI Budget and Acounting Section to Thomas Ash, executive director of USIST— Walter Linberg's boss. The memo included a detailed accounting of the costs of the combined FBI–D.C. Metropolitan Police SWAT operation, as well as an operational report written by Reikoff, which outlined the origins of the operation, as well as Linberg's part in it. The memo stated quite bluntly that since the assault had been mounted on the basis of Linberg's obviously erroneous information, USIST bore at least some of the fiscal responsibility for the operation. The memo concluded with a request that, in future, employees of USIST refrain from involving themselves with Bureau matters. Half an hour after the memo reached his desk, Walter Linberg was asked to attend a meeting with Executive Director Ash later in the day.

After reading the memo over a couple of times, Linberg's initial anger turned to bitter acceptance. Although in reality the assault had been made on the basis of legitimate information gathered from the St. Augustine investigation, it was obvious that Reikoff and the Washington field office were using him as a scapegoat. Responsibility for the $20,000 fiasco had been laid quite clearly on his doorstep, and Linberg had no illusions about how Ash would handle the situation. A sacrificial lamb was required, and Walter Linberg was it. He dictated a letter of resignation to his secretary and asked her to type it up and hand-deliver it to the executive director's office. While she was doing that, he went over the preliminary forensic report, desperately looking for some clue that might give him an idea as to what the terrorists' next move might be. One way or another, if it was only for the sake of his professional pride, he was going to carry the investigation as far as he could. He was positive that the terrorist group represented a real threat. He'd gone into the Bureau as a gung-ho recruit, but his years in law enforcement had taught him that departmental bungling and whitewashing had confounded the investigation of as many crimes as the Bureau's agents had solved. He wasn't going to let it happen this time, even if he had to go to the newspapers and commit the cardinal sin of embarrassing the Bureau.

The forensic report in itself was an example of the complex bureaucracy that could often choke an investigation. A dozen people had been involved, hailing from half a dozen different sections within the FBI, from Latent Fingerprints to the Document Section. Each had its own operating methods and procedures, with all of the various material eventually filtering down to the Uniform Crime Reporting Section of the Computer Systems Division. The resulting report was a tossed salad of information that made almost no sense at all.

The Latent Prints people, for instance, had sent their findings to the technical boys, who had in turn sent them on to Fingerprint Correspondence. Correspondence reported back to Latent saying that there was no record of any of the prints from the warehouse being on file, even though Linberg had given both Swanson and Reikoff sets of the terrorists' prints. Sometimes Linberg wondered how any crimes were ever solved at all.

After spending an hour poring over the report, he could find only two pieces of information that might be leads. The first was the fact that the compressor and some of the other machinery found at the site indicated that a vehicle had been painted there sometime during the previous week. The second was a three-inch piece of cash-register tape listing four identical purchases and their inventory numbers. The tape had been sent to the Documents Section for analysis by the Checkwriter, Rubber Stamp, and Mechanical Devices Office. Possibly they would be able to trace the tape to its source.

Linberg went to the Xerox machine on the main floor, copied the entire forensic report as well as the original U.K. file, and then returned to his office. It was noon, and his secretary had gone to lunch, but she'd left an envelope in the center of his desk. It was his letter of resignation. At the bottom of the page, Ash had scrawled the word "Accepted" and then signed his name.

Smiling to himself, and not quite sure why he felt so elated, Walter Linberg packed his attaché case, took a last look around, and then left his office, closing the door quietly behind him.

Harry Maxwell lay on the floor of Daniel Pendergast's studio, staring up at the ceiling, a bottle of beer carefully balanced on his chest. Beside him on the floor a cigarette burned slowly in a tinfoil container that had once held a frozen TV dinner. A few feet away, seated on the window sill, Daniel stared out into the darkness, listening to the steady patter of rain that was falling on the city of Washington. He glanced at his watch and grunted.

"Twenty-four hours exactly," he said. "It's ten-thirty."

"Great," murmured Harry from the floor, still staring at the ceiling, trying to count the old-fashioned tin squares in the gloom. Behind him the accumulated litter of the past few weeks had been carefully cleaned up and disposed of, and Daniel's art materials had been returned to their proper places. The only jarring object was the coffin, still on its sawhorses in the center of the room, and now packed with the equipment they'd need to crack the Night Owl RPO. Harry and Daniel were alone in the studio. Martin Benovoy had taken a couple of Serax earlier in the evening and gone home to get a good night's sleep, and Adrian was out seeing if he could rustle up some last-minute action on M Street in Georgetown. Both Harry and Daniel had been worried about the actor's plans for the evening, but Adrian had assured them that it was standard operating procedure for him before a performance, and it would help calm his nerves.

"How do you feel?" asked Daniel, his slight figure outlined against the window.

"Fine."

"Nervous?"

"Sure," said Harry. He sat up on his elbow and plucked the cigarette out of the aluminum-foil ashtray. He took a deep drag and let it out slowly, sending little plumes of smoke up into the shadows. He laughed quietly and shook his head.

"What's so funny?" asked Daniel.

"Oh, nothing. But I feel just like I did before I married Carol. Horny, depressed, and scared shitless all at the same time."

"Wonderful," said Daniel. "You sure you don't want to back out of this? There's still time, you know. We're not committed to anything yet."

"Sure we are," said Harry. "I'm dead, remember? Benovoy's done the dirty work with my files. Right this minute, pathology students at Georgetown University are carving me up in the name of science."

"Well, I'm not dead," said Daniel.

"You want out?" asked Harry, peering at his friend.

"No. I've just got this dull feeling in the pit of my stomach, that's all."

"Fear?"

"More like guilt," said Daniel. "I mean, this is big-time stuff we're into."

"Smuggling coke wasn't?" asked Harry.

"It's not the same. That was . . ."

"Cool," Harry put in. "It was okay to smuggle coke because it was dope, and we were dopers, and the cops were the enemy. Up the revolution, and all that shit."

"Maybe," said Daniel.

"Maybe nothing," said Harry, crushing the remains of his cigarette into the tinfoil. "Smuggling is romantic. Theft is right there in the Bible—'thou shalt not steal.' Relax, you're just having a sociological twitch. It'll pass."

"You don't feel that way?" asked Daniel.

"Of course I do," said Harry. "Maybe worse." Harry sighed and levered himself into a sitting position on the floor. "Look, Daniel, I'm not really sure why I'm doing this. Maybe I'm tired of living in a country and in a world where there's no such thing as freedom of choice anymore, at least for me, or maybe because I've always had a criminal mind, or maybe it's because we're all losers when you come right down to it, and now we have a chance to win. I don't know. What I *do* know is that I've been dying for the last three or four years. Not physically, but mentally. I've been withering up and growing old, and that scares the shit out of me worse than any prison sentence could. If I'm going to blow it, I want to blow it with a *bang*, I want people to know that I was here. Do you understand?"

"Sure, I understand," said Daniel softly.

"You want to forget about it?" asked Harry.

"No," said Daniel. "I'm in for the distance. Fool that I am."

"Good," said Harry. He lifted his bottle of beer in a toast. "To us!"

"The Night Owl Gang!" responded Daniel, lifting an imaginary glass.

"And the Crime of the Century!" added Harry Maxwell. "Long may it remain unsolved!"

Part Two

THE CORRIDOR

*I wasn't just scared, I was terrified.
On the other hand, reading the
morning paper can be pretty scary
too, so what the hell.*

Harry Maxwell,
the Playboy Interview

Chapter 5

Sunday, June 26
Time: 8:30 P.M. EDT
Distance: 0 miles/0 km.

Frank Sagadore, Chief of the Special Operations Division of Amtrak Security Services, sat on a stool behind the Master Panel Operator in the CTC room at New York's Penn Station, sipping his coffee and enjoying a moment of relative peace before he went to work for the night. Central Traffic Control was the only place in Penn Station where he had the feeling that everything was under control. The low light, the huge U-shaped operations console, and the blinking lights of the Model Board spread out on the wall gave the tall, dark-haired security man a feeling that here at least there was order in an otherwise insane world, especially when Mac Donovan was the Master Panel Operator. The pudgy MPO handled the glowing push-buttons on the panel in front of him like a concert pianist, glancing up to check the model board occasionally to confirm that his interpretation of the score was correct.

Sagadore was constantly amazed that one man at the desk could control the activities of virtually the entire Northeast Corridor from Washington to Boston, although Donovan's actual zone of responsibility covered only the division between Newark and Port Chester. The CTC system, which had been in a constant state of development from its crude beginnings in the twenties, was now so refined that some trains could actually be controlled without engineers or any human input other than the MPO. Switches could be thrown automatically, signals changed or overridden, and through special in-cab relays trains could be slowed, stopped, or even reversed. The days of the lone operator in his tower and the brakeman with his swinging lamp were long gone. Simply by glancing at the model board, Donovan or any other MPO could survey the status of the entire Northeast Corridor and see exactly where each train on the double-track system was located.

Sagadore took another sip of his coffee and squinted up at the model board. At a rough guess, it looked as though Donovan was working close to a dozen trains on the system. "Looks like things are cooking pretty good," he said to the MPO's back.

"Nothing out of the ordinary," mumbled Donovan, without turning around. Sagadore was used to talking to the back of Donovan's balding head; the system was automatic, but the man rarely took his eyes off the master panel and the model board. In a sense, the MPO was a railroad version of an air traffic controller, and his job was just as critical. Without Donovan and the three other people quietly working the telephones, the telex, and the computer console, the whole system would fall apart.

"How many running?" asked Sagadore.

"Nine," said Donovan. "This is peak time. It'll drop off in a while. We've got a Metroliner, the Bankers, the Merchants, a Clocker, and the Montrealer northbound; the Mount Vernon, the Boston Merchants, the Connecticut Valley, and the Bay State going south. Give it a couple of hours and the board'll be clear except for you and a couple of others."

The "you" to which Donovan was referring was the Night Owl, the train that had been ruining the broad-shouldered security man's Sundays for the three years he'd held the job of Special Operations Chief. Between the Federal Reserve shipment and the gaggle of diplomats who rode the tail-end sleeper, Sagadore had to act as liaison for half a dozen federal, state, and city police forces, not to mention the Secret Service. During the past three years there hadn't been a single incident, but that only seemed to make the various cops even more paranoid. One of the Secret Service men guarding the diplomats had once told Sagadore that his job was like babysitting the San Andreas Fault. He *knew* that something would happen eventually, and the longer he was on the job, the shorter the odds became.

Sagadore checked his watch; there was still time for a bowl of chowder at Paddy's before it closed, and it would be his last chance to get away from the station until the Night Owl reached Boston at ten to eight the next morning. It seemed ridiculous to spend the whole night on duty, since there wasn't a hell of a lot he could do if something did happen to the train, but the Night Owl was his responsibility from departure to final arrival at Boston's South Station.

He stood up, tipped his empty coffee cup into the wastebasket beside Donovan, and said good-bye to the MPO. A few moments later he was striding across the wide expanse of the upper concourse and heading for the escalators that would take him up to street level.

Until 1966, Penn Station had been a regular aboveground terminal, condemned as a grimy eyesore by some and revered as a historic landmark by others. Eventually the winds of change and financial expediency had won out and the great, hulking station was demolished, the glittering monolith of the new Madison Square Garden rising in its place. The station was banished underground. Amtrak took possession of the subterranean facility in 1976 and spent almost a million dollars on renovations that included a major cleanup, extensive repairs to the tunnels, and a revamping of the upper and lower concourses, complete with boutiques, restaurants, coffee shops, and a lower-level Amtrak Lounge for waiting passengers.

The new station, unromantic as it was, was open twenty-four hours a day, and in that day efficiently handled 750 trains, including four Metropolitan Transit Authority subway lines. According to a few old-timers who worked in Maintenance, the only thing left of the old station were the rats that still infested the warren of heating ducts. Rats, according to the veterans, which were the size of small dogs and capable of taking a finger off if you weren't careful. Sagadore could believe it; soon after taking the job as Special Operations Chief, he'd checked over the original foundation plans for the building, and he'd been astounded by the complex maze of abandoned tunnels and ducts that still existed behind the newly created façade.

As he rode the escalator to the street, the security man turned and looked back down at the concourse. By weekday standards the wide, low-ceilinged chamber was virtually deserted. He could pick out a few regulars among the people coming up from the MTA: Benny, the lanky black pickpocket in his inevitable raincoat; Princess Hat-

71

tie, one of several bag ladies who use Penn Central as a combination home and scavenging ground; and a small group of Puerto Ricans in jeans and faded denim jackets. Sagadore grinned despite himself; he knew beyond a shadow of a doubt that the young boys were carrying aerosol paint cans in their jackets, and within five minutes they'd be busy "decorating" the exterior of subway cars as they came into the station far below. He didn't condone the graffiti artists' delinquency, but it was an innocent enough crime when you compared it to some of the things that went on in the area. If paint-can bandits were all he had to worry about, he wouldn't be chewing his way through two rolls of Tums each day for the incipient ulcer his doctor had warned him about.

On any given morning or afternoon, Sagadore had to face at least a dozen crises. In addition to jobs like babysitting the Night Owl, he had to deal with ticket security, movement of cash from various ticket agents, the wire mobs of pickpockets that plagued the Penn Plaza parking garage, ripoffs, and smash-and-grabs from the stores and restaurants on the upper concourse, and a mind-boggling array of loonies, junkies, perverts, and psychos. Sometimes it made the two years he'd spent as an investigator for the Inspector General's office in Saigon seem like a rest cure.

He reached the top of the escalator, went through the glass doors, and stepped out onto the plaza, the looming bulk of Madison Square Garden and the office tower at his back, its thousand windows gleaming golden in the last of the sun. He shivered slightly in the cool evening breeze and turned down Thirty-fourth Street, casting up a silent prayer that the night ahead would be an uneventful one.

Mark Cavendish stared out the window, even though there was nothing to see except his own reflection and the slightly blurred lights of North Philadelphia. He liked to travel alone, and usually the forward seats on the lead coach of the Night Owl were empty. Tonight, however, someone had sat down beside him, even though most of the coach was vacant. He'd thought of moving, but more than a decade spent making sure that he didn't draw attention to himself kept him where he was. At least his seatmate hadn't tried to start up a conversation.

Flexing his shoulder, he lifted his arm and snagged the package of cigarettes in his windbreaker pocket. He tapped the package lightly on the window ledge, and flexing his shoulder again, he brought the package up to his mouth, uncomfortably aware that the man beside him was watching every movement. He reached into his jacket again, replacing the cigarettes, and clamped the twin steel calipers onto his Zippo. Bringing the lighter out of his pocket, he rolled it on the thigh of his jeans until the hinge snapped back with a small clicking sound. He rolled the lighter again, this time brushing the wheel against the flint, then brought the lighter up to his cigarette. He doused the lighter by reversing the process, then slipped the Zippo back into his pocket. Rolling his left hand on his knee to turn the palm upward, he used the Dorrance hook on his right to transfer the cigarette and position it between the first and second fingers of the cosmetic prosthesis. Finally, after a complex series of actions that a normal person would go through without thinking, he was able to smoke the cigarette. The Mark Cavendish Freak Show, he thought to himself bitterly, brought to you by a Russian SA-2 Guideline missile and the good folks in the bilateral amputee ward of the Washington Veterans Administration Hospital.

Sometimes, caught off guard with nothing to distract him or to occupy his mind, as at this moment, he found himself thinking about the depth of his anger and was amazed at its virulence. A dozen years had passed, and it was still enough to make him grit his teeth in fury. The psychiatrists at the VA had told him that the feelings he had stemmed from the year and a half he'd spent as a POW, and would fade in time, but even a decade ago he'd known they were wrong. The POW camp had been effect, not cause. The true reason for his anger and bitterness came from the knowledge that his sacrifice had been futile—not just because the United States had eventually lost the war, but more because the war had been irrelevant in the first place. He'd paid dearly for a debt he didn't owe, and worse, the payment had never been acknowledged. Once he'd thought that the loss of both his hands and lower arms was the worst thing he would ever experience, but now he knew that they were the smallest part of what he'd given up. He'd lost his youth, his dreams, and his future, and they could never be regained. He'd joined the navy at eighteen, and by his twenty-first birthday his life was over.

With the exception of the girl to whom he'd lost his virginity in his hometown, he'd only slept with Saigon whores, and since his release from the POW camp, he hadn't even had enough desire to pay for sex, let alone seek any real relationship. Beyond that, the only job he was trained for—flying navy recon jets, was obviously impossible. Ironically, the only job he'd been qualified to do after leaving the hospital was counseling other wounded vets, and that was what he'd been doing ever since. Now, more than a decade after the war had officially ended, he was still living it every day in his own memories and the memories of the mentally and physically crippled people who were his clients.

Cavendish took a last drag from the cigarette and then squeezed out the butt between the jaws of the Dorrance hook. He dropped the remains into the built-in ashtray on the armrest, noticing as he did so that the man who'd been sitting beside him was now gone. He leaned back against the headrest and closed his eyes, letting the rhythmic movement of the train ease the tension within him. At least now, alone, he might get some rest.

"Time?" asked Harry Maxwell, the bottom half of his face lit eerily by the battery-powered lantern on the floor of the baggage car.

"Twelve-forty-one," said Daniel Pendergast, raising his voice slightly over the echoing rattle of the swaying car.

"You're early," said Harry, hauling out the last of the equipment from the coffin. He grunted as he picked up the makeshift harness that held the nitrous oxide tank and began to strap it on.

"I was sitting beside this guy who started to spook me," Daniel explained as he started to assemble the conveyor. "He had a hook where one hand should have been, and the other one looked like it was made of plastic. I couldn't handle it anymore. I mean, I'm freaked out enough by this as it is."

"We on schedule otherwise?"

"About two minutes off, I think," answered Daniel.

"No sweat," murmured Harry. He did up the last buckle. "There you go, Lloyd Bridges," he said, standing back so Daniel could see.

"Terrific," said his friend. "You have everything?"

Harry bent over and checked the tools on his belt. "Bolt cutters, knife, pliers, and Vise-Grips. Yeah."

Daniel checked his watch. "Okay. It's twelve-forty-five. You've got about fifteen minutes before we go through Bristol. You've got to be off the roof of the RPO by then. All we need is some station agent seeing somebody riding on top of the train."

Harry nodded and went to the forward door of the baggage car. He turned, gave a little wave to Daniel, and then pulled open the door. He stepped into the vestibule and paused, staring at the door to the RPO, only a yard away. He took a deep breath and then let it out slowly. On the other side of the door there was either sudden death or a king's ransom. Standing there, jerking back and forth on the overlapping plates of the connector floor, he was almost overwhelmed by the enormity of their crime. He looked over his shoulder and glanced at the blank face of the baggage car door. Once he climbed up onto the RPO and gassed the two guards, there would be no turning back.

"This is crazy," he whispered, the sound of his voice lost in the clanking rattle of the vestibule. Finally, gritting his teeth, he shrugged off the feeling of impending doom that was threatening to throw him into total panic, and bent down, drawing the heavy-bladed knife out of its sheath on his belt.

Plunging the knife into the thick rubber, he began to saw upward, the serrated blade slicing easily. In less than a minute he'd slashed an opening six feet high. He put the knife back in its sheath, took out the bolt cutters, and began snapping the metal struts at the top and bottom of his newly created hole. The metal was stronger than he'd thought, and the job wasn't done until 12:50, which put him behind schedule. He blinked, squinting out through the opening, the harsh wind drying the sweat that had begun flowing freely down his forehead and jawline. Bracing himself against the door frame of the baggage car, he lifted one heavily booted foot and wedged it against the last of the struts. He lifted himself and pushed back hard against the door, straightening his leg at the same time and locking his knee. The strut bent, widening the space even further.

Harry slipped the plastic athlete's safety goggles out of the pocket of his windbreaker and put them on to protect his eyes from the wind. He stepped forward and leaned out, the thunder of the hammering wheels below roaring in his ears.

The first move was going to be the most dangerous. He had to balance on the diaphragm and then stretch out across a five-foot gap to reach the first of the grab bars with his hands. If he missed, he would be too far off balance to pull himself back, and he'd fall between the cars. There would be no second chances. Tightening the belt of the harness by another notch, he shrugged, settling the bottle between his shoulder blades. Then he stepped up onto the diaphragm, swaying erratically with the motion of the train. Beyond the aperture there was nothing but darkness and the faint glint of the row of grab bars that led up to the roof of the RPO. Muscles tensing, his heart like a clenched fist in his throat, Harry dropped forward, his arms outstretched.

The train lurched heavily at the exact moment he moved, and he flailed wildly, the horror of the yawning space below rushing up to meet him. One hand caught a grab bar and clenched desperately as his legs were pulled off the diaphragm by the sudden movement. He swung wide and his grip almost failed, but he managed to get his other hand onto the next U-shaped support and he hung there, his legs dangling in space. It felt as though his arms were going to tear out of their sockets, but the prospect of what would happen if he let go was far more horrifying than any pain. He dragged himself up, his feet seeking purchase, the bottle on his back feeling like a ten-ton weight. Finally his feet hit the bottom grab bar, and by hooking his elbow around the one at chest level, he was able to relieve some of the tension on his arms.

He hung rigidly for a moment, fighting to slow his breathing and stop the shaking of his arms and legs. He knew he had to move soon, or fear and the cold air tearing through the thin fabric of his jacket would bring on muscle cramps that could freeze him to the side of the car. He unhooked one elbow and reached up for the next grab bar. When he had a tight grip with both hands, he forced himself to lift his foot and plant it on the bar above. After an eternity he reached the last grab bar and hauled himself up onto the roof of the RPO.

The rushing wind roared painfully in his ears, and the combination of the towers flicking by on the edge of his vision and the erratic rocking and rolling of the car beneath him set his stomach roiling. With his feet still grimly hooked on the top grab bar for support and his body spread-eagled across the roof, he reached up with one hand and freed the hose from its clip mount on the tank harness. Peering ahead into the darkness, he could make out the darker shadow of the vent housing on his left, and he realized that he was going to have to let go of the grab bar to reach it.

Taking a deep breath, he let go with his feet and began to inch forward over the roof, his eyes fixed on the small hump of the ventilator, acutely aware that he was completely unsupported. If the train hit a sharp enough curve, he'd be thrown off the roof into the blackness beyond. He gritted his teeth, silently cursing his overactive imagination. Spread out on the roof of a speeding train was not the ideal place to have regrets.

He reached the ventilator and grabbed the curved housing with one clawing hand, grateful for any handhold, no matter how slight. With his free hand he pulled on the hose, giving himself some slack. Lifting his belly up, he groped for his knife and pulled it out of the sheath on his belt. He hauled himself forward a little farther and then stabbed at the light wire grillwork over the vent with a single firm jab. The wire parted and Harry let out a long, shuddering breath. He had no more use for the knife, so rather than waste time putting it back in his belt, he simply tossed it away into the darkness. Throughout the whole exercise he'd been counting off seconds in his head, and he knew he was running out of time. By his rough calculation he had less than five minutes before they went through the station at Brighton, and it was going to take three and a half minutes to empty the tank of nitrous oxide into the vent with the valve cracked fully open. That left him only ninety seconds to get off the roof of the RPO.

Still hanging on to the vent, he used his other hand to push the open end of the hose down into it. When all the slack was taken up, he reached back and, working blind, found the small valve lever and turned it fully open, beginning to count out loud. He hit two hundred ten, then added another ten for good measure. When he was positive the tank was empty, he let go of the vent housing and began unbuckling the tank harness. At the edge of panic now, he rolled over on his side, ignoring the danger, shrugged out of the harness, and levered himself up into a crouching position, bracing his knees on the shifting metal surface of the roof. Using both hands, he picked up the tank and the harness, and with all his strength he flung it as far as he could, praying that it wouldn't strike one of the passing high-voltage catenary towers. Without waiting to see where the tank fell, he dropped down onto his stomach again and began to crab backwards toward the rear of the RPO.

His feet found the edge of the car and he kept moving back, feeling around for the grab bars. One foot connected and he almost fainted with relief. He eased himself over the side, heart pounding, feeling for each of the bars until he was completely over the side.

Now came the part he was dreading. With his left foot firmly planted on the lowest grab bar and his left hand gripping another bar at shoulder height, he pushed out to his right, squinting into the rushing darkness between the cars, searching for the narrow slit he'd cut in the diaphragm. His foot found the aperture and he wedged it in tightly, leaving him spread-eagled between the side of the RPO and the vestibule. Drenched in sweat now, his mouth cotton-dry, he waited until the train headed into a slight left curve. As it lurched away from him, he used the centrifugal force and launched himself outward, his right hand flailing for support. His fingers found the edge of the tear he'd created, gripped, and with the train still leaning to the left he released his hold on the upper grab bar with his left hand and hauled himself back through the hole, collapsing on the floor of the vestibule, panting with the sudden release of tension.

Daniel got his hands under Harry's arms and dragged

him to his feet. "Christ!" he whispered harshly. "I thought you'd died up there or something. I was going out of my mind. We're almost five minutes behind schedule."

"Sorry," Harry grunted, still fighting for breath. "You ready?"

"Yeah. Here." He handed Harry a gas mask and slid his own over his head, making sure the straps were tight. Martin Benovoy had liberated the masks from a paramedic van parked in the emergency lot at Georgetown Hospital the week before. The masks were multiple-use types fitted with both particle and gas filters. The ambulance driver had assured Harry that the masks were more than adequate for the job.

Daniel waited until Harry had his mask on firmly and then handed him the small sledge and the cold chisel. Together they approached the blank face of the RPO door. Harry butted the end of the cold chisel against the lock mechanism and nodded to Daniel. His friend stepped up, gripped the chisel with his right hand, and moved back out of the way. Harry took a deep breath, sucking air in through the chin valve of the gas mask, then brought the sledge around in a wide sidearm arc. The force of the blow slammed the lock mechanism inward a good inch, creasing the metal of the door around it, but the lock held.

"Again," said Daniel, his voice muffled by the mask.

Harry brought the sledge up for another try, putting all his strength behind the blow. There was a dull snapping sound and the lock punched inward, disappearing into the hole. Harry dropped the sledge onto the floor of the vestibule, took the small crowbar Daniel had removed from his belt, and slid the bar into the hole. He wrenched hard and the door swung open. Trying not to think about what the consequences would be if the gas hadn't worked, Harry stepped into the RPO, the crowbar clutched in his hand and Daniel right behind him.

"Holy shit!" said Harry, stopping dead in his tracks, the crowbar falling with a clatter from his suddenly nerveless fingers.

The interior of the RPO was an abattoir. There were great splashes of blood on the side wall, sprayed up to the ceiling, and even more blood pooling around the two bodies. One lay on the floor with most of its head missing, slime and gray porridge around the stump of the neck like some obscene halo; the second was slumped over the radio table with the left arm and shoulder blown to shreds, the man's bloody scalp flipped over across his face, obscuring the dead features. A third body was lying on the floor of the car a dozen feet away, the nylon pistol-grip butt of a Siles nickel-barreled police shotgun a few inches from its outstretched hand. Unlike the two uniformed corpses, the third man was dressed from head to toe in black—combat boots, paratrooper pants, and a black shirt-and-combat-vest combination.

The two men stood transfixed, legs bracing automatically against the jerking sway of the car. Harry felt his stomach roiling, and for a moment he thought he was going to vomit. He swallowed hard, eyes flicking back and forth over the carnage as his brain tried to cope with the reality of the horror before him.

"I think I'm going to be sick," muttered Daniel, standing at his side.

"We've got to get out," said Harry dully.

"What?"

"We've got to get out," he repeated, panic rising in his gut and squeezing his throat. He backed up a pace, eyes still glued on the corpses. "I just wanted to rob the train," he whispered. "This . . . this is . . ."

"Murder," Daniel supplied.

"Who?" asked Harry.

"I don't know," his friend answered. "Does it matter?" He took a deep, shuddering breath. "All I know is that this wasn't part of the plan, Harry. We're into some heavy shit here."

"That guy on the floor has got a shotgun, and from the way he's dressed I don't think he's a good guy. Maybe he's got friends," said Harry.

"Is he alive?"

"I don't know," said Harry. "Jesus! Now what do we do?"

"You said it before. We get out. It's a bust, Harry. Abort time. This is way out of our league. My life of crime just came to an end. *Finito*. Right now. A cop on the other side of the door would be an answer to a prayer."

"I need to think," said Harry. "Back into the baggage car."

"Lead the way," said Daniel.

They retreated, Harry pulling the door of the RPO closed as best he could. In the baggage car, they stripped off the gas masks and began changing into the clothes Harry had carried with him in the coffin. Three minutes later they were standing at the coach-end door of the baggage car. Harry checked his watch.

"Ten after one," he said softly. "Tucker's not due to come out of the room for another eleven minutes." He reached forward and grabbed the door handle.

"Wait a second," said Daniel. "Think it out. We can assume the guy we gassed, the one with the shotgun, wasn't working by himself, so where are his pals?"

"Either on board or at a stop," said Harry.

"Or both," said Daniel. "We came up with a plan to get the money off the train, and it stands to reason they did, too."

"You're missing something obvious," said Harry, his voice wavering, the image of the two bodies in the RPO still frighteningly clear. "The guy with the shotgun didn't give a shit if he blew away the radio or not, and you can bet these people are aware that the guards are supposed to check in regularly. The next transmission is set for one-twenty-six, so whatever they're planning is going to happen within the next ten minutes and you and I are right in the way of it. I'm not waiting for Adrian and his diversion. I'm getting out of here right now." He turned the handle and pulled the door open. A few feet away, on the far side of the vestibule, he could see the brightly lit interior of the first coach.

"Now what?" asked Daniel, standing behind Harry in the jolting, vibrating space between the cars.

"We bluff it out," said Harry. "We walk in there and take the first two seats we find. When the train stops at Princeton Junction to offload our coffin, we get off too. Benovoy should be there by now. We get into the hearse and drive off, pronto."

"We'll get caught," said Daniel.

"Maybe," said Harry. "But if we stay here, the chances are pretty good that we'll get killed. Take your choice."

"All right," Daniel muttered. "The first two seats on the left as we go in should be empty."

Harry nodded, and with Daniel behind him he went to

the coach door, pulled it open, and walked into the car. A few people looked up as the two men appeared, but no one seemed unduly interested. On rubber legs, Harry and Daniel swung into the two left-hand seats and sat down, every muscle wire-taut.

A long moment passed as the two men waited, holding their breath. Nothing happened. No outcry, no shouts, nothing.

"Time," said Harry.

"One-seventeen," said Daniel, looking at his watch.

"Okay. If we're on time, that means we hit Princeton Junction in nine minutes. The coffin is open, there's tools and crap lying around all over the place. They're bound to figure out that something's wrong."

"So?" asked Daniel.

"So we're too close to the scene of the crime," said Harry. "I think we should stick it out here for another couple of minutes and then head down to Adrian's room. If we get off from his car, we'll have a chance."

"What do we tell him?" Daniel asked.

"We tell him the truth. If he's smart, he'll stay in the room and ride it out to New York. We can take the radio and the other stuff off for him. There won't be anything to connect him to what happened in the mail car."

"If the other people don't appear first," said Daniel.

"Pray," muttered Harry, lighting a cigarette. As he spoke, a young man dressed in a casual suit but carrying an attaché case walked by their seats and paused at the ice-water dispenser beside the toilets. He put the attaché case down, bracing it with his foot, and filled a paper cup with water. He drank, picked up the attaché case, and then, balancing it on his raised knee, he flicked open the catches.

"Shit," whispered Harry, his gut twisting as he realized what was about to happen.

The man tipped back the top of the case, reached inside, and pulled out a short-barreled Valmet machine gun. He dropped the case and his knee in a single motion, raising the black stamped-metal weapon and tilting back the cocking lever with his free hand. His voice, when he spoke, was heavily accented.

"Ladies and gentlemen, may I have your attention, please?" He waited as people looked up and took in the sight of a man in Ralph Lauren jeans carrying a machine gun. There was a flurry of whispering that died as the man gently swung the barrel of the Valmet back and forth across the aisle. When he had everyone's eyes riveted to him, he spoke again. "Thank you, ladies and gentlemen. I would like to make an announcement. This train is now under the control of the World People's Army. Any attempt to violate that control will be dealt with severely. Please remain calm. We do not wish to hurt anyone. You may talk among yourselves, but under no circumstances will anyone leave his seat until further notice. I shall make a further announcement in a few minutes. Thank you."

The man walked carefully down the aisle and disappeared from view. Harry and Daniel remained exactly as they were, staring at the wall ahead.

"Shit," Harry said again, his voice low.

"Yeah," said Daniel Pendergast.

Frank Sagadore sat beside Mac Donovan at the Master Panel in the CTC room and squinted up at the maze of lights and lines on the Model Board. Five minutes before, Sagadore had been checking out his duty roster and wondering how he was going to keep his eyes open for the rest of the night; now he was wide awake, his jaw tight with concentration, the knotted muscles of his stomach making him regret the bowl of chowder he'd had at Paddy's.

"Where are they?" asked the security chief.

Donovan reached forward and tapped a button on the panel in front of him. Instantly a light glowed red on the Model Board. "Just this side of Princeton Junction, about a mile out of Monmouth. The stationmaster at Princeton Junction was waiting for a special stop, but they went right on through. We tried to raise the engineer, but there was nothing."

"The Mobile can't raise them either," said Sagadore.

"There has to be somebody unauthorized in the cab," Donovan said. "The train slowed down three minutes ago. It's only doing about thirty."

"But it hasn't stopped?"

"Not yet," Donovan answered.

"Who's in the cab?"

"Charles McClure. McClure's been with the railroad for

twenty years. Penn Central and then Amtrak. Solid as a rock."

"What about this Devine person?" asked Sagadore. "Know anything about him?"

"Not yet," said the Master Panel Operator. "But I thought you'd want to know, so I buzzed personnel to send up a file."

"What's your best guess on this?" asked Sagadore.

The heavyset MPO shrugged. "I don't have one," he said slowly. "It *could* be some kind of radio screw-up. Those overhead catenaries sometimes act up, but I doubt it. It's the loss of speed that concerns me. McClure knows that kind of slowdown can throw off a schedule from one end of the corridor to the other. He wouldn't do it unless he had a hell of a good reason, and he doesn't." Donovan waved a hand at the Model Board. "Everything's green right into Newark."

"Engine problems?"

"*And* the radio?" The MPO shook his head. "Not a chance."

"So?"

"So, a fin says that McClure's not at the handle." Donovan turned and stared at Sagadore, the MPO's eyes goggling out behind the thick lenses of his glasses. A phone set burred at Donovan's elbow and he turned away to pick it up. He listened for a moment and then hung up.

"That was Communications, next door. They're getting a breaker call on the Night Owl cab frequency. I told them to respond and then patch it in here." He reached across his board, punched a pair of buttons, and indicated a telephone receiver on the panel in front of Sagadore's position. The security chief picked up the phone, and then Donovan punched another set of buttons. Instantly a voice sounded from the loudspeakers set into the ceiling.

"This is the Night Owl cab. Who am I speaking to?" The voice was muffled and mechanical, giving no clue as to age, nationality, or even sex.

"Frank Sagadore, Security Services." Sagadore watched as a young man in shirtsleeves to his right started up the large Ampex log recorder that was used to tape all conversations between trains and the CTC headquarters.

"Mr. Sagadore, I presume you are in some position of authority with Amtrak?"

84

"I'll do for the moment," the security man answered dryly. He frowned. The voice was strong, but there was a hint of the feminine. A woman? The choice of words was interesting, too. As though the person wasn't used to English as a first language.

"Mr. Sagadore, as you are obviously aware, the Night Owl, your Amtrak train number sixty-six, is no longer under your control. To put it bluntly, it has been hijacked."

Sagadore kept his mouth shut with an effort of will. The more the other person talked, the better, in this kind of situation. There was a brief, static-filled silence, and then the voice came again.

"Your train has been taken over by members of the World People's Army. Thus far no one has been hurt, and no one will be hurt if you follow our instructions."

Frank Sagadore kept the telephone to his ear and reached out for a pad of scratch paper. He scribbled a brief message and showed it to Donovan. *Get me the Secret Service in Washington and notify the FBI regional office.* Donovan read the message, nodded, and waved for one of his people.

"At this point," the voice on the loudspeaker went on, "you need to know only that we are entirely capable of killing everyone aboard the Night Owl instantly. I assume that you have already notified the FBI and the Secret Service, or will soon do so. When you meet with them, you can tell them that we have planted a number of DTAT antitank mines throughout the train, which can be triggered automatically. The coach doors are all wired with PRB-413 antipersonnel mines, and the exterior of the train is protected by RCA portable surveillance radar. Any attempt to interfere with the train in any way will result in the immediate deaths of all passengers, and any attempt to contravene our instructions will have the same result. Do you understand, Mr. Sagadore?"

"I understand," said the security chief. "What are the instructions?"

"For the moment you need only concern yourself with the routing of the train." There was a short pause, as though the person was waiting for something, or perhaps consulting somebody else.

"All right," said Sagadore. A few seconds later the voice returned.

"You will see to it that all tracks and signals are cleared to double green status on the following lines. On your present track to Elizabeth, New Jersey. From Elizabeth to Summit on the Rahway Valley and Consolidated Rail line. From Summit to Morristown and Denville on Consolidated Rail, and then East on Conrail to Lake Hopatcong and Andover Junction. From there the line should be cleared along the Consolidated track to Albany. You will receive additional information at that point. We are aware that your Master Panel Operator has no direct control over much of the track I've just mentioned, but you can inform the local tower operators by telex or telephone in plenty of time. To expedite the procedure, your Master Panel Operator should know that we will be traveling at a constant speed of twenty-five miles per hour until we reach the junction at Andover. Are there any questions?"

Sagadore turned to Donovan. The MPO shook his head. "No," said Sagadore.

"Excellent," said the voice. "This will be the last transmission until the train reaches Andover. Let me stress once again that any attempt to interfere with the train will result in the immediate execution of all the passengers. Thank you."

There was a click and then the static hiss of dead air. Frank Sagadore stared at the telephone receiver in his hand and then replaced it in the cradle on the Master Panel. He turned to Donovan again.

"What was that all about?" he asked.

"He's avoiding New York City," said the MPO. The paunchy man tapped at the keyboard in front of him for a few seconds, and a glittering line of red lights began to appear on the complex web of lines on the Model Board. "The way he's planned it, he even avoids Newark. Look," said Donovan, pointing at the lights on the board. "He hopscotches north up to Denville and west to Lake Hopatcong and Andover Junction. South on that line would take him back to New York. North gives him Troy and Albany."

"So those are the two options for a destination?" asked Sagadore.

Donovan shrugged. "Not necessarily," he answered. "He could keep on going north up to Rouses Point and go into

Canada, or he could meander around on any of a hundred lines in upstate New York. Who's to say whether he has a destination at all, for that matter? Maybe he's just moving around until he gets what he wants."

"Whatever that is," said Sagadore. "Christ! A Federal Reserve bank shipment and a sleeping car full of diplomats!"

"You're going to be on the front page and on the six o'clock news, Frank," grunted Donovan. "I don't envy you your job right now."

"Right," said Sagadore. "I think I'd rather be on that train, as a matter of fact. At least then I'd know just what the hell was going on." He looked at his watch. Less than fifteen minutes had passed since the call came down to him.

"Where are they now?" asked the security man.

"Mile or so the other side of New Brunswick. About eighteen miles from the switch point at Elizabeth. That's when the controls go out of my hands. If he keeps to the thirty miles an hour, it's going to take him almost forty minutes."

"That's something, anyway," muttered Sagadore. "A bit of breathing space." He frowned, thinking hard. "Look," he said finally. "I've got to go and deal with the Feds. They should be piling up in my office by now. Can you get one of your people to ring Reservations and find out just who's on that train?"

Donovan nodded. "No problem. You'll have a printout in your office within ten minutes."

"Great," said the security man, standing up. "I'll need a copy of that tape as soon as you can get it, too. And if there's any change in the train's status, let me know immediately, okay?" He looked at his watch again. It was 1:46 in the morning.

Chapter 6

Monday, June 27
Time: 1:52 A.M. EDT
Distance: 192 miles/307 km.

Annalise Shenker sat sprawled in one of the armchairs
in bedroom A of the tail-end observation car of the Night
Owl, frowning as she went over the checklist pinned to
the clipboard on her lap. In the other chair, Mohamet
Kawi, the hawk-faced Libyan demolitions expert, waited
patiently, his long bony fingers steepled beneath his dark-
stubbled chin. Dressed in a perfectly fitted two-piece denim
suit, complete with a white shirt and a raw silk tie, Kawi
contrasted sharply with Shenker, who was wearing tight-
fitting jeans, a faded light green T-shirt, and a bleached-
out denim jacket. Even dressed informally, Shenker was
darkly beautiful, and not for the first time the Libyan
found himself wondering how a woman so obviously feminine could be so bitterly hard, as tough as any man he'd
ever known. Most people within the terrorist establishment assumed she was a lesbian, especially considering
her long association with Ulrike Meinhof, but from personal experience he knew that she was unreservedly and
sometimes frighteningly heterosexual. So much so, in fact,
that he avoided any situation that might lead him to her
bed. She used sex the way some people used drugs, and
he found the intensity of her addiction almost obscene.
Her sexual proclivities aside, however, she was by far the
best cell leader he'd ever worked with.

Shenker flipped back her long fall of jet black hair with
a practiced motion of one hand and looked up from the
clipboard, frowning. "A status report, please," she said
crisply, speaking in heavily accented English, the group's
common language.

"The train is secure," said Kawi. "Dieter has established a communications headquarters in room A in the
next car. Both radar units have been set up, and he will

monitor them from there, as well as the radio. Raoul is watching the coaches, and Sheila is still in the cab with the engineer. Lisa has our diplomatic friends under control here. The charges have been set as you ordered, and the passengers have been instructed to keep all the window shades down on pain of death. We have also told the passengers that there are several of us who will remain anonymous among them to ensure that our orders are followed. Except to use the toilets, no one has moved a muscle."

"No word from Amal?" asked Shenker.

"No," answered Kawi. "Dieter says that there have been no further transmissions from the car containing the guards, so we must assume that he was successful."

"We assume nothing," Shenker said coldly. "The men in the Treasury car were armed. Together with the two Secret Service agents guarding this car, they represent the greatest threat to our operation. They might well have managed to kill Amal. They could be waiting to make their move."

"Amal had the locomotive end key to the RPO that our friend 'Mr. White' gave us," said Kawi. "If he is alive, he will know that the charges have been set by now. He had a walkie-talkie like the rest of us. If the two guards try to leave the car, they will be blown to ashes. The same applies to the locomotive. Sheila set two charges with a transverse tripwire across the rear doorway of the engine after Amal went into the RPO. The explosion could kill the Treasury guards, but at worst it would only destroy the heating boiler. The guards are trapped. There is nothing to worry about."

"There is everything to worry about, Mohamet. There are millions of dollars in that mail car. Enough to finance a dozen major operations. This project was chosen because of that shipment. The diplomats we have as hostages are nothing more than a buffer between us and the authorities. Unless we have possession of that shipment, we have accomplished nothing."

"So what do you suggest?" asked Kawi. "You know as well as I do that we haven't the manpower to risk an assault on the mail car. By my count there are over two hundred passengers on board, as well as fifteen train crew. Without Amal there are only six of us. To lose even one more in such an attack would be disastrous. Remember, Anna, we have a long way to go yet before this is over. Leave the guards alone for now. We have them contained, that is enough."

"It is too great a risk, Mohamet. The removal of the guards was the key to our plan, you know that."

There was a firm double knock on the door of the room. "Enter," said Shenker. Mohamet Kawi shifted slightly in his seat and drew a heavy, foot-long Interdynamic 9mm Parabellum out of its shoulder sling beneath his jacket. He pushed back the safety and leveled the vicious-looking weapon at the door. It opened slowly and Dieter Haas appeared.

"What is it?" asked Shenker.

"Amal," said Haas, his pale oval face expressionless. "He has reported in. The guards have been dealt with."

"Did he say what took him so long?" Kawi interrupted.

"No. But he wants Annalise to come to the mail car at once. He says we may have a problem. His voice was slurred. He may be hurt."

The German woman thought for a moment, then nodded. "I will come."

"Mohamet, take the manacles from the case in Room B and have Lisa handcuff our diplomats to their seats. We can't spare a guard for them. If they have to shit, they can do it in their pants. A little humiliation might do them some good." She stood, turned, and reached up onto the luggage rack over the toilet cubicle. She brought down a soft-sided overnight bag with a Gucci logo and laid it on the armchair. She unzipped it and withdrew one of the small Ingram MAC-11's they had taken from the St. Augustine weapons cache. She slipped the web-sling over her head, letting the machine gun dangle at her waist, and stuffed the pockets of her denim jacket with extra magazines. Unable to help himself, Kawi realized that he was becoming aroused. The combination of beauty and violence was undeniably erotic. Shenker smiled coldly, seeing the expression on the Libyan's face.

"*Int'a bela-sharra'f Mohamet*," she said in Arabic. "You have no shame." She followed Dieter Haas out of the room and into the corridor. They turned and headed up the train toward the RPO.

"Ai, Annalise, ne int'a kha'a'ter," he whispered. "And you are dangerous."

Within five minutes after he returned to his office, the burgeoning crowd of railway officials and various police authorities had become so large that Frank Sagadore shifted his base of operations to an empty conference room on the same floor as Donovan's CTC headquarters. While the security chief tried to keep some kind of order among the dozen people around the elongated oval of the large table, a dozen more were hard at work installing a telex hookup and a radio link that was patched into Donovan's network, as well as a battery of telephones and tape recorders. The bustling activity beyond the table and the babbling of those seated around it was only one step away from chaos, and Sagadore knew that unless he did something drastic, nothing at all was going to be accomplished. Finally, as the sound in the room began to reach a panic level, he stood up and slammed his fist down hard on the hardwood surface of the table.

"All right. Shut the fuck up!" he bellowed. Instantly there was silence, and every face in the room turned toward him. "Much better," he said, remaining on his feet. "Now look," he continued. "We have an extremely complex situation here and no amount of talk about jurisdiction or authority is going to simplify it. Until someone tells me otherwise, I'm taking over as Crisis Manager here, and you'll all follow my directions or you can get the hell out right now." He looked around the table, but no one said anything. "Good," he muttered, and sat down again. "First off, I want somebody to take some notes. Boswell, you can do it for now." He nodded down the table at the broad, rumple-suited figure of the Penn Station stationmaster. The man seemed surprised at the secretarial role he'd been given, but he didn't balk. Instead he pulled the yellow pad in front of him closer and silently took a ballpoint pen from the sheath in his breast pocket.

"Now then, let's have a situation report. What we need right now, more than anything else, is information. Rabinovich, you're Treasury. Where do we stand from your end?"

A tall, dark-suited figure halfway down the table on

Sagadore's right nodded, tapping the eraser tip of his pencil nervously on the pad in front of him. "We're still a bit confused," he began hesitantly. "As far as we can tell, things went pretty normally right up until train time. The money was brought onto the Railway Post Office out in the coach yard, just like always. No problem. The car was shunted in and coupled to the rest of the train, and then it left. SOP. We sent out the Mobile and Dodds and MacMillan. The two guards in the RPO reported in right on schedule until Trenton. That's when we lost them. They should have given us a preliminary advisory just outside Princeton Junction, but it never came. That's when they must have been hit."

"Can anybody tell me exactly why the train was stopping at Princeton?" asked a conservatively dressed man in his forties who sat across from Rabinovich. It was Wesler, the Manhattan FBI officer-in-charge.

"It was to offload a coffin," said Vaughn, Penn Station's scheduling manager. He flipped through a binder of computer printouts in front of him until he came to the one he wanted. "Here it is. Order came in from the Arlington Memorial Gardens. Coffin carrying the embalmed remains of a Mr. Frederick Dettrick for transshipment from Washington, D.C., to Princeton Junction. Pickup by another funeral home, the Woodglen Funeral Parlor."

"Is that kind of thing normal?" asked the FBI man.

Vaughn shrugged. "It doesn't happen too often, but it's not oddball or anything."

"I'll check it out anyway," said Wesler.

"Do that," said Sagadore. He looked down the table at Boswell, the stationmaster. "Terry, can you give us a rundown of the consist? It might help to give us all a better idea of what we're up against."

The stationmaster cleared his throat nervously. "Nine cars. Motive power is an F-40PH diesel-electric. Two head-end cars, the RPO, and a baggage. Two Amfleet coaches, an Amdinette, a section sleeper, two sleeper combines, and the observation car. The three sleepers are old Penn Central stock, and the observation car is a Pullman Standard."

"How many passengers?" asked Sagadore.

"Two hundred and twenty-five. Seventeen crew, not counting the two men in the RPO or the two Secret Service men."

"What about the diplomats?" asked Sagadore. "Do we know exactly who they are?"

"I can answer that," said a man at the far end of the table.

"And who are you, exactly?" asked Sagadore.

"Anthony Neal, United States Secret Service," said the man.

"Where's Dempsey?" asked Sagadore. "He's my Secret Service liaison."

"On the phone to Washington," answered Neal. "I'm his number two."

"Okay," said Sagadore, nodding. "Who are they?"

"There are five of them on board. Kiyoshi Katsuki, the Japanese trade delegate, Helmut Klassen, the West German U.N. ambassador, Giuseppe Franchia, the Italian naval attaché in Washington, Monsignor David Chilton, secretary to the Vatican ambassador at the U.N., and General Enrique Sanchez, the Argentinian defense minister."

"Shit," said Sagadore. "It couldn't have been a few lightweight couriers. What a cargo!"

"It'll get worse before it gets better," commented Wesler, the FBI man. "Things are bad enough without them, but you can bet dollars to doughnuts on five outraged phone calls from five different embassies pretty soon."

"I don't mean to pull rank," said Neal, choosing his words carefully, "but I think it also means that this is all going to be taken out of your hands, Mr. Sagadore. Ours too, for that matter. We're getting into the Secretary of State's backyard here. This is going to get a lot of international attention."

"Which brings up the question of press relations," said the young woman sitting directly opposite Sagadore at the far end of the table. "The news is going to leak out pretty soon, and you can bet all hell's going to break loose."

"Frankly, Mrs. Youngman, that's your problem. I don't want to see a single camera within a hundred yards of this place, and anyone at this table who gives out any information is on my personal shit list. Terrorists live on publicity, and I don't intend to give these creeps any at all. Got it?"

"Absolutely," said the woman. "But don't expect miracles. I can't control all the other agencies and groups involved here."

"Do your best," said the security chief.

"I'm interested in your choice of labels," said Wesler. "Why do you assume that these people are terrorists? Why not just train robbers?"

"Thieves don't announce themselves," replied Sagadore. "They're talking about mines, explosives, and portable radar units."

"Bluff?" Neal suggested.

"You want to take that risk?" asked Sagadore. "Which brings me to my next question. If we accept the premise that these people *are* terrorists, we can also assume that they're top class. There aren't too many of those around. How can we find out exactly who we're dealing with? Any suggestions as to just who the World People's Army might be?"

"You can try USIST," said Wesler.

"What the hell is a USIST?" asked Sagadore.

"The United States Institute for Studies in Terrorism," explained the FBI agent. "They keep files on just about everyone in the business."

"Find me somebody there I can talk to," said the security chief. "And not some horseshitter either. I want someone who *knows* something."

Sagadore looked around the table. "If there's nothing more, I suggest we get to our various chores. We should meet back here in an hour. If any of you want me before then, I'm on my beeper." He stood up and then leaned over, his palms spread flat on the table. "One more thing. I don't want any of you acting on your own. If you get any flak from your superiors, come to me with it. This is an Amtrak problem, and I'm the boss, at least for now. Anyone who wants to tell me differently better work in the Oval Office." With that, Sagadore straightened and walked out of the room.

"Draconian son of a bitch, isn't he?" commented Wesler, as the security chief stalked out the door.

"Better than a Mary Poppins, though, don't you think?" said Neal, the Secret Service man.

At 2:16 A.M. the Night Owl tripped a sensor as it passed

94

into the last "block" of track before Elizabeth, New Jersey, and instantly a light appeared on Mac Donovan's Model Board, alerting the Master Panel Operator that the train was within two miles of the designated Rahway Valley Line switchpoint. Donovan punched the button on the Master Panel for the switch, and the wye track automatically opened.

At 2:20 A.M., still traveling at a sedate thirty miles per hour, the Night Owl reached the junction and angled northward off the mainline and out of Donovan's direct control. From that point on the MPO would have to rely on telephone and telex links to insure the required switching of the train from one track to another. The area between Elizabeth and Newark was a maze of tracks and yards woven like steel threads through the industrialized district on the outskirts of New York, and there were literally dozens of switchpoints and towers to be dealt with if they were going to comply with the terrorists' routing of the train. Donovan couldn't help but be impressed with the planning that had obviously gone into the hijacking; simply working the train through the mind-boggling grid was going to require all his concentration, and there wasn't going to be time for any fancy work that Frank Sagadore might dream up. As he stared up at the Model Board and watched the indicator lights flicker to green, announcing the Night Owl's departure from the main line, the MPO also found himself wondering if the passengers on the train knew how little could be done to help them now.

In sociological terms, a North American passenger train is a closed hierarchical system that is a microcosm of the society it travels through. Sleeping-car passengers, with their private bathrooms, beds, and servants to care for them, form an upper class that is usually separated from the rest of the train by a dining car or a lounge. The middle and lower classes travel in the coach seats, and all passengers are policed by a chain of command that works down from the conductor to the trainmen and eventually the various stewards. The system, established with the invention of the first true sleeping car by George Mortimer Pullman in 1858, is old-fashioned, elitist, and often racist. But by and large it is effective, and over the long history of the North American railroad there have been few complaints. The hijacking of the train by Annalise Shenker and her companions changed that system drastically, at least for the 250-odd people on board.

With the demand that the window blinds be pulled down, the passengers and crew of the train were completely cut off from the outside world; with the takeover of the locomotive, the official power of the conductor and the rest of his crew was nullified. Everyone on board—crew and passengers alike—was in the same situation.

The impotence of that situation was augmented by the announcement that there were other members of the terrorist group aboard the train who had not shown themselves, thus defusing any chance for the development of a common front among the hostages. The closed system was still closed, but the hierarchy had been removed. There were no rules and regulations anymore, except the law of sudden death that was apparent from the weapons carried by Shenker and her companions. Shenker had further compounded the bizarre state of affairs by doing the unexpected; instead of demanding that all the passengers remain in their seats, she had allowed free movement throughout the train after the charges had been set on the exterior doors.

At first no one had tested this apparent liberty, but by the time the train reached the Rahway Valley switchpoint, the dinette was lined up three deep with anxious passengers demanding free rations of Amtrak liquor. The only evidence of anything unusual was the hard-faced terrorist, Sheila Teng, guarding the entrance to the rear observation sleeper, a Canadian Arsenals FN automatic rifle clutched in her small hands.

"We're really up the creek, aren't we?" said Daniel Pendergast, seated on the lower bunk in Adrian Tucker's bedroom. Harry Maxwell, perched on the small sink, a cigarette in his hand, shrugged.

"It could be a hell of a lot worse," he said. "At least we can move around."

"I don't understand that," said Tucker, squeezed into the other corner of the bunk, his hands working nervously on his bent knees. "Why are they letting us go where we want? It's crazy."

"No, it's not," said Daniel. "It's pretty damn smart, really. We're a captive audience anyway. Even if those mines or whatever they are on the outer doors between the cars are fakes, I don't think anyone is going to jump out of the train."

"They've obviously thought it out right down the line," said Harry Maxwell from his perch. "It's not like an airplane hijacking, where you've got everybody in a small area. The passengers are spread out over almost a dozen cars, and from what I've seen, they don't have the manpower to keep that many people in that many seats under any kind of effective control. I'm willing to bet that the line about these other terrorists traveling incognito is a lot of horseshit, but even so, I'm not going to chance anything. Nope, they've got us right where they want us."

"What I don't understand is why," said Daniel. "You said it yourself, Harry, this isn't like a plane hijacking. The train has to stop sometime, and when it does the cops will be all over it. The whole thing is suicidal."

"Maybe," said Harry. "But these people have been smooth so far, and that dark-haired woman in the jeans who we saw going into the baggage car looked as smart as she was beautiful. Believe me, they've got something cooking."

"Speaking of the woman in the jeans, what's going to happen when she finds her buddy snoozing in the money car? It's not going to take any smarts for them to figure out there was a heist in progress."

"It's going to worry her," Harry answered. "We're a factor they hadn't counted on."

"Do you think they'll come after us?" asked Daniel.

"I doubt it," said Harry. "Not actively, anyway. Like I said before—not enough manpower. They'll have their eyes open, though. Which means we should probably get rid of the radio and anything else that might associate us with the RPO."

"And then what?" asked Adrian Tucker, anxiety putting a tremor in his voice. "Do we just sit here and wait?"

"No," said Harry, leaning down and stubbing out his cigarette in the wall-mounted ashtray. "No, we don't just sit and wait. We can't."

"Why not?" said Daniel. "If we lie low and don't make any waves, these people will treat us like any of the other passengers."

"We don't just sit here because people are going to get

hurt before this is over. Maybe a lot of people. I don't know what the goons who took over this train are demanding, but you can bet your ass someone is going to call in the marines sooner or later. And these people are nuts. Loonies. They might let the passengers go, but on the other hand they might blow us all to hell for the greater joy of their cause, whatever that is. And on top of that, I'm pretty pissed off."

"Explain that," said Daniel.

"We busted our cranks getting this robbery together, and I'm not about to give up now. I want that money."

"You're nuts," whispered Tucker, his eyes widening.

"No, just angry," said Harry. "One way or another, I intend to survive this, and I want to come out of it with more than just a good story to tell the guy from *Time* magazine."

"Just what are you proposing?" asked Daniel, frowning.

"A counterattack," said Harry. "These people took the train, and so far they've managed to hang onto it." Harry lit another cigarette and blew a plume of smoke up toward the ceiling vent, then looked down at his two companions. "What I'm proposing is that we take it back again."

Mark Cavendish sat at one of the small tables in the wildly overcrowded dinette, trying to shut out the roaring babble of the voices around him. He rocked easily back and forth as the train lumbered over the irregularly used Rahway Valley track, and tried to formulate some kind of plan of action. The dinette—noisy, filled to overflowing, and hazy with cigarette smoke—was hardly the place to do any creative thinking, but it was better than sitting in the coach with nothing to do except stare at the fabric of the window blind. Beside him, an overweight man smelling faintly of Lectric Shave and drinking Schlitz was babbling about his "human rights" to a uniformed Amtrak steward on the other side of the table, while directly across from Cavendish a slight, balding man with glasses was quietly reading a book, its title obscured by a neatly folded protective paper cover that was obviously homemade. The little man in his rumpled suit looked completely relaxed, an island of calm in a sea of near hysteria. Cavendish was enthralled by the man's composure.

"Good book?" he asked.

The man looked up from his reading and smiled politely. "I beg your pardon?" he said pleasantly.

Cavendish raised his voice above the din and repeated his question. "I asked if the book was any good," he said. "I'm surprised you can read at all under the circumstances."

"It's *Marshall's Rail Facts and Feats*," replied the man, smiling. "It's rather like a *Guinness Book of Records* for trains."

"You're interested in trains?" asked Cavendish.

"Yes," said the man. He closed the book, marking his place with the flap from the dust cover. "I'm an engineer, you see."

"A train engineer?" asked Cavendish, not quite believing it. The man couldn't have weighed much over a hundred pounds, and the rumpled, somewhat frayed blue suit he was wearing didn't fit the standard image of a Casey Jones type.

"Not that kind of engineer," said the man. "I'm a mechanical engineer. I design elements for air conditioners, mostly. Trains are my hobby. I'm a model railroad enthusiast. Passenger consists, actually."

"Oh," said Cavendish, his interest waning. "Models."

"That's right," said the man. "But only prototype designs. I like them to be as close to the real thing as possible."

"So you know a lot about trains, then?"

"Quite a bit," said the man, flushing slightly. "For instance, I have a fairly good idea of where we are."

"You're kidding," said Cavendish, interested again.

"No, I'm not. As far as I can tell, we're on the old Rahway Valley line that links up at Summit to the route between Gladstone and Newark."

"How do you know all that with the blinds down?" asked Cavendish, intrigued.

"The Washington–New York Corridor is my specialty," said the man. "Most rail fans have one area they concentrate on. Anyway, I've traveled most of the Corridor lines at one time or another, and I'm quite familiar with the switchpoints. The hoodlums who took over the train began slowing us down just after we went through New Brunswick. By the feel of it, we're going at about thirty miles per hour, so if the speed is constant, that lurch we felt a while ago was the wye switchpoint at Elizabeth. We've gone about ten miles since then, so by my calculations we should be coming up on Summit in a couple of minutes."

"Amazing!" said Cavendish, impressed. "What happens at Summit?"

"Not too much, I'm afraid," said the man. "It's not much more than a junction, as I recall. The Rahway line joins the Consolidated right-of-way going in three directions—west toward Gladstone, which is end-of-track, east to Newark, and north toward the Denville junction and then Scranton."

"Which way do you think we'll go?" asked Cavendish.

"I don't have the slightest idea," said the man. "Although I assume we won't head toward Gladstone, since it's a dead end."

"So it's Newark or Scranton," said Cavendish.

"Not necessarily," the man said thoughtfully. "The choices are almost infinite, really. By switching often enough, we could go almost anywhere."

"Terrific," muttered Cavendish.

"By the way," said the man, "my name is Mottbrown, Howard Mottbrown." He extended a hand across the table. Cavendish looked at it for a long moment and then lifted his right arm, bringing the Dorrance hook off his lap. He tapped the gleaming, dulled point of the mechanism into Mottbrown's hand and then withdrew it.

"Mark Cavendish."

"Good lord," the small man said softly.

"The other one is even better," said Cavendish, lifting the arm fitted with the cosmetic prosthesis. Out of the corner of his eye he caught the reaction of the fat man sitting next to him. There was a frozen instant, and then he felt the man move almost imperceptibly away from him. Mottbrown, on the other hand, didn't show the slightest embarrassment.

"That's amazing," he said, peering at the prosthesis. "It's very lifelike. Does it work as well as the hook?"

"Not really," said Cavendish, pleasantly surprised by Mottbrown's forthright interest. "It's not much more than a hinged armature with a latex covering. I can mold the fingers to hold things and turn the palm, but that's about it. I was right-handed before, so I use the hook for anything that needs a light touch." He lifted his right hand and clicked the Dorrance hook open and shut a few times, mostly for the benefit of the fat man next to him. A few seconds later the man mumbled inaudibly and left the table, followed by the man across from him. No one took their place.

"Those two seemed a little upset," said Mottbrown, watching them go.

"Being an amputee has a few good points," said Cavendish, grinning. He shifted slightly on his seat. "At least now we have some breathing space."

"How did you lose your hands?" asked Mottbrown.

"Vietnam," said Cavendish. "I haven't jerked off since."

Mottbrown lowered his eyes and blushed again. Cavendish, realizing that he had embarrassed the man, cleared his throat and changed the subject. "You want something to drink? It looks like it's on the house."

"No thank you," said Mottbrown. "Most people get dry-mouthed and thirsty when they're scared. I worry about my weak bladder."

"This scares you?" asked Cavendish.

Mottbrown nodded slowly. "Yes," he said. "Of course."

"Me too," said Cavendish. "I've got a pretty active imagination."

"What do you mean?"

"We've been hijacked by terrorists. Every terrorist incident I've ever heard of wound up with hostages getting hurt. I've also had some personal experience with this kind of thing before."

"You've been hijacked before?" said Mottbrown.

"POW camp. A place called Lang Son on the Nanning railroad line, way up north by the Chinese border," said Cavendish, a steady parade of images dancing fresh and painful in his mind's eye. "I learned a lot about terrorism there. And physical torture was the least of it, let me tell you. Those guys could have you writhing in mental agony. That was worse, in a lot of ways. And that's what we have here. It's the reason for them letting us have free access to most of the train. It's a variation on the 'hard cop/soft cop' routine."

"I'm afraid I don't understand what you mean," said Mottbrown.

"In a police interrogation you often have one policeman who comes on like he's going to give you the third degree. That's the 'hard cop.' Then he goes away and leaves you with the 'soft cop,' the one who's sympathetic, gives you a cup of coffee and a cigarette. You go through the routine a few times and you wind up being willing to tell the soft cop anything he wants to know, just to keep the hard cop off your back. Here it's a bit different. They're letting us have the run of the place, making it seem as though we're barely hostages at all. That's the soft part. It's going to make it all the worse when they lower the boom, and they will, you just watch. Hard."

"So what do you think we should do about it?" asked Mottbrown.

"What do you mean?" said Cavendish. "What can we do? They're holding all the aces."

"Well, we have to do something," said Mottbrown. "If what you say is true, then we're all in very great danger."

"I don't have to do anything except cover my ass, Howard, and as far as I'm concerned that means keeping a low profile and ducking any bullets that come along. I played hero once, and I wound up with my arms rotting off in a tin hut in the middle of a godforsaken jungle, ten thousand miles from home. I don't mean to be a shit about it, Howard, but you've had a nice soft life designing air conditioners, so maybe you haven't figured out that in this world no one gives a crap about anyone else. It's what they call a simple truth. We're on our own, each and every one of us."

"I'm sorry you feel that way," said Mottbrown.

Cavendish shrugged and slid out from behind the table. He stood up, the plastic fingers of his left hand supporting him as he stood for a moment in the aisle. "If you come up with any bright ideas, give me a shout. I'm in seat thirty-six in the next car."

"I'll do that," Mottbrown murmured thoughtfully. Cavendish stared down at the mousy little man for a second and shook his head. Then he turned and made his way through the crush of people around the service counter in the dinette, heading for the door leading to the next car.

Walter Linberg was roused from a troubled sleep by the ringing of the telephone beside his bed. He felt around for the bedside lamp and switched it on, wincing in the sudden glare. He groaned, reached out with stiff fingers for the phone, and dragged it to his ear.

"What?" he managed, his mouth gummy.

"Walt? Dave Wesler. Sorry to wake you, but I've got an emergency."

"Wesler?" Linberg's brain struggled with the name and finally came up with an association. Dave Wesler was the USIST-FBI liaison contact for New York. A name on a memo list and a half-remembered face at meetings. Linberg let his eyes open slightly and lifted his wrist up in front of his face. It was after two. "An emergency?"

"We need someone with some background on recent terrorist actions. I know I should have phoned your boss, but there isn't any time."

"I don't have a boss," grunted Linberg. "I'm not with USIST anymore."

"Damn!" Wesler breathed, his voice anxious on the other end of the line.

"What's the problem?" asked Linberg. "Maybe I can put you onto somebody you can use instead."

"We've had a hijacking. A bad one. The Amtrak Night Owl from Washington to New York. Two hundred passengers, half a dozen top diplomats on their way back to the UN for today's session, and a goddamn Federal Reserve currency shipment. It couldn't be much worse."

"Shenker," said Linberg, suddenly wide awake.

"What?" said Wesler, confused.

"Annalise Shenker," said Linberg, dragging himself up into a sitting position. "Something I was working on before I quit USIST."

"You mean you know who these people are?" said Wesler, astounded.

"I think so," said Linberg. "It fits. There was a raid on a private armory a while back, and then we hit a possible arms cache here in D.C."

"I remember that," said Wesler. "It was on the last circulating sheet. It came up empty, right?"

"Not quite," said Linberg. "Both raids were leads out of a report that came in to USIST about a month ago. Six top terrorists had their own private little summit

103

meeting in Algiers, then came to the States. The only thing we found after the D.C. raid was a cash register tape. I pulled some strings and National Office ran it down for me. The inventory codes on the tape were from a place in Alexandria that makes uniforms. The purchase in question was three Amtrak maintenance coveralls. I couldn't take it any further without resources, and nobody seemed interested, so I dropped it and quit. They would have fired me anyway for the D.C. fiasco."

"To hell with that," said Wesler. "You're back on it now. If you really do know who these people are, then maybe we have a bit of an edge. I want your ass up here on the double."

"On whose authority?" asked Linberg.

"Mine," Wesler snapped back. "You can be a consultant or something. We'll deal with the paperwork later."

"Talk like that and they'll boot you out of the Bureau," said Linberg, grinning evilly into the telephone receiver.

"Take your shots," said Wesler. "There'll be a helicopter at Fort McNair in twenty minutes. Be there."

"Where am I going?" asked Linberg, swinging his legs out from under the covers and onto the floor.

"Penn Station," said Wesler, and suddenly the line was dead.

"That makes sense," said Linberg to himself. "Taking a chopper to a railway station." Laughing, adrenaline pumping through his veins at the prospect of action, he began to dress.

As the helicopter carrying Walter Linberg took off for New York City, a small group of men were meeting in the otherwise vacant State Department offices on Virginia Avenue. The four men in attendance were Norman Gregg, the Presidential Security Advisor; Thomas Watt Kellog, Assistant Secretary of State for Domestic Affairs; General Frederick Bowman, from the office of the Joint Chiefs of Staff; and Carl Holloway, Assistant Director of the National Security Agency. Gregg, the senior official present, acted as chairman of the meeting. The three other men sat quietly, sipping hastily brewed cups of coffee while the birdlike man in the perfectly tailored gray suit read the slim preliminary report that had been prepared for him. Of the four men, Gregg was the only one who seemed fully awake and alert.

"All right," the dapper man said finally, carefully closing the red folder and arranging it neatly in front of him on the small conference table. "I am now acquainted with the problem. I see several options open to us at this point, but I would like your suggestions before I proceed. Mr. Kellog?" Gregg turned to the short, slope-shouldered figure on his left. Kellog, the Assistant Secretary of State, ran a hand through his unruly mass of salt-and-pepper curls and shrugged. "I don't think there's much we can do. Not yet anyway. I'm still not sure of jurisdiction here. At first glance it looks like one for the FBI—strictly internal, and considering both the Federal Reserve shipment and the ownership of Amtrak itself, it seems to be a case of either kidnapping or the theft of government property, or both. The Bureau seems to be operating under that assumption so far, although I gather that one of Amtrak's security people in New York is carrying the ball at the moment."

"General Bowman?" said Gregg, nodding toward the heavyset man at the far end of the table. Bowman was dressed in what appeared to be golf pants and a brightly colored Hawaiian shirt, an outfit that somewhat diminished his usual imposing, uniformed image.

"I don't think we can afford to wait. And I don't give a shit for jurisdiction. This has been coming for a long time now, and we've been caught with our pants down to our ankles. Every other country in the world has some kind of antiterrorist contingency planning operation except us. I can just imagine what's going on in New York right now. There's a dozen mother-lovers up there running around getting in each other's way and accomplishing nothing. We've all seen these terrorist scenarios work in other countries, and we all know that the longer you wait before you hit, the more people get hurt. Not to mention the fact that another limp-wrist operation like Carter's try for the Iranian hostages is going to make us look like utter fools all over the world. I say we hit and hit hard. Now."

"Carl?" said Gregg, turning to the NSA man.

The assistant director cleared his throat and looked around the table, his lean, almost hawklike features cut and crosscut with lines and wrinkles that were the battle scars of more than twenty years in the forefront of the intelligence field. Methodically he reached into the pocket of his Harris tweed jacket, took out a package of Chesterfields, and lit one, twin spears of smoke coming from the nostrils of his aquiline nose. When he spoke, his voice was low and harsh with half a century of tobacco.

"I agree with General Bowman's assessment of the bad national image this situation will almost surely create if the terrorists keep the train for too much longer. On the other hand, I doubt that any ill-advised attack on the train will do much for the nation's public relations, either.

"I think the first thing we all have to understand is the nature of the beast we're dealing with here. As you are aware, most hostage-taking incidents are short-term; the longer they go on, the more lives are lost, and the less chance there is of success on the part of the terrorists. But that isn't the case here. Hostages are usually taken as leverage for certain demands: money or the release of so-called political prisoners. In this instance I think you'll find that the terrorists' needs have already been met. So far there have been no demands and no manifestoes—we still don't even know who we're dealing with. I think the reason for that is simple: the terrorists already have what they want—to wit, the Federal Reserve shipment. If that is true, and there are no other demands, then they have the upper hand. There won't be any long, drawn-out negotiations, because they won't be necessary. The terrorists will have a single, simple goal—to get away with the money, using the hostages as a blind to keep us at arm's length. That *does* give us an advantage, though, since it means that these people are almost certainly working within a time limit of some kind. They're not simply wandering around on any available stretch of railroad track they can find—they have a destination, and they have to be there at a certain time. Our problem is to find out where that is and stop them."

"Interesting," murmured Gregg. "Thank you, Carl." Gregg pursed his lips and stared down thoughtfully at the report on the table in front of him. Then he looked up.

"There is no time to quibble about jurisdiction here. Nominally, of course, it is an FBI situation, but they sim-

106

ply don't have the resources or capabilities necessary. I also agree that a quick and poorly planned operation against the train would probably result in a number of deaths and a public relations nightmare. However—action is required. I assume your Black Berets are ready and waiting, General Bowman?"

"Of course, sir," said the military man. "There's a Starlifter on tap that can have them within spitting distance of the train in less than two hours."

"What about one of those Spectre surveillance airplanes we used in Vietnam?" asked Carl Holloway.

"Already thought of that," said Bowman, smiling. "There's one in for evaluation at Wright Field now. Full complement."

"Yes," agreed Gregg. "Even if the operation fails, intelligence at close hand would be advisable." The Presidential advisor flipped open the report on the table and glanced at it briefly. "According to the hypothetical schedule outlined here, the train should be in the vicinity of Andover, New Jersey, at approximately four-forty A.M. shortly before dawn. That gives us slightly less than two hours before the information we now have runs out. By General Bowman's estimation, he can have his people in the vicinity of Andover within that time limit. To proceed rashly, however, would be unwise. If the train continues on its way, and for the sake of argument we can assume that it will, our terrorists will need to give the Amtrak office in New York further instructions concerning which tracks they wish to use. I suggest that General Bowman's Black Berets take off immediately, as well as the surveillance aircraft. In the meantime, using what information we have at hand, we will form some kind of plan of attack. With any luck it will succeed, and we can have an end to this before the evening editions are printed. A *fait accompli* is no news story, gentlemen."

"And if it doesn't work?" asked Holloway, a slightly sour note creeping into his voice.

"I think we should cross that bridge if and when it becomes necessary, Mr. Holloway. To assume failure is hardly the American way, now is it?"

Chapter 7

Monday, June 27
Time: 3:46 A.M. EDT
Distance: 233 miles/375 km.

In the two hours since the first notification that the train had been hijacked, a considerable amount of information had been gathered by Frank Sagadore and the various officials involved with the incident. By comparing the preliminary reports from the FBI, the Secret Service, Treasury, and his own people at Amtrak, Sagadore had been able to piece together what he assumed was a reasonably close approximation of what had happened to the Night Owl.

A thorough check of the D.C. Terminal Yard had revealed the bodies of two maintenance men, throats slit, bundled into an equipment shed. It was assumed that two if not more of the terrorists had boarded the train while it was being assembled in the yards. A third body, this one that of an oiler from the diesel sheds, had also been found, throat cut like the other two, so presumably a third and possibly a fourth terrorist had managed to hide in the rear engine compartment of the Night Owl locomotive. Since there was no real security involved in ticketing boarding passengers, there was no way to know how many other terrorists were on board the train, but the FBI's best guess was that there were at least five more involved. Wesler, the New York FBI agent-in-charge, had reported that they might have a lead on at least some of the terrorists involved, but they wouldn't know for sure until the expert from D.C. arrived.

The Night Owl's run had proceeded normally from its departure until its arrival in Trenton, so logically the hijacking must have taken place between there and Princeton Junction, where the train was supposed to have stopped to offload a coffin.

The question of the Princeton Junction stop bothered

Sagadore. The FBI had checked with both the Arlington Memorial Gardens in D.C. and the Woodglen Funeral Parlor in Kendall Park, New Jersey, and neither company had ever heard of Fred Dettrick, embalmed or otherwise. Suspicious, perhaps, but also anomalous, since the train hadn't stopped at Princeton Junction to offload the alleged corpse. Agent Wesler came up with the possibility that the coffin, which *had* been loaded in Washington by a bona fide hearse, might have been used as a weapons cache, but Sagadore had pointed out that there was no reason to go to all the trouble; it was just as easy to pack whatever weapons were necessary in a suitcase and carry them onto the train, since there were no metal detectors or any other security procedures for baggage. Eventually, Wesler had dismissed the question of the coffin as irrelevant.

By 3:30 A.M. the conference-room headquarters had been fully established, with Frank Sagadore as its pivot. He found himself in the unlikely and uncomfortable position of being not much more than a dispatcher, fielding calls from tower switchers along the line, routing memo slips to the appropriate people and listening to complaints from just about everyone, including Jennifer Youngman, the Amtrak PR lady, who was having a hard time keeping the press at bay. The Treasury and the FBI both had their noses out of joint at Sagadore's arbitrary assumption of control, and she'd had several irate calls, from both Wesler's boss at FBI headquarters in Washington and from the Treasury, complaining about it. Both agencies had press conferences scheduled for 9:00 A.M. Sagadore was praying that the crisis would be over by then, but he doubted it, and being tied to the conference room was making him more and more agitated with each passing minute. Where he really wanted to be was up in one of the helicopters trailing the Night Owl.

The helicopter surveillance and the reports from switch towers along the line were the only concrete points of reference in a sea of hypotheses. According to the visual reports the train was proceeding along its chosen route at an inexorable thirty miles per hour, running without lights and with all the blinds in all cars pulled shut. Three sharp-eyed switchers had confirmed that the windows in the vestibules between the cars seemed to have been painted over, making any kind of interior view impossible. All the surveillance reports mentioned that there appeared to be some kind of boxlike device mounted on the rear quarter of the diesel roof—presumably the radar that the voice on the radio had mentioned. It really was beginning to look as though the hijackers had thought of everything; the Amtrak Night Owl was a locked box and they held the key.

Working independently, Frank Sagadore had come to the same conclusion as the secret group that had met at the State Department: the hijacking was a *fait accompli*. There would be no demands. The terrorists already had their ransom, and the hostages' only value now was as a shield and a publicity device. He'd also concluded that given the precise planning demonstrated by the terrorists so far, it was a sure bet they had a way of getting away with their crime unharmed, which in turn meant that somewhere along the line, literally, the Night Owl was going to reach some prearranged destination.

The only problem with that was the almost infinite number of potential places the train could go. So far the route chosen by the nameless voice in the cab of the Night Owl diesel was telling Sagadore nothing except the obvious: by heading north, the terrorists were avoiding New York City. Once they reached the junction at Andover they could go either northeast up into New York State, west and north toward Scranton, Pennsylvania, or southwest toward Bethlehem. With the fuel they had on hand, the train could be taken four or five hundred miles in any of those directions.

Sitting at the conference table, Sagadore stared at the large North American route atlas in front of him, trying to think ahead of the terrorists, the spiderweb of tracks on the pale green pages of the atlas blurring, name crowding on name until his head felt as though it was stuffed with cotton wool. He closed his eyes finally, and sat back in his chair, trying to ignore the bustling people around him. If he wanted to get away with it, which way would he go? The terrorists either knew for certain or could easily assume that they would be under surveillance and that any change in their pattern, speed, or position would be instantly reported. Railroads in the United States are an urban transportation system, and except for some areas in Texas, Nevada, and Montana, thousands of miles away, there is

110

virtually nowhere in the country that isn't within a relatively short distance from an urban center. With the state police alerted and the FBI on full alert, the terrorists didn't stand a chance. Even if they did manage to get off the train, they'd be caught within a matter of hours, if not less. They didn't have a hope in hell of getting out of whatever state they stopped in, let alone the country.

So?

He sat forward and opened his eyes, looking down at the route atlas. He flipped to the first page of the large binder and scanned the map, which showed the entire North American continent. In the lower portion the map was almost a solid mass of black lines from the Atlantic Ocean to Kansas City. To the north, though, there was almost nothing. From Montreal to Vancouver, a distance of three thousand miles, there were only two main lines and a few secondaries. On one section, between Sudbury and Thunder Bay on the far side of Lake Superior, there was a stretch of track almost seven hundred miles long that looked as though it didn't go through any town larger than a few hundred people. Perfect. Away from concentrated population areas and out of the country, just like that. Simple.

"The bastards are going into Canada," he whispered.

At 4:00 A.M., slightly less than an hour before dawn, a Lockheed C-141 Starlifter, traveling at an altitude of 5,500 feet, dropped eighteen of General Bowman's Black Berets over the isolated community of Andover Junction, New Jersey. Their target was the mouth of a double tunnel three miles to the east of the small freight station on the rarely used section of Conrail track that ran from Belvidere to Franklin. Of the eighteen men, twelve landed within five hundred yards of the target, four became disoriented and landed almost three miles away, one broke his ankle landing badly, and one, Master Sergeant Leonard Nelms, a forty-one-year-old ex-Special Forces Vietnam veteran, died when his parachute failed to open and he plummeted to the forest floor almost a mile below. The Starlifter, which had brought its passengers to the drop zone a full half hour ahead of schedule, continued on toward Griffiss Air Force Base in Rome, New York.

Ten thousand feet above the Starlifter and completely invisible and inaudible from the ground, a second aircraft slowly circled the drop zone. The plane was a much-modified C-130 Hercules transport, transformed into a Spectre gunship of the type used in the last years of the Vietnam war. The 25-million-dollar aircraft, which was usually based at the Sixty-fourth Fighter Weapons Squadron at Nellis Air Force Base in Nevada, had been deadheading at Wright Field when the call came in from General Bowman. In addition to an awesome range of weapons, from 12,000-round-per-minute machine guns to a 105mm howitzer, the Hercules was also equipped with a full complement of electronic surveillance and warfare equipment including Pave Spike video tape recorders, Pave Strike laser target designators, infrared Linescan cameras, and Compass Link data transmission facilities that tied all the electronics on board to the Initial Defense Communications Satellite System, which in turn relayed any or all information to Washington. The Compass Link System, originally brought into service in 1968, was so fast that an operator in the Pentagon war room could actually "see" the action taking place as much as four thousand miles away within eight seconds of real time.

"They're down," murmured a uniformed weapons officer in his cubicle at the center of the broad-bellied aircraft. In front of him, the pale colors of the IR Linescan screen turned his features a washed-out pink.

"Where are the toads?" asked the voice of the pilot in the man's headset. The weapons officer shifted his glance to the smaller surveillance scope to the left of the linescan screen. He punched a sequence of buttons on the console in front of him and the dimly lit cubicle was brightened with a muted green glare as the monitor came on. The weapons officer punched in a grid-coordinate overlay on the screen and watched as a square of numbers and letters appeared in the upper right-hand corner of the screen.

"Thirteen miles east of the target. Ten miles from the junction."

"You getting anything else?" asked the pilot's crackling voice.

"Just a little heat from a few cars. Not much traffic up in the backwoods this time of night, I guess."

"Keep watching," said the pilot. "Anything gets close to the train, I want to know about it."

"We flying close support?" asked the weapons officer.

"Don't be stupid," said the pilot. "This is fucking New Jersey, for Christ's sake. Those are Americans on that train, not gooks. We hang around and do surveillance, that's all. We just do what we're told."

"Sorry," said the weapons officer.

"Right," said the pilot. "Just keep watching."

Within five minutes of reaching the ground, the twelve remaining members of Bowman's squad had assembled on the roadbed close to the mouth of the tunnel. The group, minus a third of its complement, began to deploy without further instructions. The plan of attack—devised by three of Bowman's best tactical people back in Georgia and relayed to the Starlifter via satellite—was straightforward and without any frills. The tunnel, which cut through a large hill almost a mile long, exited at a crossover in the tracks designed to accommodate a freight consist waiting to move through the small yards at Andover Junction. The twin mouths of the tunnel each contained a separate track, both of which joined on the crossover a hundred and fifty yards from the mouth. At the crossover there was also an overhead signal gantry. The complex tracking, and the angle at which the two tracks joined close to the tunnel entrance, would force the train to slow to about fifteen miles per hour as it came out from underground. Bowman's squad, located on the hill above the tunnel mouth and on top of the signal gantry as well as beside the track itself, would storm the train as it slowed. Four men on the ground close to the tunnel mouth would try and climb onto the train between cars, four more would drop onto the roofs of the rear cars from the hill above, in an effort to rescue the diplomats in the observation car, and a three-man weapons team stationed on the signal gantry would take out the locomotive. The eleven men would be directed via walkie-talkie from a small knoll to the right of the tracks, some seventy-five yards out from the tunnel mouth. The twelfth man, the squad's leader, was equipped with a tripod-mounted Rank passive night sight capable of magnifying existing light some forty thousand times. By staring into the battery-powered device, the squad leader

113

could see clearly for almost fifty yards down the apparently pitch-black tunnel. Acting on his instructions, the squad would attack the train simultaneously, the three men on the gantry stopping it dead while the others went on board. Using flash grenades, tear gas, and low-velocity bullets, they hoped to retake the train within three to four minutes, taking acceptable losses of two or three of their own men and less than a dozen hostages.

That was the plan.

Harry Maxwell moved slowly along the swaying corridor, heading for the Amlounge car. He took his time, trying to assimilate as much information as he could. With all the blinds drawn and the vestibule windows between the cars blackened, there was no way of telling where they were, but he had kept count of the time it took for the train to click over each section of rail, and as far as he could tell they were traveling at a steady rate of just under thirty miles per hour. In the past hour and a half they also seemed to have traveled over quite a few bridges, which probably meant they were upcountry somewhere and well off the main line.

He pulled open the door at the end of the corridor and stepped into the vestibule, where he was instantly assailed by the hammering of the bogies below his feet. Looking left and right, he saw that here, as in the previous space between cars, the windows had been roughly painted over and the doors leading off the train hung with an obvious booby trap. No way off the train there, at thirty miles per hour or any other speed.

He dragged open the door into the next car and stepped into the section sleeper, coyly referred to by Amtrak as a "Slumbercoach." The beds, all of which had been made up when the train left Washington, had now been folded away by order of the terrorists, and the passengers were sitting up in their seats, most of them in their nightclothes. As he walked slowly through the car, several of the passengers threw him suspicious glances and he realized that they were wondering if he was one of the hijackers. Harry nodded to himself as he reached the end of the car and crossed to the lounge. The claim by the

114

terrorists that there were more of them traveling incognito was obviously working.

The lounge was almost completely empty, except for a pair of nervous men in wrinkled business suits and a small Walter Mitty type at the far end of the car, who was busily scribbling in some kind of book. The earlier, fear-induced excitement that had filled the bar a couple of hours before had disappeared, to be replaced by the deeper fear that the people on the train were involved in something totally out of their control. The terrorists had ordered that the doors to all roomettes and bedrooms be left ajar, and walking through the train Harry had seen expressions on faces that ranged from rigid fear to barely controlled panic. He'd begun his meandering reconnaissance of the train with the faint hope of finding a few passengers with enough chutzpah to gang up on the hijackers, but so far he hadn't seen anybody who looked capable of walking without his knees knocking, let alone with the guts to take on their captors. Harry had a sneaking suspicion he wasn't going to find anybody cut from different cloth in the coaches beyond the lounge, either.

He stepped up to the bar midway along the car and ordered a Scotch, straight up, noticing as he did so that the bartender was the same man who'd been their night porter on the first Night Owl trip. Harry recognized the black man's tired face, as well as the name on his jacket: Hamilton Stackpole.

"We meet again," smiled Harry.

Stackpole's lip curled up automatically. "What?" There wasn't even the faintest trace of stewardly courtesy in the man's voice. Hamilton Stackpole, the porter/steward, had obviously booked off for the night.

"I was on the Night Owl a while back," explained Harry. "You were the sleeping-car porter."

"Yeah," said Stackpole.

"You have a grip on any of this?" asked Harry, sipping his drink.

"No," said Stackpole.

"And you don't give a shit, either, do you?" grinned Harry.

"If I did, you think I'd tell you?" said Stackpole.

"Why not?"

"Because you could be one of them, that's why," answered the black man, wiping the already spotless counter.

"But I'm not."

"Which makes it a conundrum," said Stackpole. "You say you aren't, I say you could be, and both might be just as true as false."

"A profound bartender," said Harry, finishing off his drink.

"You bet your ass," said Stackpole. "Three years fighting in World War II, a bachelor's degree in English literature, and I wind up on the Florida east coast polishing other people's shoes. *That's* profound, my friend."

Harry toyed with his glass, elbows on the counter, his body riding easily on the steady back-and-forth lurching of the train. "How many of them do you count?" he asked after a moment.

"I'm not sure," Stackpole said carefully, his eyes on Harry and his voice low. He poured out another drink without being asked, and then poured one for himself. "At least six. Could be more."

Harry mentally added the man he and Daniel had seen lying unconscious in the RPO.

"How do you know?" asked Harry.

"Jungle telegraph," said Stackpole, with a note of disdain.

"Where are they?"

"One in the observation car. The boss lady is in a bedroom in the next car up, with a third monitoring a radio in another bedroom. There's a fourth standing guard in the corridor. Number five is in between the dinette and the first coach. Number six, the Spanish looking woman, seems to wander around from car to car with that big machine pistol of hers."

With number seven in the RPO, and eight and maybe nine in the cab of the locomotive, thought Harry. "You've got good information," said Harry after a moment, looking down at the drink in front of him, the glass shivering slightly with the vibration of the train.

Stackpole shrugged. "Part of the job. Why are you so interested?"

"I guess I'm just your basic American individualist," said Harry, looking up and grinning at the black man. "I don't like being cooped up."

"You going to do anything about it?" asked Stackpole.

"The thought occurred to me," said Harry.

" 'The never-failing vice of fools,' " said Stackpole.

"Pardon?"

"Thinking," explained the black man. "Alexander Pope, 'An Essay on Criticism.' These are mean people. You'd be a late-night snack for the boss woman. A couple of the others look like real crazies, too."

"So we sit back and take it?" asked Harry.

"I didn't say that," said Stackpole with a genuine smile. "I just said you'd be out of your mind to try to take the train back from them. On the other hand, you might be just as crazy not to."

"Explain that," said Harry.

"They're killers," said Stackpole. "They off people the way you or I might squash a roach. We've got more than two hundred on board right now. All of them uptight, nervous, frightened. Something is bound to blow pretty soon. Some idiot will do something really stupid, and they're going to have at it with all that fancy ordnance they're toting around. There's going to be blood on the walls before this is over, one way or another. People like that feed on it like vampires."

"So if I'm going to be a victim anyway, it's better not to be passive ones, is that what you mean?" put in Harry.

"Something like that," said Stackpole, tossing off his drink in a single swallow.

"Care to lay out any specifics?" asked Harry. "What with that three years of World War II you had."

"It's going to take more than just you, that's the first thing," said Stackpole.

"I've got two others," said Harry.

"Makes three," Stackpole said thoughtfully. "Still not enough. And you don't have any weapons, either. There's one guy you might try. He was sitting at that table behind you, talking to the little guy with the book. I couldn't hear much of what they were saying, but I think he was in Vietnam."

"The one with the book?" asked Harry.

Stackpole shook his his head. "No, the other one. Big, tough looking. Only problem is, he's got hooks where his hands should be. He headed into the coach."

"An amputee?" Harry sighed. "Maybe we better sit it out after all."

"He looks like he can handle himself," said Stackpole. "Hands or no hands. It's worth a try. It's a good bet he's not one of the hijackers, anyway."

"All right." Harry nodded, pushing away from the bar. "I'll go and have a chat with him."

"Good enough," Stackpole answered. "Where are you and these other two recruits located?"

"The first sleeper. Bedroom B."

"All right, I'll find you there later. But be cool. If these people see a little coffee club starting up, you're done, my friend."

Harry nodded and moved away from the counter. He went to the end of the nearly deserted car and pulled open the heavy door, wondering if their plan had the slightest chance of success, or if it was just a complicated way of committing suicide. He shrugged the thought off; they really didn't have any choice, and if he was going to die, he wanted to die fighting. He swallowed hard and dragged open the door leading into the coach.

"I should have done what good old dad wanted," he muttered under his breath as he eased through the doorway. "I should have gone into sheet-metal work."

Annalise Shenker surveyed the carnage within the RPO, her mouth drawn down in a hard line and her hands clenched tightly at her hips. Amal Akbar, still bleary-eyed from the nitrous oxide, was slumped in the chair recently and violently vacated by one of the two guards now piled in the corner. The blood and brains on the wall behind the Libyan had dried to a thin crust. At the far end of the car, Dieter Haas was loading the paper-wrapped "bricks" of currency into a number of pale green duffel bags.

"They were very good, whoever they were," said Shenker thoughtfully. She had spent the better part of an hour moving back and forth between the RPO and the baggage car, trying to figure out what had happened.

Akbar, the Siles shotgun in his lap, nodded dully. "I knew I was being gassed," he said slowly, speaking in Arabic. "I thought it was some kind of security measure we hadn't been told about. I thought we had failed."

118

"It was not the police, our Mr. White said nothing of that."

"From the smell and from the way you described your symptoms, it must have been nitrous oxide. Laughing gas. It would not have been my choice, nor that of the security people."

"I don't understand," said Akbar.

"The chance of error is too great," she explained. "Nitrous oxide is only an incapacitating agent. Much better to have used a potassium compound, or perhaps cyanide. Clearly they did not want to kill anyone."

"So?" said Akbar.

"So it gives us some sense of whom we are dealing with," responded Shenker. "It would appear they are not willing to kill."

"Thieves," said Dieter Haas, still filling the duffel bags.

Shenker nodded. "Yes. Thieves. But intelligent thieves, and resourceful ones." She inclined her head toward the door leading to the baggage car. "The idea of smuggling a man aboard in a coffin is quite brilliant. Presumably they were going to take the money off the same way."

"What does it matter?" Akbar grumbled. "You say they are thieves, and you say they were not willing to kill."

"They have intelligence, and obviously they are very brave even to have tried such a thing," said Shenker, smiling faintly. "That makes them potentially dangerous."

"What about your Mr. White?" asked Akbar. "The man who sold us the information."

"White is our only source of intelligence among the passengers," said Shenker. "It is far too soon to compromise his position. We may need him. And we can deal with this ourselves."

"And if we find the people, what then?" said Akbar.

"We kill them, of course. Nothing must interfere with Montreal."

Sheila Teng, seated in the fireman's position beside the engineer, reacted instantly as they came out of the tunnel. She had trained for more than a month in a dummy of the F-40 locomotive, and she knew exactly what to do under the circumstances.

Although the train was traveling without lights, Teng

119

had a more than adequate view of the terrain ahead by using a Smith & Wesson Star-Tron night vision system that was one-third again as powerful as the one being used by Bowman's man on the knoll two hundred yards distant. Instead of a monocular eyepiece, the system was connected to a small television monitor that gave her a wide angle view of one thousand meters in starlight and slightly more in the moonlight conditions they were presently operating under. Shenker had chosen the TV monitor because it left both of the operator's hands free.

As they exited the tunnel at seventeen miles per hour, the young Japanese saw the three men on the signal tower ahead, and on the edges of the screen she spotted the movement of the four-man squad on the ground. Following procedure and without hesitation, she raised her left hand and squeezed the trigger of the sawed-off shotgun. The unchoked pellets struck Charles McClure, the engineer, in the face and chest, blowing him out of his chair. Dropping left, out of the line of fire from the tower ahead, Teng thumbed the transmit switch on the walkie-talkie in her right hand and spoke a single word:

"Hinterhalt!" Ambush!

Above her the windshield of the F-40 disintegrated as the three-man squad on the tower opened fire, filling the cab's interior with hexagonal shards of flying safety glass. Still keeping her head down, Teng reached up with her left hand, grabbed McClure's body by the belt, and dragged him away from the control station. With the corpse out of the way, she blindly dragged the throttle lever around, remembering to release the handle slightly as it hit each of the eight running notches. There was a tooth-rattling lurch as the giant diesel increased power, dragging the train forward. As the firing from the tower continued, Teng reached out and twisted the knurled knob of the headlight switch to the "on" position, hoping to blind anyone ahead with the sudden burst of light. With that accomplished, she rolled herself into as small a target as she could, and squeezed close in under the dashboard, ignoring the splattered patches of McClure's blood that seemed to be everywhere. She had done her job for the moment; it was up to the others now.

Unlike the terrorists, Bowman's twelve-man assault team was completely unprepared, beyond the most basic of briefings and an attack plan that had been developed in a very short time. Bowman's men—again unlike the terrorists—had all come out of the regular army and were used to strict military order and tactics, so when the battle plan began to change radically within fifteen seconds of the train's appearance at the tunnel mouth, the men's ability to react to the new situation was limited.

Instead of the train stopping, as they had planned, the three men on the signal tower saw that it was accelerating. A split second later the F-40's headlight flared, blinding the snipers. By the time they had recovered, the locomotive was already under the signal tower and pulling away, leaving them without a target.

The men on the ground didn't fare much better. They too had been expecting a sudden deceleration, or at least enough speed to let them mount the forward cars. As it was, two of the men never even managed to find a handhold while the other pair, one on either side of the head-end coach, were only barely hanging on. As the train swung onto the crossover track beneath the signal tower, the left-hand man lost his hold on the vertical handrail and slipped under the car body, the heavy wheels chewing into his legs just above the knees, while the rest of his body was tossed outward by centrifugal force. The fourth member of the ground team, on the right side of the coach, had managed to get a better hold, and with his feet braced on the doorsill and one arm wrapped around the handrail, he pulled down on the door handle, pushing inward with his right shoulder.

As the door opened, the thin wire that ran from the doorframe to the explosive bundle taped to the inner latch parted. There was a tiny, high-pitched 'ping' as the plunger in the detonator snapped down, and the nine-ounce package of plastique went off.

Most of the blast effect was directed outward, blowing the door off its hinges and killing the man outside instantly, but there was enough force in the explosion to fill the alcove between the cars with a hail of shrapnel, a small piece of which cut into the wire on the door opposite, setting off the second charge an instant later. The double blast ripped off most of the diaphragm connecting the two cars, took out the doors leading into the coach, and peeled open the coach toilets like sardine cans.

The blast also tore through the electrical panels at the head end of the coach, plunging the car into instant darkness. As the sound of the earsplitting explosion faded, it was replaced by the screams of passengers who had been unlucky enough to be sitting within range of the blast. Less than a minute had passed since the first shots were fired by the team on the signal tower.

Shenker, Haas, and Akbar were in motion within an instant of hearing Sheila Teng's one-word warning. Shenker and Haas headed back through the baggage car to the coach, while Akbar went in the opposite direction to help Teng in the cab. Shenker and Haas, running hard, weapons cocked and ready, were at the far end of the first coach when the plastique exploded, but they barely paused. Both terrorists presumed, and correctly, that any assault on the train would center on the locomotive and the diplomatic hostages in the rear observation car. The diesel was Teng and Akbar's responsibility; the diplomats were theirs.

Three minutes after the initial warning, Shenker and Haas, trailed by Raoul Attendera and Lisa Ruffio, made it to the Bedroom A communications center in the next-to-last car of the train. Mohamet Kawi, monitoring the radar sets, calmly reported the situation.

"Four on the roof. They must have been waiting above the tunnel entrance. When we speeded up, one of them slipped off, so now there are only three."

"Window charges and flash grenades," Shenker predicted. "Just like the Iranian Embassy in London. Where are they exactly?"

"Almost directly above us," said Kawi. In a reflex action the four other terrorists looked up toward the ceiling. "They are moving cautiously," the Libyan continued. "I don't think they were expecting the speed."

"What about Sheila?" asked the terrorist leader.

"She is fine. I spoke with her a moment ago. The engineer is dead. According to her, there were three men on the signal tower and three or four on the ground."

"The door charges," Haas commented, nodding. "Two of them went off at the head of the lead coach."

Shenker turned and spoke quietly to Lisa Ruffio. "Go back through the cars and keep an eye on things," she said.

122

"What about the men on the roof?" asked the heavy-breasted Italian woman.

"They will be no problem," Shenker answered. "They have lost the element of surprise. We can take care of them."

Ruffio nodded and backed out of the small room. Shenker turned her attention to the others. "All right. We have three minutes, perhaps less. Nothing is any different from what we expected. We've practiced for this a hundred times. Are there any questions?"

There were none. Shenker turned on her heel and left the compartment, followed by the others, including Mohamet Kawi. Shenker unlocked the door to the next compartment, using one of the keys taken from the conductor. Laid out on both the upper and lower bunks were four identical suitcases with two more half hidden under the lower bunk. The two suitcases on the upper bunk were empty, for they held the weapons initially used by the terrorists when they took over the train, but the two lower suitcases contained lightweight Kevlar body armor and enough respirator masks for every member of the group. The Kevlar vests had originally come from the Second Chance Body Armor Corporation of Chicago and had been picked up by the terrorists during their raid on the St. Augustine arsenal, while the respirators had come from a Washington safety supply company. The masks were normally used by people working with toxic chemicals, and the double filters were more than enough to deal with any CN, CS, or aerosol Mace normally used by police SWAT teams and the military. Since the masks were of the full-face variety and covered the entire head, they had the added advantage of providing protection against the blast effects of the "flash-bangs" that Annalise Shenker knew the men on the roof of the car above them would be using. She and the other three terrorists managed to get into the vests and slip on the respirators in forty-five seconds, two seconds short of the record they had set while practicing in the Washington warehouse. It took another twenty seconds for them to take up their positions—Shenker and Haas halfway down the short corridor leading to the rear observation section of the tail-end car, and Raoul Attendera and Mohamet Kawi directly behind them, facing in the opposite direction. All four were armed with short-barreled Ingrams.

Shenker had adopted a squatting position in the corridor, her right shoulder braced against the Bedroom E door to steady her against the lurching of the rapidly moving train. From where she knelt she could see the terrified figure of Helmut Klassen, the West German ambassador to the United Nations. The short, barrel-chested diplomat was manacled to the lounge chair just in front of the rear window of the car. It was an obvious entry point for one of the men on the roof.

"*Tapferkeit, mein freund*," she called out, grinning, raising her voice against the constant battering roar of the wheels and the mask covering her face. "Have courage, my friend, nobody lives forever." She checked the sweep hand of the large man's watch she wore on her right wrist. If Kawi was correct in his estimate, they would be getting into position above her.

"Remember," she said, speaking quickly. "Three men. The window charges will go off first. Locate the point of entry, and then heads down. When the flash from the stun grenade passes, begin to fire. Aim low. Continue firing until you run out of ammunition or I order you to stop. Ignore everything except your own—"

The rest of her sentence was drowned out by the triple explosion of the window charges slapped on by the three remaining members of Bowman's squad. As she had predicted, one of the charges went off on the window directly behind Ambassador Klassen, the force of the explosion blowing the handcuffed man and his chair face forward. A second window blew in on the right-hand side, less than ten feet from where she was kneeling, and there was a third explosion behind her. She was best located to take the window on the right, and she swung the small machine gun in that direction before lowering her head against the inevitable flash of the stun grenade to follow, leaving the rear window for Haas.

Bowman's men, working in perfect unison and hanging from rappel ropes secured to the roof ventilator scoops, tipped in their stun grenades simultaneously, following them a four-count later as they had been trained to, coming in feet first, then tucking into a roll and coming up in a half crouch, M-60s at the full ready position. The

M-60, weighing slightly more than twenty-two pounds, is a heavy weapon for use in counterterrorist operations, but it had been chosen by the Delta Group for its high rate of fire—more than two hundred rounds a minute. Theoretically it could hose a closed environment with enough lead to kill several score of terrorists. Unfortunately, theory was all that Bowman's men, or any other members of the Delta Group at Fort Bragg, had to go on, since none of them had any practical knowledge of terrorist tactics. On the other hand, Annalise Shenker and her companions were working from long experience.

Before the full effect of the flash-bangs had faded, Shenker and the others were already firing blindly at their chosen targets, concentrating on pulling down the lifting barrels of the Ingrams. The trooper who came in behind Shenker and Haas took the worst of it, since he entered the observation car with both Attendera and Mohamet Kawi aiming in his direction. The lower half of his body had barely made it through the shattered remains of the window before the concentrated force of fire from the two machine guns literally threw him out again. Both Shenker's target and the trooper who came in behind Ambassador Klassen actually made it into the observation car, but neither was able to get off even a single shot. Shenker, stitching her fire from right to left and upward, caught her man eleven times before he fell, while Haas, the marksman of the group, concentrated his fire on the head of his chosen prey. Eighteen seconds after the window charges went off, the interior of the observation car was a smoking ruin and the three Group Delta troopers were dead. Franchia, the naval attaché, Chilton, the Vatican secretary, and Sanchez, the Argentinian defense minister had thrown themselves to the floor, taking their chairs with them as the window charges went off, but the stun grenades had left them blind and whimpering in the choking haze that filled the car. Judging by the spreading pool of blood around the motionless head of the West German ambassador, he was either dead or dying, victim of the explosion that had taken place less than a foot behind him.

Annalise Shenker stood up slowly, her weapon still tense in her hand, and aimed at the motionless figure of the trooper she'd been firing at. The cold dawn wind blowing in through the shattered windows was already beginning to sweep away the acrid smoke within the car. She waited a full thirty seconds before she spoke, her eyes still on the man a few feet away.

"Take their weapons," she said at last. "And then have Sheila stop the train." She walked forward and nudged the corpse of the trooper. "Take this one and rope him to the front handrails of the engine. Arms and legs spread. Make sure his head is up. When we come into Montreal, I want the television cameras to have the best possible shot. I want his superiors to witness the wages of their sin."

Part Three

THE MEET

*You'd probably oe surprised at what
you think about when something like
that happens. Mark reacted a lot faster
than I did, dragging me down out of
the way of the flying bits and pieces
with those can-opener hands of his.
All I can remember thinking is, "How
the hell does he go to the bathroom?"*

Harry Maxwell,
the Playboy Interview

Chapter 8

Monday, June 27
Time: 12:30 P.M. EDT
Distance: 673 miles/1,083 km.

Bleary-eyed with fatigue, Frank Sagadore sat at the conference table, its surface littered from one end to the other with a hodgepodge of half-empty coffee cups, overflowing ashtrays, and scraps of paper. In addition to the security chief, there were four others present: Wesler from the FBI; Walter Linberg; Mac Donovan, who had given over his shift at the Master Panel to another MPO; and John Boswell, the Penn Station stationmaster. All of them looked much the worse for wear.

"What's the latest from the surveillance choppers?" Sagadore asked wearily.

"Ugly," said Wesler. He stood up and went to the diagram of the Night Owl consist that Boswell had made up and arranged on an easel. "At least we now know for certain that they really do have charges on the doors. It looks like a good ten or twelve feet of the first coach has been blown open, and the whole rear of the baggage car. It must have blown some of the electrical connections as well, because the chopper observer said the interior of the car was dark."

"And the rear?" asked Sagadore.

"Blown to hell," Wesler said briskly. "Half the windows gone, and some smoke damage. They couldn't see inside, though, so we don't know if anyone was hurt."

"According to the previous report, they've got somebody roped to the front of the engine," said Sagadore, a sour note in his voice. "The assumption is that he's dead. I think we can assume casualties without having a body count, Inspector Wesler."

"I don't assume anything," Wesler answered. "What I'm waiting for is some kind of communication from the terrorists."

"I doubt that you'll get it," Walter Linberg put in slowly. "At least not yet."

"Why do you say that?" asked Sagadore.

"They're letting us stew," said Linberg. "The attack was a mistake; they know it and so do we. They want us to squirm. That's why they roped the soldier to the locomotive."

"I think they're a bunch of crazies," muttered Boswell from the far end of the table.

"Not really," said Linberg, turning to him. "They might be termed insane if you use the normal checks and balances of civilization as your criteria for sanity, but in this situation they're as mentally competent as you or me. They're following definite, logical patterns. There's nothing erratic here. It's all planned, every detail."

"You call hopping all over the map at twenty-five miles an hour logical?" asked Wesler. "I brought you in as an expert, Walter, but I don't think you can explain that one."

"Not yet," Linberg said, shrugging. "But that doesn't mean it's not logical."

"Horseshit!" said Wesler. "They don't know what they're doing. They were spooked by that idiotic Delta Group attack."

"I doubt it," replied Linberg, still calm. "These people have been in tight situations before, everything from the Munich operation to the OPEC kidnappings. They're not spooked at all, don't kid yourself."

"You still think they're going to head into Canada?" asked Boswell. "Because if they are, we'd better get onto the VIA Rail people in Montreal, not to mention the Canadian State Department."

"Secretary of State," corrected Sagadore. "I've already done it. They're fully aware of the situation. They say they're going to wait and see how it develops."

"Sounds just like our people," muttered Wesler.

"I still don't see why they'd want to go to Montreal," said Boswell.

"They don't want to go to Montreal," said Linberg. "Frank is probably right. Crossing an international border, even a friendly one like the U.S.-Canada, still complicates things incredibly. Two bureaucracies, God knows how many police forces, two different rail authorities to work through. Chaos. Which is exactly their intention. I think they'll bypass Montreal like they went around New York and Albany."

"Can they do that?" asked Wesler.

"Sure," Sagadore replied. "Montreal is a major railhead. Half a dozen mainlines in and out, not to mention a few hundred miles of switch line."

"But we'll still be able to track them?" added the FBI man.

"We won't, but the Canadians will," said Mac Donovan. "They've got Central Traffic Control, just like we do." The MPO took a bite out of a stale doughnut and washed it down with some lukewarm coffee. "But as soon as they cross the border, it's out of our hands."

"I hope the Canadians are up to it," said Sagadore. "I did some quick checking. Montreal has almost a hundred passenger trains a day going in and out, and that's not counting the suburban lines or the freights. They'll have to do some fancy juggling. If they screw up and the Night Owl goes onto the wrong track, or has to stop, God knows what those maniacs will do."

"They'll kill everybody on board," Walter Linberg said simply. "They'd have no other choice, at least in their minds."

"Jesus," Wesler whispered.

"It might not be so bad," Donovan commented. "What's the ETA for Montreal?" Frank Sagadore riffled through the spread of papers in front of him. He picked up a scrap of paper and peered at it.

"As of half an hour ago, they were just south of Westport, New York. Following the normal schedule, that's about three hours from Montreal. The way they're traveling, it could be five, maybe more. Canada could stick to their scheduled runs up until, oh, say an hour before that, then clear the board until they're gone through. It's not impossible." He gave a sour smile. "On the other hand, I'm glad it's not my baby to handle. The Montreal MPO is going to be sweating."

A young man padded self-consciously into the conference room and wordlessly handed Frank Sagadore a note. The security chief read it, then dropped the sheet into the maelstrom of others like it in front of him.

"Well, that's that, gentlemen," he said, standing up.

"It is the considered opinion of the State Department, the Canadian Secretary of State, Amtrak, and the VIA people in Montreal that the Night Owl *is* going into Canada. According to them, the terrorists have no other clear option."

"And?" asked Mac Donovan.

"And so," continued Sagadore, hooking his jacket off the back of the chair and shrugging it on, "Mr. Wesler, Mr. Linberg, and I have been asked to get our asses to Montreal as fast as possible. I'm supposed to look out for a couple of million dollars' worth of Amtrak rolling stock, and Mr. Wesler will act as liaison with the federal police in Canada and the U.S. Embassy. Mr. Linberg is supposed to bring along his crystal ball, since he's the only one around who seems to know anything about the terrorists. There's a helicopter on its way to the port by the U.N. and there's a government jet at JFK."

"For all this talk about trains, I wind up spending all my time in helicopters," said Walter Linberg, shoveling papers back into his briefcase.

"Amtrak gets you there," drawled Mac Donovan, leaning back in his chair. "They just don't tell you how."

Oberleutnant Wolfgang Groz shifted slightly in the hard seat of the Messerschmitt Me-109, wincing as he stared ahead into the faintly starlit sky. As usual they were flying in a two-man *Rotte* or cell, with Werner in the lead tonight, playing *Rotteführer*, while Groz was the slightly trailing *Katchmarek*, or wingman. Twenty minutes before, they had taken off from the small rutted field at Eglise-sur-Mer, and were now acting as escorts for a flight of Heinkels from the KG-100.

Once upon a time Groz had been of the opinion that anything was better than slogging around with his boots full of water in the infantry, but after seven months flying the Me-109 through flak over the Thames and battling the British Nightfighters, he wasn't so sure. The Messerschmitt was a marvelous aircraft, and in many ways it was superior to the slower Spitfires and Hurricanes that the Tommies used, but flying escort to Heinkels was a job that left the fighter pilots extremely vulnerable during close attacks. So far Groz had been lucky, but he was no fool. Sooner or later his luck was going to run out; all he cared about was that when he was hit it was over land and not the Channel.

So far, things had gone according to plan. The flight of Heinkels were pathfinders, well ahead of the main bomber force and equipped with the new X-Geraet radio target-finding system. It was their job to locate the target and then drop incendiaries for the following force. The incendiaries were light in comparison to the 2,500-pound "Max" bombs carried by the bombers following them, and because of that, the Heinkels could move faster, a fact that Groz appreciated and was grateful for. He was an enthusiastic flier and an ardent defender of the Luftwaffe as a gentleman's military force, but he was far from being a Nazi, and unlike some of his companions, he was even farther from being willing to give his all to the Führer and the Fatherland. At the age of twenty, Wolfgang Groz considered that his life and his balls, in that order, were worth considerably more than a posthumous *Ritterkreuz*, with or without the oak leaves. Which was why, before each and every mission, no matter how hurried the scramble, he always took care to see that his parachute harness was in good order, and the cockpit canopy well greased.

For Groz, the end of the world came in the form of a British Spitfire directly in front of him, a screaming needle-nosed shape less than two hundred yards ahead, all eight machine guns and cannon flaring along the knife-edge wing like a solid row of angry, flaming teeth.

Out of the corner of his eye Groz saw Werner's plane turned instantly into a fireball by the British craft; then he was pushing the stick between his legs as far forward as it would go, his left hand instinctively slapping the throttle lever to full power, sending the Messerschmitt into a screaming power dive as he tried to gain speed to escape.

Without warning the world seemed to explode around him; the 109 shuddered as it was hit from behind by another Spitfire. Groz twisted into a neck-snapping roll, but the aircraft on his tail stayed on, pumping round after round into the already stricken plane. Glycol began to stream out of the engine and over the canopy, and the engine sputtered, then seized. Fumes began to fill the cockpit. Barely conscious, Groz hit the canopy release and dragged it up and to the right. The smoke cleared, but it was followed by a roaring gout of flame that swept in through the firewall from the engine, engulfing Groz and setting fire to his flight jacket. Clothes smoldering, he managed to unbuckle his safety harness and throw himself out of the plane before it began to roll away in an uncontrolled spin toward the barely visible ground below. As his parachute opened, Groz beat at the flames on his chest, the heat searing the right side of his face. Then, mercifully, consciousness faded.

Wolfgang Groz—sixty-five years old, the scars of that night still faintly visible on his tanned and weathered face—stared out of the portside window of the Lufthansa 747 and watched as the immense aircraft banked over the dark green woodlands around Mirabel International Airport, outside Montreal. It wasn't often that he thought about that night almost half a century before, but whenever he flew, even in as unlikely a beast as a Jumbo, the old memories came back.

It was fitting, too, that he should remember it now, for this was a time for memory and nostalgia. A holiday, perhaps, but more than a simple two-week vacation away from his printshop in Stettin; this was a homecoming in a way, for he'd spent almost four years in this country as a prisoner of war. He smiled to himself, still watching out the window as the jet lost altitude rapidly. Before that night when the phantom Spitfire had shot him all to hell, he'd never even heard of a place called Medicine Hat, let alone considered that he would ever call it home.

"*Medizin Hut*," he whispered, grinning. It sounded just as ridiculous in German as it did in English. Ridiculous or not, it *had* been home, and he remembered it well. He also remembered the long train trip that had taken him from the docks at Halifax to the camp, three thousand miles into the heartland of the giant country.

It was a journey he was about to repeat, although, thank God, only from Montreal, and not from Halifax, and in a wagon-lit car this time, not sitting hour after hour, day after day, on a hard wood-slat bench, with only a single woodstove to heat the freezing car. He had seen the countryside only in midwinter then, and at the time he was hardly interested in the sights. Now he would be able to enjoy the trip, to see the country as it should be seen. A certain sadness came into his smile. So many of his companions were dead now, and there were so few to share the old times with. He wondered if that might not be the real reason for his return to Canada, and the best one. He would go back to Medicine Hat for all the ones who had never had the chance; his journey would be their eulogy.

The 747 began its final approach.

Jake Sloane walked stiffly down the football-field-size concourse of Montreal's Central Station, uncomfortably aware that a lot of eyes were on him. Every few yards, almost against his will, he found himself adjusting the crisp dark blue uniform—straightening his tie, twitching at his cap, or making sure enough cuff was showing. Acting as casually as he could under the circumstances, he veered to the right and stopped at the open-stall smoke shop. He bought a package of Export A cigarettes and breath mints, then headed for the stairs that led down to Track 19.

He was early. The departure board hadn't even been pulled up out of the base of the track number sign. He lifted his wrist and checked his watch, thankful that he hadn't given in to his mother's insistence that he use the pocket watch and chain she'd given him when he was promoted to conductor. It was hard enough being the youngest conductor to be given the company's premier train and giving orders to men twice his age, some of them with over thirty years on the railroad; wearing an old-fashioned watch and chain would have made him look and feel like an idiot.

There was still over an hour to departure time. Officially he didn't have to be on board until the first passengers came down onto the platform, but it didn't hurt to check things out, especially since this was his first trip out on the Canadian as conductor. He reached over, slipped the latch on the waist-high brass-and-glass gate, and went through, closing it carefully behind him. Then, trying not to look too eager, he went down the dogleg stairway to the platform.

The train was waiting for him, and no amount of will-power could keep the spring out of his step as he walked along beside the rumbling, steam-hissing behemoth that was to be in his charge for the next four days. He'd loved trains as long as he could remember, and that love hadn't faded with age. Through school and college, to work for the railway had always been his goal, and he'd proved his interest by taking any kind of summer job he could get, first with the Canadian National, and then, after the formation of a single national rail passenger company, with VIA. Now, after being six years with the company, full-time, his interest was as strong as ever. He'd risen quickly through the ranks, first as an assistant trainman working short hauls to Ottawa, Quebec City, and Toronto, and then as a full trainman working the same runs. They'd put him on the Canadian Transcontinental for a year, then switched him over to the Ocean, going from Halifax to Montreal. Finally, two years ago, they'd promoted him to conductor and, much to his mother's joy, put him back on the short runs along the Quebec-Montreal-Ottawa-Toronto corridor. That way he was rarely gone for more than thirty-six hours at a time and she could keep him under her watchful eye. At thirty, Jake was reasonably sure he didn't need watching, but his mother had different ideas—he wasn't married, and until he was, she seemed hellbent on keeping him her "baby."

Eventually he reached the head end and stood for a moment, staring up at the massive blue and yellow PA-4 diesel, its idling 2,400-horsepower engines and venting brake hoses making her sound like some giant sleeping dragon. Jake resisted an urge to reach out and pat the side of the huge steel creature, and turned back, going down the platform past the baggage car and crew dorm combine to the first of the coaches. He swung himself up the short ladder and stepped onto the train to begin his long checking tour down the eight-car consist.

The Canadian, traveling 2,900 miles in four days, covers more mileage than any other train in the world, with the exception of the Soviet Trans-Siberian Express. Leaving Montreal on a daily basis, the train normally has between eight and ten cars, depending on the season, but by the time the transcontinental reaches the Rocky Mountains, it has picked up additional cars in Toronto, Winnipeg, and Calgary, often bringing the total consist

136

up to as many as twenty-one cars, making it not only one of the longest-running, but also one of the largest passenger trains in the world.

The train's roots go back to the Canadian Pacific's Pacific Express, inaugurated in 1886 and following roughly the same route as the present-day version. The CP continued to dominate the cross-country travel scene for the first half of the twentieth century, with trains like the all-Pullman Imperial Limited, and later the Dominion. In the early fifties, the CP announced that it was ordering a massive stock of the new streamlined Budd cars of the same type used by the American Zephyrs, and in 1955 the cars made their first Canadian run. Not to be outdone, Canadian National, the government-owned railway, started up its own transcontinental run, the Super Continental, at roughly the same time. The CN train was slightly more austere, using a combination of Canadian Car Foundry cars and flat-sided Pullman Standard equipment. During the sixties and early seventies, both services began to lose money heavily, and finally, in October 1977, by order of the Canadian government, the two trains were merged.

Jake made his way through the cars, checking to make sure that everything was in order, from air conditioning to the direction the seats were facing. The cleaning crews back in the passenger yards had done a good job, and considering that most of the cars were twenty-five and thirty years old, things didn't look half bad.

The first two cars were old CN coaches, each one capable of seating eighty people in relative comfort. The third car, now bustling with activity as stewards loaded supplies on board, was a Budd Skyline combination snack bar and sightseeing dome car. The Skyline lounge—in this case the refurbished buffet-solarium car *Antigua*—was the division point between first class and tourist on the train. Following it was a Daynighter, in reality an old CN coach that had been gutted and refitted with airline-style seats for fifty passengers, as well as improved sound-proofing and better lighting. Traveling Daynighter was slightly more expensive than straight coach, but it usually removed the passenger from the crying-baby brigade and the inevitable teenager with his cassette machine.

Beyond the Daynighter was a Budd diner, the *Empress*,

with seating for forty-eight passengers at each of three sittings. The dining car was normally used only by sleeping-car occupants, but in the enlightened eighties the old practice of preventing coach passengers from using it had been abolished. The dining car was followed by two sleeping cars: the *Château Radisson*, with eight duplex roomettes, a drawing room, six bedrooms, and four berths; and the *Riverdale*, with ten roomettes and five double bedrooms. The last car in the train, which would remain last throughout the various switchings and additions during the trip, was the *Tremblant Park*, a scenic dome car with two lounges, a drawing room, and six bedrooms. There were twenty-four seats in the upstairs dome. The drawing room in the *Tremblant Park* would be Jake's home for the duration of the trip, since no one had booked it, and he found it preferable to the rather crowded crew accommodations in the dormitory car at the head end.

Upon reaching the end of the train, he let himself into the drawing room, located beside the mid-car lounge. He grinned; the stewards, aware that it was his first time as master of the train, had made things easier for him. A folding table had been set up in front of the forward-facing couch, complete with the latest passenger printout and stores inventory. Peeking behind the door, he saw that two fresh uniforms were hanging ready in the small closet. Leaving the door open, Jake slipped out of his jacket and hung it on a hook beside the toilet cubicle along with his cap. He unclipped the *Motorola two-way* from his belt, set it down on the table, and sank down onto the couch. It was time to do some work.

He ran through the staff sheet first, checking to make sure that all forty-three members of the crew were accounted for. In fact, they were short two stewards in the dining car, but according to a notation on the list, the men would be picked up in Toronto along with the rest of the crew needed for the other section of the train. Except for that, they were running with a full complement. With that out of the way, he turned his attention to the stores inventory, checking out the chief steward's computation of stock already on board, as well as new foodstuffs, liquor, and tableware for the dining room, and extra linen taken on in Montreal. It was boring work, but necessary, and he'd have to do it several more times over the next four days. Additional supplies were taken on in Toronto, Winnipeg, and Calgary, and it was important to keep an accurate running total of supplies to avoid either overstocking or running short.

Surprisingly, perhaps, there was rarely a mistake made in the inventories, and the occasional mistotals were almost invariably simple errors of multiplication or addition—only once since he'd been with VIA had he ever found evidence of any kind of pilfering, and even that was small potatoes. It seemed that unlike the airlines, which had to cope with huge inventory losses, especially of liquor, the men and women who worked the trains were pretty honest.

Having completed the inventory check, Jake picked up the long folded passenger manifest and began working through it, comparing it to the previous one from earlier that day, checking for dropouts that would leave him with freed-up accommodations as well as giving him a sense of who would be on board. It didn't hurt to know if there were doctors traveling and where they were located in the train, in case of an emergency, and it was helpful to find out about any other special needs of the passengers: people with seeing-eye dogs; the deaf, wheelchair cases, and even women who were far enough along in their pregnancies to warrant special attention.

Running down the sheet, Jake saw that although they were traveling light—less than half full, in fact—they were going to be carrying quite a mixed bag. Coach reservations stood at ninety-four out of a possible 160, most of them booked only as far as Toronto, but with a few going to Winnipeg and two who were going the full distance to Vancouver. Fortunately there were no school tours, Boy Scout groups, or football teams; once, by some hideous twist of fate, he'd worked the Canadian as a trainman with all three: sixty private-school girls going from Montreal to a summer adventure camp outside Thunder Bay, forty pubescent boy scouts on their way to a Jamboree in Brandon, Manitoba, and an entire Canadian Football League team traveling to Alberta for a game with the Calgary Stampeders and using the train because of a strike on the airlines. It had been three days of shrill, rock-and-roll filled, drunken madness. By the time they reached Banff and unloaded the last of them, Jake had thought he was going to die of exhaustion.

Daynighter bookings were light too, running at just over two-thirds, but there was at least one interesting passenger, a Sergeant Norman Kettering of the Metropolitan Toronto Police, traveling home. The code beside the reservation indicated that the man was carrying a weapon. Jake red-penciled a line under his name, just in case.

There were two doctors in the *Château Radisson*, a man named Bellows in Bedroom C, and another one named Strong in D. Bedroom A was being held for a pair of nuns, and B was empty until Toronto. The drawing room was also vacant, but all eight roomettes were filled, and so were the eight berths in the four sections. Jake tagged the two doctors' names on the list and made a note to have Forrest, the *Radisson* steward, see if he could find out if they were medical doctors.

The young conductor's eyebrows rose when he saw the occupants of the *Riverdale*. All the roomettes and four out of the five bedrooms had been booked in a block by Le Groupe Astrale, a Montreal modern dance company, leaving only the single drawing room vacant. Corrigan, the steward listed for the *Riverdale*, was well known on the line as a pretty heavy-handed redneck, and Jake smelled trouble. He decided to switch Corrigan to the *Radisson* and Forrest to the *Riverdale* as preventive medicine. Forrest was the senior of the two stewards by a good ten years, but Jake was sure that the older man would understand the situation when it was explained to him. Forrest had spent fifteen years with the Pennsylvania Railroad before coming to Canadian Pacific in the early seventies, and Jake knew that a modern dance group wouldn't even ruffle the man's feathers. With twenty-five years on the railway under his belt, Forrest had seen everything at least twice.

That left the *Tremblant Park*. Of the three bedrooms, only one was taken, and the last name on the manifest made him smile with pleasure. Wanda Jenkins Margay, off on another one of her transcontinental voyages. Jake had first run into the septuagenarian traveler when he was working as a snack-bar steward while he was in college, and he'd seen her at least once a year ever since. She'd followed his career with interest, giving him endless tidbits of advice and also telling him railroad stories that went back half a century. Born rich, Wanda had married even richer and been widowed early. With no need to work, and almost unlimited money at her disposal, she had begun traveling, but because of a deathly fear of water and an even more incapacitating fear of heights, she was chained to the North American continent. Undaunted, she had begun taking trains, going from her home in Montreal to Vancouver, then transferring onto the old Burlington Northern line and heading south through Washington and Oregon to California. According to Wanda, she'd traveled every one of the BN's 25,000 miles of track, and that was only the beginning; every state of the Union serviced by a railroad had been seen by Wanda, and she had friends everywhere. Her journeys took anywhere from three weeks to three months to complete, and she usually finished off the year by migrating to Florida.

After wintering in Miami, she'd return to Montreal and start all over again, sometimes heading east, sometimes west, and sometimes south. To keep herself busy while she traveled, she knitted constantly, and Jake knew dozens of railroad men, himself included, who wore Wanda's patented double-toe-thickness winter socks.

Jake dropped the passenger manifest onto the table and leaned back on the couch. He lit a cigarette from the almost empty package in his vest and grinned happily. The next four days were going to involve a lot of hard work, but with Wanda only two doors down, Jake Sloane knew he wasn't going to be bored.

Kenzie McLeod was, in the jargon of social workers, a bona fide member of the "target population" they serviced. Born illegitimately of a union between a black draft dodger and a commune hippie from British Columbia in the last great days of the "revolution" that never happened, she had lived in the grinding cycle of welfare single parenthood all her life. She'd never known her father, and his only legacy to her was her permanently deep-tanned complexion. Together with her mother's Irish good looks and jet black hair, the result was a young woman of exceptional beauty, with what most people assumed was some North American Indian in her background.

The Canadian Department of Employment and Immigration listed Kenzie's mother as a seamstress, but the only sewing Kenzie had ever seen her do was the odd bit of embroidery on the shirts of her endless succession of boyfriends. Sometimes Kenzie wondered if the inevitable butterfly on a collar or rainbow on a pocket wasn't some kind of magic her mother tried to use in an attempt to keep the man interested. If it was magic, it was pretty weak, because they never seemed to last more than a few months at best, and lately they'd been showing as much interest in Kenzie as they did in her mother.

When Kenzie had been younger, her mother had been proud of her daughter's looks, but as she went through puberty and it became obvious that her beauty far exceeded that of her mother, their relationship began to falter. At first Kenzie didn't understand her mother's sudden distance, but eventually she realized that her mother was jealous. As her mother's looks faded with age, Kenzie's blossomed, as though the young woman were somehow spiriting away her mother's only asset.

The week before, the situation had reached a peak. Kenzie's mother, out peddling quarter-ounces of grass to stretch the welfare check, had forgotten that she'd invited her current boyfriend over for dinner. The man, purportedly a musician for a band Kenzie had never heard of, showed up on time, but Kenzie's mother didn't. The musician, already ripped on some hideous combination of drugs and liquor, made a pass at Kenzie, which she was in the process of fighting off as her mother came in the door of their third-floor walkup in Montreal's St. Henri slums. There was a lot of screaming when Kenzie's mother saw what was going on, but in the end her mother sided with her boyfriend, who insisted that Kenzie had been cock-teasing. She hadn't been, but there was no point arguing. Then and there, Kenzie decided that she'd had enough of her mother, her mother's boyfriends, and the squalor she'd been living in all her life.

She bided her time for a few days, waiting for the weekend. As usual, during the summer her mother had found a place to crash in the country for a few days, leaving Kenzie behind. It was illegal to leave a minor child unattended, and Kenzie knew it, but she wasn't about to complain. When she was sure her mother was gone for the weekend, she made a beeline for the dope stash in the closet and cleaned it out. For the next two days she circulated among her friends, selling the grass, hash, and hash oil at rock-bottom prices. By Sunday night she'd pulled together two hundred dollars. She threw her few clothes into a knapsack, ripped off her mother's best jewelry and portable tape deck, and split. She spent Sunday night in the basement locker of a friend's building, and by noon on Monday she was in Central Station, wondering what to do next. She was reasonably sure her mother wouldn't report her to the welfare people, since that would mean she'd catch hell for leaving Kenzie for the weekend, not to mention the fact that she'd probably lose the child welfare allowance. Still, staying around Montreal wasn't a good idea; there were too many of her mother's friends on the street, and eventually she'd be spotted by one of them if the cops or the juvenile authorities didn't pick her up first.

Central Station and the maze of boutique-lined corridors and tunnels connecting it to the Place Ville Marie shopping complex and the Place Bonaventure Hotel was familiar turf for Kenzie. She'd cut classes to spend entire days in the underground arcades, and she knew how to avoid drawing attention to herself. With the knapsack on her back she immediately became just another kid bumming around for the summer, and with the addition of an empty VIA folder she found in one of the pedestal ashtrays, her disguise was complete. With the folder sticking out of one of the knapsack's side pockets, she knew she could stay in the station without being hassled by the security cops until the last train had left, and according to the big spaghetti-board schedule by the baggage room, the last train out of the station was something called the Cavalier at 11:35, an overnight train to Toronto.

Seated on one of the hard plastic seats across from the schedule board, Kenzie munched on a doughnut, and sipped at a cup of heavily sweetened coffee. She stared at the schedule, ignoring the steady stream of people crossing back and forth in front of her.

She could take any one of a dozen trains leaving that day for Toronto or Ottawa, but neither city appealed to her. Ottawa was only a hundred-odd miles from home, and that was too close for comfort, while Toronto was just too damned big. As she sat thinking over her options, a pair of red caps came by, wheeling along a portable ticket counter. The sign on it said VANCOUVER. She nodded to herself; that was more like it. For one thing, she'd been born there, and for another it was just about as far as you could get from Montreal and still be in Canada. The chances of her old lady finding her there were almost zero. From what she'd heard, it was a pretty easygoing city too, and if she couldn't get some kind of job there, she could always go south into California.

She stood up and followed the men wheeling the counter down the concourse. They stopped at the steps leading down to Track 19, locked the wheels, and wandered off. A moment later a potbellied man in a VIA uniform appeared, carrying a high stool, and sat down behind the counter. According to the flash on his cap, he was a sleeping-car conductor. Sitting down again, Kenzie tried to make up her mind, her fifteen-year-old's anxieties about leaving home battling with an almost overwhelming desire to change her life once and for all. She was a bright girl, and living with her mother had given her the street smarts of someone a lot older than her years. She knew that staying with her mother in Montreal was like signing her life away. Another couple of years and despair would overcome good sense; she'd be ready to get pregnant by some loser so she could live on her own. She had to act, and act now.

A recorded voice echoed over the PA system, announcing that sleeping-car passengers were now able to board the VIA Canadian. It was enough to tip the scales. Kenzie stood up and walked across to the glass-enclosed ticket windows as a steady stream of people began to line up at the portable counter beside the Track 19 entrance.

Fifteen minutes later, after waiting for a dozen people in front of her, Kenzie was back in her seat, her face clouded with anger. The price of a ticket to Vancouver was $210. She could get to Calgary for a little less, but it was her entire stake. Being poor in Montreal was one thing, but arriving penniless in an unknown city was courting disaster. She slumped down in the chair, her knapsack between her knees. Now what the hell was she supposed to do? She bit her lip, fighting to keep back the tears of frustration forming in her eyes.

She was vaguely aware of a young couple beside her, obviously in the midst of some kind of romantic farewell.

As their embrace deepened, Kenzie turned slightly so that she could watch. The man was in his late teens, shaggy-haired and wearing jeans and workboots. From what Kenzie could tell, the girl wasn't much older than she was. As their clutching hug deepened, Kenzie dropped her eyes, embarrassed at being an inadvertent party to the passionate caressing. Her glance fell on the man's knapsack, battered green canvas much like her own. There, poking out of the near side pocket, was a VIA folder like the one she'd picked up earlier for protective coloration.

The next few seconds passed like a strange dream. Hardly believing what she was doing, Kenzie reached down as though to adjust the cuff of her jeans, slid the folder out of the side pocket, and stood, almost in one continuous motion, picking up her own knapsack and walking slowly away, her heart pounding beneath her ribs, her breath held hard. The echoing sounds of the huge station blended into a single cicada whine, like the sound of a high-tension cable. Mingling with the crowd of non-sleeping-car passengers, milling around the entrance to Track 19, Kenzie chanced a glance back over her shoulder. The two figures were partially hidden by the retaining wall of the next track, but from the way their heads were glued together it didn't look as though they'd noticed either the theft or Kenzie's abrupt departure from the adjoining seat. She slipped the knapsack onto her back and pushed her way deeper into the crowd of passengers waiting for the gate to open. When she was completely surrounded, she flipped open the ticket folder in her hand and glanced down at it.

Unreserved coach seat to Winnipeg. She barely controlled a whoop of glee. More than halfway there! She took a closer look at the ticket. There was nothing in the slot for the passenger's name, and the date of issue was June 30. The rectangular space beside the date showed a time of issue that read 1530 hours—less than half an hour ago. The method of payment space said CASH in neatly typed computer print. No check, no credit card, and no name. She was almost positive the ticket would be untraceable. Kenzie also knew enough about bureaucracies to realize that even if there was a list of tickets sold to various destinations used by some official on the train, the chances of its being updated so close to departure time were slim. If the guy kept on making out with his girlfriend for a few minutes longer, she was going to be home free. When he did notice that the ticket was gone, he'd assume he'd lost it and go back to the ticket window. The hair, the jeans, and the workboots wouldn't win him much sympathy, and if she was lucky he'd still be trying to get another ticket when the train pulled out of the station.

A few seconds later, another recorded announcement boomed out across the concourse. VIA Rail's Train Number One, the Canadian, was now accepting passengers on Track 19. Ahead of her the brass gate opened, and Kenzie McLeod let herself be pulled forward by the surging flow of the crowd. She was on her way.

As Kenzie McLeod began her long-dreamed-of escape from Montreal, and while Jake Sloane was settling his old friend Wanda Jenkins Margay into her compartment in the tail-end car of the Canadian before getting down to work, two people stepped out of a Diamond taxi at the concourse-level cab stand. The woman, short, well dressed, and blond, paid the driver and declined any help with her single piece of luggage, a medium-sized dark green Samsonite suitcase. She followed her companion, a man in his late twenties, dark-haired and French looking, as he went through the glass doors leading into the concourse proper. The man carried a large aluminum case of the kind used by photographers, and anyone touching the side of the case would have been surprised at how cold it was, as though it had been kept in a freezer for some time. Although the case was clearly quite heavy, the man carried it almost delicately, his hand carefully grasping the vinyl-padded handle, his wrist slightly bent to keep the case from brushing his leg as he walked.

The two people, separated by several yards and barely identifiable as a couple, reached the entrance to Track 19, showed their tickets, and went down the stairs. They were the last people through the gate, and as they disappeared from view, the digital clock suspended from the high ceiling over the entrance to tracks 11 and 12 clicked loudly, the numbers flipping to show 16:25.

146

Chapter 9

Monday, June 27
Time: 4:40 P.M. EDT
Distance: 780 miles/1,255 km.

At 4:10 P.M. the Amtrak Night Owl, roughly following the route of Amtrak's Train 69, the Adirondack, reached Rouses Point, New York, still traveling at approximately thirty miles per hour. A few minutes later the train crossed the border into Canada and the hijacking officially became an international incident. The crossing was reported by the customs officials at Rouses Point, who would normally have boarded the train at that point. An FBI surveillance team from the field office in Albany was also on hand, and utilizing a farmhouse within a hundred yards of the track, its members managed to obtain several dozen photographs as well as a videotape recording of the train's passage. The photographs and tape were the first pieces of hard evidence demonstrating that the ill-advised Black Beret attack on the Night Owl had resulted in fatalities. A clear shot of the body of the unfortunate Delta Group trooper roped to the front grab bars of the F-40 was indisputable proof that the raid had been something short of successful.

At four-thirty, only a few seconds after the VIA Canadian pulled out on Track 19, Frank Sagadore, Walter Linberg, and FBI Inspector Wesler arrived under police escort at the Dorchester Street entrance to Central Station. They were taken to a conference room on the lobby floor of the Queen Elizabeth Hotel, which rises directly above the underground terminal.

They were met by a hastily assembled welcoming committee composed of a VIA vice-president, the chief dispatcher for Canadian National Railways' Montreal Yards, and the senior officer of the Montreal detachment of the RCMP. All of them looked worried. They seated themselves around the rectangular table, and Frank Sagadore saw trouble brewing right from the start. The Canadians were fanned out on the left-hand side of the table, and the Americans were all on the right. Patrick Mason, the Via vice-president, appeared to be heading up the Canadian group. Sagadore sat directly across the table from the fiftyish, conservatively dressed executive.

Mason cleared his throat and fiddled with a sheaf of papers on the table in front of him, eyes down as though not quite sure where to begin. Sagadore had seen the look before. Mason knew that anything he said now was going to set a precedent, and like every bureaucrat the security man had ever known, Mason looked scared as hell at the thought of taking any kind of responsibility. Before the man could speak, Sagadore took the bull by the horns himself. "We've been out of touch for the past few hours," he said. "I think we'd all appreciate a status report."

Mason cleared his throat again. "Yes, of course," he said slowly. He turned to his right, looking down the table at Jean LaSalle, the man who'd been introduced to Sagadore as the chief yard dispatcher. LaSalle appeared to be in his late forties, his face tanned and weathered. Up the hard way, Sagadore thought to himself.

The dispatcher nodded; when he spoke, his voice was calm and controlled, with only a faint hint of a French accent. "As of a few moments ago," he began, "your consist was just outside Napierville, about sixty kilometers from Montreal."

"What's that in miles?" asked Wesler.

"Thirty-five," LaSalle answered evenly. "There has been no increase in speed, and so far there has been no communication with the cab, although we have kept all our frequencies clear."

"What about other trains on the line?" Sagadore asked.

"We have cleared them all the way to Verdun," the man replied.

"We thought it was wiser to keep most of the other trains moving, at least for the time being," Mason put in. "We've kept on schedule so far, at least the VIA trains have. The Canadian just pulled out a minute ago, and so did the Bonaventure, one of our Toronto trains. We have an Ottawa Rapido leaving in about an hour, but that's about it for the main line traffic."

"What about commuters?" asked Sagadore.

"No problem," said LaSalle, taking over again. "Most

of it goes through the mountain, then heads east and west."

"There won't be a problem unless your train wants to come into the station," said Mason. "God help us if it does," he added.

"We don't think there's much chance of that," said Sagadore, lighting a cigarette. "If they'd wanted to do some damage, they'd have done it in Penn Station. They could have raised ten times as much hell there."

"Do you have any real idea what they'll do?" asked Gore, the RCMP officer. Although the gray-haired, wide-shouldered man was wearing a plain dark blue suit rather than a uniform, Sagadore could have picked out the man as a cop from a mile off. The short razor haircut and the military posture were like a cap and badge.

"We think they'll head for the hills, basically," said Walter Linberg, speaking for the first time. He slid a copy of his file on the terrorists across the table to the RCMP inspector. "Read about them for yourself. We think the leader of the group is a woman named Annalise Shenker. Old-guard terrorist. I'm no psychiatrist, but she doesn't strike me as the suicidal type. She wants to get away with this."

"I don't know a damn thing about the trackage here," said Sagadore. "If these people want to get around Montreal, what are the options?"

"They would have to make some kind of decision before they crossed the St. Lawrence River," said LaSalle. "They could go toward the east, which would take them to the Gaspé or to New Brunswick, or they could turn west and then south and go back into the United States through Huntingdon, on the Consolidated tracks."

"What about this side of the river?" asked Sagadore.

"To the east they could go to Quebec City, but to do so they would have to travel the entire length of the city, perhaps along the docks," said LaSalle. "If you say they are trying to avoid the city, then that would not be very logical, yes?"

"What about west?"

"Ah, west," murmured LaSalle. "Well, that is very different. "They would come across at the Pont Mercier junction into Montreal West. From there they would head along the main line to Dorval. The line goes past the classification yards at Lachine."

"Dorval?" asked Wesler. "The airport?"

"That is correct," answered LaSalle.

"Shit!" said the FBI man. "How far is the track from the airport?"

"Not far, m'sieu, perhaps half a mile to the terminal. You can see it quite easily from the station there."

"Could that be it?" asked Wesler, turning to Linberg.

"What's in between the station and the airport?" he asked.

"A six-lane highway, among other things," said Sagadore, recalling their drive in from the airport. "There are concrete guard rails and a lot of turf after you get across the expressway. It's wide open. I don't think our Ms. Shenker sees herself as an Olympic runner, especially if she wants to get clear with all that money. And what would they do when they got to the airport? Hijack a plane? Why bother when you've already got a trainload of hostages? No, they'll stick with the train."

"We're off our own ground here," Linberg said slowly. "Why don't we ask somebody who knows? Mr. LaSalle?"

"*Pardon?*"

"Put yourself in their place. If you wanted to get away clean, how would you do it? Where would you ditch the train?"

The dispatcher thought for a moment, then shrugged. "It is not a question that has ever occurred to me before," he said, "but I think I would be most likely to travel to the north. Out of the corridor as quickly as possible. That would mean going to Ottawa, and then beyond, where the line crosses back into Quebec from Ontario. Traveling at a reasonable speed, they could be—how would you say it?—in the middle of nowhere by dark tonight. Two hours to Ottawa, another four or five to North Bay. By midnight they would be deep into northern Ontario."

"Then that's what they'll do," said Linberg, nodding positively.

"It makes sense," Chilton agreed, still reading Linberg's file on the terrorists. "It says here that this man Mohamet Kawi has a pilot's license. There are a thousand lakes up there. If they've got a floatplane waiting . . ." he let the rest of the sentence dangle.

There was a high-pitched beeping sound. LaSalle frowned, reached down to the pager clipped to his belt, and turned it off. "You will pardon me," he said. "I have to make a telephone call." The dispatcher left the room. Less than five minutes later he was back, his return breaking the icy silence that had grown between the two sides of the table.

"That was Jacques Normand at CTC," he explained, sitting down again, his face pale and his expression even more worried than it had been before. "Your Amtrak train has increased its speed and has demanded double greens and switching across Pont Mercier, then west at the 480 junction into the south end of the classification yard at Meadowbrook."

"Yes?" asked Mason, the VIA executive. "That puts them close to the main line to Ottawa, doesn't it?"

"*Oui*," answered LaSalle, inadvertently dropping into French. "*C'est vrai. Mais* . . . but there is something else. Jacques says the Canadian has stopped, with a clear signal for the block beyond the 480 junction. He telephoned the tower operator in the yard. He says the train is just sitting there. The engineer does not respond, either."

"I think I've been in this nightmare before," said Frank Sagadore. "And it's getting worse every minute."

Half an hour previously, as the Canadian moved out into the daylight, Jake Sloane left the drawing room at the *Tremblant Park* and headed toward the head end of the consist. The first order of the day would be the collection of tickets, assisted by one of the trainmen. He went through the vestibule and into the *Riverdale* sleeper. The car, booked by Le Groupe Astrale, was buzzing with activity as the fourteen dancers and their support staff settled in, and within a few seconds the young conductor was fighting an upstream battle against a swarm of men and women dressed in everything from skintight leather jeans to iridescent kaftans. Jake made no attempt to try to figure out which sex was which, and he ignored several fairly broad comments about his uniform as he passed through the car. He finally managed to squeeze through to the head of the car, and slipped into the *Radisson*, breathing a sigh of relief as the heavy door blanked out the bilingual pandemonium at his back.

He walked down the roomette corridor, balancing easily as the train lurched through the crossover, then he took the dogleg around the drawing room, turning sideways with his back against the bulkhead as a passenger appeared from Bedroom B and headed his way. He was surprised when the passenger stopped directly in front of him, their chests almost touching, and he was even more surprised to hear himself addressed by name.

"Mr. Sloane?" The man was in his late twenties, dark-haired and wearing tinted, horn-rimmed glasses.

"Yes?" said Jake, feeling a little uncomfortable speaking to someone whose face was less than a foot from his own. The man's arm came up, and Jake stiffened as he felt something hard prod into his side.

"Mr. Sloane, I have a small pistol against a spot between your fourth and fifth ribs. If I shot you now, you would be dead before you hit the floor. I want you to do exactly as I tell you, and without comment. Do you understand?"

Jake nodded, the blood draining from his face and his mind tumbling madly.

"Please move up the corridor to Bedroom B and go inside," said the man. Once again Jake nodded, then did as he was told, the pressure of the gun never varying. He backed into the room, his eyes locked with the stranger's. Once inside the small room, the man closed the door and flipped the latch, working by feel with his left hand, the right aiming the black, palm-sized gun at Jake's chest. The bunks were still flush in the bulkhead, and Jake saw that the room was empty except for the two regulation arm chairs and a single aluminum photographer's case.

"Sit," said the man. Jake did so, taking the chair closest to the window. The man hit the toggle switch over the sink, and the overhead light came on. "Pull down the blind."

Jake did, then turned back to the man, his stomach knotting painfully. He laid his arms out along the arms of the chair, grasping at the worn tartan fabric in an effort to stop his hands from shaking.

"Good," said the man. "Now we can talk." He sat down in the other chair, first turning it to face Jake, but only using his free hand. Even as he sat down, the gun never wavered.

"My senior trainman is going to wonder where I am," said Jake, his voice no more than a croak as he jerked out the words. It was fact, not bravado; if he didn't show up soon, his second-in-command was going to come looking for him, and the last thing Jake wanted right now was an interruption. The blank expression on the face of the man seated across from him was that of a killer or a madman. Or both.

"Mr. Vermette will have to wait," the man said easily. Jake started at the use of his senior trainman's name. First his own name, and now Bertrand's. The man with the gun had good information. It was unnerving. "All right," said the man. "Now I want you to listen very closely, because it is important that you understand the situation you are now in." He paused, obviously waiting for a response.

"I'll listen," said Jake.

"Good. My name is Cyr. Jacques Cyr. You see, we have something in common. We have the same first name." Cyr smiled pleasantly. "You will be given an opportunity to talk to your superiors later on, so I should also tell you that for the last three years I have been an employee of the Canadian National Railways, working as a junior dispatcher. I have been involved in this operation for the last ten months. You and your people can rest assured that I have every piece of information necessary concerning the operations of the Canadian. I know the junctions, block signals, and radio frequencies. Everything. If necessary, I can also act as the engineer. You can tell your superiors that. You can also tell them that the RCMP probably has my name in their Section G files. They should look under the name Paul Etienne Cyr, who was my father. I think that will establish my credentials. But that is beside the point. I want you to know what is happening to you right now. You see that case on the couch?"

"Yes," said Jake.

"I want you to reach over and put your hand on it."

Jake did. "It's cold," he said, frowning.

"Dry ice," said Cyr. "Do you know what anthrax is?" he added.

"It's an animal disease, isn't it?"

"Yes. Among other things," agreed Cyr. "I'm only repeating what my partner has told me, but it will interest the authorities." Cyr leaned back in his chair, the gun still in his hand but resting on the arm of the seat. "Anthrax.

Bacillus anthracis. An aerobic microbe. That means it survives in the open air. Unlike many other microbes, it also survives in a vacuum by producing spores. It is one of the hardiest of all contagious diseases. As a spore, it is resistant to both heat and cold. During a British biological warfare test in the Hebrides, an island was so infected that nothing can live there for the next hundred and fifty years or so. Boats are not even allowed to land there. It is as deadly to humans as it is to cows and sheep. You die of pneumonia very rapidly. I understand it is quite horrible."

"Why are you telling me this?" Jake asked hoarsely.

"The case you touched holds eight containers of *Bacillus anthracis* spores in an agar culture base. Right now the spores are dormant. When I remove the canisters from the case, the containers will warm to room temperature and the bacillus will begin to propagate. Within twelve hours there will be enough of the bacilli to be seen with the naked eye. In twenty-four hours the agar will be like soup. In forty-eight hours there will be enough of the bacilli to infect an area of several hundred square miles for at least a century. That is one canister. There are eight here. My partner has six more." Cyr glanced at his watch. "Seventy hours from now the bacilli will be almost bursting out of the canisters. The canisters are extremely fragile. The bacilli, trillions of them, will be very widely spread. At the very least, everyone still within this train will be fatally infected. Wherever the train is at that time will become a no-man's land. I have a remote switch which will open each one. Even now, a single spore inhaled by one of your passengers would be enough to kill him. So, as they used to say in the movies, let's not have any false heroics."

"What do you want me to do?" asked Jake.

"In a few seconds we will leave this room. My partner will then take the case and prepare to place the canisters." He checked his watch again. "By this time she will have already placed the first three from her own case. While she is completing her task, you and I will move to the head end of the train. I will escort you through the baggage and dormitory cars and we will cross the B unit and then the engine itself. Your task is to make sure we aren't stopped. If we are, I will shoot you and flip on my remote switch. Do you understand?"

"Yes."

"Good. Once we have reached the engine you will tell the engineer enough to acquaint him with the seriousness of what is happening. You will order him to slow the train as we pass the 480 junction and then stop so that the engine is just beyond the wye track leading out of the Meadowbrook Yards. At that point you will tell Mr. Vermette the situation. You may tell him anything you want, so long as what you say results in the passengers and the rest of the crew believing that we have stopped for some small mechanical problem."

"Then what?" Jake asked woodenly, hardly able to believe the horror of what was happening.

"Then we wait, Mr. Sloane."

After twenty-two years on the Metropolitan Toronto Police, Norm Kettering had developed a near-infallible nose for trouble, and a chronic backache. The backache was making him grimace as he shifted around on the Daynighter seat of Car 1823, and his trouble-sniffing nose was making him nervous.

At first he'd put the nervousness down to the fact that he'd just spent slightly over two weeks in Montreal as a witness for the prosecution in an involved drug case. He didn't like Montreal much, since he didn't speak any French at all, and the case itself had been nerve-racking; he had been a key witness, and had known that his testimony could make the difference between the five defendants taking a walk or being put away for seven to nine years.

But the trial was over, the case won, and the tension he was feeling had a harder, more immediate edge, a faint feeling that something wasn't quite right here and now. Idly he examined the hunch, the way he did when he was working on something. It was a habit that had driven his wife to distraction for fifteen years; she'd complained that he didn't even stop being a cop while they were making love. That and a lot of other factors had led to a divorce that was now almost ten years old.

Three things itched and didn't respond to logical scratching. For one thing, they'd been stopped now for almost fifteen minutes without any apparent reason. No other train had gone by on either side, and looking out the window, he couldn't see anybody working on the train. They were just sitting there, as though they were waiting for something. The second thing was the woman. Two or three minutes after they'd left the station, with the tenement slums packed in around the tracks and down the narrow, desolate streets of St. Antoine, the woman, dressed in a VIA blue blazer and slacks, had appeared at the rear of the car, carrying what looked like a toolbox. She'd gone down the length of the car, opened an access panel to the circuit-breaker switch box, and fiddled around for a moment. Then she'd moved on to the next car. Kettering wasn't positive, but he'd never heard of a woman maintenance worker on a train before, and if they did exist, they wouldn't be wearing uniforms like that. The third thing was the conductor. He'd come through the car just before they stopped, accompanied by a young man carrying a metal photographer's case. At the time, the heavyset policeman hadn't paid much attention, but in thinking about it now he realized that the conductor had been white as a sheet. Either he was sick and the man with the case was a doctor, or the conductor had been scared shitless. Kettering had seen the same expression of abject fear lots of times over the years, usually on the faces of rookies under fire for the first time.

Still, there was no obvious problem at hand. The other people in the Daynighter didn't seem to be upset, beyond a bit of grumbling at the delay, and anyway, what *could* be wrong? This was hardly the era of the train robber. On the other hand, his nose was rarely wrong. Casually he stood up, reached for his briefcase on the rack above him, and brought it down to the seat. He sat down again, turning the case so its contents were masked by the hinged top, and brought out his pistol, a standard if somewhat old-fashioned Smith & Wesson .38 Police Special, fitted into a worn, spring-clip belt holster. He slipped the pistol into the waistband of his suit trousers, buttoned his jacket, and closed the briefcase. Armed, he put the briefcase back onto the luggage rack and sat down.

Most of his colleagues on the force would have laughed themselves sick at his apparent paranoia, but that didn't bother him at all. In twenty-two years he'd never been shot, never been hurt, never had a traffic accident, and had always taken good physical care of himself. Mr. Careful, they called him, and that was just fine with Norman Kettering.

"Better safe than sorry," he whispered to himself.

Chapter 10

Monday, June 27
Time: 5:25 P.M. EDT
Distance: 821 miles/1,321 km.

To the average person, unacquainted with terrorist tactics and strategy, the secondary hijacking of the VIA Rail Canadian and the subsequent coupling of that train to the Amtrak Night Owl might have appeared to be the final aberrant act of a group of lunatics. Most people would also assume that after sixteen hours the authorities would have developed a workable game plan to deal with the situation, or at the very least would have provided some sort of security to prevent the VIA train from being taken. It would seem impossible that fewer than a dozen men and women could foil the efforts of two large governmental organizations like VIA and Amtrak, the resources of the armed forces of the United States, the manpower and facilities of the Federal Bureau of Investigation, the United States Treasury forces, the Royal Canadian Mounted Police, and the entire Montreal Police Department. After all, what were a handful of malcontent thugs when you compared them to North America's best and brightest?

In point of fact, Annalise Shenker, who had first begun planning the operation more than a year before, was a highly trained political and military strategist, as well as a brilliant operational tactician whose services would have fetched a very high price indeed from any of a dozen major intelligence organizations. When the operation was barely more than a shadowy concept in Shenker's mind, she had realized that the hijacking of the Night Owl had a far greater chance of success than most terrorist actions, and offered an unparalleled opportunity in both financial and media benefits. The plan, which had originated in a chance reading of an article in an old copy of *The National Geographic*, and which was later confirmed by a simple telephone call to the public relations office of the U.S. Bureau of Printing and Engraving, hinged on the fact that bureaucracies, whether corporate or governmental, were made vulnerable by their inability to cross-communicate.

In addition, Shenker knew that the hijacking of the Night Owl would constitute the first major terrorist operation ever mounted within the United States. As such, she knew it would draw a great deal of unhealthy attention as well as the more useful media coverage. On the other hand, with the exception of occasional aircraft hijackings and anomalous incidents such as the bizarre and pointless efforts of groups like the Symbionese Liberation Army, the Americans — both armed forces and police — had virtually no experience with international terrorism.

Using the computer research facilities of the Arab Liaison Bureau in Tripoli, which was operated by the Libyan secret police, Shenker went over all past incidences of terrorism that involved the United States. Within a few weeks she had gathered a file of information that showed that historically the United States authorities were incapable of cutting through their own legal and bureaucratic structures when faced with a crisis. There was no single organization that actively monitored terrorist activities, and no police or military group having the powers necessary to deal with an operation such as the hijacking of the Night Owl. The only efforts that had been made to counteract a terrorist threat were some rather loose security precautions at major airports, and even those could be dealt with, given enough time. Using the same hindsight logic that plagues most bureaucracies, American authorities had initiated no security precautions to safeguard the Amtrak system or any other potential terrorist targets in the United States. Public figures were rarely protected; there were virtually no gun-control laws, and unlike most countries in Europe and the rest of the world, no identification or police documentation was required to purchase firearms. The Americans naïvely assumed that although terrorism could strike anywhere else, it was impossible in the United States. Going over the various data she had assembled, Shenker knew that a major terrorist act in the United States would initiate tremendous confusion, and the added complication of taking the train across an international border and coupling it to a Canadian train would simply compound that confusion. The chances of any serious counterattack being mounted, at least within the time frame she had allowed for, were minimal. According to the statistics she'd gathered, as well as information regarding European operations in the past, Shenker estimated that it would take a minimum of twenty hours to coordinate a serious counterattack, and before that the scenario would have been radically changed by the addition of Paulette Baxter and Jacques Cyr.

Cyr had been on the periphery of the international terrorist scene for a number of years, an association due mainly to his father's involvement in the Front de la Libération de Québec, the FLQ, a quasi-terrorist organization that flourished briefly in the late sixties. Cyr's father had been involved in a small way with the Cross/Laporte kidnappings of 1970, and had been accidentally killed as a result of that involvement. The biggest attraction for Shenker was the fact that the bitter young man worked for VIA Rail. As soon as Shenker was reasonably sure of the overall game plan for the operation, Cyr was recruited by Paulette Baxter.

Baxter herself had been only recently recruited. The young and not terribly attractive university student was the unhappy progeny of a wealthy Montreal couple who had divorced years before. Paulette, never particularly the apple of either parent's eye, had been shuffled from one private school to another, an ambition to be a doctor her only source of personal pride and strength. On a summer vacation in Europe after her first year of premed at McGill University, Paulette had engaged in a brief affair with a contemporary of Annalise Shenker's who was a roving agent for George Habash's Popular Front for the Liberation of Palestine. As well as taking her virginity, an encumbrance of which Baxter had been trying unsuccessfully to rid herself for several years, the Popular Front recruiter also took the young woman's rather naïve political consciousness, punctuating each bout of lovemaking with equally passionate arguments in favor of Habash's violent solution to the question of a Palestinian homeland. The PFLP's reactionary and simplistic philosophy fit Paulette like a glove, and within a few weeks she was a wholehearted convert to the cause — as much out of the knowledge of her parents' horrified reaction as out of true conviction.

The PFLP operative escorted her to the training camp at Mukalla, in the People's Republic of Yemen, on the Aden coast. There she came to the attention of Naif Hawatmeh, Habash's second-in-command, who in turn pointed her out to the East German secret police "consultants" in the camp. Intrigued by her background in medicine and realizing the resources of McGill University, the East Germans put her through an entire summer of grueling training and indoctrination, then sent her back to Montreal — forever grateful to the PFLP for the loss of her virginity and a focus for her life. She became a one-woman cell in Quebec, concentrating on developing methods of producing toxic and bacteriological material, a lack of which had been seen as a chronic failing on the part of most major terrorist groups up until that time. When Annalise Shenker returned to North America prior to the hijacking, she carried a small vacuum container of *Bacillus anthracis* spores intravaginally through customs at Mirabel Airport. Except for the weapons taken from the St. Augustine armory, the tiny vial of lethal spores was the final piece in the complex puzzle that Annalise Shenker had been assembling so methodically.

At 5:20 P.M., at the height of Montreal's early-evening rush hour, the Amtrak Night Owl crossed the Lachine Canal, then headed through the Autoroute underpass at Kirkland Park. As the train slowed prior to the Meadowbrook Yards main switch lead track, Annalise Shenker and her companions took up their positions, ready to move as soon as Sheila Teng brought the train into position. Each member of the group had practiced his or her part a hundred times in the D.C. warehouse, and as the train came to a jerking stop with the engine poised on the Route 13 overpass, they swung into action. Mohamet Kawi, Raoul Attendera, and Lisa Ruffio dropped down from the head end of the RPO. Kawi and Attendera began uncoupling the engine at breakneck speed while Ruffio, now armed with one of the dead Black Berets' M-60's, stood guard. The positioning of the train was ideal, since the raised concrete platform of the overpass gave her a view out across the railyards. At the rear of the train, Akbar was equally well positioned in the Vista Dome, with the wide-open expanse of the Meadowbrook Golf Course on one side and a cemetery and the Lachine public golf course on the other.

If any attempt was made to storm the train, either she or Akbar would see it coming from a long way off. As it was, there was nothing visible except a creeping line of automobiles moving through the underpass, and the dust-hazed expanse of the huge railyard in the distance.

The uncoupling was done in less than three minutes. With that complete, Kawi jumped back onto the RPO while Raoul ran forward to the dwarf switch on the far side of the overpass. Lisa Ruffio tensed, waiting for the dull smack of a bullet; if there were snipers hidden in the distance, this was the time they'd strike. She watched as her lover used the switch key provided by Jacques Cyr to free the manual arm. The South American heaved on the short lever, swinging the short length of switch track into position. He waved Teng on, and the Amtrak diesel began to move forward with a coughing roar, its turbo-charger blower sending up a hot blast of rusty exhaust. As the engine passed Attendera, he grabbed the rear handrails and stepped up onto the platform to ride shotgun. Ruffio watched as they moved into the distance, heading up the line to the CN/CP Piggyback Service snub siding a few hundred yards away. When they reached it, Raoul would use his keys again, throwing the upline dwarf to allow Sheila Teng to back the F-40 onto the siding and off the main line. With that done, Raoul would throw the switch back and both he and Teng would then wait for the Canadian to pull forward.

With the Amtrak diesel out of the way, the VIA locomotive was now visible on the mainline track less than fifty feet away to the left. The Italian terrorist waited until she saw the engine begin to move, then climbed back up onto the RPO. She glanced at the LED watch on her wrist. Five minutes and twenty seconds from the time they'd stopped. She closed her eyes, going over the sequence they had practiced so often.

While the VIA diesel, the B unit, and the baggage car pulled ahead, Haas, Annalise, and Kawi would be uncoupling the mutilated Amtrak observation car, now emptied of the diplomats, who had been moved forward into the last sleeper. The observation car, like the *Tremblant Park* on the Canadian, had no rear door and would have been left behind even if it hadn't been damaged, since there would be no through access if the car was coupled in the center of the train.

The VIA locomotive and its head-end cars had now moved across the still-open dwarf switch Raoul had thrown to let the Amtrak F-40 onto the main line. Once fully across, the VIA diesel would reverse down the switch lead to the RPO. If everything had gone according to plan, Cyr would have the Canadian train conductor in the cab with him, and under the barrel of Ruffio's M-60, the conductor and Cyr would couple the VIA baggage car to the RPO. The diesel would then pull ahead again, and back onto the main line, taking the Night Owl with it. Akbar would abandon his position in the now uncoupled observation car at the last minute and wait with Mohamet Kawi and Dieter Haas in the vestibule of the last sleeper. When the Night Owl had been taken forward onto the main line, it would then reverse and Akbar, Kawi, and Haas would couple the sleeper to the first VIA coach. Then, with the two trains joined, they would continue on their way.

The net result of the complex switching operation would be the replacement of the Amtrak locomotive, now dangerously low on fuel, with the VIA diesel, and the coupling of the remaining Amtrak cars with the Canadian consist. The procedure left them dangerously vulnerable to attack for almost seven minutes, but it was necessary if their plan was to proceed.

The Italian opened her eyes and squinted against the lowering sun. The silhouetted bulk of the VIA baggage car was looming only a hundred feet or so away. She braced herself against the impact of the approaching head-end car and nervously looked at her watch again. It was 5:29.

"Oh my God, it's happening again," groaned Adrian Tucker as the stationary Amdinette jerked heavily.

"We're being shunted," said Howard Mottbrown, his expression a fixed mask of concentration as he tried to deduce what was going on by sound alone. "That bumping movement a few minutes ago was the train being pulled through a crossover. The last bump came from behind, which probably means they're coupling on more cars."

"I don't understand it," said Daniel Pendergast, keeping a wary eye on the head-end door of the car. The creeps who'd taken the train had been doing a lot of running back and forth, and Pendergast was worried that eventually they'd start to get suspicious of the little group sitting around the Amdinette table. "What do they need more cars for?"

"Who knows?" said Harry Maxwell, sipping a warm can of Schlitz. He frowned thoughtfully, staring at the closed blind of the window directly across the aisle. "You're sure we're in Montreal?" he asked Mottbrown.

"I don't see where else we could be," said the small man. "I've tried to keep track of directional changes, and I'd swear that we've traveled north ever since — "

He stopped, his voice trailing off. Harry knew what the little man was thinking. The terrorists had made a point of dragging the bloody corpses of the Delta Group troopers through every car as a demonstration of what would happen to those who opposed them, and the section sleeper two cars back had been turned into a makeshift infirmary for the dozen or more passengers who'd been injured when the demolition charges on the coach doors exploded. The coach itself had been abandoned and declared a prohibited area by the terrorists, forcing the passengers who'd been seated there to crowd back into the other cars. The possibility of the "Stockholm syndrome" appearing, in which the hostages in a terrorist operation begin to identify and empathize with their captors, had effectively been ruled out by the events of the previous night. The Delta Group's bodies and the coach explosion victims were ample proof to the passengers of the Night Owl that the fix they were in was dangerous and potentially fatal. Half an hour after the Delta Group attack, a terrible quiet had fallen over the train, unbroken except for whispers between seatmates, and there was virtually no movement between the cars. The lounge was empty, and except for Harry's group, so was the Amdinette, although occasionally a passenger would appear, rummage behind the counter, and then disappear again, clutching some cellophane-wrapped sandwich booty.

"I still think we stick out like a sore thumb here," Pendergast complained. "I read an article once that said the last thing you should do if you're held hostage is draw any attention to yourself. It sounds like good advice."

"We'd draw even more attention if we were all squeezed into your bedroom back in the sleeper," said Mark Cavendish. "If anybody asks, we tell them we're together. We were going to a Mets game. Don't worry about it; I think these people have other things on their mind right now."

The train gave another crunching lurch and then began to move forward smoothly.

"On our way again," said Pendergast. "The question is where."

"West," said Mark Cavendish. "You can tell by the way the sun is coming through the cracks at the bottom of the blinds."

"You learn that in the marines?" asked Daniel sourly.

"Boy scouts," answered the amputee.

"West out of Montreal," Harry brooded. He turned to Mottbrown, who had gone back to reading his book. "That mean anything to you, Howard?"

The mousy little man closed his book, carefully marking his place with a folded paper napkin. He pursed his lips and stared thoughtfully at the ceiling. "I don't know an awful lot about the Canadian lines, but it probably means they're heading to Toronto, or farther north. I think they call it the Lakehead Route."

"The Lakehead? You mean Superior?" asked Cavendish.

"I believe so. It's the transcontinental line. Winnipeg and then across their midwest."

"Bush country," said Cavendish.

"Then that's how they'll go," said Harry, nodding. "I think the whole point of this moving around has been to get them away from built-up areas. They have some kind of escape route planned."

"What about us?" said Adrian Tucker. "What will they do to us?"

"Forget about us or kill us," said Cavendish. "Depends on what mood they're in at the time, I think."

"They won't forget about us," said Harry Maxwell. "They aren't like the PLO or the IRA. They don't need any public support. The bigger the atrocity the better, as far as they're concerned. They've got enough high explosives planted on this train to blow us all to hell, and I think that's exactly what they're intending."

"Don't overdramatize," Pendergast cautioned. "I read you like a book, Harry — you're just getting antsy, you want to *do* something. The only trouble is, it might get us all killed."

"I think Harry's right," Cavendish commented, spearing a cigarette from the open pack in front of Tucker.

"Nobody asked for your opinion," the artist said coldly.

Harry looked across the table at his old friend and shook his head almost imperceptibly, signaling Daniel to calm down. He knew why his friend was so antagonistic toward the veteran; Cavendish was an outsider. It was bad enough to be trapped on the train, but once they were off, *if* they got off, the fewer people who knew about the attempted robbery of the currency shipment the better.

"I really don't think we have very much choice in the matter," Howard Mottbrown said quietly. "The authorities have already tried to recapture the train, and it ended in disaster. The doctor that Mr. Stackpole found told me that there are several people who were very badly hurt when the explosives went off in the coach. I'm not an expert or anything, but it stands to reason that the police or the army will try to retake the train again, and that means even more people are going to get hurt."

"Us," Adrian Tucker muttered gloomily.

"Perhaps," said Mottbrown. "Whatever the case, I think it's up to us to deal with the situation."

Daniel shook his head, sighing. "Look," he began, "you may want — "

The muted clattering rhythm of the train increased in volume as the door at the tail end of the Amdinette opened. Hearing it, the group at the table tried to look like the baseball fans they were supposed to be. They relaxed when they saw it was only Stackpole.

"Well, look at that," said the gray-haired steward, approaching. "If it ain't Hogan's Heroes all together in a bunch." He shook his head and made a clucking noise with his tongue and teeth. "Now that ain't what I'd call wise, groupin' together like eggs in a basket. These folks, they might think you *conspirin'*, and that wouldn't be healthy, nossir."

"What's with the Step'n' Fetchit routine?" asked Harry.

"I have been chosen by our captors to act as a messenger boy. I think they figure that because I'm black I'm on their side or something. They were very buddy-buddy."

"So what's the message you're supposed to be spreading?" asked Daniel cautiously.

"I'm supposed to tell everyone that we are now in Canada — just outside Montreal, to be precise. They had a few of their comrades on the VIA Canadian, which is now hanging on our ass end. About three hundred more hostages to add to the list."

"Good Lord!" whispered Mottbrown.

"That's nothing," said Stackpole, standing in the aisle and swaying easily with the motion of the train. "I'm also supposed to advise all the passengers that this train is now playing host to enough anthrax germs to waste everyone on board and a couple of hundred thousand besides."

"Holy shit!" said Daniel.

"One more thing," continued Stackpole. "Everybody's got to move into the Canadian end of the train. It's going to be crowded, let me tell you."

"Why are they doing that?" asked Tucker. "It's just going to make everybody uncomfortable."

"Maybe that's the idea," said Harry.

Stackpole shrugged. "Who knows? That's just what they told me. Get yourself at least four cars back and find what space you can. No luggage except what you can carry. Anyway, I have to go forward and tell everyone else."

The black man lowered his voice. "I don't suppose you people have come up with anything yet?" he asked. "I don't know how much longer I can keep up this 'yassuh, boss' routine."

"We don't have much, Hamilton," said Harry. "We know who's wearing the black hats and who's wearing the white ones, but that's about it, so far."

"Well, let me know when you're cooking," muttered the Amtrak steward. "These people make me nervous."

"Will do," said Harry. Stackpole nodded and then he

166

was gone, pushing through the forward door of the Amdinette.

"What we need to know is the layout of the train," Daniel mused. "We can't figure out any strategy blind."

"I think that perhaps we might be able to deduce the consist fairly accurately," Mottbrown said. He plucked a felt-tipped pen out of the little plastic holder in his shirt pocket and began sketching on a place mat in front of him, drawing out a neat line of rectangles in a row and labeling them.

"We can assume that the shunting in Montreal was to replace the Amtrak engine, which would have been low on fuel, with a VIA Rail engine from the Canadian, which is the VIA transcontinental train. Further, they would have coupled the Night Owl consist to the Canadian, and that means they would have dropped the rear observation car from the Night Owl."

"Why?" asked Mark Cavendish. "How can you assume that?"

"It's quite simple, actually," said Mottbrown, smiling shyly.

"There's no connecting platform for the rear of the observation car. It's always a tail end, so they'd have to drop it if they wanted to join the Amtrak and the VIA consists together at that point."

"Okay," said Harry. "What else can we deduce, Howard?"

"Well, the standard VIA Canadian consist would probably be a baggage car, two standard coaches, a Skyline Lounge, which is a dinette like this one but with a dome observation platform on an upper level, a Daynighter, which is really just a fancy kind of coach with reclining airline-style seats, probably a full dining car, a couple of sleeping cars, and perhaps a sleeper/dome combination at the tail end."

"Okay," said Harry, leaning over and checking the diagram that was taking shape on the place mat. "You figure we've lost the Amtrak observation car and the baggage, so that gives us the RPO and two coaches up ahead, the Amdinette right here, and the sleeper behind us before we hit the Canadian cars, right?"

"Approximately," Mottbrown replied. "The consist for

167

the VIA train might be a little different, I can't really say for sure."

"A good guess is better than a blank," said Harry, scanning the layout on the place mat. "The question is, where are the terrorists?"

"The ones up forward will be the same ones we've had so far," said Cavendish, pointing with his hook at the forward cars on the diagram. "That means one in the engine, or maybe two. Because no one has come forward since Montreal, we can figure on the rest of them being in the cars behind us."

"You can bet they'll have lookouts in the two dome cars," said Daniel.

"Makes sense," Harry agreed. "So that's three at least. Out of how many, seven?"

"Or more," said Daniel. "We don't know how many got on in Montreal, and we still don't know if they've got people undercover among the passengers. This is foolishness, Harry. It doesn't tell us a damn thing."

"Speak for yourself," said Mark Cavendish. He crushed the butt of his cigarette out between his pincers and dropped the mangled end into an ashtray on the table. "It's better than doing nothing. If you can't take it, why don't you go back and sit with the other passengers?"

"Stop bickering," Harry snapped. "If we start fighting among ourselves, we might as well quit. At least now we have some idea of the environment we have to work in. I don't care how many came on board at Montreal, this train is now at least fifteen or sixteen cars long. That's a lot of space to control, and a lot of people."

"If the Canadian was full leaving Montreal, we'd be carrying about six hundred passengers now," Mottbrown offered.

"Right. Sixteen cars and six hundred people. Our creepy friends are going to be spread pretty thin, and they'll be worrying more about what's going on outside than about us."

"So what do we do?" asked Mottbrown.

"A little snooping, maybe," said Harry. He pursed his lips, staring down at the diagram thoughtfully. "These people must have some kind of headquarters. Odds are they've got radios and a lot of other junk. Anybody got any ideas?"

"One of the dome cars," said Cavendish.

"The one at the end of the train," said Daniel. "The other one is too vulnerable; if it's where Howard here says it is, that means it would be almost in the middle of the train, open to attack from both ends. They'll have a guy up there, but it won't be their main base."

"I think Pendergast is right," said Mottbrown. "The sleeper domes they use in Canada are very spacious. Several bedrooms and a large rear lounge."

"Okay," Harry interrupted. "Then we split up and start pinpointing exactly where these people are . . . " his voice trailed off as the rear door of the Amdinette swung open.

A heavyset man in an out-of-date suit appeared. The man closed the door carefully behind him and paused, looking down the car at the small group assembled at the far table. After a few seconds he came down the aisle, large hands held away from his body, guarding against the erratic swaying of the train. He stopped in front of the table and looked down at the group.

"Is one of you Harry Maxwell?" he asked.

"Why?" asked Harry, trying to keep the nervousness out of his voice. The authority in the big man's tone reminded him of his high-school principal.

"One of the porters gave me the name. He said he saw who I was on the passenger list, and he figured I might be useful."

"Oh?" said Harry noncommittally.

"Yeah," said the man. He pushed back his jacket and pulled a short-barreled Police Special out of the holster in his waistband. He laid the gun carefully down on the table in front of Harry. "My name is Norm Kettering," he said. "I'm a cop."

Wanda Jenkins Margay sat in the roomette, her gnarled hands clasping her ornate walking stick, and studied the man seated across from her. He seemed uncomfortable, perched as he was on the cushioned seat that covered the toilet, but beyond that he looked angry. Almost an hour had passed since she was forced at gunpoint out of the compartment in the observation car and told to find whatever accommodation she could. In what she had at first assumed was a chivalrous gesture, the man now seated across from her had offered his seat, and she had accepted gratefully. Now she wasn't so sure; the man wasn't much younger than she was, by the looks of him, and if his expression was any indication, he was on the verge of a towering rage. She didn't know who was more frightening — the terrorists who'd forced her from her room, or the potential madman less than a yard away. She kept her eyes on him constantly, and her hands on the head of her walking stick, a gift from her husband. Her fingers were swollen and crabbed from arthritis, but they had enough strength to twist the silver head and pull out the seven-inch-long, needle-sharp stiletto blade. The custom-made cane had appalled her when her husband presented it to her, but he had insisted that she needed some form of personal protection. Now, after fifty years, it seemed that the gift might finally be of some use.

Strangely, Wanda felt no qualms about using the stick, either against the man seated across from her or against the terrorists, if it came to that. She had lived her entire seventy-six years removed from any of the violent realities of life, but even so she was neither stupid nor naïve; she knew that different times and circumstances required different responses, and here and now, violence was clearly the order of the day.

She did not, however, wish to end her days at the hands of a balding lunatic in a railroad roomette, and so she decided that it was about time she found out a little more about her companion.

"My name is Wanda Margay," she announced formally, her voice quavering slightly. She had spoken the same words an hour before, but the man's reply had been nothing more than a brief nod. "It would seem that we are both in the same boat, so to speak, and I thought we should get to know each other."

"My name is Groz," said the man. "Wolfgang Groz."

His accent was thick, but his English was excellent. "You are European?" asked Wanda.

"German," said Groz.

"You speak English very well."

"I was in Canada for almost four years. I learned then," said Groz.

"Where did you live?" asked Wanda, relieved that the

man seemed capable of sustaining a rational conversation, terse as it was.

"Just outside Medicine Hat. It was called Camp One Thirty-two. I was a prisoner of war."

"Oh," said Wanda. She cleared her throat. "I suppose that was the Second World War?"

Groz made a small choking sound, a stillborn laugh. "Yes. World War II."

"The Nazi war."

"Yes," said Groz. "But I wasn't a Nazi."

"I'm sure you weren't," Wanda said diplomatically.

"No," said Groz, his mouth drawing into a bitter smile. "I never thought of things like that. I was a *jungefleiger*, a flyboy for the Luftwaffe. We never thought about politics. It is funny, you know, I didn't learn what it was to be a Nazi until I was captured and brought to Canada. I found out in the camp what Nazism was. I saw them there, people who were supposed to be my countrymen, but who were no better than wild dogs. They controlled the camp by terror. In 1943 they murdered a man. His name was Plaszek. They were very powerful in the camp, but the Canadian authorities tried the man who had done the killing and he was hanged. I had great respect for the Canadians after that. And only loathing for the Nazis — for people like the ones who have taken this train."

"You think they are Nazis?" asked Wanda, surprised.

"They may not call themselves so," Groz responded. "Left wing, right wing, it makes no difference. To be a Nazi is to hate without discrimination, as these people do."

"Well, then," said Wanda, "I think we should do something about them."

"What?" said Groz. "I am an old man, and you are an old woman. We can have no effect."

"Don't be silly," Wanda chided. "I have a very simple philosophy of life, Mr. Groz, and it's served me very well. You're alive until you're dead, and I am just as alive now as I was when I was twenty-one. I don't drool, I don't talk to people who have been dead for years, and I don't forget things — at least not very often. Think of it, Mr. Groz, between us we have more years of experience than that entire pack of hoodlums. Surely we can think of something. Perhaps we can use our advanced years to

171

good effect. After all, they won't be expecting any threat from a pair of oldsters like us, now, will they?"

"No, that is certainly true. But to talk is easy. What can we *do*?"

"I've been thinking about that," said Wanda promptly. "Messages in bottles?"

"I beg your pardon?"

"It's what castaways do. They send out messages in bottles."

"And how do you propose to get a message away from this train, Frau Margay? They have the doors blocked, and all the window blinds drawn. We are sealed in."

"Not entirely, Mr. Groz. In fact," said Wanda, smiling broadly, "the outside world is much closer than you think."

Frank Sagadore stared down at the early-evening traffic fifteen stories below and sipped occasionally from a cup of charred coffee. On the far side of the room, Walter Linberg sat with his feet up on the coffee table, apparently asleep.

"This is just a big waste of time," said the Amtrak security chief, turning away from the hotel room window. "Wesler's up to his whatever in meetings, and we're here with our thumbs up our fannies. It's ridiculous."

"It's bureaucracy," murmured Linberg, his eyes still closed. "First they'll talk about jurisdiction. Then they'll talk about policy procedures. After that will come chain-of-command and reporting procedure. *Then* you might see some action, but don't bank on it. Dollars to doughnuts, somebody in the upper echelons is going to get cold feet about actually doing anything, and they'll have to start over from the beginning. Take it from me, Frank, these things have a life of their own; all we can do is watch it unfold."

"Shit," said Sagadore, slumping down into an upholstered chair across from the ex-FBI man.

Linberg opened his eyes, blinked, and said, "A terse but vivid description."

"So what do we do?" asked Sagadore.

Linberg shrugged, then stretched, yawning. "Nothing, my friend. Not only are we out of our depth, we're out of our country."

"So we just stand by and wait for your Ms. Shenker and her pals to blow my passengers away?"

"They might come out of it in one piece," said Linberg.

"Bull," said Sagadore. "You're the expert on terrorists, and you said yourself they didn't stand a chance unless there was some intervention."

"True," said Linberg. "They don't have much of a chance otherwise. I told Wesler the same thing. Presumably he's repeating my statement to the Canadians. We've done all we can, Frank."

"But nothing's going to happen, damn it! You know that."

Linberg nodded. "And if it does, it'll come too late. But as I said, it's out of our hands."

"So why don't we take it back into our hands?" said Sagadore.

"Right," said Linberg with a grimace. "You be the Lone Ranger and I'll be Tonto."

"I'm serious," Sagadore urged.

"You're crazy," Linberg amended. "The U.S. Special Forces blew it — why do you think you could do any better? This thing's gone from bad to worse, Frank. The train is wired up like a bomb, we've had proof of that, and according to Wesler the train is now rigged with biologicals as well. When I last talked to him on the phone, he said they were running down the woman's name to see if she checks out as being capable of doing it, but I'm willing to bet you she is."

"So how dangerous could it be?" asked Sagadore, frustrated and angry.

"Very," Linberg answered. "It's not the kind of thing you put press releases out on, but it's worried the Bureau for a long time; in a way, this was inevitable. According to the files I've read, the three best bets are anthrax, botulinus, and cholera; they're the easiest to manufacture on a limited basis. If it *is* anthrax, as Wesler says, any dissemination of it could be catastrophic. The Brits tested some on an island off the coast of Scotland back in the early forties, and it's still dangerous to land a boat there. The death rate for people close to where the stuff is released is something like ninety percent, and you can infect a huge area if the spores get any sort of widespread release. You really want to stick your oar in that?"

"If the odds are good enough," Sagadore said stubbornly. "Who's to say these creeps won't release the anthrax anyway?"

"That's a point," said Linberg. "But how do you think you'd do any good? What are you going to do, stand on the tracks and try to flag her down?"

"The train will have to stop soon," said Sagadore. "I've done a bit of investigating on my own."

"Go on," Linberg prompted him.

"The locomotive power for that train is an old rebuilt F unit with a 'B' steam generator behind to power the train's air-conditioning system. With our cars in tow as well, she's hauling a pretty heavy load. Presumably she was fully fueled when she pulled out of here, but even so, she'll be low on fuel by late tonight. I doubt these people will want to risk going through the night without refueling. She'll have to stop."

"Where?" asked Linberg.

"I checked the route map. A place called Capreol seems the most likely. It's the start of the Ruel Subdivision, about three hundred miles of bush up above Lake Superior. This Capreol place is apparently where they split a lot of freights for Toronto, as well as adding on the Toronto section of the Canadian. A big railyard, easy to fill the tanks and keep the train isolated from people at the same time."

"And if they don't stop?"

"They'll run out of gas somewhere in the bush. Maybe not where they want to be."

"So what are you proposing?" asked Linberg.

"While they stop for fuel, we get ourselves on board," said Sagadore.

"We?" said Linberg.

The security man grinned. "I thought you'd want to come along."

"Your estimation of the state of my mental health aside, how did you figure on getting aboard? The doors are booby-trapped, remember?"

"I've figured it out," said Sagadore. "I went over that plan of the train the Canadians put together. According to it, the dinette is an old Budd Vista Dome. Our terrorists are good, but unless they know an awful lot about those cars, they probably overlooked the car's slop door."

"Slop door?"

Sagadore nodded. "It's behind the counter area, down by the floor. If you were looking at it, you'd probably think it was the door to a storage cupboard or something. Anyway, it probably hasn't been used in years — they were put into the cars long before anybody worried about pollution or littering. They were used to dump garbage en route."

"You're kidding," said Linberg, interested now.

"Nope," said Sagadore, shaking his head. "About eighteen inches high and four feet long. Easily big enough for a man to get through. All you'd need is a crowbar."

"Not to mention blind faith," Linberg added. "What happens if you're crowbarring while one of the terrorists happens to be standing in the car?"

"There won't be any terrorists. Remember, they'll be vulnerable, and they'll be expecting something to go down while they're stopped. Most of them will be outside the train, and on the other side from where we'll go in."

"How do you know that?"

"Because the Canadians do it the same way we do. On an east-west run, the train will almost always fuel from the right side; west-east, they fuel from the train's left. It's the way the pumps are set up."

"You're sure?"

"I checked. I collared a senior conductor down in the station. He's worked that run for twenty-five years. The station is on the right, and most of the yard trackage is on the left. They'll be expecting any action to come from the station side. According to the conductor, there's a lot of open space to the left, and nothing but dense bush when you reach the edge of the yard. You could never hide a bunch of soldiers, but if we're in place before the train gets in, we should be able to find enough cover for the two of us."

"And how are we supposed to get there before the train does? How far is it from Montreal?"

"A little under four hundred miles. There's a guy at Dorval Airport with a Piper Navaho who says he can have us in Sudbury in under two hours. From there, it's thirty miles by road to Capréol. If we left now, we could be there by midnight."

"You found out all of this while you were on your little constitutional' a while back?" asked Linberg.

Sagadore nodded. "I got tired of doing nothing."

"What's the ETA for the train?"

"Sometime between two and three in the morning. We'd have plenty of time."

"Okay," said Linberg. "Suppose we do get to this Capreol place, hunker down behind a bush, wait for the train, and manage to sneak on board. Then what? By my count, there are now nine terrorists aboard that train. Those are pretty lousy odds, two against nine, especially since they're armed and we're not."

"I've got my S&W in my attaché case," said Sagadore.

"You brought a gun with you from New York?" said Linberg. "That's illegal."

The security man shrugged. "So is what we're planning here."

"What *you're* planning. And have you thought about that end of it?"

"Sure," said Sagadore. "It'll cost me my job. But if it works, nobody's going to complain, and if it doesn't, we're probably going to be dead anyway. Think about it, Walt — when you come right down to it, we are the only ones who *can* do something. Everyone else is tied up in bureaucratic knots. I'm just an Amtrak employee and you're not with the Bureau anymore, so we'd be acting as private citizens." He paused, smiling weakly. "Almost," he added.

"This is crazy," muttered Linberg.

"No, it's not," said Sagadore. He stood up and began pacing from his chair to the window and back again. "It's necessary. When I figured out that Shenker and her people were taking the train into Canada, I knew we were up shit creek. You were right about these people. They're smart, and they know exactly what they're doing. They've got everybody running scared. By the time anybody in authority comes to a decision, it'll be all over. We've got to act now."

"And risk our lives," Linberg said.

"That's right," Sagadore replied. "It won't be the first time for either of us. As far as I'm concerned, I'll just be doing my job. I'm supposed to protect that train and the people on it, not to mention the Federal Reserve shipment. Call it professional integrity, if you want."

"That's a bit corny," said Linberg.

"Maybe," said Sagadore. "But it's true." He stopped pacing and looked across the room at the ex-FBI man. "I would have thought you felt the same way."

"Don't give me any guilt crap," said Linberg. "I'm too old to be swayed by phrases like 'devotion to duty'. I had enough of that with the Bureau." Then he smiled. "On the other hand, I'm not so old that I've lost my bloodhound instincts. I want these people so badly I can taste it."

"So you'll go?" said Sagadore.

"There's no fool like an old fool. I should know better, but yes, I'll go."

Annalise Shenker sat at the extreme rear of the lounge in the *Tremblant Park* and stared at the sleek radio set that stood on the coffee table in front of her. As in all the other cars, the *Tremblant Park*'s blinds were closed tight, the soft lighting in the car masking the lines of fatigue that were beginning to appear on the terrorist's face. Seated in the lounge with her were Paulette Baxter, still in her VIA uniform, Mohamet Kawi, and Dieter Haas. Lisa Ruffio was acting as a roving guard through the train, keeping a general eye on the passengers, while Amal Akbar stood guard in the front dome and Raoul Attendera kept watch a few feet above them in the dome of the *Tremblant Park*. In the locomotive cab, Sheila Teng kept the F unit moving, assisted by Jacques Cyr, who was also acting as an armed forward lookout. All the terrorists were connected to Mohamet Kawi's communications center in Bedroom B of the *Tremblant Park*, next door to the drawing room, which was now being used to house the remaining diplomats from the abandoned Amtrak lounge.

"Where did you find the radio?" asked Shenker.

"Bedroom B of the first American sleeping car," said Dieter Haas, his English slurred with a guttural Dutch accent. "According to the passenger list I took away from the Amtrak conductor, the space was reserved by a W. Sparling."

"Anything else?" asked Shenker. "Proper baggage?"

"Nothing," said Haas, shaking his head. "There were

signs that one of the ventilators had been tampered with — scratches. That is all."

"An aerial?" suggested Mohamet Kawi.

The Dutchman shrugged. "*Vielleicht*. It is possible."

"Our friends again," said Shenker, sweeping her hair back and holding it bunched against her neck. "We had forgotten about them."

"Who are you talking about?" asked Paulette Baxter. "What friends?"

"Somebody was trying to steal the currency shipment. Or at least it looks that way," answered Shenker. "They almost ruined everything."

"My God!" exclaimed Baxter. "Who are they?"

"We don't know," Shenker said patiently. "That is what we are trying to find out. With the radio, it becomes even more important. They may have been sending messages out."

"It is most unlikely," said Mohamet Kawi. "Such a radio has a very limited range. Still, these people represent a dangerous unknown. They must be found as quickly as possible."

"It will be difficult," said Haas. "I think we are carrying almost five hundred people now. They are all mixed together as though on a *viehwaggon*. Your cattle car. And we have more important things to do, I think."

"Maybe you are right," said Shenker. "But I don't like it." She glanced at her watch, frowning. "How long until we reach this place where we will refuel?" she asked, turning to Kawi.

"Three hours, perhaps a little less," said the Libyan. "I spoke with Sheila a few minutes ago, and she says there are no problems. My last transmission to the authorities seems to have had its effect. The line is fully open as I demanded. There will be no interruptions."

"Good," said Shenker. She closed her eyes briefly, pinching the bridge of her nose between a thumb and forefinger. "The motion and noise all the time are making my temper very short," she said slowly. She opened her eyes and looked at her companions. "It is probably doing the same to you. I am also aware of the pressures we are all under. But we still have a long way to go, and there is no margin for error, no place for those who lose their tempers or make mistakes. To succeed, we must remain calm while the rest of the world is confused. If we can do that, we will be remembered far into the future, and this will be the political coup of the century."

Harry Maxwell stood in the tiny cubicle of the VIA Daynighter toilet, his forehead against the cool glass of the opaque window, the monotonous thunder of the wheels droning loudly in his ears. Someone had banged angrily on the door a few minutes before, but had eventually given up to seek relief elsewhere. Harry was, at least for the moment, alone with his thoughts, and any kind of solitude on the overcrowded train was a miracle.

He stood for a few moments, enjoying the cool pressure of the window, and then he sat down on the toilet and lit a cigarette, staring up at the blank, painted metal ceiling above him. There was a fly perched upside down on one of the dull green rivets, and Harry smiled weakly, wondering if the minuscule creature had the slightest idea that it was being held hostage by a gang of ruthless terrorists. Harry took a drag on his cigarette and then held his hands out in front of him, examining them.

They were shaking, and not just from the movement of the train. The tiny shiverings were half from the creeping exhaustion that was beginning to exert its toll, and half from tension. He'd expected to be afraid during the robbery, but if things had gone according to plan, that would have been over an infinity ago. He wondered how long the human mind and body could take the kind of strain he'd been under before something cracked. He looked at his watch. It was ten-thirty. Twenty-four hours had passed since he'd boarded the Night Owl in Washington, and during that time he'd slept no more than a few hours. He knew beyond a shadow of a doubt that if something didn't happen soon he was going to burst like an overinflated balloon.

And it wasn't just him. It had been bad enough when it was only the Amtrak train. With the Canadian in tow as well, the doubling up of passengers had made things even worse. Food was running out, and the drinking water was down to a trickle. Apparently fear made you thirsty.

By force of numbers, Harry and the others had managed to commandeer a compartment in the first of the two sleeping cars behind the dining car, so they had some kind of privacy, but having six people in the cramped room was tension-producing in itself, and they had fallen into a pattern of regular visits to the bathroom every fifteen minutes or so. This was Harry's time, and he was beginning to wonder if the relatively fresh air and the few minutes of solitude were worth it; the air really wasn't much better outside the compartment, and the crowded corridors and cars were like something out of a Fellini nightmare. Six hundred people, all of them frightened and some of them hysterically so, were crammed into seven available cars, which were meant to hold barely half that many passengers at best. Babies were crying, people were moaning, and the stink indicated that at least one toilet had backed up already. A few people looked as though they were sleeping, but for most, the fear and the bright lights made rest impossible. And it was going to get worse.

Harry ground out his cigarette on the floor and leaned back, closing his eyes. Six hundred people, and if his little plan went wrong, a lot of them were going to get hurt. If Mottbrown was wrong or if something else screwed up, the train was going to be a charnel house.

According to the bespectacled model railroad enthusiast, the train was going to have to refuel before very long, since, with the Amtrak consist, it was now pulling at least sixteen cars. Howard was betting on a place called Capreol, somewhere east of Lake Superior. Using his own formula of the time it took between the clicks that marked off each length of rail, Harry had figured out their approximate speed and come up with an arrival time of somewhere between two and three in the morning. Assuming that nothing else happened in the meantime, Capreol would be the place to make their move. Howard's best guess was that the refueling would take at least fifteen or twenty minutes. Both Harry and Kettering, their new recruit, agreed that although the terrorists would be most alert to danger while they were stopped, they would also be most vulnerable. Mottbrown had assured them that it would take two people to do the actual refueling, and they could reasonably expect at least two more to be on guard, if not more. With at least one in the cab of the engine and one each in the dome cars, there wouldn't be many left to guard the occupants of the train. Beyond that, it was unlikely that the terrorists would be concerned about the passengers; their worries would center around another assault from the outside. Kettering's pistol with its five bullets wasn't much, but it was better than nothing, which was what they'd had before. If they were very lucky, they might be able to pick up another weapon from one of the other terrorists, but Harry wasn't counting on it.

He sighed and stood up. Somebody was rattling the door handle desperately. Time to go. He paused, his hand on the lock release. Yesterday he'd been a criminal in the making; today he was a hostage to terrorism. What would he be tomorrow? A free man?

Or a corpse?

During the early stages of the hijacking, there had been an almost festive sense of comradeship among the passengers. This is a common response in such situations, but inevitably, as time passes, the ebullient spirits begin to decay, to be replaced by widespread depression and an almost total loss of any feelings of self-determination. The hostage has virtually no say in the progression of events around him, and recognizing his impotence, he retreats within himself, responding only to authoritarian commands from the people holding him hostage. And so it was on the Amtrak/VIA train as they moved blindly through the deep forests of northern Ontario.

Paralleling the psychological atrophying of the hostages aboard the train was a steady deterioration in their physical environment. A number of the older passengers, unable to bear the mental strain, had begun complaining of chest pains and other ailments. Some of them who were actually suffering from heart problems had been moved into the already heavily taxed medical car, which had now overflowed into the next car behind. Medical supplies, limited from the beginning, were now almost totally gone, and the passengers injured in the coach vestibule explosion were in agony. The Amtrak cars, most of them fitted with holding-tank toilets, were filled with the stench of excrement as the tanks plugged and then overflowed, and most of the toilets in the VIA consist were backing up as well. On top of that, drinking water was failing, supplies of food were beginning to give out, and several of the cars were starting to overheat as the air-conditioning systems quit. There were men on board qualified to repair the heating machinery, but no one wanted to go anywhere near the electrical panels where the anthrax canisters were fitted, so nothing was done.

"Harry, for Christ's sake, are you in there?" It was Daniel's voice, and he sounded scared.

"Yeah. I'm here," muttered Harry, pulling open the door of the toilet cubicle. Instantly his nostrils were assaulted by the stench in the car. Automatically he began breathing through his mouth. "What's the matter now?" he asked his friend.

"A guy's gone crazy in one of the coaches. He got a knife from somewhere and he's threatening to slice up anyone who comes near him."

"Shit! That's all we need," said Harry, fatigue cracking his voice. "Has anyone tried to take him?"

"Not a chance," said Daniel, shaking his head. "He's backed up against one of the electrical panels and he's threatening to rip out the germ canister."

"What does he want?" asked Harry.

"Out," answered Daniel. "He wants to get off the train."

"He's not so crazy," Harry grunted.

"This is no time for jokes," said Daniel. "The guy's a nut case. If we don't do something, he's going to kill us all."

"What does Mark say?"

"He's for shooting him, of course," Daniel answered, his lip curling. "What do you expect from the soldier boy?"

"Ease off, Daniel. I know you've got a thing about soldiers, but Mark's never done anything to you. What about Kettering?"

"The cop? He says we should wait and see. They're both up there now. We tried to clear the car, but the guy said if anyone moved he'd rip the canister off the wall."

"What about our friendly jailers?" asked Harry.

"They don't know about it yet. And we've got to do something before they find out. If one of their people see him like that, they'll blow him away and probably half a dozen other people as well."

"So what am I supposed to do?" Harry asked wearily. "This isn't 'Naked City,' for Christ's sake. I'm not going to be able to talk him out of it."

"Just come, Harry. Check it out. Please."

"All right."

Stepping discreetly into the coach three cars ahead gave Harry the queasy sensation of having walked into a "Twilight Zone" episode. The car — the coach just before the terrorists' no-man's-land — was jammed with people, their faces pale and sickly in the thin light from the overhead fixtures. Both toilets at Harry's end of the car had overflowed, and the odor in the vestibule was almost overpowering. Gagging, Harry edged forward, Daniel behind him, and stared down the length of the aisle. Everyone in the car was silent, with the exception of a single child crying noisily in its mother's arms about halfway up the car. Beyond her, standing jammed against the bulkhead at the head end, was a thin, balding man in a rumpled sweat-stained white shirt. One hand, braced against the window beside him, held a large carving knife. The other hand was touching the thermos-sized canister clipped onto the electrical panel. The open door of the panel swung with each rocking movement of the train, banging with an erratic rhythm as it hit the bulkhead every few seconds.

Harry lifted his arm and wiped away the sweat that was starting to pool under his eyes. The air conditioning in the car had given up the ghost long ago, and beyond the awful smell, the air was stiflingly close.

"Jesus," he muttered. "It's got to be a hundred degrees in here." Blinking, he peered down the aisle again. "Where are Mark and Kettering?"

"You can't see them from here," said Daniel. "Cavendish is between the two seats second from the front. The cop is across the aisle."

"I think Mark is right," said Harry. "There's no way to take him out without shooting."

"The cop doesn't want to do it. He figures if the terrorists hear a shot from one of us, we'll all get it. He's right."

"So suggest something," said Harry. The train lurched heavily into a turn, and even from eighty feet away Harry could see the standing man's hand clench on the canister.

"Another couple like that, and he's going to peel that thing off the wall and into our laps," whispered Daniel.

"Who is he?" asked Harry.

"His name is Hafner. Bob Hafner. Kettering got that from one of the other passengers."

"Anybody know what set him off?" asked Harry.

"He got into a fight with the guy next to him. The other guy broke Hafner's glasses. From the looks of it, he's half blind without them. Anyway, Hafner went up to the dining car and came back with the knife and started hacking away at the other guy. He's still there, on the floor in front of the seat. Nobody knows how badly he's hurt, but he hasn't made a move or a sound in the last ten minutes."

"Dead?"

"Maybe, or just lying low," said Daniel. "The big thing in our favor is Hafner's nearsightedness. That's why he hasn't raised hell about us coming in. He can't see this far. That's how I got out to get you."

"The blade on that knife is about a foot long," Harry commented. "He couldn't miss if he was completely blind, Daniel."

"So it's a stalemate? What happens when one of our bad guys appears? We'll be up shit creek."

"This *is* shit creek," said Harry, wrinkling his nose. He sighed. "Okay. I'll go up there and talk to him. You keep behind me so he doesn't see you. When I'm close enough, drop down onto the floor and get to Kettering. I'll try to come up with something, but if it starts to look bad, Kettering shoots. Got it?"

"Okay."

They started forward, Harry lightly gripping the back of the seats on either side as he moved. At the edges of his vision he could see the faces of the passengers, all of them taut with fear, eyes wide. By now there was nothing but the sound of the clattering wheels; even the baby had stopped crying. At thirty feet the man with the knife noticed Harry for the first time. He went rigid, his knife hand coming forward and making skewering motions. The other hand clasped the top of the canister.

"Who is it? Who's there?" he called out. Harry stopped dead in his tracks. Dropping down to the floor, Daniel Pendergast scuttled ahead, below the man's line of sight.

Harry kept his eyes up and forward, ignoring his friend's movements.

"My name is Harry Maxwell, Mr. Hafner. I understand you want to get off the train."

"You bet, you bet," said the man, sputtering. "I mean this is an outrage. Outrage. I've got obligations. Yes, yes. Obligations. Joanne, of course, she'll be worrying."

Bananas, thought Harry. "We're all in the same boat, Mr. Hafner," he said, interrupting gently. "And we're all scared. But what you're doing isn't going to help."

"I've thought it out! I know how!" bellowed the man. "We can all get out of here. Break a window. With a suitcase. They'll never know."

At the head end of the coach, Harry saw movement, and he looked away from Hafner for a moment. It was the terrorist leader, the woman. He swallowed hard and looked back at Hafner.

"Put the knife down, Mr. Hafner. Right now," he demanded. The crazed man stared myopically and then began to laugh, a long, choking bray. Harry saw the head-end door begin to open and he froze. The woman was carrying a small aluminum-colored machine gun in her hand. He made eye contact with her and his stomach twisted. He felt like some kind of animal mesmerized by a cobra; the beautiful woman's eyes were dead, and death was the only message they carried.

"Hafner! The knife!" commanded Harry in a last attempt. The man didn't pay any attention, his laugh pealing out horribly. Harry stared, dumbstruck, as the woman entered the coach, gently adjusting the slide on the weapon in her hand. She stepped forward around the toilet cubicle, ignoring the movement of the train, balancing easily, still hidden from the babbling man with the knife. Without thinking, Harry moved forward, reaching for Hafner, who immediately began brandishing the knife.

"Get away! Get away!" he screamed, lunging clumsily. Harry reeled back and the terrorist made her move, taking a final step and swinging the tiny machine gun up in a single smooth motion. Harry watched as her long, slim finger curled on the trigger and squeezed twice, carefully. Hafner's face opened up like a piece of ruptured fruit, the features pushing inward as the flailing lead, its passage marked by two brief pops, found its target.

185

Almost magically, the knife dropped from his fingers and he began to crumple. With two steps, the terrorist reached the canister and peeled the dying fingers away from the device. Hafner dropped. She stepped back, ignoring the corpse, the machine gun dropping to her side. She stared at Harry for a moment.

"You were trying to be a hero," she said, her words brittle and precise. "Heroism is for fools. I suggest you remember that. I do thank you for your distraction, though." She nudged Hafner with one booted foot. "The man is dead, and so is the other one on the floor, apparently. Remove the bodies."

She looked at Harry for a long, considered moment, then turned away, leaving as she'd come, as though the death of Hafner had been nothing more than a slightly irritating interlude. Harry slumped against the seat on his left, vaguely aware of Daniel and Norm Kettering rising from their hiding places a few feet away. The sudden violence had drained him, and he felt as though the woman's eyes had burned twin holes in his skull.

"Oh God," he whispered. "I can't take much more of this."

Part Four

THE SHIELD

Whoever said "fools rush in where angels fear to tread" hit the nail right on the head. We were fools, and Capreol, Ontario, isn't the kind of place you're likely to find an angel even at the best of times.

Harry Maxwell,
the Playboy Interview

Chapter 11

Tuesday, June 28
Time: 3:13 A.M. EDT
Distance: 1,274 miles/2,050 km.

If Harry Maxwell and the other passengers of the hostage train had been able to see out of the shrouded windows of the cars, they would have noticed a slow but inexorable change in the landscape across which they were traveling, and someone like Harry might well have made the observation that as the situation deteriorated on board, the countryside was also becoming less and less civilized.

For the bulk of their journey, the captives had moved through territory that had been tamed by man for centuries, and some kind of human settlement was never more than ten or twenty miles away. But it was different now. For the first hundred miles or so after they skirted Ottawa, there were still farms and settlements strung along the twisting thread of the Ottawa River; but as the train swung northwest through Chalk River and Mattawa, the terrain became rugged, dense cedar forest spotted with lakes, always with the somber bulk of the Laurentian Mountains rising in the distance on the right. Indian legends called it Nipissing, the Land of the Sorcerers, while less romantically inclined geologists identified it as the Mattawa Fault, a 600-million-year-old fracture valley known for its ochre deposits, on the southern fringe of the massive granite landform known as the Canadian Shield.

The stations on the main line, all of which had been advised of the situation aboard the train, were dark, and no attempt was made to interfere with the consist as it streamed through the gathering darkness at a steady *fifty* miles per hour, just about the maximum speed for the poorly traveled roadbed.

There were eyes in the night, however, even though no direct action was being taken. A recon group from the

Canadian Forces base at Petawawa watched as the train sped through the camp artillery range, and Ontario Provincial Police detachments from Renfrew, Chalk River, and North Bay also monitored its progress.

Not that there was anything to see. The train was a ghost, windowshades drawn, running lights extinguished, and moaning air horns silent as she passed eerily by, the thunder of her wheels on the rails echoing for a moment, then fading as though the train had never been there at all.

It was full night as the consist reached North Bay on the eastern end of Lake Nipissing, moving above the town and switching onto the Canadian Pacific line, pausing briefly while Jacques Cyr used his master switch key to put them on the northern tracks. The change went unseen, since the three OPP spotter planes had been recalled half an hour before because of the increasing darkness and the danger of a crash into the gloomy, all-encompassing forest that stretched north to James Bay and south to Lake Huron. It was an area larger than the entire state of New York and had a population density roughly equivalent to that of Outer Mongolia. Ahead lay nothing but almost a thousand miles of virtually impenetrable bush. A surveyor, mapping the route a hundred years before, had described it as "a monstrous terrain, empty wasteland as savage as any on the planet, where rocky ribs burst through scanty soil as in a decayed skeleton. Intervening hollows hold muskeg swamps which gulp down yards of fill before providing firm footing for a roadbed." In a century, nothing had happened to change that description.

Wesler, the FBI inspector who had come to Montreal with Frank Sagadore and Walter Linberg, sat at the all-night lunch counter in Central Station drinking coffee and halfheartedly picking at something that superficially resembled a cinnamon Danish. The last meeting had broken up over two hours before, but the troubled man had been unable to sleep. Frustrated, he'd come down from the hotel into the virtually empty main concourse of the station to think, his only companions the lunch-counter waitress and an occasional sweeper working his way across the huge, vault-roofed station.

Swiveling around on the chrome and vinyl stool, Wesler rested his back against the counter and sipped at his coffee, his eyes finding the clock suspended from the ceiling a hundred yards away down the concourse. It was 3:21; according to the last estimate from the Montreal Central Traffic Control office, the train would be almost into Capreol now, ready to take on more fuel.

The meetings had accomplished nothing except to muddy an already complex situation. Wesler had argued for immediate action of some kind, but no one had backed him. The RCMP and the Canadian military seemed content to wait for the terrorists to make some kind of move away from the train. For some reason they assumed that the terrorists wouldn't harm the passengers before making a break, but Wesler wasn't so confident. The Canadians, and the U.S. State Department representative from their embassy in Ottawa, were adamant. With the added complication of a potential anthrax outbreak, they weren't going to take any chances. The terrorists would be allowed to move as they wished, and when they left the relative safety of the train they would be followed. Only when they were absolutely sure that there was no danger to either the hostages or the public at large would the authorities act. Until then, there would be nothing except surveillance by teams assembled in Capreol, Sioux Lookout, and Winnipeg on the northern line, and Thunder Bay and Kenora on the lower route, in case they switched the train that way. It was generally assumed that the terrorists would try to leave the train somewhere between Capreol and Winnipeg, and several large surveillance and tracking aircraft were being flown into Thunder Bay to begin a grid search as soon as it was light. In addition, Ontario Provincial Police detachments at Gogama, Folyet, Hornepayne, Nakina, Armstrong, and Sioux Lookout had also been put on alert since they were the closest police authorities to the main line.

None of which made the slightest sense to Wesler. He'd been shown the route of the train on a regular Rolph McNally road map of Ontario, and the Canadian Forces bases and OPP detachments were clearly marked. If he could see them, so could the terrorists, which meant that it was unlikely they'd try to escape anywhere along that part of the line. It was equally absurd to assign forces to Winnipeg and Thunder Bay; so far the terrorists had done

191

everything they could to avoid major urban centers, and Wesler doubted that they had any intention of changing their strategy now.

When the possibility that the terrorists might try to escape into northern Ontario had first been broached, it seemed reasonably logical, but the more Wesler thought about it, the less convinced he became. To escape meant that they would almost certainly have a plane stashed somewhere, and while they might avoid the normal radar nets by flying low, just where would they fly? To the north there was nothing but the Arctic Circle, and south meant the major centers of the United States. Wesler was sure that the headlong flight of the Night Owl was far from over.

The FBI man turned around in his seat again, dropped a quarter tip beside his empty cup, and left the lunch counter, walking slowly back across the concourse to the tunnel exit that led back to the Queen Elizabeth Hotel. He decided to phone Linberg's room first thing in the morning and talk over the situation with him. If it didn't look as though any definite action was about to be taken in the case, he was going to ask to be taken off it. After almost twenty years with the Bureau, he could smell a fiasco from a mile off, and this case was already stinking to high heaven.

"How much farther?" whispered Harry, his voice barely audible over the whirring of the fan in the darkened compartment. The small rubber-bladed fan, high in the upper corner of the tiny room, did little more than shift the stale air around, but it was better than nothing. Mottbrown, crouched on the floor, peeked out through a half-inch crack in the blind covering the window.

"Two miles," he whispered back. "We just went by the post, and we're slowing down."

"Quiet!" breathed Mark Cavendish from his position beside the half-open door leading into the corridor. "Someone's coming!"

Howard Mottbrown eased the blind down carefully, and everyone in the room settled back into a position of sleep. Harry fought off the urge to open his eyes as the footsteps passed by, and waited until he heard the far door of the sleeping car open and then shut again.

"Catch anything?" he asked when he was sure they were gone. Cavendish levered himself up off the floor and peeked around the door.

"Yeah," he said, easing back into the room. "Three of them. The good-looking one, the German, and one of the Arabs."

"They're going out through the blown door in the coach," Pendergast suggested. "That way they won't have to fiddle with any of their booby traps."

"Makes sense," Harry agreed. "But how many more are there?"

"I haven't seen the other Arab or the Spanish-looking one for a long time," said Adrian Tucker. "Maybe they're the ones in the dome cars."

"And the man who got on in Montreal went forward with the conductor just after we left the station. He hasn't come back, so he's probably up in the engine."

"That leaves the Italian woman and the one you saw in the VIA uniform. Figure them to be in the rear observation car," said Cavendish. "Unless there's someone we don't know about, that covers it."

"Okay," said Harry. "Howard says it'll take two people to gas up the train and one to stand guard. That'll be the good-looking one. She's no fool, so you can bet she'll stay pretty close to the coach entrance, just in case something goes wrong."

"They've got it pretty well covered," said Norm Kettering, wincing as he shifted his back into a more comfortable position against the wall of the compartment. "Two in front, two in back, and the two guys in the dome cars; they'll be able to see anything coming."

"From outside, but not from in here," said Harry.

"So how do we play it?" asked Kettering.

"It's got to be the guy in the front dome," Harry answered. "Like we talked about. If we can get him, we can hold the whole back of the train and keep most of their firepower forward. Then all we have to worry about are the two in the rear observation car and the guy in the other dome."

"Who probably has a machine gun," muttered Daniel.

"It doesn't matter what he's got," said Harry. "You can

bet your socks they'll haul ass as soon as the fighting starts and then we've got the train working for us. It's going to be just as much of a bottleneck for them to get to us as the other way around."

"So we sweat it out?" asked Kettering.

"Until someone comes up with a better idea," said Harry. "The trouble is, we've got to make sure we keep the people in the observation car from coming forward. Every time I've seen any of these people, they've been carrying walkie-talkies, so if the guy in the front dome gets wise before we take him out, the others'll be all over us."

"So we take him out silently," said Cavendish out of the semi-darkness.

"How are we going to do that?" asked Daniel.

"With this," said the Vietnam veteran, holding up his right hand, the twin hooks gleaming in the dim light from the corridor.

"Jesus!" whispered Harry.

"Crude," said Cavendish. "But it'll work."

"As long as you can get to him," murmured Daniel.

"The lights will be off in the dome," answered Cavendish. "He wouldn't be able to see out if they were on. And there should be enough background noise to cover me."

"Go for the eyes," Kettering said calmly. "Those hooks aren't sharp enough to cut through his clothes, and maybe not even his skin. See if you can dig the hooks into an eye socket and then fish around. It might not kill him right away, but it'll keep him away from the walkie-talkie. You'll need somebody to back you, too, preferably with something heavy enough to beat the guy's brains in."

"I'll do it," Adrian Tucker said thickly, horrified apprehension in every syllable.

"Thanks, Adrian, but — " Cavendish began.

"I want you to go and find Stackpole," Harry cut in. "I want you to stick to him. If we get into trouble, we might just need a hole card the bad guys don't know about."

"Don't bullshit me, Harry," said the actor. "Why don't you just admit you want me out?"

"Because it's not true," Harry lied. "I want you hidden

away, not out of the way." There was a cold silence between the two men, but finally Tucker nodded.

"All right, Harry," he said softly. "If that's how you want it."

"Why three at the head end?" asked Howard Mottbrown, breaking the tension. "And what should I be doing?" he added.

"Daniel is going to keep watch at the foot of the stairs leading up to the dome," Harry answered. "If any of the terrorists climb back on board too soon, we're cooked. And I want you just inside the next car back. As soon as we take care of the creep upstairs, I want to build a barricade. Luggage, seat cushions, whatever you can find. Adrian, you do the same at your end. Any questions?" There was a momentary silence and then Howard Mottbrown spoke up. "I have a suggestion," he offered quietly. "It might increase your chances of . . . dealing with the man in the dome car."

"Shoot," said Harry.

"Well, you may have noticed that there are glassed-in fire boxes in most of the cars. All you have to do is break the seals to get into them."

"Axes," said Norman Kettering. "They've got great bloody axes in each one."

"That's right," said Mottbrown. "And the fire extinguishers themselves might be useful. If Mr. Pendergast had one ready, he could delay anyone getting back onto the train for a few moments at least."

"You're a wonder, Howard," said Harry, grinning. "Axes, hooks, and fire extinguishers. What a crew."

"I gather I'm supposed to hold my position," said Kettering.

"I can't see any other way," said Harry. "You've only got one gun, and any kind of firefight is going to get you killed, not to mention a whole bunch of other people. In fact, it might not be a bad idea to tell the people in that car to move up some."

"It's a sleeper, isn't it?" said the policeman. "It's crowded enough already without making it worse, and anyone in there should be able to keep out of the line of fire."

"All right," said Harry. "Use your own judgment."

The train gave a heavy clanking lurch and slowed even more, the brake shoes beginning to squeal against the bare metal of the wheels. Howard Mottbrown tipped up the blind fractionally and looked out. "This is it," he said. "We're still on the main line, just going past the station, I think." There was a pause. "Yes, that's it. It's all dark. They've got all the lights off in the station."

"Nobody wants to be a target," said Cavendish. "Let's just hope they don't try to rush the train."

"We're going past the station, into the switchyard," said Mottbrown. "Three — no, four tracks on this side. There'll be more on the other."

"I wonder how far ahead the gas line is?" murmured Harry.

"There'll be more than one," answered Mottbrown, still crouched at the window. "They'll use the one deepest into the yard, I expect, to keep the train as far away from the station as they can."

"You think they have soldiers out there?" asked Adrian Tucker.

"Probably," said Cavendish. "But they won't be any help to us."

The train lurched again, brakes squealing, and then came to a jarring stop.

"All right, that's it," said Harry. "Let's go."

They moved out of the compartment, checking first to make sure the corridor was clear. Harry, Mark Cavendish, Howard Mottbrown, and Daniel turned right, moving toward the head end, while Kettering and Adrian Tucker went in the opposite direction. Except for the steady rumbling vibration of the idling diesel, and the hiss of air bleeding from the brake valves, the train was silent.

Harry paused at the door leading out of the sleeping car and closed his eyes, trying to visualize the plan Howard Mottbrown had sketched for them. They had been in the second sleeper forward from the observation car, which left the Canadian dining car and the Daynighter between them and the forward lounge/dome car. Beyond that were the two regular Canadian coaches and then the Night Owl, minus its own observation car. If the terrorists were using the demolished front end of the first Amtrak coach as an entry/exit point, that meant there should be two sleepers, the dinette, and a coach between the first coach and the Canadian train. Almost four hundred feet of no-man's-land for the terrorists to cross if the man in the dome/lounge managed to raise an alarm. A minute and a half at a dead run — not much of a margin.

Turning his head, Harry saw Mark Cavendish using his pincer hand to twist off the wire-and-lead seal on the glass-fronted emergency case. Once it snapped, Daniel opened the door and pulled the small ax from its retaining clips, hefting the tool in his hand. It had a blade on one end of the head, and a pick on the other.

"Welcome to the Lizzie Borden Amateur Hour," muttered the artist, grinning wolfishly.

"We take out the guy in the dome as fast as we can," said Harry, ignoring his friend's comment. "If things are still quiet, we go up to the head of the Canadian train and help Howard with the barricade. Mark and I will bring down whatever weapons the guy has up there. Let's hope he's got enough firepower to fend off his pals up front."

"What about the people in the coaches?" asked Mottbrown. "Do I say anything?"

"No," said Harry, shaking his head. "Not yet. The last thing we need is for a herd of freaked-out passengers to come swarming back into that dome lounge before we've offed the one upstairs. Just ignore them for the time being. I don't think anyone will so much as say boo. I guarantee you they're just as scared as we are."

"Yeah, shitless," said Cavendish.

"Let's get moving," said Daniel nervously. "We're wasting time. And as far as I'm concerned, any passengers who don't want to help better not get in the way."

"Agreed," said Cavendish.

As quietly as possible, Harry pulled up on the handle of the door and dragged it back. Behind him, Daniel reached up and clipped the door into an open position against the bulkhead. Harry moved quickly across the open vestibule and peered into the car ahead — the dining car. It was eerily empty, the lights dimmed, each table set, right down to crowned napkins and baskets of sugar packets for the first dinner sitting, which had never come. As in all the other cars, the blinds were fully drawn, blocking any view of the outside.

"It's clear," said Harry, turning his head. He opened the door and went into the car, followed by Cavendish and Mottbrown. Once again, Daniel paused to lock back the door. If they had to beat a retreat, he didn't want to waste time hauling open doors.

They walked the length of the car to the far door, and as he'd done before, Harry crossed the vestibule first. The next car was the Daynighter, now being used as a makeshift infirmary for the passengers wounded in the explosion the night before. Here, too, the lights were dimmed; peering through the glass, Harry couldn't see much activity. The seats nearest to the door had been fully reclined and Harry could make out their occupants — bodies with faces covered by blankets. He swallowed hard and motioned his friends ahead.

As they went down the aisle, Harry counted eighteen patients, some of them roughly bandaged and all of them apparently asleep. Upon reaching the midpoint of the car, Harry stopped as a figure rose into the aisle, blocking his path. It was a man in his mid-forties, dressed in suit pants, a white shirt, and a rumpled vest. There was a stethoscope looped around his neck, and Harry could see the dim outline of a doctor's bag on the seat beside him.

"May I ask what you think you're doing?" said the man.

"Please get out of my way," said Harry.

"I asked you a question," snapped the man. "Don't you realize that there are people with guns up there?" he said, jerking a thumb over his shoulder. "I won't let you jeopardize these patients and the other passengers on this train with any false heroics from a — "

Mark Cavendish stepped forward and tucked the twin hooks of his prosthesis into the man's collar. He twisted, pulling the man forward until their faces were only an inch apart.

"Get out of our way, doctor, or I'll rip your fucking throat out." He removed his claw and pushed the man backwards slightly.

"Vietnam veteran," said Harry. "You never know with them. He might do it." Wordlessly the doctor stepped aside.

"Mad as a hatter," said Daniel, lifting the ax up onto his shoulder as he slipped past the goggle-eyed physician. Howard Mottbrown, following the other three, simply raised his eyebrows and smiled. The doctor sat down in his seat and stared after them.

The group assembled at the head of the car, waiting for Harry's next move.

"I thought we could barricade here," he whispered. "But the doctor is right. These people can't be moved, and there's too much chance of someone getting hurt."

"So what do we do?" asked Daniel.

"Same as before," replied Harry, "except Howard waits at the bottom of the steps with you. When I give the word that we've nailed the sucker upstairs, you and Howard get your asses up to the front of the car. It'll work even better there — you can pile up tables and some of those armchairs. Cram them into the space right in front of the door. It opens inward, doesn't it, Howard?"

"That's right," said the little man.

"Anything we should know about the dome car?" asked Harry.

"There's only one way up to it," answered Mottbrown. "A half-twist spiral staircase at the end of the car closest to us. Eight or nine steps to the top. The dome is about sixty feet long, with two rows of double seats, twelve on each side. The seats are raised up about a foot, so the aisle is recessed. Unless he's broken the windows, he'll only have two ways to fire, through the front or through the rear; they're the only two windows that open."

"He's almost sure to have broken them," said Cavendish. "He wouldn't restrict his field of fire like that."

"Great," said Harry. "If the windows are out, that means there'll be more sound from outside to cover us."

"We hope," muttered Daniel.

"Let's go," said Harry. "And for Christ's sake, keep it quiet."

Amal Akbar stood at the front of the dome car's upper level, his eye glued to the viewfinder of the tripod-mounted Rank SS-32 night sight as he moved it through a slow 180 degrees from right to left, his view encompassing everything on the south side of the train and each sweep taking a carefully counted-out nine seconds. He knew that Raoul Attendera was doing the same thing in the rear dome, covering the station side and thus protecting Akbar's back. The Libyan's walkie-talkie was within a few inches of his right hand on the shelf created by the forward curve of the dome, set to the Channel One frequency that would immediately alert the others in case there was trouble. Beside it on the shelf, his square-barreled Walther Olympic pistol lay ready, slide drawn and released, a .32-caliber wad-cutter already in the chamber. The pistol looked more like something you'd see at a shooting match, but Akbar fancied himself a marksman, and the two-and-a-half-pound weapon had been his personal choice from the St. Augustine haul. More to the point, considering his present situation, one of the M-60s "liberated" from the Delta Group squad was propped up on the seat in front of him in case there was an attack. Hours before, he had taken the precaution of using the machine gun's heavy butt to smash out the thick windows of the dome, giving him a full range of fire. Unfortunately the broken windows also let in the cool night air, and he'd spent the last four hours of his duty chilled to the bone as the wind and the northern latitude conspired to drop the temperature down into the high forties. Akbar, raised in a climate where it rarely went below eighty, was suffering, every muscle and joint stiff with the unaccustomed cold.

For the last few minutes, though, his chill had been forgotten, lost in the general anxiety of being stopped in the station, the dome and his position an obvious target if any of the men out there in the shadows decided to take a potshot at him. So far, the steady track of the night sight had revealed nothing except rows of barren track, random groupings of boxcars and tankers, and finally the dark line of trees at the outer perimeter of the switchyard.

But they were there, he knew that. *L'ihudi halluf*. Jew pigs, all of them, waiting in the darkness. *Mayoukounsh*. Cowards, too afraid to come out of the shadows and fight like men. Afraid to die. He wiped the line of sweat off his upper lip and felt a chill go down his back. How many? A dozen, twenty, fifty? How many to kill Amal Atsuk Akbar? How many bullets would stitch his body, and how many would die at his hand before he fell?

"Weld l'gahba!" — son of a whore — he muttered, wiping the recurring line of sweat away once more. How much longer would they be? It had been hours since he'd been relieved, and his bladder was near bursting.

Several years before, Amal Akbar had watched a television news report about a Soviet athlete, a high diver. The diver had tried a particularly difficult combination, and as he somersaulted down toward the water, his head had smashed into the concrete diving platform. The man was knocked instantly unconscious, and after a couple of days in a coma, he died. Akbar had been fascinated by the tape of the accident, and many times since, he'd found himself thinking about it, wondering if the last thought, the final reality in the man's brain, had been the terrible pain as his skull was shattered by the diving board. One moment, the almost orgasmic feeling as the dive began. Then, a fraction of a second later, overwhelming agony; a near instantaneous turnabout from pleasure to pain, life to death, without warning or premonition. Akbar, who had never consciously feared death, simply because he refused to accept the possibility of it for himself, had been annoyed by the diver's end. To him, dying was a time for ritual and not just a matter-of-fact erasure of existence. In the end, of course, an individual has very little say in the matter, and so it was for Amal Akbar.

The stainless-steel hooks caught Akbar in the corner of his right eye socket then twisted downward, snagging the globe of the eye and rupturing it as well as crushing the optic nerve and tearing through the internal carotid artery. The hooks dragged Akbar away from the night sight, shrieking with agony, the steel biting deeper into the frontal lobe of his brain. His entire consciousness was concentrated on the raging horror of his eye, and he was barely aware of the second blow as Harry's ax sliced into his neck, cutting through the thick muscles of the trapezius and splenius, finally lodging at an angle with the near end of the blade against the sixth cervical vertebra, while the far edge lay in the foaming, bloody mess of Akbar's esophagus and trachea. Had the blow come more from the side, the Libyan probably would have been decapitated, but as it was, when Harry released his single-handed grip on the handle, the ax remained in Akbar's neck, a grotesque centerpiece for the fountain of blood that was spraying in all directions. Dead now, the terrorist sagged to the floor of the dome, dragging Mark Cavendish off balance as the man's partially severed head flopped forward. The Vietnam vet grunted harshly and pulled the deadly prosthesis out of Akbar's eye socket. Harry, on the verge of being sick, tugged at the ax handle, silently wishing that he was anywhere else but where he was. As the ax came free and Akbar's corpse slithered completely prone, there was a stuttering flash of light up ahead, followed by the popcorn crackle of automatic weapons fire.

"Forget the ax!" Cavendish yelled. "Grab the guns!"

Harry nodded and grabbed the match pistol off the shelf, then dragged the M-60 off the seat across from Akbar's night sight. By the time he had them both, Cavendish was already heading down the stairs to the lower level of the car, and as Harry hit the top step there was a powerful lurch. An instant later the train began to move again.

During the long hours since the capturing of the VIA Rail Canadian in Montreal, Wanda Jenkins Margay and Wolfgang Groz had done more than simply exchange their life stories. Wanda had revealed the toilet hidden by the drop-seat that Groz was sitting on, and using a seemingly infinite supply of vitamin and patent medicine bottles, she had kept herself busy flushing messages down the waste pipe, which lead directly to the tracks below. The messages, repeated several times, explained the situation and gave what little information they had about the composition of the terrorist group. It wasn't much, but it kept her from feeling totally useless. For his part, Groz had made a complete inventory of both his own and Wanda's personal belongings. By the time the train had reached the Petawawa River, a little more than a hundred miles west of Ottawa, the fighter-pilot-turned-chemist was busy at work on what he hoped would be an effective weapon to use against the terrorists if the opportunity arose.

After half an hour, Wanda Jenkins Margay could no longer control her curiosity. She'd said nothing when he emptied a rather large bottle of schnapps from his own suitcase into the sink, and she had remained silent when, using a makeshift funnel contrived from his ticket folder, he'd replaced the liquor with a small bottle of rubbing alcohol from her own belongings; but the crumbled charcoal tablets she used for occasional flatulence, and the bar of hand soap powdered with the edge of his Swiss Army knife, couldn't reasonably be ignored.

"I hope you don't think it rude, but may I ask what you're doing?" she said.

Groz, using the Formica shelf over the washbasin as a workbench, looked across the small cubicle and smiled. "Napalm," he replied. "Or at least an ersatz form of it."

"I'm afraid I don't understand," said the old lady politely. "What exactly is napalm?"

"Jellied gasoline," answered Groz. "An incendiary." Using the edge of his hand, he brushed the soap powder onto a sheet of paper torn from his address book, then transferred it to the funnel. "*Volkommen*," he muttered wryly. "Perfect. I have everything now except the petrol."

"Must it be gasoline?" asked Wanda.

"Not necessarily," said Groz, sitting back on the toilet-cover seat. "Anything with a hydrocarbon base would do. Benzol, benzene, toluene."

"I don't know about any of those," said Wanda. "But would cleaning solvent be of any use? I understand it's quite flammable."

"Most certainly," said Groz, raising an eyebrow. "Don't tell me you also carry cleaning fluid with you on your travels."

"No," Wanda said primly. "Although there have been times when it would have been useful. But I think I know where you might obtain some."

"Yes?" prompted Groz.

"Just outside the door," said Wanda. "At the end of the car. They have little maintenance cupboards. I think I've seen cleaning materials there."

"Wonderful!" said Groz. He stood up, went to the door of the roomette, and opened it. He disappeared for a few moments and then returned, grinning broadly and carrying a half-gallon plastic container of Varsol. An hour later, with the soap, alcohol, charcoal, and rubbing alcohol mixed in their proper ratios, the schnapps bottle, the bottle containing the rubbing alcohol, and an economy-sized jar of Vitamin B-12 capsules had been transformed into lethal firebombs, each one sealed with wadded toilet paper and topped with an igniter made of wooden match heads.

"Now what?" asked Wanda, eyeing the pitifully small arsenal of bottles arranged on the washbasin shelf.

"We wait for the right moment," answered Groz.

Both Wanda and Wolfgang Groz had dozed off by the time the train reached Capreol, but the sudden stop brought them out of their light slumber and they were both wide awake a few moments later when the knock came. Wanda opened her mouth to answer, but Groz put a finger to his lips, gesturing for silence.

"The stick," he whispered. She nodded and handed him the walking stick. He twisted the handle carefully and slid the blade out of its camouflaged sheath. Standing, he reached out and flipped the toggle switch on the wall panel, killing everything but the faint blue night light in the ceiling. The knock came again.

"Yes?" said Groz.

The door handle rattled, but Groz had taken the precaution of throwing the latch before he made his fire bottles.

"Open the door, please," said a muffled voice.

"Just a moment," said Groz. Holding the dagger in one hand, he unlatched the door and stepped back. He kept the stick low, angled upward at his side. "It is open," he said.

The door slid back. A man stood silhouetted in the opening, a gun in his hand. He was tall and broad-shouldered. Groz moved away from the wall in a single motion, bringing the knife up quickly, the point slipping in under the man's chin, the needle point just touching the skin. The man jerked back, but the ex-fighter pilot moved with him, keeping the point where it was. The big man's gun hand never moved.

"Please put that down," said the big man. "I'm a policeman. My name is Kettering."

"*Sicher*," said Groz. "So you say."

"I can prove it," said the man, speaking urgently. "Look, mister, we don't have any time to waste. I'm trying to save all our asses, and you're getting in the way. All I'm trying to do is get anyone in this car out of the line of fire."

"You said you could prove you were a policeman," said Groz calmly. "Please do so."

"In my inside breast pocket," said Kettering. "My ID case."

"Frau Margay, if you please," said Groz.

Hesitantly, Wanda stood up and approached the burly

204

man in the doorway. She looked at Groz, and he smiled encouragingly. As delicately as possible, trying not to actually come in contact with the man, she pinched back his lapel and reached into the inside pocket of his suit jacket. She pulled out a small leather case and opened it.

"Norman Kettering," she read, squinting in the dim light. "Metropolitan Toronto Police Department. There's a photograph and a badge as well. Detective Sergeant."

"Good enough for you?" asked Kettering.

"Not entirely," said Groz, leaving the point of the dagger against the policeman's neck. "But it will have to do. I would appreciate it if you would put that revolver back in your pocket."

"Christ!" muttered Kettering. He slowly lifted his hand and slid the gun into the waistband holster. "Satisfied?" he asked.

"For now," said Groz. "Please step in to the roomette so that we can speak privately."

"Look," began Kettering, "I don't have time to — "

"Please," murmured Groz, moving the point of the dagger slightly. Kettering swallowed carefully, aware that if the train lurched or began to move, he'd be impaled on the razor-sharp blade. He nodded, and Groz stepped back. Kettering came forward into the roomette, and Wanda Margay slid the door shut. Only when that had been done did Groz remove the knife. Kettering opened his mouth to speak but Groz shook his head.

"I will ask the questions," he said firmly. "First of all, are you part of some sort of official rescue attempt by the authorities?"

"No," said Kettering. "I was a passenger."

"I see," said Groz. "Then you are acting on your own."

"No," said Kettering. "There are others. I'm supposed to be dealing with the terrorists back here while they take on the ones up front."

"You expect to attack these people with a single pistol?" asked Groz.

"It's all I've got," replied Kettering.

"Perhaps we can help, then," said Groz.

Kettering looked at Wanda Margay and then back to Groz. "Oh?"

"Two old people, yes," said the ex-pilot, smiling. "But

we are not without our resources." He reached behind Kettering and picked up one of the incendiary bottles. "I have managed to create three of these."

"Molotovs?" asked Kettering with disbelief.

"Of a sort. Somewhat more effective, I would think," said Groz. "Napalm is a closer approximation. Given a little more time, I might have been able to produce an actual explosive, since Frau Margay here has a good supply of potassium chloride tablets among her medicines."

"Good Lord!" said Kettering.

"Pardon me," said Wanda from her seat. "I don't mean to interrupt, but I wonder if you intend to go into the observation car after these people."

"No," answered Kettering. "Too dangerous. I'm just supposed to keep them contained."

"I think that's wise," said Wanda, furrowing her brow. "By my count, there are at least three of them back there, as well as their hostages. The layout wouldn't lend itself to any kind of offensive action, either, in my opinion."

"Really?" said Kettering.

"No," Wanda continued. "I've read extensively about the Napoleonic Wars and the American Civil War, and this strikes me as one of the blind bottleneck situations that was so common in those unfortunate hostilities."

"Oh," said the policeman.

"Indeed," said Wanda. "There is what I believe is commonly called a dogleg in the corridor of the observation car, shortly before you reach the lounge, giving you very little room to maneuver. On the other hand, it presents the same problem to the enemy."

"The enemy," said Kettering, bemused by the old lady, who was now rummaging in the large, ancient portmanteau that rested between her feet. She pulled out an old-fashioned and ornately decorated hand mirror and held it out to Kettering, smiling triumphantly. "This, however, should be enough to turn the tide in our favor."

"How's that?" asked Kettering.

"There is a circuit-breaker panel just before you reach the door leading out of this car," Wanda explained. "You can use it to turn out the lights in the car. If you situate yourself in one of the roomettes across the corridor and place this mirror in the doorway, facing toward the rear of the train, you will be able to see anyone coming out of the observation car without their seeing you." She looked up at Kettering and beamed. "What do you think?" she asked. Kettering thought for a moment and then grinned.

"Actually," he said, "I think it's one hell of a good idea."

The L34A1 silenced Sterling submachine gun has been in regular use by the British Army and the Canadian armed forces since 1953, and is so well designed that almost no modifications have been made to it since that time. Like any other weapon that has been loaded and cocked, however, it has an unfortunate tendency to go off when it is dropped on the ground. This is exactly what happened when Corporal Dwayne Corrigan of the Second Airborne Commando of the Canadian Special Service Force tripped on a switch rod in the darkness of the Capreol yards some two hundred yards from the point where Jacques Cyr and Sheila Teng were refueling the VIA diesel, aided by Jake Sloane and guarded by Dieter Haas and Annalise Shenker. Corrigan was one of a twenty-man Mobile Strike Squad airlifted from Camp Petawawa and dropped into Capreol ahead of the train to keep tabs on the terrorists. The group was purely for reconnaissance, and the men had orders not to shoot under any circumstances.

The terrorists acted instantly at the sound of the shot. Teng and Cyr raced back to the diesel and began climbing up into the cab, covered by Haas and Shenker, who kept up continuous fire as they moved backwards to the half-open cargo door of the VIA baggage car. Several of Corrigan's colleagues, spread out along the northern perimeter of the yards, opened fire in response, two of them choosing the standing, petrified figure of Jake Sloane as a target, while a third began firing at Cyr and Sheila Teng. Cyr had reached the engine before Teng, and his head came over the top of the gangway first, a slightly darker shadow against the blue and yellow of the cab. A single shot from a Canadian soldier's night-sight-equipped Parker-Hale sniping rifle killed him instantly. Before the sniper had time to reload the bolt-action weapon, Sheila Teng managed to claw her way over Cyr's body and make it into the safety of the cab. Jake Sloane, the innocent

VIA conductor, dressed in shirtsleeves and without his cap, was mowed down by automatic weapons fire from the other two men. Within thirty seconds of Corrigan's ill-timed misfire, Annalise Shenker and Dieter Haas had managed to get back onto the baggage car, and Teng had the train under way. Three minutes after that, the train was well on its way out of the yard, and Annalise Shenker was on the radio, trying to find out what had happened.

Norm Kettering crouched in the dark roomette, his back braced against the back of the single seat, his eyes glued on the mirror he'd been given by Wanda Jenkins Margay. He's heard the shots a few minutes before, and when the train suddenly and violently lurched into motion, he knew that it had begun. He prayed that Harry Maxwell and the others had managed to take out the man in the forward dome car, because he knew he wasn't going to be able to hold his position in the sleeper for long. By everyone's estimate, there were at least two of the terrorists in the rear observation car, plus a third in the observation dome.

The observation car was clearly the terrorists' headquarters and almost surely their arsenal; six shots from the S&W weren't going to keep them at bay for long. He did have the German's firebombs, two of them nestled safely on the pillow of the seat behind him and the third ready in the pocket of his jacket, and he had the darkness in his favor as well; Wanda had been right about the circuit breakers, and now the whole car was in darkness. He swallowed hard and wiped the oily sweat from his forehead with the back of his free hand. On the force, he'd always had the reasonable assurance of backup when he was in a tight situation; this time there were no guarantees, and what backup he did have was amateur.

He wondered, crouching in the darkness, if he wasn't within a few moments of the end of his life. He frowned; at least the two old people were out of it, for now anyway. The old lady had wanted to stay in the roomette, but he and the German had finally convinced her that they'd better make it forward to the relative safety of the next car while they had the chance. Not that it was going to matter much in the end. Kettering knew that he and the others were in an all-or-nothing situation. The shots from outside, and Maxwell and Cavendish's attack on the forward dome, meant that the rest of the terrorists would be on the war path. He'd been involved in enough SWAT operations and attended enough "psychology of violence" seminars to know that they were beyond the point of no return now. The terrorists were going to want revenge, and all logic and reason would be replaced by that single violent desire. Unless he and the others could either contain or kill the terrorists, the lives of all the hostages were forfeit.

Kettering tensed, suddenly aware of a phantom movement in the small oval of glass. He moved forward on his haunches, peering into the mirror, not quite sure whether the movement had been real or just an illusion conjured from his anxiety. He reached out and steadied the mirror against the constant vibration of the train and looked again. There it was, a shape outlined against the light of the observation car — a face against the glass of the far door, and then more movement as the observation car door was opened, then hooked back.

"Smart," murmured the policeman. The terrorist wasn't taking any chances. If he or she had to beat a quick retreat, the door would already be open. It was likely that the same thing would be done with the inner door to the sleeping car as well. Kettering loosened his grip on the revolver, letting it sit easily in his palm. He thumbed off the safety and waited, breathing deeply, trying to project his thoughts onto the pistol range where he still practiced twice a month, imagining the shot. The range was less than thirty feet, but he was going to be shooting from a difficult position and from a low angle. There'd be no risking a head shot; he'd shoot for the middle of the chest, and with luck the bullet would slip in under the ribcage and catch a corner of the heart. He forced himself to see the target in the mirror as a paper cutout and not a flesh-and-blood human being. Terrorist or not, killing someone wasn't easy, and there was no room for hesitation now.

He slid down onto the floor, tucking his legs back in between the toilet and the cater-corner sink. He turned his head, watching the mirror, and braced his gun hand at the wrist, supporting the weight of his upper body on his elbows. More than a couple of minutes in that position and he would begin to cramp, but there was no choice; he wouldn't be able to draw a bead down the barrel, so he'd be shooting by feel rather than aim. The sweat was pouring down his face now, stinging his eyes, but he didn't move. In the mirror he saw the figure approaching, the shadowy outline of a small automatic weapon in one hand. An Ingram or an Uzi, judging by the shape, professionally slung at the elbow, bent arm extended. Both the Uzi and the American Ingram tended to pull up and to the right, but at six hundred rounds a minute, and with a forty-round magazine, either gun was capable of tearing the sleeping car to shreds within three or four seconds.

The figure opened the door of the observation car and stepped carefully into the vestibule, moving side-on to present the smallest target to whatever might be waiting in the darkened car beyond. Kettering took a deep breath and let it out slowly, his trigger finger tightening. He was going to get only one shot, and if he missed the terrorist was going to hose the car with bullets as he retreated. The cop prayed that the terrorist would do the expected and keep his sight at eye level rather than looking down; the mirror barely showed, but it would be enough of a tipoff.

The terrorist reached out and pushed open the door into Kettering's car, the sudden increase in noise hammering into the policeman's ears. The terrorist leaned his shoulder into the heavy door and pushed hard, the barrel of the submachine gun pointing to one side. In any other circumstances Kettering would have fired, but he wanted to be absolutely sure, and the target the figure presented wasn't good enough. He waited. The terrorist came fully into the car, and as the figure pressed the door back against its restraining clip, Kettering realized it was a woman. Then he fired.

The range was less than twenty feet between Kettering and his target, and the .38-caliber bullet had barely reached its optimum velocity before it tore into the woman's body, doing exactly what Kettering had hoped, angling up under the ribcage, ripping into the soft flesh of her belly and into the thoracic organs, finally exiting through the spinal cord just below her shoulder blades. Paulette Baxter was dead before the monstrous ringing explosion of the gun had time to reach her ears.

Kettering dived forward out of the roomette, and in a stumbling crouch he reached the slumped body and tore the submachine gun out of an unresisting hand. Some part of his brain noted that it was an Ingram, and then, without thinking, he fired the deadly instrument down the corridor into the observation car, using it one-handed while he stuffed the Smith & Wesson blindly into his waistband. He fired another burst from the Ingram while he fumbled in his jacket pocket for the incendiary bomb Groz had created. Finding it, he pulled the bottle out of his pocket and tossed it underhand through the open vestibule doors and into the corridor of the observation car. There was a split-second pause as the match-head igniter sputtered, and then Kettering was thrown back by a furious white-hot blast of air as the device exploded, spitting trails of the viscous jellied solvent in all directions. Almost at once, billowing clouds of acrid smoke began to roll down the corridor toward the vestibule. The incendiary had burst onto the wall and floor of the observation car corridor at the dogleg, instantly igniting the carpeting and the plastic ceiling tile, creating an impenetrable curtain of flame. Coughing hard in the increasingly dense smoke, Kettering stepped over Baxter's body and into the vestibule. The open door of the car was already hot to the touch, but the policeman managed to free it from its restraining clip and close it, sealing off the burning car from the rest of the train. He stumbled back into the sleeper and began stripping equipment from the corpse of Paulette Baxter, satisfied that the terrorists in the observation car were contained by the fire, at least for the moment. Crouched over the crumpled body of the young woman, his features were set into a frozen death's-head grin; the victims had become the victors, and now the odds were tipping in their favor. He began to laugh, the sound of it choked and raw from the smoke he'd inhaled, realizing that the old adage was true: only in the face of death do you really understand what living is.

211

Chapter 12

Tuesday, June 28
Time: 4:35 A.M. EDT
Distance: 1,445 miles/2,929 km.

Frank Sagadore and Walter Linberg managed to get aboard
the hostage train exactly as they'd planned, forcing the
simple latch on the small service door behind the counter
of the Skyliner car. Sagadore went in first, with Linberg
right behind him. The Amtrak man stood up carefully,
gun in hand, while Linberg swung the slop door shut.
The car was completely dark, the shuttered windows
blocking out even the dim illumination of the yard lights.

"I thought I heard shooting," whispered Linberg, rising
from behind the counter.

Sagadore paused, listening. From outside he heard the
unmistakable ripping-cloth sound of automatic weapons
fire. "Shit," he breathed. He lifted himself up onto the
counter and was in the process of swinging his legs over
it when he froze, reacting to a loud shriek followed by a
shout, directly over his head in the dome. Before he could
bring his gun to bear, he was confronted by the sight of
Mark Cavendish, his face and the hook and sleeve of his
right arm drenched with blood as he came down the
spiral stairs from the dome. Harry Maxwell was hard on
his heels. Cavendish froze, and Sagadore used the moment to bring his gun up two-handed, the stubby barrel
pointing at the Vietnam vet's chest. The Amtrak security
man swung his legs over the counter, keeping his eyes
and the gun on Cavendish.

"Move down, slowly," Sagadore instructed them.

"Who the hell are you?" asked Cavendish. Behind him,
Harry shifted the weight of the M-60 in his arms, wondering
if he could get it aimed before the man in front of the
counter blew their brains out. He ruled out that idea almost
as fast as it came to him; not only was the guy already

212

aiming at Mark, but he didn't have the slightest idea how to fire the machine gun, let alone fire it accurately.

"I told you to move down," repeated Sagadore.

Cavendish glared at him angrily. "You're a cop, aren't you? You've got the Look."

"Not quite," said Sagadore, caught off guard. "But it'll do for now."

"We're good guys too," Harry put in, two steps higher. "So you can put away the gun."

"I don't see any white hats," said Walter Linberg, coming out from behind the counter. As he did so, the train heaved and began to move, picking up speed quickly. Cavendish threw an anxious look toward the head end of the train.

"We left the white hats upstairs with the Arab we just offed," said Cavendish.

"Arab?" asked Linberg.

"That's right," said Harry.

"Akbar or Kawi," Linberg muttered thoughtfully.

"You know these people?" said Harry.

"Look," Cavendish broke in, "the longer we stand around here making noises at each other, the more dangerous it's getting. There are at least four more of these crazies in the forward end of the train, and you can bet your ass they're out for blood right now. There's maybe a hundred or a hundred fifty innocent passengers between them and us, and they're going to be dead meat unless we can get this M-60 up there."

"So you're passengers?" asked Sagadore, wavering.

"No, we're fucking birdwatchers," Mark fumed. "*Of course* we're passengers, for Christ's sake. So can we *please* get moving?"

"Walt?" said Sagadore, still keeping the gun on Cavendish.

"They're not part of the original group," said the ex-FBI man. "I'm sure of that. I think they're clean."

"Okay," said Sagadore, lowering the gun. "Lead the way."

Dave Wesler, the FBI liaison in Montreal, sat in the makeshift situation room in the Queen Elizabeth Hotel and listened for the third time to the taped report from the

Capreol surveillance team. His stomach had been numbed by half a dozen Rolaids, but his mouth still tasted like the bottom of a birdcage and his eyes were gluey from the restless sleep he'd fallen into only an hour or so before. Except for a duty officer dozing at the radio, the conference room was empty; the RCMP people had gone off to report to their superiors, and both the Canadian External Affairs people and the man from the Secretary of State had taken a shuttle back to Ottawa for briefings there.

The tapes had been recorded off the radio less than an hour before, and came from the surveillance team on the ground as well as a Canadian Forces chopper that had gone up within a few minutes of the train's leaving Capreol. The ground force said that there had been a firefight with the terrorists ten minutes after the train arrived in Capreol, and that two of them had been killed. So far, neither body had been identified. There had been no armed forces casualties.

There was no mention in the report of what had started the fight, but it didn't really matter much now; the implicit violence had become overt. If Walter Linberg's estimation of the terrorists was correct, the reprisal killings would have begun by now.

The helicopter report was interesting; according to the pilot, he had picked up the train as it curved around Bass Lake, no more than a mile or two out of Capreol. The pilot had hung back slightly, following the dark snake of the train as it hammered along the rocky right-of-way beside the Vermilion River. As the train reached the small dam at the head of Fraser Lake, the copilot, watching the train through night glasses, reported that there was a bright flash in the rear observation car, followed by what seemed to be smoke streaming out of the rooftop ventilator ducts. The helicopter followed the train for another few miles, and according to the copilot, it seemed as though the fire died down. Then, fearing a collision with high-tension wires in the unfamiliar darkness, the pilot returned to Capreol.

Wesler turned off the tape machine and sat back in his chair, frowning uneasily. An exchange of shots between the terrorists and the ground recon group, and then, a few minutes later, an apparent fire in the rear car. What did that add up to? What the hell was going on aboard that train?

214

The FBI man leaned forward, picked up the telephone, and dialed the front desk of the hotel. He asked for Linberg's room and listened as the phone rang a dozen times. Finally he hung up, annoyed at the man's ability to sleep through the ringing. He checked his watch. Just past four. Soon it would be dawn, and in the north woods of Ontario, people were dying.

Harry and Mark Cavendish led Linberg and Sagadore toward the head end of the train, the Vietnam vet leading the way with the M-60 cradled in his arms, the bloody hook of his right hand resting on the trigger, and a two-hundred-round link belt of shells draped over his shoulder. With Amal Akbar's blood spattered freely on his arm, chest, and face, he was a vision out of hell. As they passed through the two crowded coaches, the passengers — already frightened and exhausted by their ordeal — drew back silently, letting the group pass without interference.

They eventually found Howard Mottbrown and Daniel Pendergast in the Amdinette, the two empty Amtrak sleepers between them and the filled coaches. The two men had managed to rip the tops off half a dozen tables to form a barricade at the rear of the car. Leaving Cavendish, Sagadore, and the M-60 to defend the head end with Daniel and Mottbrown, Harry and the ex-FBI man turned around and headed for the rear of the train and Norman Kettering. Linberg took Sagadore's Smith & Wesson; Harry still carried Akbar's heavy Walther Olympic.

They found Kettering resting comfortably in the doorway of one of the roomettes in the next-to-last car of the train, a VIA Rail issue pillow at his back and the boxy little Ingram in his lap. The car was shrouded in darkness, without even the spill of light from the observation car corridor to offer illumination, and Paulette Baxter's corpse was no more than a lumpy shadow in the still-open doorway of the sleeper.

"How we doing?" asked Harry, crouching down beside the burly man.

"Good enough," answered Kettering, shifting his weight slightly against the pillow. "I dropped one of them, anyway." He peered up at Linberg. "Who's the new recruit?"

"Walter Linberg, FBI." He didn't bother to explain the complexities of his position. "Two of us managed to get on board at Capreol."

"The other one's an Amtrak security officer," said Harry.

"Two? That's all?" asked Kettering. "I knew you people were on a pretty tight austerity program, but isn't that shortchanging the situation a bit?"

"Probably," Linberg said with a grin. "But Frank and I were acting on our own. We decided to cut through a bit of the red tape."

"Well, I guess two is better than none. How are we doing up front?"

"Barricade in the Amtrak diner, and a great big machine gun. Mark's holding the fort with Daniel and Mottbrown. What's it like here?"

"She's the only one who's showed so far," said Kettering, gesturing with the short barrel of the Ingram at Baxter's body. "I chucked a firebomb down the corridor of the back car there, and it must have done something. It burned for about five minutes and then all the lights went out."

"A firebomb?" asked Linberg, startled.

Kettering laughed. "That's right. I found an old couple in one of the roomettes putting together an arsenal. The guy's a German — a chemist, I think. I've got two more."

"Did it work?" asked Harry.

"Like gangbusters," Kettering replied. "At least until the lights went down. There was an awful lot of smoke."

"Sprinklers probably cut in and shorted the lights," said Linberg. "There's been no action since?"

"Not a peep," said the policeman, shaking his head.

"There were some diplomats these people were holding hostage," said Linberg. "Would they have been in that car?"

"They'd have to be," Harry put in. "They never took anybody forward that any of us saw, and the observation car is the only one we haven't been in."

"Not good," said Linberg. "They'll be using them as shields. It means we can't just go in there in a frontal assault."

"Crap," said Kettering from his position on the floor. "Diplomats or not, that's exactly what we have to do." The train lurched and swayed as they went around a tighter-than-usual curve, throwing the policeman off balance. He winced as the edge of the door dug into his back, and then adjusted his pillow again.

"Why don't you explain that," said Linberg.

"It's simple," Kettering replied. "This is a war, Mr. FBI man. Not cops and robbers. We can't afford to fight on two fronts. If there's somebody in there with any kind of firepower, they can come up on our asses anytime they want. Divide and conquer, and all that. We get them before they get us."

"And just how are you going to do that?" asked Linberg.

"There's a little old lady up front with my chemist friend," said Kettering. "She seems to know a lot about trains. According to her, and according to what I've seen, there's a dogleg corridor that leads into the car proper. I think we should go in there, stick our necks out, and let off a few rounds. Any return fire, and we lob in another one of the firebombs and burn the bastards into bacon fat."

"And the hostages?"

"How many are there?"

"We're not sure. Four, perhaps five."

"And how many passengers? Six hundred? As far as I'm concerned, a hostage is a hostage, and some diplomat has the same value as any other passenger. It's no contest. A few politicians against hundreds of innocent people?"

"I'm afraid I can't go along with that. These people are important," said Linberg, realizing as soon as the words were out of his mouth how sanctimonious he sounded.

"We're playing by different rules here," Harry observed. "You may be an FBI agent in the real world, but that doesn't count for much right now. What counts is getting out of this with our asses intact. The game is simple. Norm here has the biggest gun, so what he says goes."

"All right," Linberg said. "But just remember, if you *do* get out of this with your asses intact, as you put it, the rules in the real world are going to apply again."

Harry smiled sourly. "Don't worry, I'm well aware of that. More than you could ever know, Horatio."

"Pardon?" Linberg said quizzically.

"Forget it," Harry muttered. He reached out a hand to Kettering. "Come on, let's get this over with before my sphincter gives out."

The policeman grasped Harry's wrist and pulled himself up, groaning as he rose. "I'll go in first," he said, grunting and putting a supporting hand on the small of his back. "Harry second, and Linberg, you come last. Gun in one hand, firebomb in the other. I fire first. If there's return fire, you throw the bottles and get the hell out. Okay?"

"Whatever you say," said Linberg.

"All right, let's do it," said Kettering.

The three men crossed the vestibule and slipped into the observation car, trying to ease the door back quietly as they went in. The interior walls of the corridor were scorched badly, and there was still an acrid pall of smoke in the air. The overhead sprinklers had quenched the fire quickly, turning the carpet at their feet into a charred and soggy mess, but it was obvious that the incendiary had done a good deal of damage, including the complete destruction of the circuit-breaker panels to the left and right of the vestibule door.

They reached the end of the dogleg, working their way forward by feel, then paused. Except for the rattling hammer of the wheels and the rhythmic creaking noises as the car swayed back and forth, everything was quiet. Without exposing himself, Kettering bent his arm around the wall and fired a deafening burst from the Ingram, the muzzle flash throwing the men's faces into sharp relief for an instant before the darkness shuttered in again. There was no response to the firing of the submachine gun.

"Maybe there's nobody home," Harry whispered, his ears still ringing from the blast.

"Or maybe they're just waiting for someone to stick his nose out into the corridor," answered Linberg from behind him. "Do we have any idea what the layout of the car is?"

"Four bedrooms, a lounge, and then the rear lounge. The corridor runs all the way down the right-hand side."

"So if they're waiting in the rear lounge they can pick you off as you come toward them," said Linberg.

"It's as dark for them as it is for us. I'm going to go from bedroom to bedroom and fire a burst like I just did. If I get to the lounge without any trouble, you follow."

"Fine," said Linberg.

"Good luck," said Harry.

Kettering moved off.

"He's nuts," whispered Linberg, his back against the wall of the dogleg. "What if he hits one of those canisters?"

"We don't have much of a choice," answered Harry. A few seconds later there was another burst from the Ingram. Harry squeezed his eyes shut and held his breath, waiting for a response. There was nothing. "I think I'm going to be sick," he groaned softly, the tension and fear working on his guts like a twisting knife, the memory of Amal Akbar's terrible death still as harsh and burning as the bile rising in his throat. Before he'd headed up the stairs to the dome, he thought he'd reached the limits of fear; now he knew differently; it got worse every time, not better. As far as he was concerned, fear was a bottomless well. There was a second burst of fire as Kettering made his way down the corridor, and once again there was no reply. Suddenly, and with no apparent cause, Harry found himself remembering why he had come aboard the train in the first place, and he began to giggle.

"What's so funny?" asked Linberg, his voice low.

"Nothing," Harry replied, trying to suppress the panic-tinged laughter. "I think I just started to believe in God, that's all, or at least divine retribution."

"Christ," muttered Linberg, "you're both crazy!"

The furious chattering of the Ingram came again, definitely more distant, and then, a few seconds later, the sound of Kettering's voice.

"All clear, you can come down!"

"I was right," said Harry. "There's nobody home." He edged around the corner of the corridor, pulling his lighter out of his pocket as he went. He flicked it on and held it up like a lamp, the broad flame from the Zippo lighting his way. He'd expected to find bodies somewhere, but there was nothing. Finally he and Linberg reached the large half-oval of the rear observation lounge. Kettering was standing at the foot of the stairs leading up to the dome, waiting for them. The swaying of the train was much worse at the rear of the car, and Harry had to spread his legs wide to keep his balance.

"Up in the dome?" asked Harry.

Kettering shook his head. "Nobody. But I think that's how they got out of here. Come on up and take a look."

"What about the hostages?" asked Linberg, appearing in the small circle of light thrown by the lighter.

"I didn't see anyone," said Kettering.

"I'm going to look around," said Linberg.

"Suit yourself," Kettering replied, shrugging. "You can get some light by opening the blinds; there's no reason to keep them down now." He turned and headed up the stairs to the dome. Harry followed.

Most of the lower panes of glass in the dome had been smashed, presumably for a better field of fire, and the breeze was cold enough to make Harry squint. Outside, dawn was beginning to break, the black of the night sky now turning to a deep transluscent purple. There was no horizon in either direction; the landscape was a wilderness of clotted stands of cedar and immense, jutting spurs of tumbled glacial rock. The train was running through a deep cut in the rock, and only occasionally could Harry see the threading line of the Vermilion River as they rocked heavily along.

"That's how they got out," said Kettering, raising his voice against the whining rush of the wind. He pointed to the forward end of the dome. Beyond the last pairs of elevated seats, the front window — the only window in the dome that could actually be opened — was gaping. Beside the window, on the wide shelf of the dome interior, stood an empty tripod mount for an M-60.

"Jesus! You don't think they went over the top of the cars, do you?"

Kettering shrugged. "It's the only way out."

"I don't get it, though," said Harry. "Why bother taking off at all? That fire didn't do too much damage."

"I think they panicked," answered Kettering. "There was one hell of a lot of smoke. They probably figured it was a full-scale assault."

"You think they made it?"

"Who knows?" said Kettering. "Maybe. Or maybe they never even tried. Maybe they just jumped off."

"So what do we do now?" asked Harry, dropping into one of the dome seats.

"Post a guard so they don't try to sneak in the back way," said Kettering. "I didn't really take a close look, but I think there's a whole bloody arsenal down there in the rear lounge."

220

"Well, we're no farther ahead," said Harry, his voice tired. "They're still in the driver's seat, literally."

"We're ahead of the game. At least now it's going to cost them if they want to take any of us out. They had us cold before. Now it's a little better odds. A draw's better than a defeat."

"I suppose," said Harry. He gave a jaw-cracking yawn. "I'm going to drop if I don't get some sleep pretty soon."

"They must be in the same boat. No problem. We can take things in shifts."

"I'm going to get some kind of meeting together first," Harry said thoughtfully. "We've got to have some kind of plan if we're going to get out of this — "

"With our asses intact?" Kettering grinned. "Yeah. I think you're right."

Walter Linberg appeared at the head of the stairs.

"Find anything?" asked Harry.

"The hostages," said the ex-FBI man, cold anger in his voice. "In one of the big bedrooms. They're all dead. Murdered. The bedroom looks like a slaughterhouse."

"We think they went out over the top of the train," said Harry.

Linberg grimaced. "They destroyed their radio before they went. No calls for help." He took a deep breath and let it out slowly. "We're going to have to do something about the bodies. We can't just leave them there."

"The other two as well. Your man in the dome and the one I took out," said Kettering. Outside, the dawn was fully breaking, the purple of the sky gone to a deep blue, the ragged tops of the trees tinged with gold. In the half-light, Harry saw that the policeman's face was drawn with fatigue, and Linberg didn't look much better. "We can't leave them on the train, you know that, don't you?" said Kettering, looking Linberg directly in the eye.

"Yes. I know that," he answered. "Like Harry said, we're playing by different rules now. Throw them out before they start to rot."

Annalise Shenker paced up and down the length of the RPO, her features taut with anger and tension. Seated on a trunk at one end of the car, Mohamet Kawi watched his colleague and wondered when the fury boiling within her would finally erupt. Of all the people he had ever worked with, she was by far the most professional, but now he was seeing another side of her, and he was worried. Failure was coloring her judgment and making her angry, and that kind of unfocused rage was dangerous. Fortunately, Raoul and Lisa were staying out of her way by guarding the vestibule between the first Amtrak coach and the dinette, while Dieter was forward in the engine with Sheila Teng. He knew he could deal with Annalise, but he wasn't too sure of the others, especially Haas. The Dutchman was a fool who killed for the sake of killing and not out of conviction.

"We still control the train," Kawi said evenly. "Remember that, Annalise."

"No!" snarled Shenker, stopping in the middle of the car and staring hotly at the Libyan. "*You* remember. Remember Amal. Remember Jacques. Remember Paulette. Our comrades have been killed, Mohamet!"

"I cannot remember people I never knew, Annalise," he replied slowly. "Cyr and Baxter were nothing to me, and if Amal died at the hands of the passengers, then it was what he deserved. Don't expect me to respond to sentiment, Annalise. It has no place in what we are doing."

"So they are to remain unavenged?"

"No, certainly not. But the best revenge is for us to complete our mission as it was planned long ago. Nothing has happened to change that."

"We are cut off from our supplies and our ammunition, we have lost three of our people. Men and women who were once our hostages now have our weapons. You don't call that change?"

"Tactically perhaps, but not strategically. As I said, we still control the train. Weapons or not, the passengers are still hostages, the doors are still mined, and the train moves in the direction in which we want it to. And then there is Mr. White, our secret weapon, of course," he added wryly.

"How much longer do we have?" asked Shenker, ignoring him.

Kawi looked at his watch and then closed his eyes, calculating the distance left to their destination. "If we maintain our present speed on an average, approximately thirty-eight hours."

"Can we last that long?"

"There is no reason why not," the Libyan replied. "Lisa and Raoul destroyed the radio before they abandoned the observation car. The authorities will have no way of knowing what has gone on. If anything, we are in an even better position in some ways. According to Sheila, we took on enough fuel at Capreol to take us most of the way. If we fuel again at Carberry — which was one of our alternates — we will not have to stop again. The authorities have failed to take us on two occasions now; it is unlikely they will try again so soon."

"And the hostages? We make no attempt to take back the rest of the train?"

"As a balm to the bruises on our egos? No. We have already won the war — why should we fight unnecessary battles?"

"You have a way of making profundities out of nothing, Mohamet," said Shenker, a smile breaking through the anger on her face.

"And you of seeing demons where there are none," countered the Libyan. Shenker moved across the swaying car and stood in front of Kawi, looking down at him. She reached out with one hand and let her fingers trail down his chest to the taut fabric over his groin. Cupping him with one hand, she leaned forward and kissed him lightly on the stubbled line of his jaw.

"I see what I wish to see, Mohamet son of Khalil."

"Is this wise?" asked Kawi, feeling himself harden against her hand.

"Perhaps not," whispered Shenker, her mouth against his ear. "But wisdom has nothing to do with desire."

The meeting convened in the VIA Rail dining car at noon that day was by invitation only. After the Battle of Capreol, as Harry called it, a number of people had come forward, insisting that they be told what was going on, including the belligerent doctor who had tried to stand in Mark Cavendish's way. After trying to satisfy a dozen people at once, Walter Linberg stepped forward and arbitrarily announced that until further notice everyone was to do precisely as he or she was told, without question. Anyone who didn't agree was welcome to go forward and join the terrorists. It was at this point that the same man who had tried to stop Cavendish asked Linberg who had given him the authority to decide the fate of innocent people. He was booed back into his seat by a score of other passengers, and the matter was settled. Harry's first command decision after the battle was to inform the passengers that they should keep the blinds down; if there was another rescue attempt, the authorities wouldn't be able to differentiate between good guys with guns and bad guys, and Harry didn't want anyone getting hurt.

There were nine people at the meeting, including Harry. Groz and Margay had been asked because of their specialized knowledge — Groz of chemicals, and Wanda because she was so well acquainted with both the train and the route it followed. Howard Mottbrown was there for much the same reason, and also because he had offered to take notes during the meeting. Linberg and Sagadore represented the outside, Mark Cavendish acted as Harry's second-in-command, and Hamilton Stackpole represented the crews of both the Amtrak and the VIA train. Three tables were pushed together, with Harry at the head and Mark Cavendish beside him. The Vietnam veteran spoke first.

"I think we should get one thing clear right away," he said, looking over the other members of the group. "As of now, democracy has been thrown out the window. What Harry says goes, and I don't want any shit from anyone on that score. He's the boss because he was the only one of us who had the guts to make a play for these people in the beginning, and also because he's got brains. Understood?"

There were nods of assent from around the table. Cavendish sat down, and then it was Harry's turn. "I'm not sure I want to be the star player here," he began, "but I guess it's irrelevant. What I really want is to get off this train alive. So far we've been lucky, but the goons up front still hold most of the cards. They've got the doors mined, and according to Walter Linberg and Frank Sagadore, those canisters we saw them placing have got some kind of plague or something in them. Walter?"

"According to our information, it's anthrax," said the ex-FBI man from his chair. "I'm no bomb expert, but the one I saw attached to the wiring panel in the Daynighter car looks like it's radio remote-controlled. We've got to assume that the terrorists still have the remote-control unit, and also that they're willing to use it."

"I am a chemist," said Groz, "and I have some experience with munitions. Herr Linberg showed me the device of which he just spoke. I know very little about anthrax, but from the appearance of the canister, I would say the vector for the germs would be compressed air. Also, according to Mr. Linberg, there are a number of these canisters throughout the train, so I would think that if these people decided to explode them, we would all be dead very quickly."

"Is there any way we can defuse them or something?" asked Harry.

"I doubt it," answered Cavendish. "They've got the same kind of release mechanism as the mines on the doors of the cars. They're spring-loaded. Cut the wires or move them, and bang."

"So we have to get the remote device," said Harry.

"Look," said Frank Sagadore. "All this GI Joe stuff is fine, but has anyone stopped to ask just what these people are doing?"

"Hijacking a train," said Cavendish. "I thought that was obvious."

"I didn't mean that," said the Amtrak man. "We already know they're trying to take the currency shipment that's on board."

"What currency shipment?" Harry asked innocently.

"There's a major currency shipment on the Amtrak train," explained Linberg. "What I think Frank is getting at is what is their final objective for all of this."

"Simple terrorism? Bucks?" suggested Harry.

"Okay," Sagadore said, "but I don't think these people are suicidal. I think they want to get away with it, and that means they've got some way out. The question is *what*."

"They've got two choices," said Cavendish. "They detonate the anthrax canisters and split, or they *don't* detonate them and split."

"But where?" Sagadore insisted. "If we had some idea where they planned to end this whole thing, then maybe we could protect ourselves."

"It would be somewhere in the mountains, I should think," said Wanda Jenkins Margay quietly. "One presumes they would want some isolated area rather than an urban center."

Linberg looked at the old lady, impressed. He'd needed

a lot more information than she had to reach the same conclusion. "I agree," he said, nodding.

"Mark?" asked Harry.

"It makes sense," he answered. "But I don't think you can depend on it. The mountains would certainly give them more cover than anywhere else. But are they going to try to hang on that long?"

"Maybe they don't have any choice," said Harry. "If they've got some particular escape route planned through the mountains, they might just be committed to it."

"How much time would that give us?" asked Linberg.

"Thirty hours to get into the mountains. Around night-fall tomorrow," said Mottbrown.

"And what's in between?" asked Harry.

"Winnipeg, initially," said Wanda. "Although I expect they would try to skirt the city proper. After that, there isn't anything of note until one reaches Calgary."

"And then?" asked Harry.

"The mountains," said Mottbrown.

"We've got some fairly urgent problems to deal with before that," Hamilton Stackpole interjected.

"Such as?" asked Harry.

"We're going to run out of food long before that, and we're already short on drinking water. We've also got six toilets plugged in the sleepers, and two more in the coaches. It's already starting to stink. You're going to have a lot of pretty low people on this train. Hungry and thirsty, too."

"What about the injured?" asked Harry.

"Your Mr. Tucker says two have died, and another one's likely to before long. Other than that, there's not too much to worry about. There's lots of first-aid kits available, and there are three doctors on the train."

"Where have you got the bodies?" asked Linberg.

"Up in the dome car with the others. They're going to start stinking pretty soon too, if you'll pardon me," answered the black man, turning to Wanda Jenkins Margay.

"I'm not quite sure why you're keeping them on the train at all," said the old woman. "I mean, they have burials at sea. Why not on the train?"

"Pardon me?" said Harry.

"Chuck them off, dear boy," she said, smiling brightly. "Someone will be along to deal with them, I'm sure."

"All right," said Harry. "Maybe we'll do that." He turned

back to Stackpole. "There's not much we can do about the food and water except ration them. As far as the toilets are concerned, close them off and bust the windows; that should keep the smell down for a while."

"I think maybe we should move people even farther back in the train," said Frank Sagadore. "Say from the Daynighter back to the observation car. It'll be cramped even worse than it is now, but I think we're better off if we concentrate the passengers in case we have to evacuate suddenly. There's also only one of the canisters between here and the last car, and that's in the middle sleeper. Maybe we can figure out a way to unhook that one, and then we'd be more isolated from the others."

"How badly would it be crowded?" asked Harry.

"We left Washington pretty light," answered Stackpole. "It'll be tight, but I think the man is right: We've only got a limited number of weapons, and it'll be safer if all the passengers are all together."

"Then do it," said Harry. "Clear the coaches and take the wounded people back to the observation car. Old people get priority. If it gets really bad, the younger passengers can stand. Anything else?"

No one else spoke. Harry stood up. "Okay, that's it, then. I'm going to move Norm Kettering up from the observation dome to the one in the lounge. Everybody else is going to take guard duty in shifts. Mark here is in charge of that." The others in the group stood up as well, and the meeting began to break up. A few moments later, Harry was alone in the dining car with Mark Cavendish. The Vietnam veteran looked worried.

"Something on your mind, Mark?" asked Harry.

"Yeah," said Cavendish, dropping into a chair and beginning the ritual of lighting a cigarette. Harry followed suit. "I didn't want to talk about it in front of the others — not yet, anyway."

"So what is it?"

"The terrorists aren't the only thing we're up against. We've got another problem."

"Go on," Harry prompted.

"I was talking to Linberg about the anthrax canisters. He says they've got the brass hats petrified. Scared shitless, in fact. Linberg thinks they might be scared enough to do something about it."

"I don't get you," said Harry, frowning. He sucked in a long drag of smoke and let it roll out of his nostrils.

"We've gone from being a trainload of hostages to being a moving time bomb," explained the veteran. "So the next time anybody from the outside tries to take on the train, it's not going to be a rescue attempt. Their first priority will be to deal with the problem of containing the anthrax, even if that means taking us out as well."

"What are they going to do, drop a bomb on us?" scoffed Harry. "Come on, Mark, this isn't science fiction."

Using his hook, Cavendish deftly reached into the inside pocket of his jacket, removed a small book, and tossed it down on the table in front of Harry, who picked it up and read the title: *Scenic Rail Guide to Western Canada*.

"I found it on one of the seats in the front coach," said Cavendish. "It's a mile-by-mile description of the route we're taking. Lots of interesting material. And you can bet your ass the terrorists have a copy of it too."

"Get to the point, Mark."

"I read most of it this morning," he replied slowly. "And then I checked with Mrs. Margay and a couple of the Canadian trainmen. If the terrorists want to use the mountains as a shield, then they're going to wait until they're pretty deep before they make their move. That means no big towns. The first place on our route that fits the bill is a stretch between somewhere called Golden and the town of Revelstoke. It's about a ninety-mile-long wilderness. Now if I can figure that out, so can the people on the outside."

"So?"

"So there's a spot about halfway between the two towns called the Connaught Tunnel. It's five miles long, and it's only ventilated from the east and west portals. It's perfect."

"For what?"

"A cemetery," Cavendish said grimly. "Or better yet, a mass grave that's hermetically sealed. Plug the vents and blow up the entrance and exit, and the anthrax isn't a problem any-more. Apparently the railroad is halfway through digging another tunnel that's even better, so it wouldn't even be much of an economic loss."

"You think they'd bury us?" asked Harry.

"Unless we do something about it before we hit that

tunnel, I think that's exactly what they're going to do," he answered.

The hours passed without incident, the land outside an unending wilderness of rocks, trees, scattered lakes, and muskeg swamp. The diesel maintained a constant speed, disregarding changes in the roadbed and without the slightest interest in the comfort of the passengers. Mile after swaying, rocking, jerking mile, the long, snaking train made its way through an ominous landscape that was almost completely devoid of humanity.

By midafternoon they had reached the Sturgeon River and Abram Lake, passing the empty mock-Tudor passenger station at Sioux Lookout, then slipping quickly in and out of the twin 525-foot tunnels at Canyon Lake and continuing westward. It was fully dark again as they crossed the border between Ontario and Manitoba, unmarked except for a sign standing among the trees.

Less than two hours later, just after midnight, Central Daylight Time, the train reached the nine-hundred-foot-long bridge that spanned the Red River Floodway. In the distance, the lights of the city of Winnipeg hazed the pitch-black sky.

The train, working off the Central Traffic Control board in the CPR Transcon Yards, followed the main line through the Nairn Overpass, and then crossed the Red River into the city proper. Luckily the city was asleep for the most part, and only a very few people were aware of the train's horrifying potential. No attempt had been made to evacuate the areas adjacent to the main line as it moved by the Winnipeg and Weston yards, and the only indication that something was in the wind were the roadblocks and police cordons set up at the major intersections. During the twenty-minute journey through the heart of the sprawling city, no attempt was made to interfere with the consist, and just before 1:00 A.M., it crossed the city limits at Omand's Creek and disappeared into the night. There was also no attempt made while the train stopped briefly just outside Carberry, Manitoba, to take on more fuel.

The drawing room in the first sleeper back from the VIA dining car had been taken over by the members of Harry's group on guard duty, and Harry himself had been asleep in the lower bunk for only an hour when he was awakened by Daniel Pendergast.

"What's up?" he mumbled blearily.

Daniel shook his head, putting a finger to his lips. Harry nodded. Walter Linberg was asleep in the upper bunk, and Mark Cavendish was snoring on the pull-out bed a few feet away. Harry, still fully dressed, swung off the bed, slipped into his boots, and followed his friend out into the quiet corridor. The train, still traveling at high speed, was rocking back and forth heavily, the incessant squeaking and rattling of the cars a constant background to any conversation.

Wordlessly, Daniel moved up the corridor, pausing at the door to the left-hand roomette closest to the vestibule that led forward to the dining car.

"It's one of the roomettes closed up because of the toilets," Pendergast explained in a whisper. "It was really stinking. I figured another toilet was plugged."

"No kidding," Harry agreed, wrinkling his nose. The stench rolling out from the small grille inset into the bottom section of the sliding door was foul.

"Take a deep breath," said Harry's friend. "It gets worse."

Harry did as he was told, and Pendergast slid back the door. Harry peered inside. The window blind was up, and he could instantly see that the glass had not been broken. Harry gagged, but not at the powerful odor of human excrement.

"Oh Christ!" he whispered, staring. Adrian Tucker, lit from above by the roomette's pale blue night light, was sprawled on the bench seat, his shirtfront and lap soaked with blood that shone darkly in the dull illumination, his head thrown back to reveal the white-edged lips of the horrible gaping slash that reached from his left ear to his right.

Harry threw up.

Part Five

THE TUNNEL

*I think anger is probably the best an-
tidote for fear. . . . After we found
Adrian, I wasn't scared anymore, I
was just mad — fighting mad.*

Harry Maxwell,
the Playboy Interview

Chapter 13

Wednesday, June 29
Time: 10:20 A.M. CDT
Distance: 2,482 miles/3,994 km.

Dave Wesler sat in the rear of the briefing room, listening to the uniformed officer outlining the Canadian contingency plan for dealing with the hostage train. There were a score of other people in the room, representing the various military, police, and diplomatic agencies concerned with the problem. For the past fifteen minutes the briefing officer had been going over past history, but now, with a small-scale map of British Columbia on the rear-projection screen behind him, he was getting down to particulars. The officer, a colonel, spoke in a monotone that made him sound as though he were describing a game plan for taking out the daily garbage.

"With the exception of specific transmission from the train relating to regulation of traffic control and movement of switches, we have had no hard information relating to the status of the passengers or the terrorists on board the train since it left Capreol early yesterday morning. Bearing this in mind, it must be understood that this is only a hypothetical plan and might well be changed at any time."

In other words, thought Wesler, they didn't know diddly-squat about what was going on, and they were hoping like hell that the terrorists did exactly as predicted. Not the most accurate way to plan an assault.

"We are assuming that at a constant rate of speed together with certain fluctuations in that speed as a result of grade changes as the train enters the Rocky Mountains, the train will reach Field, British Columbia, at approximately ten P.M. this date. According to our information on fuel consumption by the locomotive and based on the distance traveled we can also assume that the terrorists have no intention of proceeding with the train past Revelstoke, British Columbia."

"Unless they decide to refuel again," muttered Wesler under his breath.

"Knowing this, and in light of the potential danger to the general civilian population which the train now represents, we have decided to contain the train within the Connaught Tunnel, here." Using a pointer, he indicated a position just past the Big Bend area of the Columbia River, almost midway between Field and Revelstoke. He paused, and a second later the map changed to an even smaller-scale view of the area.

"As you can see, the east portal of the tunnel is bounded on all sides by mountains. Mount Dauntless to the east, the Hermit, Mount Rogers, and Mount Tupper to the west. The tunnel itself goes under Mount MacDonald and Avalanche Mountain, the west portal opening at the foot of Mount Cheops to the west and Mount Abbot to the east. Both east and west portals of the tunnel are within two hundred yards of the Trans-Canada Highway, so there is no difficulty concerning access to the area.

"The tunnel itself is 26,517 feet long, a little more than five miles, and is twenty-nine feet wide by twenty-one and a half feet high. The structure was originally designed for two tracks, but has been run as a single-track tunnel since 1959. Entry into the tunnel automatically trips a switch that activates two large ventilating fans at the west portal entrance, which force air through the tunnel as the train passes through and for twenty minutes thereafter. These fans are the only form of ventilation in the tunnel.

"Emergency operation of the fans and all traffic movements through this area are controlled from Field and from the Traffic Control Center at the Revelstoke yards." The briefing officer turned away from the map and faced his select audience. "What we propose is to stop the train within the Connaught Tunnel. This can be done without warning to the terrorists, since that area of track uses a cab-control-signaling system whereby, in passing a double red signal indication, a train may be stopped automatically if the crew does not acknowledge the signal. Once the brakes on the train are 'dynamited,' as it is called, there is no way to restart the train until the signals have cleared. Since the terrorists would see a double red signal as they entered the tunnel, we will simply remove the red lenses from the signal lights, turning the signal to a double white, or all clear."

At this point the officer flashed a brief and, to Wesler's mind, a completely insincere smile before going on. "We do realize that we are dealing with a very large group of hostages in this situation, and because of that we have decided to make a last assault on the terrorists. This will be done from within the tunnel, using a volunteer group of British Special Air Services personnel from the SAS Twenty-second Regiment at Hereford. These men have been on call since the train entered Canadian territory, and are presently en route to Trail, British Columbia, where they will then go by helicopter to the tunnel. There has been opposition both from the United States Secretary of State's office and a number of our own people on this point, but neither the U.S. Delta Group nor our own Group Red units have had any experience with terrorist train hijackings. These men have, specifically with the Dutch-South Mollucan hijacking. They have also done a number of exercises on potential train operations. Beyond that, this particular group has completed several exercises in British Columbia and is familiar with the terrain. The group, which consists of fifteen men, will be aided by a demolitions unit from CFB Chilliwack. If, for any reason, the SAS unit is unsuccessful, the demolitions unit will seal both the east and west portals of the tunnel, thus containing any possible release of the anthrax bacilli, although unfortunately at the expense of the hostages' lives. However, such a loss would most certainly be the lesser of two evils, and the economic repercussions would be minimal, since the Canadian Pacific will complete its new Rogers Pass Tunnel within the next year. Until such time, trains could utilize the old Big Hill right-of-way.

"Demolition charges will be in place by six P.M. Mountain Time, and the operation will begin at approximately midnight, or three A.M. here. There will be a debriefing at four A.M. in this room, if you would like to attend. Thank you."

The colonel gathered up the sheaf of papers from the podium in front of him, the map disappeared from the rear screen, and the briefing session was over. The people in the room began to leave, and Wesler stood up. As he followed the crowd out into the corridor, he checked his watch. In fifteen hours it would all be over, one way or another.

"I think it's a stupid idea, and I think he's full of shit," said Daniel Pendergast, fuming. Harry Maxwell stubbed out his cigarette in the drawing room's wall-mounted ashtray and stared out the window. Outside, there was nothing to see but endless sheets of rippling wheat toasting under the immense, hard blue bowl of the eastern Alberta sky.

"It's not a stupid idea and he's not full of shit," answered Harry, still staring out the window. In the distance he could see the shimmering mirage of an Alberta Wheat Pool grain elevator, rising out of the monotonous landscape like some surreal fortress tower. "If we just sit here and let things unroll around us, we're just as much victims as we were before — except now we're behind barricades. We've got to do something before the goons up front do it to us, or the authorities decide to lower the boom. We're a plague ship, for Christ's sake, Daniel. Nobody's going to let us land anywhere. It's kill or be killed."

"You're beginning to sound like our Viet-vet friend. I think maybe he's warped your brain, Harry. Maybe he never got over his taste for strafing jungle villages."

"Ease off, Daniel. Mark isn't influencing me. I'm not turning into a Green Beret or anything. But he's right."

"I don't suppose getting revenge on whoever killed Adrian has anything to do with it?"

"No," said Harry firmly. "But that is a problem we've got to figure out too. I don't think one of the terrorists managed to sneak back here just to slit Adrian's throat."

"A spy in the house of love?" asked Daniel. "You think we've got some kind of psychotic, gay-hating loony among the passengers?"

"Not that either," said Harry, shaking his head. He lit another cigarette and leaned back against the bench seat. "I think the goons were telling the truth when they said there were others among the passengers, keeping tabs. I think either they decided to give us a jolt, or maybe Adrian stumbled onto something."

"Any idea who?" asked Daniel.

"Adrian was spending a lot of time with the wounded."

"One of the doctors?"

"No, I don't think so. But we've got to find out."

"We don't have time for twenty questions with all the passengers," said Daniel. "So what are we going to do?"

"We're going to keep any plans to ourselves, for one thing," replied Harry. "We're the only ones who even know he's dead, and I want to keep it that way, at least for now." Outside, the grain elevator was looming larger with each passing second, and Harry could see a small cluster of houses to one side. He could imagine someone in one of those houses, a kid maybe, watching the train go by, wondering why almost all the blinds were shut and why the train looked as though it had been in a war. On the other hand, maybe the whole world knew about them by now, in which case the little village beside the grain elevator had probably been evacuated. The Flying Dutchman of the Rails.

"You're sure you want to attack these people?" asked Daniel.

"We have to," said Harry. "I think it's the only chance we've got."

"But what if this Linberg guy and his friends are wrong?" asked Daniel. "Maybe those canisters are empty."

"Wishful thinking," said Harry. "These people aren't bullshitters, Daniel. If they said it was anthrax, you can bet on it."

"So we attack, and one of them decides to push the button. What then?"

"We're dead," Harry said simply. The grain elevator tore by, the giant silo filling the window for a spinning instant and then disappearing, leaving nothing but the empty prairie.

Harry, Mark Cavendish, and Howard Mottbrown sat at a table in the empty VIA dining car and went over the sketch of the train drawn by Mottbrown. The meek-faced man had neatly drawn in all the important details he could think of, and had carefully noted their own defensive positions, including Kettering in the forward dome, and the barricaded café lounge beneath him.

"Okay," said Cavendish, "tell me again what I've got in front of me. This is only for reconnaissance, but I don't want to run into something I wasn't expecting."

Mottbrown nodded, his small mouth pursed thoughtfully. "Ahead of the Vista Dome you have two of the Canadian coaches and then the Amtrak portion of the train. They've dropped the original observation car, so that gives you two sleepers, the Amdinette, and two coaches. Five cars in all, or about four hundred feet to cover. Past that you should have the baggage car and the RPO I saw when I got on board in Washington. The last car is the Canadian baggage car."

"I don't understand that," said Harry. "Why would they hang on to the Canadian baggage car?"

"Simple," said Mottbrown. "It's considerably easier to hook two cars together than to hook a car to a locomotive or a B unit. They left it on the Canadian diesel to save time."

"Okay," Mark cut in, "so after that we should have the diesel, right?"

"Yes. According to the trainman I talked to, it's a PA-4. Quite old-fashioned by American standards, but a highly effective piece of equipment nonetheless."

"So we can expect a couple of them in the locomotive," murmured Cavendish, using the pencil clamped in his twin hook to deftly place an X marking their position on the diagram. "Logically, they'll have at least one person as an observer in a forward position close to us, say here." Again he put an X on the diagram, this time at the tail end of the first Amtrak sleeper. "They could be even closer," he mused, "but they'll probably leave the two coaches as a kind of no-man's-land."

"How many more does that leave us?" asked Harry.

"There's no way of being absolutely sure, but I'd say three or maybe four."

"And that includes this Shenker woman, the good-looking one that Linberg says is the leader," said Harry.

Cavendish nodded. "She's the one who'll probably be in charge of blowing out those canisters."

"Where is she likely to be?" asked Harry.

"Here," said Cavendish firmly, putting another X on the drawing. "The first of the Amtrak coaches, where the booby traps went off. We'll be coming into Calgary, according to Howard here, and that means they'll be expecting trouble. With that big hole in the side of the car, they're vulnerable to attack."

"I want this one alive," said Harry, tapping the X on the diagram marking Cavendish's hypothetical forward observer. "I want to squeeze some hard information out of one of these bastards so we can get a grip on how this thing is going to end."

"I think I've got an idea," said Mottbrown. He reached into his jacket pocket and took out a neatly folded map. He spread it out on the table. Reading the legend, Harry saw that it was a street map of Calgary. "I borrowed this from Mrs. Margay," he said with a small smile. "It really is astounding what she carries in that bag of hers. At any rate, here is the main line we're traveling along," he said, indicating a gray line threading up from the southeast. "The Canadian Pacific main line comes in from this direction and then roughly follows the line of this irrigation canal before it joins with the Bow River. There are a number of industrial parks in the area and a lot of spur lines, but their most likely course is straight through the center of the city and then along the main line. Mrs. Margay says the route follows the Bow River all the way into the foothills."

"I don't see the point of all this," said Harry.

"Well, it's the curves, you see," Mottbrown said quietly. "There appear to be quite a number of them, especially as you move through the industrial section on the eastern side of the city. If the train is curving along the track, that means the Amtrak coach with the hole in its side will be visible from the rear of the train."

"So?" said Mark Cavendish.

"So presumably Mr. Kettering, as a policeman, must be at least an adequate marksman, and if he were to use one of the weapons you captured to fire from the Vista Dome . . . "

"He's right," said Mark Cavendish, turning to Harry. "Kettering could keep them busy by potshotting into the hole every time the train curved."

"Okay, so we've got the two or three in the forward end pinned down. Now how do we nab the sucker waiting in the sleeper? He's not going to throw down his gun and come running to us with open arms."

"Pepper gas and a smokescreen," Cavendish answered promptly, a grin spreading across his face. "I asked Groz to come up with something right after we first talked about this. He's dissolved about a hundred of those little packets of pepper into some of Wanda's rubbing alcohol and taped the bottle to one of his incendiaries. He says the smoke from it will be blinding and incapacitating. How's that?"

"Marvelous," Harry said wryly.

"We picked up a couple of those short-handled shotguns in the observation car," Cavendish went on. "We can blow out the glass in the doors between the cars, toss in the firebomb, and then go in and get him. One, two, three."

"Or four," said Harry. "We found some gas masks in the observation car, too. What if he's wearing one?"

"It's a chance we'll have to take," said Cavendish, shrugging. "They had those things in case somebody from outside used tear gas on them; they aren't going to be worrying about us using pepper."

"Okay," said Harry. "You blow the windows, I'll toss in the bottle, and we'll both go in and get him. Kettering's upstairs, keeping the heavies off our backs and Linberg, Sagadore, and Daniel hold the fort at the barricade in case this whole thing blows up in our faces." He turned to Mottbrown. "How much longer to Calgary?"

"We just went through a place called Strangmuir," answered the little man, consulting his VIA schedule. "That puts us about forty miles out. At this speed we'll be there in about half an hour."

What had begun as an escape for Kenzie McLeod, when she stole the young man's ticket in Montreal's Central Station, had turned into a nightmare that showed no signs of ending. When she became aware that the train had been hijacked shortly after leaving the station, she had been as scared as anyone else on board, and the sight of the wounded passengers, and later the blanket-covered corpses being moved up to the snack-bar car for disposal, had made her sick with fear. But it was worse now. As she sat huddled with half a dozen other passengers in the crowded sleeper, she was almost petrified. The constant swaying of the train, and the combination of murmuring voices and the body odors of the hundred or so people packed like sardines in every available space in the car were making her physically ill. Unable to take it any longer, she stood, and by twisting her way through the dense mass of humanity she was able to reach the vestibule door at the end of the car. Stepping over a pair of dozing passengers lying in the aisle, she pulled back the door and went into the vestibule, finally alone. It was the one place in the train that wasn't carpeted with people, but was avoided by everyone because of the grim devices attached to the outer doors. Kenzie didn't care; she had other things on her mind, specifically what to do about what she had accidentally witnessed the night before.

Keeping well away from the booby-trapped doors, she leaned back against the vestibule bulkhead and breathed in the relatively fresh air that leaked in through the vibrating floor plates and around the door seals. Even the constant roar of the wheels didn't bother her, now that she was alone.

Eyes closed, she slipped her hand into the pocket of her jeans and fingered the small object nestled there. The man she'd seen coming out of the roomette had dropped it, and the key chain had almost been her undoing. She'd seen it fall in the dim light of the corridor, and she'd actually started to call out to the man when something stopped her.

At fifteen, Kenzie McLeod was a virgin, beautiful and intelligent. She also had a highly developed sense of survival that had come from living her life on what amounted to the bottom rung of the social ladder. The same street smarts that had kept her from losing her virginity, and perhaps getting pregnant by any one of the losers she traveled with, also intuitively kept her from calling out to the man she'd seen slipping out of the roomette. The set of his shoulders and the way he moved, even with his back to her, set off all sorts of alarms and she hung back, staying in the shadows at the rear of the car until the man had disappeared, moving forward into the next car. A few minutes before, Kenzie had been looking for a toilet that hadn't been utterly fouled, but now the ache in her bladder was forgotten. When she was sure the man was gone, she walked forward quickly and retrieved the object

241

she'd seen falling out of his pocket onto the carpeted floor of the corridor. Fittingly, the decoration on the end of the chain was itself a key, although unlike any Kenzie had ever seen before. It was two inches long, made out of cast iron, and the tang end was solid. There were three letters stamped into the metal: FEC.

Curious, she knocked lightly on the door of the roomette the man had just left, and when she didn't get an answer she gently twisted the handle and slid the door back. What she saw would remain in her mind for the rest of her life, coming back to haunt her in a thousand nightmares. If she lived long enough to have them.

Standing in the vestibule, Kenzie opened her eyes and for the first time in her life wished that she smoked cigarettes. At least it would give her something to do. She lifted her wrist and checked the time. Four-thirty. Not that it meant anything, they'd passed through at least one time zone since leaving Montreal, and she hadn't changed the hands. What it did tell her was that she'd been a witness to an unholy murder for almost exactly twelve hours.

She crossed her arms over her chest, hugging herself, pacing back and forth across the tiny space between the cars. Sooner or later she knew she was going to have to tell someone about what she had seen, but the question was *who*.

"How much time?" whispered Mark Cavendish, the ugly shape of the Siles shotgun cradled in his arms. He squatted on the floor in front of the first pair of seats in the head-end VIA coach, while Harry Maxwell did the same across the aisle. Ahead of them there was nothing but the toilet on the right and the cloakroom on the left. Beyond that was the vestibule leading to the first of the Amtrak sleepers.

"Two minutes," Harry answered, checking his watch. "Kettering's going to start firing, the next curve we come to after that."

"I hope it works," muttered Cavendish.

"What do you mean, you *hope* it works? Jesus, man, it was your plan!"

"I flew jets, Harry, I wasn't a platoon leader," Cavendish replied.

"Oh God! How did I get into this?" Harry moaned.

"You were in the wrong place at the wrong time," answered Cavendish. "How much time?"

"Ninety seconds," said Harry.

"Mottbrown says we'll feel the train lurch when we hit the curve," said Cavendish. "According to him, the driver up there is pretty good, but at this speed it's going to be jumpy. When you feel the lurch I'll start counting. We should be able to hear old Norm blasting away from here. If we do, when I hit five, light the wick on that bomb of yours. On six I'm going to stand, fire through the glass — twice, to make sure I get both doors — and then I'm going to roll right onto the seat behind you. When I jump, you move into the aisle, toss the bomb, and roll left. Take your time; the guy up there isn't going to be looking around too much after a couple of 12-gauge loads. Make sure you get the bottle through *both* doors. A fire in between the cars isn't going to do us any good. Okay?"

"Roger, Red Leader."

"Smartass. Time?"

"Thirty."

"Let's hope your lighter doesn't run out of fluid."

"Ha-ha," Harry grunted. But he gave the Zippo a test flick to make sure it still worked.

The last few seconds went by, and then, after what felt like an eternity, the train lurched drunkenly to the right. Another few seconds went by, and then both men heard the dull, muffled chatter from above and behind them as Norman Kettering began firing bursts from the M-60. Counting out loud, Mark Cavendish stood up, his prosthetic hand gripping the slide of the shotgun while the hooked hand was fitted into the trigger guard. The short pistol-grip butt of the weapon was wedged tightly into the arm's mechanical elbow joint. At the five-count, Harry lit the wick of the bomb, the flame touching the long solvent-soaked rag flaring almost invisibly. Out of the corner of his eye, Harry was aware of Cavendish standing, and then the entire car was filled with the incredible double blast of the shotgun. As Cavendish rolled past him into the seat, Harry stood up, praying that he wasn't about to find himself staring down the barrel of a gun.

Feeling as though every move was in slow motion, he slipped into the aisle, the shattered glass of the vestibule doors a few feet away. There was no sign of anyone in the corridor of the far car, and he cocked his arm, ready to throw.

Discussing it later, neither Harry nor Mark Cavendish could actually remember hearing the sound of the door opening behind them, but obviously some part of their subconscious minds, keyed to some primeval survival instinct, had rung a warning bell somewhere, since both men turned toward the rear of the train almost as one, Harry with the firebomb in his hand, Cavendish rising out of the seat, holding the Siles.

The figure stepping out of the toilet cubicle behind them was a short woman with closely cropped black hair, wearing what appeared to be some sort of combat fatigues. Cavendish, who had instinctively pumped another round into the chamber of the shotgun, fired, and Harry came within an instant of tossing the firebomb in her direction. At the last second, realizing that Mark had already blown the greater part of the woman's right leg off, Harry turned and lobbed the firebomb through the door closest to him, and into the lap of Raoul Attendera, who had been standing hidden in the vestibule. The double bottle of incendiary smashed on the slide of the Ingram submachine gun in the terrorist's hands, spraying the volatile liquid over him from head to toe. There was a powerful sucking noise, and then the ex-Sandinista became a Roman candle, the screams from his rapidly cindering mouth swallowed up by the blast-furnace rush of the flames that were consuming him. Attendera slumped to his knees and then fell forward, smothering the delayed explosion of the Ingram's ammunition with the caramelized remains of his chest, and then the vestibule began to fill with oily black smoke, the pepper mixture making Harry's eyes stream with tears and forcing him back along the aisle.

Mark Cavendish was already with the wounded terrorist, deftly stripping off the belt of her fatigues and wrapping it around the stump of her leg. His single round had taken her just above the knee, the choked spread of heavy pellets at such close range tearing the lower half of her leg completely away. The foot, still neatly laced into a combat boot, had been thrown under one of the seats where, for the sake of Harry's already churning stomach, it lay mercifully in shadow. Trying to avoid actually looking at the wound, Harry helped Cavendish twist the tourniquet on. The woman was unconscious, her face ashen with shock and her eyes rolled back so that nothing but the whites were showing.

The pepper gas created by the explosion of the firebomb was rolling down the car toward them in a faint, foaming mist, and like Harry, Mark Cavendish was beginning to feel the effects.

"Get her under the arms, Harry!" instructed the veteran, coughing. Harry did as he was told and together they dragged the terrorist out of enemy territory and back into their own domain. They had a prisoner.

The eight-man demolition team and the thirteen-man SAS antiterrorist unit from Hereford met at the Trail, British Columbia, airport at 3:00 P.M., Mountain Daylight Time. From there, utilizing four Huey helicopters from the Canadian Forces base at Comox, they were flown to the Connaught Tunnel site, high in the Selkirk Mountains. They landed behind the unused Glacier Siding station, which they had commandeered as a staging base. By five-thirty, both groups had offloaded their equipment and begun their assigned tasks. Four of the eight demolitions men made their way two hundred yards down the right-of-way to the west portal of the tunnel, where they began attaching charges to the portal entrance and the ventilator fan housing above it. The other four demolitions men and the majority of the SAS team then boarded two self-propelled maintenance trolleys at the siding and entered the tunnel itself. A three-man SAS sniping team remained on the sloping ground just beyond the west portal to prevent anyone from exiting the tunnel, once the train had entered from the other end.

Another six of the SAS group deployed themselves along the tunnel's interior at eighty-foot intervals, working back from the east portal entrance. According to the Canadian Pacific traffic control office, the train would come to a full stop with the last car two hundred feet within the tunnel. The SAS men, who intended to board the train through the windows, were all equipped with frame charges, stun grenades, and submachine guns. Six of the men would go into the train itself, while a seventh man, equipped with a U.S.-made Dragon recoilless antitank weapon, would remain in the center of the tunnel where he would be able to destroy the cab of the train and whoever was inside it at the time. The last three members of the SAS group continued on through and out of the tunnel, taking up a position behind a small, windowless tool shed beside the right-of-way about a hundred feet from the entrance. Like their companions at the west portal, their job was to ensure that none of the terrorists escaped in that direction — or anyone at all, if the anthrax canisters exploded. All of the men were aware of the dangers, and each one knew that unless the train was taken very quickly, they stood little or no chance of survival. Also, unless a coded success message was radioed by the SAS commander within six minutes of the train's entering the tunnel, the commander of the demolitions group had orders to explode his charges, sealing the tunnel forever. For his part, the SAS commander had instructions that if for any reason he thought the anthrax canisters had been detonated during the operation, he was to radio a failure message immediately to the demolitions group in the Glacier station, who would then explode the charges at the east and west portals.

By 7:00 P.M., Mountain Daylight Time, everything and everyone was in place. Half an hour later a message was received from the Field, B.C., control tower; according to the CTC office in Calgary, the train had reached the Sawback siding at the eighty-eight mile mark of the Laggan Division. At its present rate of speed, it was expected to arrive at the east portal of the Connaught Tunnel in almost exactly three hours.

At 8:15 P.M., a Tilden Rent-a-Truck, which had been painted to resemble a CP maintenance vehicle, passed behind the old log building that had once been the railway station at Glacier, British Columbia. The driver of the truck, a man named Murak Shirad Azziz, was enjoying the scenery, so radically different from that of his native Libya, which he had left a week before. Although the first shadows of dusk were already gathering in the mountain valleys, Azziz had no difficulty spotting the activity around the Glacier station. Seeing the helicopters and men, he smiled.

Fifteen minutes later, having followed the twisting line of the highway around the base of Mount MacDonald, through the Rogers Pass, the Libyan flicked on his right-turn indicator and swung the truck smoothly off the Trans-Canada and onto a gravel road that headed up into the trees, and then swung east around the four-thousand-foot level of Mount Tupper. Through occasional breaks in the trees he could see the rail line and beyond it, even lower, the Trans-Canada. The road, obviously rarely used, began to slope down after four or five miles, and a few minutes later it ran out altogether in a small clearing beside a large signal box. Fifty feet beyond that, almost lost in the gloom, was the giant expanse of the Stony Creek Bridge, a five-hundred-foot-long, steel-and-concrete double arch that spanned the deep notch created by the narrow stream after which it had been named in 1893.

Azziz parked the truck, turned on the parking lights, then thrust the keys into his pocket. Leaving the vehicle, he crossed the rail line, following a barely visible track that led down through the trees. Half a mile farther on, the path came out on the verge of the Trans-Canada. He waited until there was no traffic in either direction and then crossed, disappearing into the undergrowth on the far side. After a dozen yards, the path reappeared and he paused to check his watch. The last time he'd made the journey it had taken him only a little more than an hour and a half, even climbing the relatively steep grade. He breathed in a deep lungful of the fresh mountain air, and smiled again. There was going to be lots of time.

Chapter 14

‖‖

Wednesday, June 29
Time: 8:45 P.M. MDT
Distance: 3,050 miles/4,908 km.

"I want to know her condition," said Harry Maxwell, seated in the dining car. The doctor, an elderly man named Kerwald, lifted his shoulders wearily.

"It's very difficult to say," he replied, pausing to sip at the cup of boiling hot coffee Stackpole had set before him a few moments before. "The tourniquet was applied quickly, so there was not a massive loss of blood, but she is in deep shock."

"Is she sleeping or unconscious?" asked Daniel Pendergast. At the next table, Mark Cavendish was checking over their weapons, taking inventory of their remaining ammunition. The pile of hardware in front of him was in bizarre contrast to the spray of plastic flowers set in a small vase between the salt and pepper containers.

"She is asleep," said the doctor. "I gave her a sedative. Meperidine hydrochloride."

"Will it keep her under?" asked Harry.

"For the time being."

"I want to talk to her," said Harry. "I want you to wake her up."

"I don't think that would be wise," said Kerwald.

"Why?"

"Because she is in very serious condition," said the doctor. "Any stimulant given to her at this point might make her condition even worse. It could easily be fatal."

"She's one of the terrorists, doctor. She's responsible for inflicting the pain you've been treating. She's a killer."

"That's beside the point," said Kerwald. "I cannot treat her in any way I feel would endanger her life."

"What have you got in the way of speed in that bag of yours?" Daniel cut in. The doctor, who carried his black bag on his lap, clutched it protectively, his lips thinning as he glanced at Daniel.

"By speed, I presume you mean stimulants," he said stiffly.

"Right," said Daniel. "Amphetamines, methedrine, anything like that."

"Certainly not," replied Kerwald. "I only carry the most basic medications when I travel."

"What do you have?" asked Harry quietly.

"Ritalin. Methylphenidate hydrochloride. It's used for hyperactivity in children, but it has the reverse effect on adults."

"How much would it take to bring her out of it for a few minutes?" asked Harry.

"Perhaps thirty milligrams," said the doctor. "I only have five-milligram tablets."

"We'll need twenty of them," said Harry. "I'll give her ten first, and if that doesn't work, I'll give her five more, all right?"

"I can't let you treat her!" said the doctor, outraged.

"Give me one of those," said Daniel, turning to Mark Cavendish and holding out his hand. The veteran selected one of the Ingrams and hooked a magazine into the receiver. He handed it across the aisle to Pendergast, who pulled back the slide and shoved the gun forward under the doctor's nose. "You seem like a nice man, Dr. Kerwald, and I'm sure Hippocrates would be proud of you, but we're running out of time. I don't enjoy playing the heavy, but either you give that bitch in the next car the drugs or we will, get the picture?"

"Please, doctor," said Harry.

The old man stared at the squat device in Daniel Pendergast's hand and grimaced. Finally he nodded, "I will give it to her. In her present state it may well take a little time to work."

"How long?" asked Harry.

"Fifteen, twenty minutes."

"Okay," said Harry. He turned to Mark Cavendish. "Take him in to her. Get Stackpole to stay with them and report here when she starts waking up."

Cavendish nodded, and he and the doctor stood up. Cavendish followed the elderly man back into the sleeper behind them. A few minutes later he was back. "It's all set," he said, sitting down to his arsenal again.

"You think she'll really be able to tell us anything?" asked Daniel.

"I sure as hell hope so," muttered Harry, looking forward through the glass windows of the vestibule doors and into the next car. "We got lucky there, but I think our luck is running out. Speaking of which, do you have any idea where we are?"

"Mottbrown says we just went through a place called Field. We're slowing down, too. Howard says the grade is increasing the deeper we get into the mountains."

"How far from Field to the tunnel?"

"About eighty miles. An hour and a half at this speed, maybe a little more."

"You still think the tunnel is it?" asked Daniel.

"More and more," said Mark. "I mentioned it to Mottbrown, and he told me that they have some kind of automatic braking system; there's actually a trickle current that runs through the rails and the wheels. He says it would be no problem at all for the authorities to stop the train in the tunnel."

"That's it, then," said Harry.

"But what if they stop before the tunnel?" asked Daniel. "Maybe we've got even less time than we think."

"I doubt it," said Cavendish. "If you look at the map, the best place for them to stop is Albert Canyon, about fifteen miles past the tunnel exit. It's a couple of miles from the main highway; there's a road and there's space to land a small plane. From here to the tunnel, you're never more than a couple of hundred yards from the Trans-Canada Highway. They wouldn't chance it."

"So how the hell are we supposed to stop the train before it hits the tunnel?" said Harry. He slammed his fist down on the table, frustration and anger threatening to boil over in him. It seemed that every life choice he'd made since leaving high school had been wrong. Even if there was still some spark of optimism in him that said losers were made, not born, it didn't change the fact that once again he was on the losing end of things. Except that now losing didn't mean just a boring, mindless job or even a jail sentence; it meant death.

"Goddamn!" he roared. And at exactly that moment

Wanda Jenkins Margay and Wolfgang Groz stepped into the dining car.

"Good Lord," said Wanda. "You *do* seem very upset, Mr. Maxwell."

"Sorry," said Harry. "I've just been spending a little time wishing I'd never been born, that's all."

"Oh dear," said Wanda. "And now here I am with more bad news."

"Well, lay it on me," said Harry, in a defeated tone.

The old lady sat down across from Harry, while Groz moved up to a table beyond where Mark Cavendish was fitting magazines into automatic weapons. The German sat down, his gnarled hands clasped over the head of Wanda's walking stick, giving him a dignified Old World look that seemed out of place in the ravaged car.

"We have a young woman in our roomette," Wanda began. "She seems to be very frightened."

"So are about seven hundred other people on this train," said Harry.

"This young lady has a particularly disturbing story," Wanda continued, ignoring Harry's comment. "We found her hiding in one of the toilet cubicles. She says she witnessed a murder."

"Pardon?" said Harry.

"A murder," Wanda repeated carefully. "She may be disturbed, but on the other hand, perhaps she's telling the truth. It may seem like an odd question under the circumstances, Mr. Maxwell, but are you aware of any murders recently?"

"Several," said Harry. "Which one did she happen to witness?"

"The one in Roomette Number Five of the *Riverdale*," she answered, naming the sleeper back from the diner. The roomette Adrian Tucker had died in.

"Go on," said Harry.

"She says there was a man in the roomette. His throat had been slit."

"What the hell is she talking about?" asked Mark Cavendish.

"Adrian," said Harry, without looking at the man. "He's dead."

"Why didn't you tell me?" asked Cavendish.

"Because we didn't know who'd done it," said Daniel

251

Pendergast. "It could have been anyone, Mark, even you. Only Harry and I knew about it."

"What about you?" Cavendish asked hotly. "Maybe it was you."

"Stop it!" snapped Harry. "We don't have time for this kind of shit. Excuse me, Wanda. This girl, what did she see?"

"The girl's name is Kenzie McLeod, and both Herr Groz and I questioned her in detail. She could give no real description of the man, but she says that as he left the roomette he dropped this from his trousers pocket." Wanda reached into her purse and took a small object out of it. She laid the key on the table in front of Harry. Both Mark Cavendish and Daniel leaned forward to look at it. Harry picked it up and squinted as he read the inscription on the tag.

"What does FEC stand for, I wonder?" he asked rhetorically.

Wanda surprised him by immediately supplying the answer. "Florida East Coast," she said. "A railway I used to travel on with some frequency in my younger days. It ran from Jacksonville south along the coast through Daytona, Palm Beach, and Fort Lauderdale before arriving in Miami. Very picturesque."

"I'm sure," said Harry. "Do you know what this thing is?"

"Certainly," Wanda said promptly. "It's a switch key. A conductor would use it to open the switch boxes at various places to manually change tracks. A single key would open every switch box on the line, usually."

"But it wouldn't do anybody any good for the switch boxes here, would it?" asked Harry, trying to figure out why one of the terrorists would have been carrying such a key.

"No, of course not," said Wanda. "It is what I believe they call railroad memorabilia. People collect them."

"Who?" asked Harry.

"Train buffs," Wanda replied simply.

There was a long silence, broken only by the steady rumbling chatter of the train as it steadily clawed its way up the mountain passes toward the Connaught Tunnel.

"My God," Daniel whispered. "Mottbrown."

"I don't believe it," said Cavendish.

"Neither do I," said Harry, staring at the switch key. "It doesn't make any sense. Why would Howard help us the way he did, if he was one of them? And what reason would he have had to join them?"

"This Mottbrown," said Groz quietly. "He is the small man who looks much like the actor Donald Pleasence?"

"That's him," said Harry.

"Then he is not your murderer or a terrorist," said the German emphatically. "The young girl did notice one thing about the man. He was *schwarz*."

"I beg your pardon?" said Harry.

"*Schwarz*," explained Groz. "The man was black."

"Jesus! Hamilton Stackpole!" hissed Cavendish.

"That's crazy," said Harry, frowning. "How could he be one of them? He works for Amtrak."

"Exactly." Daniel grimaced. "It all makes sense. He's been feeding them inside information from the start. Who the hell pays any attention to stewards on a train? He could have given them security for the Night Owl, chapter and verse. He even said they'd picked him to be a messenger boy. He does that Uncle Tom act, and nobody even notices him."

"But he sent Norm Kettering to us," said Harry, still unwilling to believe that Stackpole was their man.

"Sure," Cavendish interjected. "Norm told us himself that he's required to list the fact that he carries a gun when he travels on public transportation. Stackpole didn't want a man with a gun on the loose, so he sent him to us. They were just putting all their eggs in one basket. If they knew where we were, they could keep track of us."

"I guess we got out of hand a little," said Harry. He leaned back in his seat, shaking his head. "Stackpole!"

"And he's in there now with our wounded pigeon," said Daniel. "Just what are we supposed to do about that?"

"Get him out," said Cavendish. "Get him in here on some excuse. Tell him we need his advice."

"Perhaps I should be the one to inform Mr. Stackpole," Wanda suggested to Harry. She glanced at Cavendish and Daniel Pendergast. "I don't think either of your friends here could maintain the necessary poker face."

"Okay," said Harry. "You'll be safer back there, anyway." He turned and looked over his shoulder at Groz.

"Maybe you'd better do the same, sir. It might be dangerous to stay here."

"I shall remain where I am," the German said slowly. "I assure you, this man will not make me afraid."

"All right, then, Wanda, go get him," Harry instructed. The old woman nodded and stood up, retreating down the aisle with the rolling gait of someone perfectly at ease with the shuddering sway of a train in motion.

"Now what?" said Daniel.

"Switch places with Mark and cover Stackpole from there. Mark, you move back to the table nearest the door. If he tries to get back into the passenger section, kill him."

Cavendish picked up one of the Ingrams, pulled back the slide, and sat down at a table in the rear of the dinette, the small weapon hidden on his lap. Daniel took his place across the aisle from Harry while Groz remained where he was, his old hands crossed on the gleaming knob of the walking stick, his lined and weathered face expressionless. A few moments later Stackpole appeared.

"She's not waking up," he said, coming down the aisle.

"It doesn't matter, Hamilton," said Harry, trying to keep his voice calm. "Sit down. We've got something more important to talk about."

"What's happening?" the man said easily, slipping into the seat across from Harry.

Harry Maxwell flipped the switch key onto the tablecloth. Stackpole's eyes flickered to it, and then back to Harry. "What is it?" he asked.

"You know what it is, you bastard," said Harry. "You used to work the Florida East Coast."

"I don't know what you're talking about, man," said Stackpole, frowning.

"Don't give me that hip 'man' shit," said Harry. "It's your key ring, Hamilton. The one you dropped in the corridor after you killed my friend Adrian."

Stackpole made no attempt to protest his innocence. He smiled slightly and nodded. "He heard me talking. You asked me to check to see if one of the toilets was backed up and to break one of the windows if it was, remember? Well, I used the time to try to contact my people at the head end. Adrian heard me talking and came into the roomette. I had no choice. It was him or me."

"Bullshit," Daniel snarled. "Adrian was no threat to you. You didn't have to kill him."

"He would have talked."

"You had a radio?" asked Harry.

"Sure. My people gave me good equipment."

"Why did you join up with them?" asked Cavendish. "How much did they pay you?"

"More than the fucking railroad ever did," Stackpole spat. "I fought for this fucking country and almost died for it, and when I got out of the army I thought, shit, things have changed, so I went to college and learned *nothing* had changed. I was a Little Black Sambo just like all the rest of my pickaninny friends. I wanted to be a teacher, and the best I ever got was a job on the Pennsylvania Railroad, my friend. And when that was over I got a job on Amtrak. And you know what? By then I thought I was lucky to have a job at all. And then they took that away. I was 'redundant,' they said, and they offered me half pension if I quit without giving them too much trouble. Sweet deal. I give them half my life and they want to kiss me off with four hundred bucks a month. The chance came along for me to make enough money to actually *do* something with my life, you bet your sweet ass I took it, and no regrets."

"No regrets for killing a man?" Harry asked softly. He could understand Stackpole's bitterness at the hand he'd been dealt by life, but he could neither understand nor forgive the murder of his friend.

"No regrets," said Stackpole, staring directly at Harry. "I can't afford regrets anymore." The black man stood up slowly, his left hand coming out of his jacket pocket as he rose. The hand held what appeared to be a cardboard tube the size of a small tin of fruit juice.

"Don't tell me," muttered Harry, his eyes fixed on the small device.

"Sorry," said Stackpole. "According to my people, this thing is a Belgian polyvalent hand grenade that blows out about five hundred pieces of steel wire when you set it off. There's enough here to turn you all into hamburger. Even if any of you shot me, I'd still take you out. This thing supposedly has a range of about a hundred and thirty feet. Supposed to be the same kind of explosive they've got wired to the doors, so be cool, understand?"

"No problem," Harry said wearily.

"Smart boy," said Stackpole with a smile. He turned, keeping his eyes on Harry, Daniel, and Cavendish, walking backward toward the head end, holding the grenade at arm's length. Behind him, Wolfgang Groz smiled too, as though he'd thought of something mildly amusing. Silently he twisted the head of the walking stick between his legs and withdrew the blade, the soft snicking sound of the steel leaving its ebony sheath masked by the incessant beating of the wheels below.

As Stackpole moved beside his table, the grenade outstretched in his hand, Groz lifted the blade. Still holding the head of the stick in both hands, he turned slightly and rose smoothly from his seat, the point of the blade cutting through Stackpole's jacket and shirt, then pressing home between his third and fourth ribs to lodge finally in the left ventricle of the man's heart. Groz then used the dagger as a lever and pushed back slightly. The blade, made almost a hundred years before by a company that had long since seen more profit in razor blades, sliced upward within Stackpole's chest, virtually cutting the man's heart in two. With almost offhanded casualness, Wolfgang Groz let go of the dagger and leaned forward, taking the hand grenade out of the man's unresisting hand. Stackpole made a small coughing sound that was followed by a silent gout of blood that spurted from his mouth. Then he fell face forward onto the floor of the car. Groz stared at the body, which was lying in a steadily growing pool of blood.

"*Scheisse*," he spat, scowling. He looked up at the stunned men, frozen in their seats a few feet away.

"There was no problem, really," he said, a smile broadening across his weathered face. "He still had the safety pin through the arming lever."

"Jesus Christ!" whispered Daniel Pendergast. "I think I wet my pants!"

"No word from Mr. White?" asked Annalise Shenker, coming back into the RPO from the engine. Mohamet Kawi shook his head and continued to check the bindings on the four large duffel bags laid out in front of the shipping doors. On the table, which had once been used as the communications center for the Treasury Department guards, a small military transceiver sat silently, its long whip antenna vibrating constantly from the racketing movement of the train. This close to the straining diesel and its B unit, the terrorist leader had to raise her voice to be heard.

"What about Raoul and Lisa?" she asked, frowning.

"Nothing," said Kawi. He stood up, satisfied that the bundles were secure. "I think we must assume that they have been killed or captured."

"Then it is just the three of us," said Shenker. "And it is almost over."

"How is Sheila?" asked Kawi.

"Very tired. The Dexedrine has kept her going until now, but even with the drug she is finding it difficult." Shenker dropped into the chair in front of the radio table, the muscles of her face slack with fatigue. Looking at her, Kawi wondered how he could ever have found her attractive. Here, now, with the strain of the last days so visible on her face, he could see the real woman beneath the façade of her beauty. It was the face of someone who had died a long time ago, and the Libyan found himself wondering what could have made a woman like her into the stone-hearted creature she was. Their lovemaking of a few hours before had been repellant, the sucking desire of a female spider that is about to eat its mate. To kiss her was to taste the first clod of earth thrown into a grave. His own commitment was much easier to understand; with both parents killed in a refugee camp when he was only six, he had been an easy victim of Qaddafi's revolutionary rhetoric. By the age of twenty, the only job he was fit to do was murder. The rhetoric had long since worn off. The work remained, and he took a certain professional satisfaction in it, but nothing more.

"How much longer?" he asked.

"Sheila says that we have just passed the Rogers siding. Less than ten miles more. Fifteen or twenty minutes."

"And the tunnel?" asked Kawi.

"We shall know soon enough. Sheila knows what to look for. If the truck lights are on, then they will be at the tunnel as we expected."

"If Azziz arrived on time," said Kawi.

"He will have arrived," said Shenker, smiling coldly.

257

"He has the best of incentives, Mohamet. If he does not arrive, then his life is forfeit. The world is full of those who would be most happy to avenge our deaths."

"To be avenged is an honor I would just as soon avoid," Kawi commented.

"You grow weary of the game, then?" she asked.

The Libyan shrugged. "It was never a game for me, Annalise. It is only what I do."

"A toiler in the fields, Mohamet?" Shenker said with a sneer. "A faceless member of the great proletariat? The image hardly suits you."

"Don't try to bait me, Annalise," Kawi warned. "There is no time."

"You are right," said Shenker. She turned in her seat and picked up the small radio handset from the table. She stood up, slipping it into the breast pocket of her jacket, pushing down the snap. "You know the routine?"

Kawi nodded. "The charge will be set on the coach door within five minutes. Once the train has stopped, no one will be able to leave unless he is willing to come across the tops of the cars, as Raoul and Lisa did. Even if they blow out some of the windows, only a very few will be able to escape, and those people will find themselves three hundred feet in the air with nowhere to go. When the charge has been set, I return here and wait until the train has come to a halt, then I open the doors. If the truck is there and Azziz is at the rendezvous, we should be all right." The Libyan gestured at the transmitter in Shenker's pocket. "Do you intend to use that?" he asked.

"Of course," she said, seemingly surprised that he would even ask. "If we encounter any difficulties, it will be a useful bargaining tool, and once we have escaped, it will be a final gesture. Perhaps the Americans will think twice about their new policies on chemical and biological warfare when they see it used so close to home."

"Americans only think twice about sex and money," said Kawi. "It is their greatest strength and their tragic flaw."

Shenker ignored the comment and checked her watch. "Set the charge," she said. "It is time."

"Come on, come on!" Harry insisted, leaning over Daniel's shoulder.

"Shut up! I'm going as fast as I can!" The artist flipped through the pages of the slim paperback, his fingers fumbling, sweat stinging his eyes and dampening his armpits. Norm Kettering, Frank Sagadore, and Walter Linberg had joined the others in the dining car after Wanda Jenkins raised the alarm.

Sagadore was at one of the windows, its blind now up and his hands cupping the glass so he could catch a glimpse of the terrain outside. "We just went over a bridge!" he called out.

"Big fucking help!" Daniel groaned. "There's a dozen goddamn bridges in this book. What else do you see?"

"A lot of great big shadows," Sagadore answered. "Mountains, a river way down there. No, wait. Shit, yes! Half a dozen tracks. Some kind of siding! A long bridge and then a siding!"

"Hang on," Pendergast muttered. "Beaver River ... Cupola Creek ... Alder Creek ... Here it is! Mountain Creek Bridge, and then right after it a place called Griffith! A 114-car siding. Christ, I hope this book has got it right."

"Forget that," said Harry. "What's between it and the tunnel?"

"Right. Right. Okay, um ... Bryant's Creek Bridge."

"How long?" asked Harry.

"Says eighty-three feet."

"No good, keep going."

"Cedar Creek, 222 feet. Sturdee — that's a water tower station. Raspberry Creek, 107 feet ... Mud Chute Bridge, forty feet — shit, that's no good. Uh, Cutbank, another siding. Wait, here's something. Stoney Creek Bridge, 484-foot triple span over Stoney Creek. Yeah ... yeah ... the highest bridge on the Canadian Pacific Railway, 325 feet above the creekbed, and right after it, on the far side of the bridge, there's an old car siding and water tank station."

"After that?" asked Linberg.

"Nothing. The next point of interest in the book is the Connaught Tunnel."

"Okay," said Harry. "We go with this Stoney Creek Bridge place. How far are we from it?"

"Griffith is at mile seventy-one in this division. According to this, Stoney Creek Bridge is 76.2."

"Five miles," said Sagadore, still scanning the dark landscape outside. "I've been counting poles. We're not going over thirty-five or forty on this grade. That gives us about seven or eight minutes."

"Time for a good long prayer," grunted Linberg, who was slumped in one of the dining car chairs.

"Better than that," said Harry. "Figure it out. They're probably going to stop on the bridge. Maybe they're going to blow it up, I don't know. Anyway, it's our best bet. This train is a hell of a lot longer than 484 feet, which means there are going to be cars on solid ground, probably at either end. As soon as the train stops, we can start getting people off."

"How the hell are we going to do that?" asked Cavendish.

"We can do it," Harry insisted, the adrenaline rushing through his system, giving him an almost overwhelming feeling of euphoria and raw power. "Keep an eye on where we stop relative to the bridge. If it looks like there are more forward cars on solid ground, move the people forward. You can bet your ass they'll have mined one of the doors up there, so be careful. When you get to a car that's not on the bridge, somebody's going to have to trip the charge on the outer door."

"How?" asked Daniel.

"Tie a string around it and pull. Tie your shoelaces together. I don't care, just blow it open and start getting the people out as soon as the smoke clears."

"I saw a reel of wire in the stores cupboard in our car," said Wolfgang Groz. "I think that would do."

"Then get it," said Harry. The old man nodded and stood up, heading toward the rear of the train.

"What if the only car is one of the ones with a canister of anthrax?" asked Linberg.

"Keep going forward until you come to a car that doesn't have one. It doesn't matter, just so long as you start getting the people off as soon as the train stops."

"You're talking about a lot of people," said Linberg. "It's going to take a while."

"Better we save some than none," said Harry. "What do you want to do, sit here and wait for whatever they've got in store for us?"

"That kind of sounds like what you're going to be doing," drawled Kettering. "You keep on giving orders to everyone else. What's your part in all of this?"

"I'm going out through the dome car window," said Harry. "Right now."

"Over the tops of the cars?" Linberg said incredulously. "You've got to be crazy. This thing is rocking around curves every thirty seconds."

"Those two in the observation car did it a while back," said Harry. "So can I. One of the terrorists has got whatever kind of radio control is needed to pop those canisters. I'm betting on Shenker — the good-looking one. I want to get to her before she can pull the plug on the whole goddamn train."

"Alone?" asked Kettering.

"Yeah, unless someone else wants to volunteer," said Harry, looking around at the other people in the car.

The Selkirk Mountains of British Columbia lie in an area just west of the Rocky Mountain Trench, and in geological terms they are among some of the youngest mountains in the world. During the Jurassic and early Tertiary period, 195 million years ago, the mountains, already immense, were subjected to a series of tortuous batterings and foldings that twisted and tore the monstrous spikes of rock into spurs and ridges, canyons and immense, sloping plateaus as large as cities, and were able to turn a river's course from north to south with the ease of a child creating tiny worlds on an ocean beach. Ice ages came and went, huge dinosaurs plodded through the cavernous gorges, and eventually, seventy or eighty million years ago, the giant forests began to shroud the torn rocks like a thick green blanket as Sitka spruce, the Douglas fir, the western hemlock, and cedar flourished. As recently as 1900, virtually none of the area had even been explored, and less than a century of man's presence has made almost no visible impact on a land where time is best measured in millennia. During the daylight hours it is possible to see the faint imprint of man's hand: narrow highways, power lines, and the two main rail lines cling to the flanks of the gigantic peaks, but as darkness falls, time spins back and humanity fades away. The mountains become huge dragon's teeth, rivers turn to moonlit glass, and the forests range everywhere, brooding gloomily in the silent night.

The wind created by the steady motion of the train as it stuttered up through the Rogers Pass tore at Harry Maxwell's clothes, and even in June the temperature had fallen low enough to numb his hands. Each movement of the train as it took another curve threatened to swing him off the narrow roof of the car, and with each passing second he expected to hear a shout from either Daniel or Mark Cavendish as one or the other was thrown into the gorge yawning on the left, or was crushed against the rock wall rising steeply on the right.

He stiffened, terrified, as the train lurched around a tight curve, then hit the echoing plates of yet another bridge. He kept his eyes focused forward on the barely visible hump of the diesel far ahead, and a small part of his brain wondered if the horrible gauntlet of railroad cars would ever end. He told himself that the first step out of the shattered window of the forward dome had been the hardest, and kept on, waiting for a straight stretch of track before he jumped the gap between each car. Moving as quickly as they could, the three men crabbed their way toward the head end, hunched over, legs spread and fingers grabbing at the tiny hand grips offered by the fluted ridges that ran along the top surface of each car. None of the men had any concept of how much time had passed; their entire beings were caught up in the single act of maintaining their balance from the moment they had crawled out of the dome.

Harry reached the end of yet another car and paused, spread-eagled on the roof, his heart slamming painfully in his chest as he breathed deeply, trying to conjure up the will to keep moving. Suddenly he realized that the roof of the car ahead was different from the others he'd traversed. He'd gone from the relatively flat roofs of the Canadian cars to the much more dangerous, rounded roofs of the Amtrak rolling stock, and now the roof ahead was flat again. Staring in the almost total darkness, he saw the twin rows of ventilator ports and recognized the car. It was the RPO.

A few moments later, the other two men reached the end of the last car as well.

"Why have we stopped?" yelled Daniel, his mouth an inch away from Harry's ear as he tried to make himself understood above the deafening roar of the train. Harry pointed forward, keeping one hand firmly on the roof of the car. "The RPO!" he answered. "End of the line!"

"What do we do now?" Mark Cavendish called out, kneeling a foot behind Harry and flexing his aching shoulders where the harness holding his arms had chafed his skin into burning agony.

"This has got to be the coach with the hole blown in the doors!" said Harry. "We can climb down into the space between the cars, and go in that way!"

"Why not keep going?" barked Daniel.

Harry shook his head. "Too risky! They could hear us moving over the roof! Don't worry. I've done it before, remember? There's handgrips on the side of the car. We can climb down and swing over through the hole!"

"You're nuts!" called Cavendish.

"Right!" answered Harry. "That's how I got here in the first place."

"Hey! We're slowing down!" yelled Daniel.

Harry lifted his head and stared forward. Daniel was right, the vibration of the car beneath him was changing, and so was the sound of the engine. Craning his neck, he stared upward; there was nothing to see but the looming bulk of the tree-covered slope on his right, and the thin, twisting line of the Beaver River far below him on the left. "This has to be it!" he bellowed. Then, desperately trying not to think about what he was doing, he stood up and stepped onto the swinging accordion folds of the diaphragm between the head-end coach and the RPO. Kneeling, he inched forward until he could see the first of the grab bars on the side of the coach. He slid his legs forward, one hand grasping for the U-shaped metal grip, letting himself drop off the edge of the diaphragm.

For a terrible moment he thought his hands had grown too numb to grip the bar, but then his dangling feet found one of the lower rungs and he was safe. By now the train had slowed to a snail's pace. Looking upward, he could see a dark shadow blotting out his vision: Daniel, following behind him. Then he looked down and the world ended.

The train had begun its approach to the Stoney Creek Bridge, heading out over the first of the three spans. The bridge, originally constructed in 1893 and rebuilt several times since, had left no allowance on either side, and Harry suddenly found himself suspended over the dark pit of Stoney Creek Canyon, the thread of the creek almost invisible more than three hundred feet below his heels. He felt his stomach rising in his throat, and knew that the only way he was going to survive was by getting the hell off the bulkhead as quickly as he could. Closing his eyes, he went down another rung and then eased his left leg out, searching for the opening created by the explosion of the door-bomb. Every muscle in his body wire-taut, he groped with his foot, the sudden feeling of metal against the sole of his shoe so much of a relief that he almost lost his hold on the grab bar. He opened his eyes, staring at the painted metal wall of the car, then let go with his left hand, searching for a hold within the car. His fingers touched the rounded end of a dangling cable, and after a single pull to see if it would hold his weight, he took a deep breath and swung himself around. As he did so, the upraised barrel of the Ingram strapped to his back clipped him behind the ear, stunning him. He swayed, almost blacking out, then recovered, hauling himself inside. He slumped against the inner wall of the car, sobbing for breath as the train slowed even more. A moment later, Daniel Pendergast swung around the side of the car, dropping to the floor of the exploded vestibule in a gasping heap. He raised himself to his knees and looked up at Harry.

"Never again, Maxwell. Never again will I listen to one of your stupid ideas!" he groaned.

"What about Mark?" asked Harry, still trying to catch his breath.

"Up top," said Daniel, climbing to his feet and pulling his Ingram around to a firing position. "Said there was no way for his arms on those rungs. He'll cover us from the roof."

"All right," said Harry. As he spoke, the train jerked and almost stopped, moving at less than a walking pace.

Daniel leaned out through the gaping hole in the side of the car.

"Almost off the bridge," he said, turning back to Harry. "What now?"

"Move back so nobody sees us," Harry instructed, keeping his voice down now that the train was almost at a halt. "Give them a couple of minutes to get clear, and then we go in through the door." He pointed the barrel of his submachine gun at the blank door of the RPO.

"What if it's locked?" asked Daniel.

"It won't be," said Harry, shaking his head. "And if it is, we go out the side." The wheels shrieked as the brakes were applied and at long last the train came to a jerking halt. Almost immediately, both Harry and Pendergast could hear a grating, rumbling sound.

"What the hell is that?" asked Daniel.

"The RPO doors," Harry murmured. "The sons of bitches are stealing our money!"

"*Our* money?" Daniel gaped. "Jesus Christ, Harry, you're not still thinking about *that*, are you?"

"You're goddamn right I am, Daniel. I didn't go through all of this for a fucking boy scout merit badge. I'm going to get what's mine."

"I could have had a good job as a grade-school art teacher, and here I am, stuck in the middle of the Rocky Mountains with a lunatic," whispered Pendergast, shaking his head in disbelief. "I'm going to die so Harry Maxwell can prove something to the world. Shit!"

"You're not going to die, damn it!" said Harry in a grating whisper. "Just shut up and do what I tell you." He moved in closer to the door, waiting tensely, Daniel behind him and both figures lost in the shadows of the vestibule. The only sound now was the asthmatic heaving of the idling engine and the uneven metallic clanking as the heated bearings in the wheels began to cool in the chill night air. Harry held his breath, expecting to hear gunfire at any moment, either from the terrorists or from Cavendish up above. There was nothing. Easing forward a single step, he reached out with his free hand and tried the handle of the RPO door. The latch gave slightly — unlocked. He nodded to Daniel, now standing beside him. He closed his eyes, letting his breath out slowly. He had a sudden vivid image in his mind of the thermos-like canisters strung through the train. If he didn't reach the Shenker woman in time . . .

Abruptly, the relative silence was split by the crackling roar of an engine, the mechanical chatter so unexpected that Harry flinched, almost dropping his weapon.

"Motorcycle?" whispered Daniel, confused. Then from above them came the sputtering of Mark's Ingram. The waiting was over. Harry thumbed down the latch, put his shoulder to the door, and slammed into the RPO, his own weapon up and ready, Daniel rushing in beside him. The lights in the car blinded Harry for a moment, and he squinted against the sudden brilliance, barely conscious of the figure at the wide RPO loading doors. The man turned, and Harry recognized the stubby shape of a sawed-off shotgun in his hands. He squeezed the trigger of the Ingram blindly, spraying the doorway as though using a garden hose. Mohamet Kawi, loaded down with the last of the duffel bags, made no sound as the almost solid stream of high-velocity bullets stitched across his chest, the shotgun discharging toward the roof of the RPO as he was blown out the doors and down onto the cinder right-of-way.

Harry and Daniel sprinted forward, keeping out of any possible line of fire, and reached the wide-open doors of the car just in time to see Annalise Shenker, mounted on a three-wheeled all-terrain vehicle, driving wildly out of the pool of light thrown by the open doors. Two more of the ATVs, each with a duffel bag strapped on its carrier, were standing beside a parked blue and white panel truck. Between the two remaining vehicles lay the body of Sheila Teng. A voice came out of the darkness above the open doors.

"Goddamn! I missed!" It was Mark.

Harry stopped and then dropped to the ground outside the RPO, Daniel right behind him. Shenker was traveling without lights, but Harry could hear the sound of the three-wheeler disappearing off to the left.

"Get down here!" he shouted up to Cavendish. Without waiting for an answer, he ran across the packed earth and straddled one of the machines, looking for a way to start it up. He found the electric start button on the handlebar and pressed, praying. The Honda fired up with a bellow. Turning around in his seat, he saw that Daniel was already on the second ATV. Behind him Harry could see the entire length of the train, trailing back over the narrow bridge to the far side of the gorge. Absurdly, a shred of verse from one of his old Comparative Religion courses came into his head: "Done is a battle on the Dragon black, our Champion Christ confoundeth he his force; the hounds of hell are broken with a crack!" He snorted noisily. He was hardly Christ, and the "battle of the Dragon black" wouldn't be over until the last hound of hell was blown away.

There was a thud, followed by a curse, as Mark Cavendish dropped from the roof of the forward coach, hitting the ground in a roll. Daniel started up the second ATV as Cavendish ran toward them.

"On the back!" yelled Harry, jerking a thumb behind him. He fumbled around with his foot until he managed to get the machine in gear, and with a neck-snapping jerk the ATV bounded forward. Harry felt Mark's steel arms hook tightly around his chest, and let out a whoofing breath.

"Sorry!" shouted the veteran. The ATV hit the tracks just ahead of the high-nosed diesel and leaped into the air, dropping down onto the pathway beyond. "Where the hell are we going?"

"You said you missed!" Harry yelled over his shoulder. "I'm going to give you another chance at her!"

"Where did she go?"

"How the hell should I know? There's nothing but this path, so she must be down there somewhere."

As Harry spoke, the open area around the bridge abutments narrowed and dropped away down the slope of the mountain. The path was barely wide enough for the machine, edged on both sides by dense cedar scrub. The engine was clearly suffering, but Harry didn't have time to learn the gears so he simply kept on going, his hand twisting the throttle as far as he dared. Harry was faintly aware of the sound of Daniel's machine behind him, and he was thankful that his friend had taken the time to find the headlight switch. The illumination from the rear ATV wasn't much, but it was enough to bring the worst of the hazards ahead into sharp relief. Even so, the steepening trail was like a nightmare as the path twisted back and forth around rocks and bramble-thick bush. Then, almost magically, the path opened up onto the surreal smooth expanse of the Trans-Canada Highway. Harry never even thought of slowing. There was no way Shenker had gone in either direction down the empty, moonlit stretch of blacktop. He whipped the ATV across the highway and into the trees on the far side, Daniel riding pell-mell behind.

For a full minute after the train came to a halt on the bridge, it seemed as though everyone on board was holding his or her breath. Except for the metallic clicking of the cooling bogies beneath the cars, everything was silent. Then, like the muttering wind before a gathering storm, the passengers, crammed into the rear coaches and sleepers, began to talk to one another, their voices low but steadily rising. One by one they began sliding up the blinds covering the windows, and as they began to realize the train's precarious position high above the gorge, panic began to build. With the sound of muffled shots in the distance, full-blown hysteria erupted. Within seconds, everyone who was able stood up and began to move toward the rear of the train, knowing intuitively that the climax of the crisis through which they had been living was at hand. Almost instantly the aisles were blocked completely. People began to scream as they were trampled by the crush of other passengers trying to reach any exit that would take them from the horror of the bridge and the yawning abyss below. It was like a scene from Dante come to life, and inevitably it resulted in tragedy. As the horde of passengers pressed toward the rear of the train, all logic and common sense were lost. There were no acts of heroism, but only fear, and any noble thoughts of "women and children first" were lost in the mass desire to survive. Several passengers, unable to keep their places, were forced to one side as they made their way into the vestibule between the first two sleeping cars of the VIA consist, and a woman's elbow struck the detonator wire of the charge on the outer door. There was a monstrous cracking sound as the device exploded, turning the vestibule into a maelstrom of metal fragments that chewed through flesh and bone. A score of people died in a split second, and a dozen more were wounded massively. Almost as bad, the explosion ignited several containers of cleaning fluid in a storage cupboard abutting the vestibule. In less than a minute the ends of the two sleepers had become an inferno that began to creep both forward and back, reversing the stampede of passengers and effectively cutting off any access to the rear of the train.

Norm Kettering and Howard Mottbrown had been on their way back to the rear observation sleeper when the explosion occurred, and it was only Kettering's brute strength that made it possible for them to clear a path back to the diner, the swarms of panicking passengers close on their heels.

"You'd better bar the door," gasped Mottbrown, staggering to a seat and taking huge breaths. "They've all gone quite mad back there."

"He's right," said Kettering, manhandling one of the tables forward and jamming it into the doorway.

"Where is Frau Margay?" asked Wolfgang Groz, apprehension in his voice.

"I saw her quite some time ago," said Mottbrown, his chest still heaving from his unaccustomed exertion. "She said she was going back to her roomette. Something about taking care of her witness."

"She's still back there?" snapped Sagadore, helping Kettering and Linberg pile up more tables and chairs in front of the door.

"I assume so," said Mottbrown.

"*Lieber Gott!*" said Groz, moving toward the doorway. Linberg put a hand on the old man's arm.

"You can't go back there," he said quietly. "You'd never get through. Don't worry, Wanda can take care of herself. If she's in the observation car she should be all right. We have our own problems, sir."

"Has anyone checked forward?" asked Kettering.

Sagadore nodded. "Yeah. Walt and me. They've got enough plastique on the door two cars up to blow us all to hell and back. It looks like Maxwell and his friends took the easy way out by going over the top."

"So what do we do?" grunted Kettering, bracing the last table in the doorway.

"They planned it pretty carefully," said Linberg. "The car with the explosive charge on the door is also one of the cars with an anthrax canister, and it's also the last car on the bridge. No matter what we do, we're trapped."

"Then we have to move the train off the bridge," said Mottbrown.

"And just how are we going to do that?" Kettering asked. "We've got six hundred–odd people panicking back there, with a fire behind them. Not to mention the anthrax canisters."

"I will take care of the anthrax," said Groz. "If we can remove the canisters in the forward cars, they can be placed in one of the toilet cubicles. Even if the canisters explode, the bacilli will be contained."

"Okay," said Sagadore. "But that still doesn't tell us how to get the train off this bridge."

"Through the service hatch," said Mottbrown. "The same way you and Mr. Linberg came onto the train. Once over the bridge we could start the engine."

"How?" said Sagadore. "I'm no engineer."

"I could do it," said Mottbrown, swallowing hard. "The controls are quite simple, really."

"You figure you could walk a hundred and fifty feet or more across an open trestle?" Kettering asked skeptically.

"I could try," Mottbrown said weakly. "I don't have much of a head for heights, but . . . "

"How simple are the controls?" Sagadore cut in.

"Very," said Mottbrown.

"Could you teach me, fast?" he asked.

"I think so."

"Okay, I'll do it. I've got excellent night vision, and heights don't bother me at all."

"You'd better get to it," said Kettering, peering over the barricade. The fleeing passengers coming toward the head end were already crowding into the Daynighter. "The natives are getting restless."

"All right, Howard, start talking. When I'm out, you stick with Norm and keep the people away from that explosive charge. Walt, you help Mr. Groz with the canisters."

A few moments later, with Howard's instructions firmly in his mind, Frank Sagadore slipped out through the service hatch and into the cold night air on the bridge. Behind him, Howard Mottbrown and Norm Kettering had taken up their positions at the barricade, while Wolfgang Groz and Walter Linberg headed forward to the first of the cars containing germ canisters.

The Stoney Creek Bridge crosses the 325-foot-deep gorge of the same name, at the seventy-six-mile mark of the Field subdivision. Originally a wooden trestle built in 1884, the crossing was later replaced by a single-span steel arch 336 feet long. The present bridge, renovated in 1929, has several additional arches to cope with heavier trains, increasing the length of the bridge to 484 feet overall. Like most of the bridges in the Rocky Mountains, the structure is very basic in design, with few frills. The span is just wide enough to carry the tracks, with less than twenty inches of freeboard on either side, rails and ties resting on open girderwork, the roadbed bare of guard rails. From inside the train, it appeared as though the coaches were suspended in midair, and from outside it wasn't much better.

As Frank Sagadore let himself out through the hatch, he found himself balanced on a twelve-inch-wide railway tie with less than an arm's length between himself and the edge of the bridge. Had the hatch been on the left-hand side of the diner, he would at least have had the illusion of relatively closed-in space, since the lower bluffs of Hermit Mountain were only a few hundred yards away in the darkness. Unfortunately, the view to the right was considerably more frightening; the yawning chasm beneath his feet spread out to a gigantic vista stretching out in all directions, the barely seen rise of the mountains on the far side of the Beaver River more than five miles away. Sagadore, who had once thought his highly acute night vision was a blessing, now cursed it silently as his eyes adjusted to the darkness and the details of his terrifyingly precarious position became clear. Without moving he reached back, letting his fingers touch the pale comfort of the dining car's metal skin. He swallowed hard, fighting off the vertigo that was beginning to sweep over him in wave after nauseating wave. He knew that if he made the slightest movement, his legs would give way and he would go spinning down into the gaping hole that beckoned darkly beneath his feet. For the first time in his life he was horribly aware of what the phrase "thin air" meant.

"*Rallentare, rallentare,*" he whispered aloud — slowly,

slowly — the Italian of his youth coming back to him like a prayer. With legs and thighs as stiff as iron, he managed to turn slightly, his feet glued to the narrow tie, his eyes searching out the far end of the bridge. When he finally managed to turn fully, it seemed as though the abutment was at least a mile away; an impossible distance to walk. But there was no choice. He had to do it. He took a single step, swaying slightly, and leaned in toward the train. Realizing that he was holding his breath, he paused and exhaled, waiting until he was breathing normally again. Then, with his eyes fixed firmly on the distant line of trees that marked safe ground, he began to walk from one tie to the next, his progress agonizingly slow.

The fire that had come as a result of the explosion in the sleeper vestibule had created much more smoke than flame, and the fire-retardant refit done on the old rolling stock in the late sixties worked well enough to confine the flames to a small area. Ironically, it was the fire more than Norm Kettering's barricade that eventually stopped the passengers' headlong rush. The most intense fire burned in the shallow maintenance cupboard that held the cleaning fluid which had originally fueled the blaze. The cupboard was located no more than five feet from the car's main electrical switch panel, and as the metal bulkhead separating the panel from the cupboard began to heat up, the wiring in the electrical box began to melt. Within five minutes of the explosion, the fire in the cupboard reached its height. The main electrical conduit supplying the box, its insulation now melted off, dropped slightly, touching the bulkhead and shorting out. The main circuit breaker snapped over, and the lights in the car went out. Since the electrical current for the entire train was generated by the VIA diesel's B unit, the gap in the circuit blew out every light in the train, and the passengers were suddenly plunged into total darkness. The primal fear of darkness, combined with the equally potent realization that they were suspended several hundred feet over nothingness, stopped them cold.

When the train came to a stop on Stoney Creek Bridge, Wanda Jenkins Margay was in the section sleeper two cars from the *Mont Tremblant*. Almost immediately the narrow corridor of the car was jammed with passengers trying to move forward, elbowing the old woman out of the way as panic began to take hold. The crush of people, combined with the almost unbelievable stench of the fetid, airless car, almost defeated the ancient passenger, but after being swept halfway back up the car, she managed to squeeze into a recently vacated roomette. She waited in the tiny space until the crowd passed, then hurried down the corridor to the next car and Kenzie McLeod.

The young girl had locked the roomette door as she had been told to and only opened it when Wanda assured her that everything was all right.

"Why have we stopped?" she asked, as Wanda slipped into the cubicle. Wanda smiled as comfortingly as she could. The child was obviously very afraid, the terror in her eyes like that of a trapped animal. "I think the situation has come to a head," replied Wanda. "But we'll be quite all right if we remain calm. Herr Groz and the others have things well in hand."

"We've got to get out of here." As Kenzie spoke, the lights flickered and then went out. She screamed and pushed forward, almost knocking Wanda to the floor.

"Young lady!" Wanda snapped in a voice that had eight decades of authority behind it. "You've survived this long. Don't be foolish now."

"I'm scared," groaned Kenzie, no more than a shadow in the darkness. "Really scared."

"Of course you are," Wanda said evenly. "You would be a very stupid girl if you weren't frightened. I'm frightened too, I can assure you."

"What do we do?" said Kenzie, her breathing slowed to a nearly normal pace, Wanda's voice having calmed her.

The old woman thought hard, a gnarled hand grasping the doorway for support. She knew herself well enough to recognize that she was very near the end of her physical resources, but the young woman was counting on her.

"We have a choice," she said at last. "We can do the intelligent thing and simply wait for someone to come and help us, or we can leave the train."

"What about the man I saw?" asked Kenzie, the fear coming back into her face. "I don't want to die like that."

"You won't, child, not if I can help it," Wanda said firmly, wondering just how she *would* help it if the Stack-

273

pole man managed to evade Maxwell and the others. Her lips firmed into a hard line of determination. She didn't have enough information to go on, and it simply wasn't in her nature to depend on other people. She came to a decision, "We'll leave, I think," she said.

"How?" asked Kenzie.

"Through the back door," Wanda said simply. She reached out in the darkness until she found Kenzie's arm. "Come with me, child." Kenzie took her hand and they went out into the corridor, Wanda in the lead.

They turned left, heading toward the *Mont Tremblant*, feeling their way along the corridor. As they reached the door leading to the last car of the train, Wanda miscalculated and her face smacked into the protruding shape of a fire extinguisher. Her old-fashioned wire-rimmed glasses shattered, and the edge of the extinguisher opened up a deep gash on her forehead. She staggered, and it was only Kenzie's quick support that kept her on her feet.

"What happened?" asked the young woman.

"I seem to have walked into something," said Wanda, biting her lip to keep back the pain. A wave of dizziness washed over her and she almost fell.

"Are you okay?" asked Kenzie.

"Not entirely," said Wanda. "I've broken my spectacles, dear. You'll have to lead the way." The near total darkness was bad enough, but without her glasses she was as good as blind.

"Just tell me what to do," said Kenzie, a sudden strength in her voice.

"Take us into the next car," said Wanda. "We should be in a short corridor. We will bear to the right for a few feet, which will take us into the main corridor leading back to the lounge. Do you understand?"

"I think so," said Kenzie. "Left and then right back to the lounge." Supporting the old woman firmly with one hand, Kenzie did as she had been instructed, and within a few minutes they had reached the rear lounge.

"Open one of the blinds," said Wanda. "Tell me what you can see." She dropped thankfully into one of the lounge seats, wincing slightly at the pain in her forehead. Kenzie pushed up one of the blinds and stared out into the darkness.

274

"We're on a bridge," she said. "There's a big mountain, and what looks like some kind of creek."

"I see," said Wanda, thinking. "All right. This is what we must do. The rear window of this car is actually a door. It will almost certainly be locked. You'll have to break it open."

"With what?" asked Kenzie, peering into the gloom of the lounge.

"Can you lift one of these chairs?" asked Wanda.

Kenzie went to the curved tail end of the car and grasped one of the heavy lounge chairs. "I think so," she grunted. She heaved the chair out of the way and pushed up the blind on the rear window. Wanda was right. Behind the chair she could see that the window was part of a narrow door. Looking out through the glass, she saw that there was a good hundred feet of bridge between them and the end of the trestle.

"See if you can smash the handle," Wanda said weakly. The pain in her head had been joined by another, much more frightening symptom. A phantom hand seemed to be clutching at her chest, squeezing her lungs and making it difficult to breathe. She knew what the pain was, but she refused to acknowledge it, concentrating all her energies on getting the young woman safely off the train. She smiled to herself in the darkness. It would be a fair trade with fate if she could manage that.

There was crashing sound as Kenzie McLeod rammed the steel leg of the lounge chair down onto the handle of the rear door. Wanda squinted, trying to see what was going on, but she could only make out faint, ill-defined shadows.

"Got it!" Kenzie said triumphantly.

"Good for you," said Wanda. "Do you think you can make it down from the car?"

"I think so," said Kenzie. She crossed the lounge to where Wanda was sitting. "Let's get going."

Wanda shook her head. "I'm afraid you'll have to make do on your own, young lady. I have no head for heights."

"I'll help you," said Kenzie.

"No, dear. I'll just wait here until Herr Groz and the others come to my rescue. I'm a little too old to be running about on bridges in the middle of the night, thank you."

"You sure you'll be okay?" asked Kenzie, concern in her voice.

"Perfectly," said Wanda, tensing as a tearing pain ripped into her chest, running down her left arm like a red-hot wire. "Run along now, child, please."

Kenzie stood in front of the old woman for a moment, and then she turned. Wanda stared into the darkness, listening. A few seconds later she heard Kenzie drop down onto the trestle.

"Good-bye, dear heart," she whispered. "And good luck." Then the last monstrous beat of her heart blossomed, consuming the old woman in a single stroke of pain beyond description.

"Shit!" hissed Walter Linberg, crouching beside Wolfgang Groz at the head end of the Amtrak sleeper. The lights had gone out just as Groz was lifting the second canister from its perch on the electrical panel. The chemist froze in the darkness, waiting for the tubular container to burst in his hand. Linberg's heart thundered in his chest as the seconds passed. After a slow count to thirty, he allowed himself to breathe again.

"Christ! I thought you'd done something to the wires!" he breathed.

"No," said Groz with relief. "It could not be the canister. There is no connection, just a small retaining clip, like the other one." The first canister had been disposed of in the Amdinette toilet, which in turn had been covered with as much movable furniture as Linberg had been able to jam into the small cubicle. As a further precaution, he'd forced paper towels into the finned vent grill at the bottom of the door. If the canister went off, the spores wouldn't go far. Or so he hoped.

"So now what do we do?" asked Linberg.

"As before," said Groz. "We must concentrate on our task and nothing else. It is up to Herr Kettering and your friend Sagadore to keep us intact until we have dealt with these devices."

"In the dark?" asked Linberg.

"Yes," answered Groz, his face barely visible in the gloom. "We will simply proceed with even more care, yes?"

"You bet," said Linberg.

"*Gut*. Now, here." Groz handed the canister to Linberg,

276

who took it gingerly, grasping it in both hands. He turned slowly, feeling his way with his feet, holding the canister close to his chest.

His imagination had no difficulty conjuring up a vision of what was going on within the container and what would happen to him if the Shenker woman decided to trip the remote-control mechanism. Slowly but surely, he began making his way to the toilet cubicle a few feet away.

"God be with you, Harry Maxwell, wherever you are right now," he whispered.

As Linberg began the delicate process of disposing of the deadly canister, Harry Maxwell was dropping down a forty-degree grade through the bush on the northern side of the Beaver River, barely in control of the hammering machine he sat astride, his mind scrubbed clean by the immediate terror that at any moment the narrow path could disappear over the edge of a cliff. All he cared about for the moment was hanging on. Squeezed onto the saddle behind him, Mark Cavendish was only slightly more aware of his surroundings, and most of his attention was given over to keeping the powerful mechanisms of his hands firmly locked together around Harry's chest. Daniel Pendergast kept his own machine at full throttle, his eyes slitted against the dust raised by Harry's trike, following his friend by blind faith and intuition as much as by his senses.

Finally the path reached the bottom of the steep grade and then began to snake back and forth in a series of switchbacks through a maze of rock outcrops and clumps of brush that tore at Harry's clothing like spiny, clutching fingers. Ignoring the scratchy gauntlet, Harry tried desperately to think.

By his estimation, Shenker had no more than a two- or three-minute start, and since she was driving without lights, it was obvious that she had a pretty good idea where she was going. Common sense told him to give up the chase, but he kept on regardless. More important than the money was the control device for the germ canisters; come hell or high water, he had to make sure she didn't activate it. So he continued on, manhandling the three-wheeler along the path as it twisted around the foot of the monolithic northeastern ridge of Mount MacDonald. Twice they crossed narrow wooden bridges, clearly part of the nature trail they were following, and then they headed south, tracing a line along the 3,500-foot level of the sausage-shaped slopes of the Prairie Hills Moraine. They were in true forest, the train long out of sight and the Beaver River, now a hundred feet below them, completely hidden as well.

The path turned sharply east after less than half a mile and then began to climb, working upward in an almost perfectly straight line through the thick stands of cedar covering the glacial hill. They kept on that way for another mile, the thick tires and strongly torqued engine dragging them up the slope steadily, nothing visible to Harry's searching eyes except the sentinel trees on either side and the narrow, moss-grown path ahead.

And then it ended. The trees simply stopped and the two ATVs were suddenly racing across a canted alpine pasture as wide as a football field and three times as long. At the far end of the clover-covered dell, Harry could make out the dark, shadowed shape of a cabin, and beside it something much larger. Goggle-eyed, Harry squeezed the brake handle and the ATV skidded to a drifting halt.

"Holy shit! They've got a plane up here!" he said.

Daniel's machine came up beside them and all three men climbed off, their legs rubbery after the madcap run up the dark mountain. The silence was total, and standing there, lungs aching and heart pounding, Harry Maxwell was terribly frightened; half the world seemed blotted out in the negative space created by the mountains surging all around him, and he felt like a tiny Jonah swallowed in the belly of some gargantuan granite whale. His ears began to hum sharply and he was just barely aware of the rumbling sound of the half-seen airplane's engine as it started up in the dense shadows at the far end of the field above them.

The pitch of the aircraft engine increased, revving up to a steady, frantic whine, and then the shape beside the cabin began to move toward them, the high cantilevered wings catching the faint light of the half moon overhead.

"It's a Centurion!" said Mark Cavendish, staring. "Christ! We've still got a chance!" He reached out and hooked the slung Ingram over Daniel's head, his eyes on the plane as he pulled back the slide. Then he was moving, running up the slope toward the approaching bat-shape of the aircraft. Daniel followed him, bellowing incoherently, and in a daze Harry followed them, ducking his head to bring his own gun into play, pulling the slide and cocking it without really knowing what he was doing.

He came out of his reverie abruptly, a last spurt of energy somehow managing to surface out of the exhaustion and fear that threatened to take him over. The sound of the Cessna's turbocharged engine blasted into his ears as its needle nose raced toward them. With the airplane fifty yards away, Harry could actually see Shenker's face reflected in the dashboard lights, another figure in the pilot's seat. The distance narrowed even more, and Harry could see that her head was bent as though she was looking at something in her lap.

"Get down!" roared Cavendish. "Go for the belly! Hit the belly!"

Harry dropped and rolled, bringing the boxlike shape of the Ingram up as he faced the sky, firing directly upward as the pale underside of the Cessna flickered past, no more than fifteen feet above his head, the tricycle landing gear already retracting. Cavendish, off to Harry's right, took a little more time, leading the airplane slightly, half-remembered lessons from Quantico Naval Air School and skills unused since his time in Vietnam coming back to him. In all, forty-five of the sixty rounds fired at the virtually point-blank target found their mark, Harry's rounds in a stream from underbelly to tail, Mark's more accurately placed in the prop, engine cowling, and cockpit. Azziz, the pilot, was hit four times and Shenker took six rounds, but both were still alive enough to taste the horror of death by fire as the wing tanks exploded, sheeting the plane with a hundred-gallon shroud of flaming high-octane fuel. A hundred feet beyond where Harry lay gasping with exertion, the nose of the aircraft dipped and fell, the ruptured Cessna striking the soft ground and tumbling. Bursting chunks of white-hot wing and fuselage spun off into the darkness, igniting a dozen bonfires in the grass.

Harry rose to his knees, mesmerized by the sight of the fireball on the downslope of the field. He felt a hand grip him under the arm, and with Daniel's help he climbed to his feet. A moment later Mark Cavendish appeared out of the shadows, his mouth twisted into a horrible grin of triumph, the spent and now useless Ingram dangling from his double hook.

The three men stared at the twisting column of flame, their pulses slowly returning to their normal rate. Around them the cool night air was filled with the crackle and hiss of superheated metal, while featherweight cinders sparked up into the dark sky like stillborn stars. Then, above the sound of the fire, they heard something else. In the distance, the triple horns of the train, no longer hostage, moaned a dozen trailing blasts that echoed across the broad river valley lying between Stoney Creek Bridge and the upland meadow where the three men stood.

"I hope we were in time," whispered Harry.

"It sounds like it," said Cavendish. "I think she was going for the remote control when we hit the plane. Another couple of seconds and it would have been too late."

"She knew," said Harry softly. "I saw her for a split second, right there at the end. She knew she was going to die and she was going to kill us all, take the whole train with her."

"Well," said Mark, grunting as he wound up and tossed the machine gun away into the darkness, "we can sit back and wait for the cavalry now. It's all over, finally."

Harry turned and looked at Daniel. The artist glanced at Cavendish, then turned back to Harry. He nodded imperceptibly.

"No," said Harry. "It's not over yet. Not quite. Come on."

Epilogue

The Playboy Interview

Playboy isn't usually in the business of interviewing criminals, but in the case of Harry Maxwell we had to make an exception. Neither a Richard Nixon nor a Robert Vesco, Harry Maxwell caught the imagination of the people, touching that usually benign streak of larceny which lies within all of us. The frustration and anger that led Harry and his companions to attempt the robbery of the Amtrak Night Owl are as much a part of the reality of the American Dream as are his courage and stubborn refusal to give in to the members of the World People's Army terrorist group. Harry, realistic to a fault, doesn't see it that way, of course, although he has taken the recent avalanche of publicity with good humor. As far as he was concerned, he "was in the right place at the wrong time," and everything else that happened was nothing more than an attempt to get out of it all in one piece.

There is certainly nothing in Harry Maxwell's background to give any hint of folk-hero potential. Born Harry James Maxwell in 1948, he had a completely normal childhood and showed reasonable academic prowess as he made his way through the Seattle, Washington, school system. When news of Harry's exploits became public, his parents reacted just like anyone else's: his mother cried and his father shook his head and couldn't believe it. They have since taken advantage of the somewhat complex trust system Harry and his financial advisers have set up, and are now living in Spain at a retirement condominium complex.

During the sixties, Harry attended Columbia University and worked on a degree in sociology when he was "overwhelmed by the recreational benefits of radical chic," and his university career came to an end. Throughout the remainder of the sixties and seventies, Harry supported himself on what he refers to as the "nuts and berries" fringe, communing, health-fooding, and consciousness-raising. By the late seventies he had made the transition to the Me Generation and began smuggling, first marijuana and hashish from Mexico and the Middle East, and then cocaine from South America. "Broke, burnt out, and nerves shot" by the drug business, Harry finally hit bottom as a car cleaner in the Washington, D.C., rail yards. The rest, as the saying goes, is history.

After a great deal of investigation, Playboy found Harry living on a small island off the coast of Honduras, and we dispatched *free-lance writer John Purdy* (Playboy *Interview, June 1984, "John Glenn"). Purdy's report:*

"Trying to describe the route that eventually brought us to the elusive Harry Maxwell invites insanity, and we can assure the reader that anyone who has flown Air Honduras and lived to tell the tale has our undying respect. You haven't experienced true fear until you've flown on an aircraft with an elderly couple cooking a freshly plucked chicken over a glowing charcoal brazier at eleven thousand feet.

"Finally, following Harry's explicit directions (16°, 06'N, 86°, 56'W), we reached Isla Utila in the Yucatan Basin and discovered our quarry on the screened porch of a six-room hotel with the unlikely name of Sony's Villa. The interview, which took place over a period of three days, was carried on entirely on the porch, interrupted regularly by leisurely diving expeditions for red snapper and the local lobster. A constant supply of Cerveza Modelo and a bizarre, locally brewed concoction of anise and honey called Xtabentun cooled us as we talked."

PLAYBOY: You hardly follow the pattern of the master criminal or a latter-day Robin Hood. How does a reasonably normal boy from Seattle wind up a fugitive from justice, filthy rich, and a folk hero?

MAXWELL: Kurt Vonnegut used to have a favorite phrase — "and so it goes." Mine is "one thing leads to another." I never wanted to be a folk hero; I just wanted to be stinking rich. I've read lots of stories about me in everything from *Time* magazine to *Rolling Stone*, and they all say that I'm a product of the sixties, as though ripping off the Federal Reserve bank was some kind of acid flash from the days when Jerry Rubin was hip. That's a lot of bullshit.

PLAYBOY: Then why did you do it?

MAXWELL: For the money, of course.

PLAYBOY: That's the short answer; how about something a little more complete?

MAXWELL: It's got a lot to do with failure. To me there are two kinds of failure, the conscious and the coopted. The conscious failure knows that he didn't make it, and it eats away at him. The coopted failure rationalizes that he never got the breaks, or that it just wasn't in the cards for him to make it, and he settles down to a life where he rarely gets any of the things he used to dream about. I was a conscious failure. I knew I'd blown it with my life, and that made me angry and frustrated. I knew it was too late for me to make a success out of my life the way I'd once seen myself when I was growing up, but I still wanted to live out some of my dreams. Dreams like sitting in a tropical paradise, drinking beer and being interviewed by *Playboy*, right down to the three or four little photographs. You are going to take those, aren't you?

PLAYBOY: Absolutely. We wouldn't want to blow your dream.

MAXWELL: Good. Anyway, when I saw the opportunity, I figured it was my last chance, and I was stupid enough to take it.

PLAYBOY: Stupid enough?

MAXWELL: Sure. Anyone who's successful has to have a certain amount of innate stupidity. I mean, think about it — how could you seriously think you were going to take a strip off the Federal Reserve bank and get away with it? By the numbers, I never should have survived. When you add in Annalise Shenker and her people, the odds become incredible. Even just as a passenger on that train, my chances of getting off at the other end were pretty slim.

PLAYBOY: There is the small matter of your heroism. You did save that train, you know.

MAXWELL: We all did. Mark, Daniel, Norm Kettering, even poor old Adrian. It was a group effort.

PLAYBOY: But you were the leader. You pulled it all together.

MAXWELL: Maybe. I was terrified most of the time, actually. I think anger is probably the best antidote for fear. After we found Adrian murdered, I wasn't scared anymore. I was just mad — fighting mad. Before that, I was just about ready to punch my ticket and turn into a puddle of jelly. Even afterwards I almost lost it. Up there on the mountain for instance. It was as though everything I'd gone through suddenly became terribly real, you know? Then it passed. Maybe it was because I remembered the money. I mean, after all, that's what I was after in the first place.

PLAYBOY: For a long time everyone thought the money had gone up in flames. It took a couple of months to sift through the ashes and find out they were short. By that time you were long gone.

MAXWELL: Right. They never suspected a thing, because when they came to take us off the mountain we were clean and there was the wreck smoldering away. We were heroes, in fact.

PLAYBOY: So give us the answer everyone's dying to know. How did you get away with it?

MAXWELL: It's no big secret, really. You've got to remember that there was about a twenty-five-minute lag between the plane going up and the choppers getting to us. It's pretty simple. There were four duffel bags of cash strapped to those ATVs we were on. The three of us just got back on the machines and kept on going up the trail past the forestry cabin. If you look on a map, you'll see that the trail goes up to the crest of a place called Bald Ridge and then hangs a right through the trees. A mile or so farther on, there's another forestry cabin. We buried the bags under the floor of the cabin, just slipped it under. Then we went back down to the plane. We had time to spare. After all the noise blew over, we came back to get it.

PLAYBOY: From what we understand, Mark Cavendish was a late convert to the theft. Is that accurate?

MAXWELL: Yeah. He was true blue up until he saw what was in those duffel bags. It took me about thirty seconds to convince him he'd just won the lottery. We offered him an equal cut and he took it. He deserved it, too — him and those Veterans Administration hands of his.

PLAYBOY: What about Stackpole? Did you ever suspect him?

MAXWELL: Adrian did, and that's what killed him. Mind you, we were warned. Shenker said there were people from her group among the passengers. But we were amateurs, after all.

PLAYBOY: So now that it's all over, what's next in Harry Maxwell's life? You have fame and fortune. Is there anything missing?

MAXWELL: Believe it or not, I think I'd like a job of some kind. I guess the old American work ethic is pretty deeply ingrained. I'm considering writing a book about the whole thing, and if it works, maybe I'll finance a movie.

PLAYBOY: Was the whole thing worth it?

MAXWELL: Personally? Sure. I can't speak for the others, though; you'd have to ask them.

PLAYBOY: If we could find them.

MAXWELL: Yeah, well, that's another story, isn't it? You might catch Mark or Daniel. They drop in once in a while, just for old times' sake.

PLAYBOY: Would you do it again?

MAXWELL: See any trains on this island?

PLAYBOY: No.

MAXWELL: There's your answer, my friend.

PLAYBOY: Thank you.

MAXWELL: De nada.